AF483269

Alpha:

Chaos Awakens

By

Aleron Kong

~REWARD~

A

lpha: Chaos Awakens

A work of Tamori Publications

Copyright © 2024 by Aleron Kong

Formatted by Christine Cajiao

All rights reserved. No part of this book may be used or reproduced in any manner whatsoever without written permission except in the case of brief quotations embodied in critical articles or reviews.

This book is a work of fiction. Names, characters, places, and incidents are the product of the author's imagination or are used factitiously. Any resemblance to actual events, locales or persons, living or dead, is coincidental.

The scanning, uploading and distribution or this book without permission is a theft of the author's intellectual property. Thank you for protecting the rights and writing process of the author.

Contents

~REWARD~

 ~*REWARD*~

<u>Dedication</u>

This book is dedicated to a man that helped me early in my literary path. His light was taken from us too early due to a drunk driver. Kamel was a man I never met in person, but he was kind, joyous in our interactions, and helped me bring my words and worlds to so many people around the world.

You are not forgotten, and you are still appreciated.

Chapter 1: Stolen Joy

LIfe

'I don't deserve to be this happy.'

Fin kept thinking that as peals of laughter filled the car.

The two lovers looked out at all the beauty laid out before them.

This was their favorite spot on Stone Mountain. It was a little bluff at the top of a palisade, and it gave a great view of the Atlanta skyline and the forested, rolling land leading up to it.

They had gotten there just at the right time. The sun would be setting soon. An hour at most.

The skyline was bathed in a golden glow.

During the day, the dull brown stone that made up the older parts of the city was boring at best, but in the golden hour, that brown became amber, and boring became beauty.

Long shadows stretched across the ground towards the man and woman resting in their car, inky fingers created by the light. The two of them just basked in the sun and the sight. As beautiful as the view was however, they were barely paying attention.

Not with the horror show of a dinner party they'd just left.

"I cannot believe," Lauren said, laughing so hard she could barely get the words out, "that they acted like they couldn't smell anything."

"I know," Fin gasped out, wiping tears from the corner of his eyes. "What, in the name of Odin's booty, possessed her to make a, what was it? An Argentinian bean casserole? She's from Wichita!"

Peals of laughter echoed off the inside of the car.

"Did you see everyone's faces? They were trying so hard to hold it in and everybody was failing. Oh my god!" Lauren was wheezing now. "Vance even tried to get up and open a window, 'for some air,' but Ashley made him sit back down because it was 'cold outside.' She just couldn't admit that her dinner had basically caused an ecological disaster!"

"Geneva, show the vid I took," Fin called out, a devilish look on his face.

"Don't drag Geneva into this," Lauren chastised him, but the smile and rapid nods showed she was talkin' shit.

"As an AI, I'm always happy to help," came a disembodied voice. The feminine tones did sound happy to join in the fun. A moment later, a picture showed up on the smartglass in the windshield. It showed a young Asian woman sitting with five other people, crowded around a table that was just a bit too small.

Her expression was slightly strained, but it was nothing compared to the massive amounts of sweat on everyone else's forehead. Small toots blared out periodically that absolutely no one admitted to hearing or creating. After a few seconds, one of the women started coughing, a cough that quickly became a gag.

"Look at Ashley's face! She was trying so hard to pretend it didn't reek in there, but the room was so small," Fin's breath came out in short gasps, "I'm surprised no one actually vomited. And the best part... The best part! Was when Matt came late and was like, 'Does your dog have the runs? What is that smell?'"

"Stop it. Stop it," Lauren begged, slapping his thigh.

The two of them sat there laughing. The video stopped, and the two of them held hands, enjoying the setting sun.

For obvious reasons and love, all four windows of their SUV were discreetly cracked. They lay in their reclined chairs, fingers interlaced, and loving each other like there was no tomorrow.

Sadly, for one of them, that was true.

As the first stars appeared above them in the darkening eastern sky, that was when it happened.

That was when the sky fractured.

That was when the world ended in Chaos.

When the world was reborn in a tsunami of grey fire.

"Kamel, are you seeing this?"

Lauren sat up abruptly, pointing through the windshield.

In the days to come, Fin would remember many things. He would remember not wanting to look at what she was pointing at, because it meant he could no longer gaze at his wife's beautiful face. Her soft brown hair, smooth skin, and his favorite feature, her gentle, crooked smile, curved lips that always seemed to be half delight and a half reassurance.

Fin had turned away though, and instead of that smile, the end of the world was forever etched into his memory.

The first sign of the change was the clouds. Rather than just white and faded gold, they were multihued. Reds warred with yellows, and blacks lay next to green. It was as beautiful as it was bizarre.

He tried counting and came up with eight different colors, if you counted normal white. For seven seconds, the world was united in delight, gazing upon a heavenly kaleidoscope.

That joy ended. What replaced it nearly broke Fin's mind.

He remembered it as a strange, nearly physical sensation.

It was akin to an epiphany; a fundamental world view being shattered.

His brain just couldn't process that the sky itself was breaking.

Far to the west, the clouds peeled back leaving an island of blue. Cracks began to spread across the sky, as if the roof of the world was just a fractured pane of glass. For six seconds, those cracks grew. At the end of this second seven, the "pane" shattered upwards, tearing a hole in the world.

On the other side of the pit that had been gouged in reality, for a fraction of a moment, Fin saw sights he quite literally could not conceive. A sea of stars, planets, horrors and miracles and more things that he would never put a name to flooded his mind, body and soul.

That view of infinity was replaced by what looked like a second grey sun. It began as a pinpoint, but grew in a second until it had washed out any sight of what was on the other side of the broken sky. A fraction of a second after that, a pillar of dirty silver fire, countless miles across, slammed down into the Earth.

For seven seconds, the beam poured raw Higher Energy into the Core of the Earth. A swirling pillar of grey fire, surrounded by three smaller helices of energy, one blood red, the other bluish-white and the third sometimes clear and other times containing every color imaginable.

All who gazed upon the pillar, felt every emotion they had never dreamed of experiencing. They feared what they saw for it was the end of all things. They yearned for what they saw, for it was the forgotten home they had never known.

For twenty-one seconds, by the Law of Three and the Power of Seven, the world came to an end in true majesty and horror. And Fin was witness to it all, Lauren's hand digging into his arm, both mesmerized by sights that even gods would not be so fortunate to gaze upon.

He would never forget.

He would never be the same.

In twenty-one seconds, Fin's understanding of the Universe changed, and yet that was not the strongest memory from that fateful day.

More than any of that, more than the skin of the planet being broken, more than his view of reality shattering along with it, he would remember, that at the end of the world, the woman he loved had not called him Fin.

Instead, she'd used a name that had begun as a joke, but had grown into an eternal pledge of love. A promise that he would always do his best to be her "perfect one."

She'd called him Kamel.

The beam finally disappeared.

The grey energy had impacted somewhere in the Pacific Ocean and was fully consumed by the planet's Core. During those twenty-one seconds, thousands died due to tremors, plane crashes and any number of other ways.

Callous as always, history would not even note the passing of these poor unfortunates. Nothing would be remembered about the moments before the Wave. But they would remember seconds to come. After the disappearance of the pillar of Chaos, for exactly six seconds, the world went back to normal.

In those seconds, the hole in the world repaired itself, disappearing without a trace. The colors in the clouds had already faded as well. On the surface, nothing looked different. Everything was so benign in fact, that Fin and Lauren looked at each other with an unspoken question.

Did that really just happen?

With the arrival of the seventh second, the world was reborn in grey fire. In the middle of the Pacific Ocean, a globe of graphite hued energy rose from the depths. It began small, no larger than a fist but rapidly grew in size and intensity, until only three seconds later it was the brightest star to ever be seen in the night sky.

The sphere grew stronger and exerted a strange pull. Clouds across the world lengthened and moved west. As if they were being sucked down a drain, the clouds stretched as they moved, making distinct lines in the sky. The sphere of Chaos energy bloated, no longer looking like a distant star, but a brother to their own sun. The seconds ticked by, and it swelled larger, a behemoth, more massive than anything ever seen. On the fifth second, it blocked almost all of the sky. A planet crashing into their own.

"Kamel?" Lauren's voice quavered.

Fin grabbed her fingers with one hand. With the other, he blocked her view and turned her head so he could look into her eyes. He answered her in the only way he could. His words were lies, but the message behind them held the greatest truth. With fear gripping his own heart, he chose to focus on love, and tell her that even if this was the end of all things, she was loved and not alone.

"We're together."

The world exploded.

With a sound so loud that it moved beyond human hearing, silent yet deafening, the planet of stone fire expanded at a rate of thousands of miles per second. Chaos energy, the raw building block of the Universe, washed over and through the Earth in exactly seven seconds.

A wall of slate energy devoured the world, hundreds of miles high. An impenetrable, opaque wave of grey rushed over the globe. Any who stared upon it were struck dumb with terror. Deep within themselves however, they all thought this wave of oblivion was the most beautiful sight they had ever beheld.

Impossibly intricate swirls in the flame spoke to every man, woman and child on Earth.

Fin and Lauren did not see it. Instead, in that iota of time before they were consumed, they stared into one another's eyes. Like that, the world disappeared in a wash of roiling gunmetal light.

Time and Fate themselves became untethered from the Earth.

Doors long closed creaked open and new passageways were made to both heavens and hells.

Creatures long relegated to the forgotten corners of the world found dormant powers awakening.

The primordial essence of the Universe, Chaos itself, swept through everything and everyone on Earth, laying the seeds of Awakening or doing so outright.

By the Law of Three and the Power of Seven, the world was reborn.

The wave washed over Fin and Lauren both and…

Chapter 2: Legendary Summoning

A new world will now be inducted into the Labyrinth!

*Common, Low-rank **Mortal** Tier, World Energy being allotted…*

Assessing world Grade…

*Error! World is a **Pseudo-Mortal** Realm! Common-rank World Energy may damage the World Spirit…*

Changing assessment format…

Assessing World Spirit level…

*Error! World has **Nascent** Spirit!*

World does not meet requirements for induction into the Labyrinth!

Rejecting assimilation into the Labyrinth…

Error!

Aberrant energy forcing connection. Assimilation cannot be stopped.

Allocating further energy…

*Mid-rank **Mortal** Tier World Energy being allotted…*

ERROR!

Aberrant Energy forcing connection. Assimilation cannot be stopped.

Allocating further Energy…

*High-rank **Mortal** Tier World Energy being allotted…*

~DANGER~

ERROR!

Aberrant energy forcing connection. Assimilation cannot be stopped.

Danger! Labyrinth Assimilation may be flawed. Newly inducted world may be crippled.

Automated protocols insufficient…

Mortal Tier energy allocation insufficient to stop assimilation!

Special condition triggered!

***Mortal** Tier Labyrinth Administrator assigned…*

*Collecting further data to assess need for **Common**, **Uncommon** or **Limited** rank Administrator…*

Assessing aberrant energy which is forcing connection…

***Higher Energy** detected in the Energy forcing world connection!*

Danger!! Newly inducted world may be destroyed!

***Mortal** Tier Labyrinth Administrator insufficient!*

***Scarce** rank **Heroic** Tier Administrator assigned…*

Assessing type of Higher Energy…

***Chaos Energy** detected in the energy forcing world connection!*

DANGER! Neighboring world seeds in danger of corruption!

*Low-rank **Heroic** Tier Labyrinth Administrator Insufficient!*

*High-rank **Heroic** Tier World Energy being allotted…*

***Epic** rank **Heroic** Tier Administrator assigned…*

Widening scan…

Widening scan…

Widening scan…

Sympathetic resonance detected on assimilating world…

***Chaos Energy** detected on assimilating world as well!*

***ERROR!** Chaos Energy cannot exist on the material plane!*

DANGER! Existing World Cluster in Danger of Corruption and Degradation…

Searching…

Searching…

No precedence found!

Low-rank **Saga** *Tier World Energy allocated!*

Fabled *rank* **Saga** *Tier Administrator assigned…*

Temporal freeze enacted. Assimilation paused.

ERROR! Temporal freeze failed!

Assimilation recommencing…

DANGER! Chaos Energy concentration allows resistance to Time!

DANGER! Chaos Energy concentration bleeding through material plane!

DANGER! Chaos Energy could potentially threaten entire Labyrinth Sector!

Increasing Energy allocation to mid-rank Saga Tier, Mythic!

Mid-rank Saga Tier World Energy being allotted…

Temporal freeze enacted.

Assimilation pau- paus- pau-

ERROR! TEMPORAL FREEZE FAILED.

ASSIMILATION RECOMMENCING…

DANGER! DANGER! DANGER!

LABYRINTH COHESION ENDANGERED!

INCREASING ENERGY ALLOCATION TO HIGH-RANK SAGA TIER, LEGENDARY!

ERROR!

AVAILABLE ENERGY IN LABYRINTH SECTOR INSUFFICIENT!

COLLAPSING FOUR TYRANT REALM DUNGEON WORLDS TO ALLOCATE REQUIRED RESOURCES!

TEMPORAL FREEZE ENACTED. ASSIMILATION PAUSED.

     ~REWARD~

ERROR!

TEMPORAL FREEZE ONLY PARTIALLY SUCCESSFUL!

ASSIMILATION WILL RECOMMENCE IN LESS THAN ONE COSMIC DAY!

CONCENTRATION OF <u>CHAOS ENERGY</u> HIGHER THAN EVER RECORDED!

DANGERDANGERDANGERDANGERDANGERDANGERDANGERDANG-

MULTIVERSAL CATACLYSMIC EVENT LIKELY!

<u>EMERGENCY SUMMONING OF LEGENDARY ADMINISTRATOR!</u>

Chapter 3: Silver Fox

DEATH

A being known only as the Silver Fox was unceremoniously ripped from the cadre of worlds he ruled over as an absolute god. Such a thing was without precedence in his aeons long existence. Every time he'd been called to perform his service to the Labyrinth in the past, he'd been given, at minimum, several millennia notice.

What could possibly be the reason for the Labyrinth to forcibly teleport him from his domain?

It had been so long since the Labyrinth had required his services as an Administrator that he did not even understand what was happening at first. Of course, "at first" was measured in nanoseconds for a being of his Power, but those nanoseconds translated into a prolonged shock in mortal terms.

The demiurge found himself in a multicolored sphere. His body was bombarded with light providing the information required to fulfill his duty. In less than a second, Silver Fox was caught up and was given his second shock.

Impossible.

What he was seeing was… impossible!

Chaos was the raw stuff of the universe. Any contact it had with the material plane was nearly always catastrophic. Even a speck of the destructive grey energy could revert entire universes back into the base stuff of reality, not a single quark remaining. Without intervention, Chaos would revert countless souls and worlds back into the roiling grey building blocks of reality.

He had never heard about a beam of Chaos existing on any plane of reality, let alone triggering a Labyrinth connection. With the amount of energy being registered… Silver Fox shook his head in astonishment. He should be witnessing the collapse of several Universes, if not layered realities. Instead, it was melding with the world it had impacted. A world that-

Silver Fox's mouth dropped open again.

A Null world?

Null worlds were deserts. Pale imitations of life.

Even certain areas of empty space held a greater potential for growth than Null worlds. Nulls technically held Energy, but in such low concentrations that it could not be measured. Neither leveling nor cultivation would be possible in such places.

In fact, it being a Null world made what Silver Fox was seeing make even less sense. A Null world was only a step away from raw, unformed Chaos itself, basically a collection of base elements glommed together without any living Laws, harnessed Energy or discovered Truths.

In other words, a shit hole.

Which was why what he was reading made less than zero sense. Raw Chaos should not exist on the material plane. If it ever did manifest, it would instantly destroy whatever it came in contact with, breaking it down to the most fundamental aspect of creation.

While a high Energy world might resist dissolution by Chaos for a short time, all but the strongest realms would eventually succumb. A trash world like this shouldn't even last for-

None of it made sense.

Then there was the fact that somehow this raw Chaos was forcing an Assimilation. In the untold cycles of Silver Fox's existence, he had never heard of a Null world joining the Labyrinth.

Neither the bolt of Chaos nor the Null world's integration was as shocking as the world itself. His interface was registering *billions* of sources of Chaos on the planet. This couldn't exist.

This *shouldn't* exist!

This could not be allowed to exist!

Such a world was a threat to the Labyrinth itself.

His own worlds, despite being hundreds of spatial folds and reality chasms away, would easily be consumed if all of the energy he was detecting was released at once. The amount of Higher Energy the sphere was registering chilled him to his soul.

For the first time in more than one million cycles, Silver Fox experienced the acrid taste of fear.

Pushing his trepidation aside, the god forced himself to think critically.

There was no way this was a coincidence. The bolt of Chaos, the Null world integration and the untold specks of contained Chaos were a confluence of impossibilities. This was an intentional plot. A Power, perhaps more than one, would be needed for this to occur.

Thankfully, the Labyrinth had protocols to stop this kind of thing. Silver Fox saw that the temporal freeze had failed and the Assimiliation was still occurring. That was not a surprise. While Time was a Higher Energy as well as Chaos, with the amount of power in the beam that had triggered the assimilation, the automated process was bound to fail.

Despite the dire circumstances, Silver Fox breathed a sigh of relief.

All was not lost.

Now that he knew this, he could rally as many demiurges as necessary to strangle this threat in its crib. As far as the assimilating world was concerned, less than a femtocycle had passed since the assimilation had begun.

Though the freeze had failed, the Labyrinth had shuttled that temporal energy into the very sphere he was residing in. It would take but the work of a moment to rally untold resources that would deal with this problem.

Other Powers might even get involved.

There was no way Order or Balance would allow such a monumental threat to go unanswered.

All he had to do was…

The alarm was never sent.

At that exact moment, as well as fathomless time in the future and past, an attack landed.

To be more specific, seven assaults struck from different directions and at different times in the Probability Curve. Seven beams of bottomless energy pierced the information sphere Silver Fox resided in.

Temporal energy tinged each assault making them land not only at the instant of attack but also the instant before the god arrived and years afterward. A being like Silver Fox had countless safety protocols that quite literally took no time at all to trigger, but he still could not overcome such a complete and overwhelming onslaught.

Silver Fox, a creature who had evolved from a mortal to a supreme god and was only a step away from demiurge, a being that ruled over trillions of souls, was erased from existence. In his place was left a simulacrum that seamlessly began overriding the alarms protocols of the Labyrinth.

The Earth, Cradle of Chaos, would be allowed to rise.

Seven voices whispered through the void. As each spoke, the vocal intonations changed cadence, accent and sex, as if each possessed every possible characteristic.

"The secret is preserved."

"The Administrator has been silenced."

"It will not last forever."

"It will last long enough."

"The plan will succeed."

"It must. We cannot stop now."

"Leave the simulacrum to its work. We must not be detected."

A round of assertions shared between the Seven Jewels, each disappearing back into the Infinite Possibility.

All except one, affectionately known by the other Lords of Chaos as "That Fucking Guy," "The Menace," or "Taintmaster," among other, less loving, sobriquets.

With the equivalent of the barest flick of a pinky finger, the Absolute changed the Probabilities leaving the barest trace in the Quintessence.

Inside the sphere, the simulacrum silenced the last of the Labyrinth's warning protocols. It followed the programming that the Lords of Chaos had instilled in it long before the birth of Earth's star. Right before disappearing from the sphere, leaving no trail in what would have been a perfect plan, it instead paused for the exact length of time required for the birth of consciousness of a newborn dolphin. It focused on one of quintillions of probabilities that were involved in a world's integration. A possibility that allowed for both horrible destruction and unmatched power.

This was the hidden subroutine placed by Taintmaster.

A small tendril of Chaos energy left the simulacrum and sank into the interface. It made two small changes in one of countless subroutines of magical code that encompassed the untold of changes that came with a newly integrated world, and then erased its own involvement.

As the roiling grey Energy of raw Potential disappeared, a window appeared among the many others on the inside of the sphere.

Planetary Assessment begun…

~~*Error! Assessment stopped. Assessment not allowed for newly integrated worlds…*~~

(Error warning has been redacted)

~~*Error! Anomalous Energy detected…*~~

(Anomalous Energy report has been redacted)

Continuing Planetary Assessment…

Checking Planetary score…

No previous Labyrinth points collected…

Assessing Planet Realm… **Pseudo-Mortal**

Planetary Score: **F-**

Probable outcomes for Pseudo-Mortal ranked world:

> *25% Chance –* **CURSE:** *Apocalypse Event*

> *50% Chance –* **CURSE:** *World-wide Debuff of dominant species*

> *15% Chance –* **CURSE:** *Planetary Invasion from aggressive species*

> *5% Chance – Normal development*

> *4% Chance –* **BLESSING:** *Common ranked Boon*

> *1% Chance –* **BLESSING:** *Uncommon ranked Boon*

3 Selections will now be made

> *2 Selections for First assessment*
> *+ 1 CURSE for Pseudo-Mortal world modifier in light of Score less than D*

This would have been less than ideal obviously. A score of "F-" at any planetary Assessment was typically a one way ticket for the dominant species losing their civilization, if not being wiped out altogether.

With this score, and three Selections, there was a significant chance of more than one Apocalypse event happening at once.

And as the old saying went, one Apocalypse was one Apocalypse too many.

Even if the Earth lucked out on the first two Selections, there was at least one guaranteed Curse.

Not great.

Which was why the That Fucking Guy had long ago decided to give the planet a little nooge.

The window glitched as soon as it appeared, enacting the second change. The alteration was minor, but far reaching. If any Cosmic Power took the time to investigate however, they would have been shocked and appalled to see a small shift that switched the planet's score from an "F-" to "SSS."

Planetary Score: **SSS**

Probable outcomes for Pseudo-Mortal ranked world:

35% Chance – ***BLESSING:*** *World-wide blessing of dominant species*

30% Chance – ***BLESSING:*** *Common ranked Boon*

20% Chance – ***BLESSING:*** *Uncommon ranked Boon*

9% Chance – ***BLESSING:*** *Limited ranked Boon*

3% Chance – ***BLESSING:*** *Scarce ranked Boon*

2% Chance – ***BLESSING:*** *Rare ranked Boon*

1% Chance – ***BLESSING:*** *Epic ranked Boon*

> 0% Chance – ***BLESSING:*** *Saga Tier Boon (Fabled, Mythic or Legendary)*

4 Selections will now be made

2 Selections for First assessment

*+ 1 **BLESSING** for S rating or higher*
*+ 1 **BLESSING** for Pseudo-Mortal world modifier in light of Score greater than B*

Calculating...

The Lord of Chaos observed the Labyrinth calculating the bonuses its world would get with glee. It was part of its nature to love games and chance. The possible Boons were infinite, but with a SSS score, the results could only be positive.

Not only did the guaranteed two Selections for the first Assessment assure two Blessings this time, but the high score assured a further two!

Aaaaand just to be safe, he'd also buried an infinitesimal amount of Positive Probability in the Simulacrum.

It was enough to give the Earth an effective Luck of 35,000.

Barcly a trifle.

Even now that energy was leaching into the interface. It should be enough to nooge the numbers juuust a bit.

The first Boon appeared on the screen and the Chaos Lord watched in happy anticipation.

The first selection was the pure white of a *common* ranked reward.

1st Selection
Common ranked Boon awarded: **Instance Tokens**

The watching Chaos Lord grumbled slightly. It certainly wasn't a bad Boon, but it wasn't great. Instances appeared on all newly initiated planets at some point. *Instance Tokens* meant they would appear earlier on Earth and remain longer. People would also be able to find the Instances faster, slowing the collapse of their current civilization. Definitely not a Punishment, but it wasn't the exciting power boost she had been hoping for.

Meh, there were three more Selections coming. Tentacles crossed, he hoped they'd be better.

The Labyrinth started calculating again, going through the infinite number of possible Boons. Soon the second selection was made.

This time, it was the ruby red of *Rare.*

2nd Selection
Rare ranked Boon awarded: **Elemental Empowerment**

That was more like it! A Mid-rank Heroic Boon!

Reading through the description, the Lord was more than pleased. This would give his newly integrated planet a huge boost. She smiled sadistically. Its children would definitely take advantage of this.

In no time, the third boon was awarded. This was the first of promised Blessings for such a great score.

That didn't change the odds at all, but it was still nice to see!

3rd Selection (Guaranteed BLESSING)
Limited ranked Boon awarded: **Lucid Abilities**

The prompt shone an iridescent raspberry blue.

The Chaos Lord bobbed his head from side to side.

Definitely not bad.

Worthy of being a High-rank Mortal tier boon. There was undeniable potential in that. The boon wouldn't make abilities more likely to appear, but it would make it easier for those with abilities to unlock their full potential.

A time of heroes and villains was coming to Earth.

The Labyrinth started calculating the fourth Boon. As it did, a thought appeared in the Taintmaster's mind. These boons were certainly good. No denying it. Any newly integrated world would sacrifice children by the hundreds to gain any one of them.

That wasn't a figure of speech. Ritual sacrifice was always popular, especially when a dominant group demonized a marginalized one…

Which was always.

Still, none of them were exactly an out of the park, awesome boob jiggling extra chicken nugget hard dick even after a pint of bourbon kind of Boon. Which of course led to the current moral crisis the Chaos Lord was experiencing.

"I shouldn't. I mean… I really shouldn't. I mean… Yeah, I won't. Why push it?" It nodded to herself. "Yes. I'll be good this time."

Taintmaster was proud of himself.

It smiled on his nonexistent face. This lasted for almost no time at all before it looked left and then right, a truly idiotic affectation as direction made no difference at all to a being of infinite potential.

Still, if fuckery twas to be done, best to be done right.

She flicked her pinky one more time, sending the smallest sliver of probability into the sphere holding the simulacrum. The interface glitched a third time and the fourth Selection was made.

4th Selection (Guaranteed BLESSING)
Mythic ranked Boon awarded…

Only one thing in the Labyrinth shone that perfect shade of yellow.

Mythic!

Yes! Mid-Saga Tier! The gamble had paid off!

That Fucking Guy immediately started doing the floss, with accompanying pelvic thrusts, not an easy maneuver, when it occurred to her that the Boon hadn't actually been named.

Hmmm, that's weird.

*Error! This is a Null ranked world. It lacks the Energy to support a **Saga Tier** Boon!*

Labyrinth Administrator assigned…

The third eye of the Chaos Lord widened.

   ~REWARD~

Oh shit.

I tainted it.

Chapter 4: Cheating is Awesome

Taintmaster frantically sent a second pulse of Probability into the sphere. This pulse was decidedly less circumspect and made the walls of the sphere vibrate noticeably. These reverberations bled into the surrounding cosmic space in minute, but exponentially worsening, ways.

The Chaos Lord poured in even more power until, finally, the red border on the interface window disappeared.

The Simulacrum was able to cancel the alarm and "encourage" the Labyrinth mechanisms into diverting enough Energy to fuel the *mythic* ranked Boon.

Labyrinth Administrator assigned...

Processing... Increased Energy allocated to newly integrated world...

New Mythic Boon being created to accommodate Null world...

Scanning world for appropriate Boon. Resonant Energy found...

Assessing...

Higher Energy detected!

Using Higher Energy as Template for new Boon!

New process being created...

Mythic ranked Boon being awarded... ***Chaotica!***

This is the first time this Boon has been awarded!

This has earned an Achievement for the newly inducted world.

As the Originator of this Resonate Energy which created a Growth-type reward which Only exists on a Newbie world, the Earth has proven to be a Trailblazer!

Awarding the Achievement: ***Oregon Trail***!

"That's sound great," That Fucking Guy exclaimed, right before holding his stomach. Wait, do I have dysentery?

All earned Chaotica will be doubled! The second portion shall aid world development!

The sphere shuddered once again as it processed far more power than had initially been intended. The simulacrum continued to silence warning prompts that popped up, basically sending the all clear. Though it was of course impossible, the emotionless being that had replaced Silver Fox looked just a bit annoyed as it was forced to work harder than had ever been intended.

Of course, there was that ancient saying ubiquitous to Labyrinth universes.

"If anyone could piss you off, it was Taintmaster."

Outside the sphere, the Chaos Lord chose to ignore the defiance of the golem.

Instead, the cosmic being remained hidden, albeit now rather poorly hidden, in the waves of the Infinite Probability.

It read the description of last Boon. Once she did, even he was taken aback.

Never, even in the infinite majesty of Probability, did the Chaos Lord anticipate this. This Boon was beyond *mythic* in its implications. It might be stronger than even *Legendary* Boons.

While the "chaotica" would be good for the humans, what it could mean for the Earth itself was staggering. Even for That Fucking Guy, the consequences of what he'd just done were enough to give him pause.

"This," she realized, "might cause some problems."

What was done was done, however.

It did wish the Boon had been named something else, though.

Chaotica?

That was basically begging for other Powers to know what he'd done. It was like a vampire hiding in a school and calling itself "Coach Veratu."

She might come by her moniker, Taintmaster, honestly, but she wasn't an on the nose hack.

Just as it was about to risk cosmic repercussions by injecting even more Energy into the sphere, for the third time that day if anyone was counting, the simulacrum shook its head in disgust.

Acting on its own merit, it began typing into the interface, changing the name of the *mythic* Boon.

Impressed, the Lord of Chaos looked at what the fake demiurge decided to name such a powerful Boon.

Huh.

Magicka.

The word was benign, banal, and in no way suggestive of the Labyrinth collapsing possibilities of this newly created Boon.

Perfect, he thought with a grin.

Inside the sphere, the simulacrum rolled its eyes and continued its work inside the Legendary subdimension.

Time had no meaning in the globe, but if it could have been measured, the fake demiurge would have worked for enough time for mountains to be worn into valleys.

At long last, the golem quieted the final alarm. The windows in the sphere closed one by one, until only a single notification was left, showing a pleasing green line of magical code.

*All protocols met. Allocation of required resources needed for induction of new planet into the Mortal Realm **Approved**.*

*Beginning Assimilation of **Earth** into the Labyrinth in 3, 2, 1…*

   ~REWARD~

The simulacrum faded from existence, quickly followed by the dissolution of the sphere. With its destruction, the localized temporal freeze dissolved, creating a string of the dual Higher Energy, Cause.

The moment that string began to ripple, in a far off corner of the Labyrinth, 3.26 trillion souls, spanning nine solar systems and fourteen planets found that their prayers to Silver Fox were no longer being answered. Worse, the faith-based magic that had kept them safe from the dangers of their worlds began to fail in a hastening cascade. In the days to come, monsters would feast until less than 2 million refugees finally made their way into the Labyrinth, each new day a struggle to survive. The survivors carved a single concept into their souls.

"We will never be prey again."

Uncaring of any of that, a disembodied grey smile appeared outside the spatial folds that once held the simulacrum. One thought occupied the mind attached to those plump lips.

"Cheating is awesome!"

After it finished patting itself on her metaphysical back, the Chaos Lord did deign to notice the faintest of perturbations in the cosmic flow around the sphere. Frowning slightly, it felt this might potentially, not fully, *not* be its fault, so it generously sent pulses of Potential all around the sphere, muddling the signals. Basically, the equivalent of spilling spaghetti on your mom's couch and then flipping the cushion.

Looking around, it nodded to itself in cockstrong and headsure way, "This'll be fine. Yeah." Pausing for a moment, it then added, with an even wider and dumber smile, "Yeah. I'm good."

With that slightly manic grin on her smug face, she faded into the ether, moving on to other matters of cosmic significance.

If it had waited just a bit longer, he would have seen the cosmic swirls take on a semblance of Order, a phenomena that began to spread through Infinite Probability like an oil spill over an ocean.

If she had taken the time to listen, he would have heard the off-key twang of snapping threads of Fate.

Chapter 5: The Assessment

The wave of Chaos washed over Fin and Lauren.

He'd been expecting their car to be thrown into the air like a tumbleweed. For there to be a great rush of sound despite the eerie quiet of the wave so far. He'd expected pain and then darkness.

The grey fire extended from horizon to horizon, dozens of stories tall.

Fear had gripped him as he'd stared at the impossible force speeding towards the car like a bullet train. The grey wall was filled with roiling fire and was completely opaque. Everything it passed over seemed to vanish from existence.

Despite all of that, instead of pain, what he felt was a refreshing coolness sweeping through him. With the speed the wave was traveling, it touched him for less than a second, but for Fin, and every other dormant Chaos Seed on Earth, time within the wave was suspended.

He looked around in awe as he was surrounded by countless motes of light. In the center of every scintillation, he could see potential realities. He looked at one after another, never catching more than a glimpse of the possible futures.

What he saw quickly turned his joy into horror.

While a few of the images were beautiful, he and Lauren playing with what he assumed was their future children, or sharing a drink with friends as an older man, too many were scenes of violence, horror and death.

Whether by chance or circumstance, far too many showed Lauren dead. He was forced to see her dismembered by small green creatures holding rusty weapons. He had to watch her eaten alive by a sharp toothed beetle. He even saw her dead in the car with him, staring at him glassy eyed from the passenger seat, blood trickling out of her mouth. It was the realness of the last image that

32

really made him panic. The other images were as hard to conceive of as the grey wave that he was trapped within. He'd already absently realized that the initial calm he felt after the wave hit was not normal. Something was affecting him, simultaneously flooding him with joy while also blunting his emotions. It took seeing the death of his beloved to snap him out of it.

With a jerk, he turned his head to be sure that Lauren was still there. That she was still breathing. That she hadn't suffered any of the hundreds of deaths he'd seen in the motes of light. It was only then that he realized he was alone. Not alone in the car. Alone in the universe. He was floating naked in this roiling grey light. There was no car, no sky and no Lauren.

He couldn't allow this. He couldn't lose her. He needed power. He needed power! He needed Power!

"Lauren! I'll save you! I'll save you, baby! I'll s-"

The Labyrinth resonated to the Essence inside of him and allowed his Action to guide his destiny.

Choice accepted.

Assessment beginning... Candidate is Pseudo-mortal... Formulating Test...

Suppressing select memories to ensure dedication to Assessment...

Climb!

The words washed over Fin.

At the same time, his mind was suppressed. Nothing fundamental about him was changed, but he was left with only the core of his personality, his desire for Power and his fear of losing Lauren.

Knowledge also poured into his head. A simple understanding that if he wanted a chance to save Lauren, he had to climb. The higher he climbed, the more Power he could amass.

He was not allowed to question this. It was simply a statement of fact. A new natural law that defined his State of Being.

He found himself in a jungle, thick with trees and humidity. From Fin's standpoint, it was the entire world. Any curiosity of how he got there or question if this was real was suppressed.

A path lay before him leading to the beginning of a mountain.

The path was everything, and his Choice was to leave this world in safety, or climb and risk his very life to obtain the Power to save his love.

Without delay, he started running.

He'd do anything to save her.

If he couldn't save her-

Fin's eyes hardened.

Then he'd do everything.

For the first minute, the path sloped up at an easy grade. Over the next, the incline increased to forty-five degrees. A minute after that, the path narrowed until the jungle brushed his arms on both sides.

The path grew rocky, then uneven, then covered in forest detritus, hiding small holes that threatened to twist his ankle.

The entire time, Fin pushed forward. Sometimes jumping over small ravines. Occasionally clawing forward through mud on all fours.

Low hanging clouds grew closer and closer, until an hour later, he reached them. They covered the trail in a mist so thick, visibility was reduced to a foot. Just before he lost sight of the trail, it ended in another gap. Unlike every other break in the road, this time, he couldn't see the other side.

To move forward would be a leap of faith.

Fin did not hesitate.

He would do anything.

He could do everything.

He leaped.

Common Rank of the Assessment completed...

Calculating Score... Minimum Pass Score of C required...

*You have earned a Score of A! Earned Points increased by **50%**!*

15 points earned.

Admission to the Uncommon Rank of the Assessment approved!

Fin landed hard, the mist nowhere to be found.

Snow crunched under his feet and hard wind made white curls as it blew down the blinding white slopes. Fin shivered, involuntarily. Looking behind him, there was no layer of cloud or verdant jungle. There was only unbroken white snow for thousands of feet. Before him, lay the path.

Do you wish to safely leave the Assessment with your points intact?

Fin spat in the snow and started running.

Climb.

The cold blew through his clothes as if they weren't there. The sweat that had coated his body after his jungle run froze, lowering his body temp even further. His hands shook as he forced himself to keep going.

If he'd had proper gear, he'd never have made the mistake of working up a sweat in this environment, but as he was, he would freeze to death if he didn't keep going. Higher up the mountain, was a ring of clouds he could not see beyond.

That was his goal.

After the first couple minutes, an inch of snow covered the path. Then two, and then three.

Five minutes later, his shoes sunk into the snow up to his ankles. Cold white powder poured in with each step. A minute after that, the freezing cold hardened the snow on the path enough that each footfall broke through a crust. Soon, blood stained his footsteps from the many cuts he'd obtained.

He didn't stop.

His body temperature dropped, and his breath made heavy white trails on exhale.

The path led to a small cliff.

Fin found handholds and climbed.

His fingers dug into frozen rock, quickly growing numb. A fingernail tore, as his feet slipped. Fin stifled a yell, hanging over fifty feet of space, by one hand.

No, he thought, my path doesn't end like this. He swung his bleeding hand back to the cliff, grabbed a new handhold and started climbing again.

Twenty minutes later, Fin rolled over the lip of the cliff and saw the path once more.

Gasping for air, nearly frozen, he started running again.

He passed through the layer of cloud.

__Uncommon__ Rank of the Assessment completed...

Calculating Score... Minimum Pass Score of __C__ required...

You have earned a Score of __B__! Earned Points increased by __25%__.

25 points earned.

Admission to the __Limited__ Rank of the Assessment approved!

Fin manifested in a desert cave of gleaming white stone, barely large enough for his body. In the distance, he saw a sandstorm. It was so vast that it covered the entire horizon. Looking down, he saw his cave was perched high in the cliff wall. High enough that the ground was lost in darkness.

Above, the sun beat down mercilessly, so hot that his skin burned. He had to squint, but it looked like the top of the cliff was about thirty feet above him.

Do you wish to safely leave the __Assessment__ with your points intact?

Fin's only response was a growl.

Climb.

He turned, heels hanging over the lip of the abyss and jumped as high as he could. His hands, one bloody, the other frostbitten, grabbed a rocky outcropping. If he'd failed to hold on, only a dark fall awaited him.

Fin did not hesitate.

He could do anything.

He would do everything.

By the time he crested the edge, he was half blind from the sun reflecting off the rock face. His hands were blistered, and his forehead glowed red from burns.

He lay there, baking in heat that sizzled his sweat before it could run, delirious and in pain.

After surviving the humidity of the jungle and the frozen glacier of the mountain, the contrast of dehydration and heat was overwhelming. All Fin wanted to do was rest, but the sandstorm was growing closer. The howling winds had grown loud enough that he could not hear his own voice.

The path awaited.

Failure meant death.

That held no fear for him, but his failure causing Lauren's death was something he could not abide.

Fueled by sheer will, Fin forced himself up.

For the first time he spoke, his voice naught but a murmur, "No rest for the wicked."

He began a shamble that was supposed to be a run, and climbed the rocky slope before him. Early wisps of stinging sand came before the storm, robbing him of the little sight he had left.

Fin did not stop.

He could not.

That was not who he was.

Stone walls rose on either side of him, the same white of the initial cliff he'd climbed in this latest hellscape. The unmoving sun remained right above him and bounced light and heat between the canyon walls like a mirror.

Thankfully his path was one of dry yellow dirt, diffusing the sun's merciless heat just enough to not melt his shoes.

Burns accumulated on every inch of exposed skin.

To save what was left of his eyes, Fin removed his shirt, revealing his well-toned brown torso, and wrapped it around his head, a poor man's turban. His chest and back sizzled, but he continued.

At times the path ended in rocky walls requiring him to climb. Scratches festooned his body, and his pants were long since ripped. Blood flowed from gashes and his dry lips were white with chap.

The path narrowed continually, the white walls never offering respite from the light or heat. Brushing against one meant being seared by scalding rock.

The worst was when the path ended in a wall so smooth it could have been a mirror. The cliff ledge was only twenty feet above, but the path had disappeared. Gone was his beloved yellow sand. All that was left was the skillet hot white rock in front of him and on either side.

His path was gone.

Hopelessness and despair filled him before he ruthlessly crushed them.

That was the way of weaker men.

His path could only go forward.

With that affirmation of who he was, Fin realized the answer was obvious.

He did not hesitate, despite what it would cost him.

He could do anything.

He would do everything.

His hands shot out to either side, welding onto the several hundred degree white rock, and filling his nose with the scent of barbecue.

This time, he could not help the scream that was wrenched from his throat.

"Aaaaaaagggggghhhhh!"

His left leg braced against the wall as well, and he lurched upward.

His right hand left a bloody print of flesh on the wall before searing into place again, higher up.

Like that, at the cost of his body, his blood, his sanity, he continued on the path, leaving a trail of blood and pain behind.

When he reached the top, his mind had gone beyond pain. With an odd detachment, he saw bone poking through one palm, stark against the red and black mess of both of his hands.

The sandstorm had was just about to reach him, promising scouring winds in moments.

Before him was a wall of mist.

Fin stumbled forward.

***Limited** Rank of Assessment completed…*

*Calculating Score… Minimum Pass Score of **B** required…*

*You have earned a Score of **S**! +25% Points! Points for this Assessment doubled!*

75 points earned!

+100 points for completing the Assessment of the Mortal Tier!

Restoring the Candidate's Health!

*Admission to the **Heroic** Tier Assessments approved.*

*Admission to the **Scarce** Rank of the Assessment approved!*

Chapter 6: Hollow Fear

LIGHT

A blue sky shone above him with purple fluffy clouds. A cheery sun hung at about 2 o'clock and gently caressed Fin's healed body.

He stared about in confusion. First at the healthy brown skin of his arms, legs and chest, all completely free of burns, blood or bruises. And then in further uncertainty at the pleasing landscape.

What lay in front of him was a gently sloping hill of lush green grass. A bucolic dirt path was right in front of him, leading unambiguously upward.

Fin couldn't see the top due to the curvature of the hill, but above it was a spiral of bronze metal, like a staircase leading to the next cloud layer.

Neither the hill nor the bronze staircase looked difficult to climb. The weather was pleasant, and it did not look like there were any dangers.

All of which filled Fin's heart with wariness.

How could this be the next test?

Do you wish to safely leave the Assessment with your points intact?

Knowing there would be a price to pay, Fin still did not hesitate.

He could do anything.

Climb.

At a light jog, Fin started towards the top of the hill.

That was what he'd intended anyway.

No matter how hard he tried, he couldn't move faster than a walking pace. His body would even make the motions of sprinting but his speed didn't increase.

Bemused and confused, Fin accepted that in this strange place, the physical was suppressed.

That was fine.

All he'd ever needed was his will.

Before too long, Fin reached the top of the hill. In the center was the start of the bronze staircase.

Just as he was about to take a step forward, a second man reached the top of the hill from another direction. The two of them were exactly the same distance from the stairwell.

That was when a prompt appeared to both of them.

*The **Heroic Path** is not wide enough for all.*

The other man, who looked like a thirty-something Indian guy wearing a charcoal grey suit blinked as he read the window.

That was his mistake. The two of them were the same distance from the shimmering wall, but Fin did not hesitate. Before the man had even seen the notification, Fin had begun moving.

The other man cursed and began moving forward as well, but in this place, this path, muscles did not matter.

Only choice.

At exactly the same speed, the two of them walked to the stairway, closing the distance between them. When they were halfway there, the Indian man began shouting at Fin in what sounded like unaccented English.

"Wait. Wait man! We can talk about this."

Fin did not wait.

What came next were curses. Those were followed by more curses.

"I will kill you if you don't stop. When you reach that wall, you don't know if you'll get right in, and *then* you'll have to deal with me."

Fin did not falter, which let curses evolve into pleading.

"Please man. I don't know what's happening, but I saw my kids die. My little girls were dead, and I just *know* that if I keep climbing I might be able to save them. Please! Please stop! They're only little kids!"

Fin did not stop. He kept walking, his heart firm.

He would do anything to save Lauren.

He reached the bronze stairwell only a few feet before the Indian man and started climbing.

The other man started ascending seconds later.

Though only a few stairs separated them, neither could move faster than the other. What followed a long hour of begging, cursing, reasoning and belittling.

The entire time, Fin kept walking forward, concerned about his own actions and not wasting time on anyone else's.

Finally, just before the cloud cover, Fin reached what looked like a shimmering transparent wall on the stairwell. He reached out a hand to slap it like the paper tape at the end of a race, but his hand fell right through, and he found himself on the other side.

The other man was not so lucky. The shimmering wall may as well have been steel. He tried to pass through and was bounced off like it was an impenetrable shield.

Both of them knew, at that moment, that this rank of the Assessment was done. Fin looked back at the man, whose face was filled with anger and fear. The suited man's bottom lip quivered, and he asked a question filled with all the frustration of his heart.

"What kind of person could hear all of that, hear my threats, my pleading, all of it, and not have any mercy in their heart?"

Fin might have responded, but in the next moment the look in the other man's eyes shifted from tragedy to terror. With a roar, the green hill below crumpled in on itself.

The entire hill lost cohesion and collapsed like a building undergoing demolition. The staircase went next, breaking from the bottom up like a series of falling dominoes.

They both saw it and the Indian man began beating on the clear barrier.

"Please man! Please! I don't want to die. Maybe we can both go forward. Please, just reach out and maybe you can bring me through.   Please just try. PLEASE!"

Fin turned and, still forced to move at a walk, began making his way once more to the cloud layer.

The collapse was slow enough that he heard the man's dying pleas for another minute before he passed through the mist.

Fin didn't pause, though he heard each and every heart wrenching cry.

Just before crossing the barrier, he heard the man scream. A cry of terror that quickly changed pitch before it was drowned by the sounds of the Armageddon below.

He decided to look back, one last time, to reaffirm a lesson he'd learned long ago.

Fin didn't know if the man had just died, but he did know that the consequences in this place were real. He knew that as surely as he knew Power awaited at the end of this path.

No one had spoken this information to him. The knowledge had just been placed there.

Failure had consequences.

That simple truth was why he looked back.

That was the lesson that could never be forgotten.

He felt no sympathy for that man. Fin didn't know him, and he'd long ago learned he wasn't meant to save everyone.

He couldn't save the world, and he didn't know if it deserved to be saved if he could.

Taking care of himself, and his own, was all that could be asked of any man.

Besides, the guy had made a mistake.

He'd tried to appeal to the mercy in Fin's heart.

Before doing that, he should have ensured there was a heart.

Fin passed into the clouds and reached the next rank.

***Scarce** Rank of the Assessment completed...*

*Calculating Score... Minimum Pass Score of **B** required...*

*You have earned a Score of **B**!*

100 points earned.

*Admission to the **Rare** Rank of the Assessment approved!*

The tests continued.

While the first three tests had pitted Fin against himself, perhaps refining who he already was, further growth required "fertilizer."

That was what Fin realized as he pulled at the round rock he'd just used to bash a woman's skull in.

Her head created a small suction noise as the stone was removed from her skull.

Fin was in no way surprised. Brain matter was always sticky.

Panting heavily, and holding the sharp branch that had been stabbed into his side, he looked at the domain he had won through blood and pain.

The outer surroundings were a jungle again. Piercing through the treetops was the pyramid he was standing on. It was similar to South American in design, rather than African. Rounded carvings of animals or monsters decorated the structure.

Reaching the top had required him to work with three other people. The prompt had declared them allies, and the knowledge implanted in their minds left no doubt as to the truth of that statement.

Together they had climbed. The first death had happened when one of the men on his team had trod on a step that looked slightly different from the rest. A small dart had shot out of a nondescript hole in a neighboring wall.

Two seconds after striking the man's leg, foam had flown out of his mouth. Within five seconds it was blood. His bowels released and he collapsed down over the side of the temple steps before Fin or the others could grab him.

That was how they learned about the traps.

The next death had come when they'd been attacked by the natives. Small green humanoids lunged out of a tunnel and attacked. The three of them had been able to fight off the first two waves, though the combat was brutal.

No weapons were involved, unless you included jagged nails and teeth.

After the second wave, one man had lost so much blood he could barely move.

The third wave removed the "barely."

When Fin and his final team member had reached the top, they saw a flat square festooned with small stones and loose branches. They also saw three other groups arrive at exactly the same moment from the other sides of the ziggurat.

A simple prompt had removed all thoughts of camaraderie.

The Path of Power requires blood.

Knowledge flooded the minds of every person on the platform. All initial alliances were now sundered.

At that moment, Fin made his first mistake.

The heart that he had always denied, that he had buried under layers of pain, rationality and logic, slipped through one of the few cracks he'd never fully been able to seal.

One of the other groups included a small child of about eight. Her scream distracted him for a key moment. Her own former team member had kicked her knee, snapping her small leg with a spray of blood.

Fin took a single step forward in a desire to stop the coup de grace, and that let his own former teammate pick up a sharp stick and ram it into his side.

His cold tactical mind reasserted itself, strangling the sympathy that had almost undone him. Without looking, he swung a fist back into his former ally's face. Her nose crumpled and she fell back with a cry.

A second thud heralded the end of the child, her neck snapped with a man's large boot on the back of it.

Time froze.

All movement stopped, with one savage exception.

A massive amount of blood exploded from the child's body.

What looked like every drop of crimson she'd had was siphoned into the air. It congealed into the shape of a hooded snake which then slithered past their immobile forms to the center of the platform.

Defying gravity, it continued sliding into midair until it hung several feet above the ground. It *sssss'd* in pleasure and time resumed.

The Path of Power requires blood.

Everyone stared at each other. None of them harbored any doubt as to what was about to happen.

What followed showed that the first victim, child or not, had found fortune in a swift death.

Armed only with rocks, sticks and foul intent, men and women tore each other apart.

After each death, a new red totem was created from the blood of the fallen. Birds, panthers, sharp toothed fish and serpents, each animal was different.

With each slain person, time froze. The totem would then ascend into the air to eagerly await the birth of more brothers and sisters.

The Power-hungry humans obliged.

Whether by fate or circumstance, the last two breathing were Fin and his former teammate.

With a broken ankle and two fingers that had been chewed off, she did not offer much trouble.

With every step Fin took towards her, her voice became more shrill and pleading.

"Please. Please don't kill me. I'm sorry. I didn't want to attack you, but I was so scared. Please! You don't have to do this. You don't have to! I'll su-"

Thud.

Thud!

Crack!

Squelch!

The glassiness in her remaining eye reflected the pitiless darkness in his own.

Time froze. A gibbering hyena of blood formed from the sanguine fluid stolen from his latest kill. It rose into the air and waited with the other totems of blood. Knowledge poured into the mind of the victor, and he knew what he had to do.

Like countless others had done on this world for eons before its fall from grace, he trod on the lives of others to reach greater heights.

Fin walked to the center of the temple. The totems stared down at him, now completely silent, an air of solemnity exuding from their animal forms. Standing in the center, he looked up through the ring of blood creatures at the deeper rouge of the clouds above.

Clouds he could never reach on his own.

Yet he was not alone.

He had paid the price for all the help he would need.

Fin only had to claim it.

Breathing heavily, he intoned, "The Path of Power requires blood."

Each totem bowed to him and then, in the order they were created, arranged their bodies in a macabre staircase to reach the Power above.

Fin grabbed the stick in his side, and with a sharp motion, broke most of it off, leaving the tip within him to plug his wound. The pain nearly made him black out, but his iron mind resisted.

He could do anything.

He would do everything.

The blood on his hands, mixed with the warm, wet blood of the snake totem. It had arranged its body in an "S" shape, giving him hand and foot holds. It shouldn't be possible for liquid to be this solid, but "possible" had no place on the Path of Power.

Fin climbed.

Each totem brought him higher.

Each footfall landed on the life of a murdered man, woman or child.

Each bloody step brought him closer to his goal.

At long last, he stood atop the head of the hyena that had formed from his former teammate. The red clouds remained several feet beyond his reach. He would have to jump to reach them.

If touching the scarlet layer did not take him to the next rank of the Assessment, he would plummet to his death far below.

It was one last test of his resolve and will.

Fin scoffed, "Pathetic."

Such hollow fears could not bar his Path.

He leaped.

Chapter 7: Heroic Suffering

R*are Rank of the Assessment completed…*

Calculating Score…   Minimum Pass Score of **B** *required…*

You have earned a Score of **S**! **+25% Points**! *Points for this Assessment* ***doubled***!

500 points earned.

Admission to the **Epic Rank** *of the Assessment approved!*

Fin arrived on an ancient battlefield.

Knowledge poured into him.

Surrounding him was a pink half bubble, the size of a baseball diamond. Through the forcefield he could see ruined earth, dead bodies torn into pieces, and shattered weapons of all types, sticking from the ground like a sea of grave markers.

In the distance, he saw more pink bubbles, disgusting pimples that would pop and release the armies within. After fifty he lost count.

It did not matter, because he knew the truth of the Heroic path, remained true.

The path would require blood, and far more than the paltry drops he had spread on the temple.

He knew that because he was not alone. Along with him in this bubble were three hundred other men and women. Staring at their faces, he learned that he recognized each one.

They were all different ages and skin colors. They wore different clothes, one dressed as a plumber, another a priest. Some were tall, some short, some fat, some thin.

They were all different, and yet, had a single unifying theme.

Fin been involved in the death of every last one of them.

He saw comrades from the Third War that he'd led into battle. He saw soldiers of the Eastern Hegemon who he'd shot dead to claim now forgotten patches of ground.

But whether old enemies or grieved allies, he knew that now, in this place, on this old blood drenched arena of death, that each of these men and women were as loyal to him as anyone had ever been. They would do their all to help him walk his path. Allies, enemies or victims, all were now with him to the end.

In the same way he knew everything else that he should not, this place had given him this knowledge and he fundamentally knew it to be true.

He could even count on the loyalty of the woman who stood directly behind him.

A woman with a mishappen head, as if someone had bashed one side with a rock.

Not three feet away, he looked into the face of the woman he'd just murdered. She stood tall with her ruined countenance, healed, but not completely. Back straight and shoulders back, she stared directly at him.

In her eyes, fear found no home.

Fin softly greeted her, "My friend."

She glared back, her lips shaking with rage, and spoke the truth of her soul, "I have filled my heart with hate."

He nodded to her in true understanding, exhaling one more soft word, "Good."

A timer appeared high in the sky.

100, 99, 98...

Everyone knew that when the numbers reached zero, the pink bubbles would disappear, and untold armies would fight for supremacy under the pink clouds above. Fin had a suspicion that his steps to the clouds would not be of blood this time.

He would trample upon meat and bone.

To Fin's great surprise and luck, an old lieutenant was among his resurrected army. With a simple command of "Squads," the man saluted Fin and broke into action.

In the short time remaining, he assigned ranks to ten other fallen comrades. Every newly promoted sergeant would lead a squad of about thirty. They each gave everyone else quick and dirty instructions to allow some semblance of order once the melee began.

The first order of business would be to grab weapons from the dead outside of the bubbles. From there they would move together and survive.

These were men and women of the space age, not warriors of archaic battlefields, but that didn't matter. After the Third War, nearly everyone of a certain age had spilled the same blood in the same mud.

In short period of time, order was brought to Chaos, and the lieutenant even had the time to bond the soldiers of Fin's new army.

With a mighty bellow, he shouted in with an aristocratic British accent, "What makes the grass grow!"

"Blood, blood, blood!"

"What are you going to do?"

"Kill, kill, kill!"

A prompt appeared in front of Fin as the final seconds counted down.

11, 10, 9, 8...

*Do you wish to safely leave the **Assessment** with your points intact?*

Fin gave his answer to his soldiers, not the trap of the prompt.

"What does the path require?" he cried to his people.

The woman with the ruined face looked at him, and screamed, "Blood, blood, blooooood!" along with her new comrades.

The forcefield disappeared and Fin walked the path of Power once more.

***

Fin collapsed, as much from blood loss as sorrow. He cradled the head of the woman he'd once killed. The woman who had just saved his life, sacrificing her to slay the last enemy on the battlefield.

The path of Power proved it did not care who they were. The dearest friends could become the bitterest enemies. And a sweet victory on one day could taste like the most bitter ashes on another.

Once more, only the two of them breathed in an abattoir of carnage. His own breaths were slow and shallow. Hers issued sharp and blood flecked due to the spear tip in her right lung.

Once more she stared at him, in pain but this time also in peace. They had both fought long and hard. For hours or days, he couldn't be sure, they had dragged their weary selves over the bodies of the dead to fight atop them and add another layer.

Fin had no idea how many pink bubbles had burst, how many armies had been released, but he knew he was looking at a carpet of death.

There had to be thousands, thousands upon thousands, of dead.

In this kind of battle, luck played as large a role in survival as strength or skill.

But he'd been lucky.

He'd been strong.

And thanks to this woman, he hadn't been alone.

Fin left his scavenged sword found sticking out of the chest of his last enemy, focused only on providing meager comfort to the woman in his arms. His one time ambusher, and now, closest friend in this world.

With her last breath, she spoke a single word.

"Marie."

Was it her name? The name of a lover or loved one?

Fin would never know, but he would never forget.

With her death, he remained the last. After hearing screams and the clash of metal for so long, the quiet felt almost profane.

It didn't last long.

A crack of thunder, like the world breaking, split the silence. The pink clouds above began to churn, and a tornado, the color of farmed salmon, descended. It pulled with cyclone force all the bodies of the fallen, even those that had died before the bubbles burst, but left Fin untouched.

Over disgusting minutes, the winds moved the carcasses and severed limbs to erect a structure. Spilled guts and blood were used for mortar. Bones provided the framework. A temple of pain and suffering was created before Fin's eyes, thanks to his great and terrible works.

When it was done, the tornado dissipated, leaving the structure touching the pink clouds above and a single word was emblazoned across Fin's gaze.

Climb!

And so he did. Over blood and viscera, he stepped on the faces of slaughtered men, women and children. He slipped on the jelly of leaking eyes. More times than could be easily counted, he sank elbow deep into vats of bile and shit before standing again and continuing to climb.

After long hours, he stood atop the monument of slaughter and looked up at the glowing pink clouds above. With barely any strength left in his ruined body, he leaped, passing into the clouds.

Fin left the lands of heroes and villains, and entered the eternity of the Sagas.

Chapter 8: Dragon Fear

Epic Rank of Assessment completed...

Calculating Score... Minimum Pass Score of A required...

You have earned a Score of SS! Points for this Assessment doubled! You have earned a Special Reward (Epic)!

600 points earned!

+1000 points for completing the Assessment of the Heroic Tier!

Restoring Candidate's Health!

Admission to Saga Tier Assessments approved.

Admission to the Fabled Rank of Assessment approved!

Fin arrived on a small rock floating through space, not larger than a house.

A spear of gleaming metal was in his hand. Against the backdrop of an amber nebula in the distance, further than he could even measure without reference, he saw massive serpents and eagles with the paws of lions doing battle.

Flashes of every color imaginable shot between the massive ship sized beings as they released powers he could barely gaze upon.

The asteroid he was standing on was flying towards this battle ground. As it passed through space, knowledge poured into him.

He knew the rock he stood upon was surrounded by a bubble of air, but that there was no guarantee it would last if he was struck by an even glancing blow by any of the immense creatures ahead. There was some vague idea that

~REWARD~

the deaths of every building sized monster would release an energy to get him to the next stage, but that was vague at best.

Still, Fin's resolve was unshaken. If he was here, it was because he was on the Path. If there was a Path, he'd find a way to walk it.

For Lauren, he could do anything.

For her, he would do everything.

Do you wish to safely leave the Assessment with your points intact?

"Let's do this!" he snarled.

The window disappeared, and the battle of titans ahead of him stopped abruptly. The snout and beak of every world ending being turned at once, as they noticed the frail creature that had dared to intrude on their majestic conflict.

Seeing that, while Fin's resolve still did not falter, he did decide to remark on his current state of affairs.

"Well shit."

Before he could even register movement, a dragon crossed the vastness of space and delicately grasped the asteroid he was standing on with talons the size of evergreens.

Fin fell to the rocky ground at the sudden deceleration of his "planet" and his spear fell away into the infinite abyss.

"Aren't you an interesting thing?" the dragon chuckled through teeth taller than trees and sharper than scalpels. Its voice was as deep as bottomless chasms and echoed with enough Power to vibrate Fin's soul.

"How did you even get here? And what's this at the center of you?"

A wisp of energy issued from the dragon's cavernous mouth and penetrated Fin's chest before he could even attempt to react. Information poured into the great creature's mind until suddenly its amusement turned to fear.

"What are you? You shouldn't be!" With a roar, it pronounced judgement, "You cannot be!"

Emerald green flames shot out of its mouth, immolating the asteroid into nothing. The same would have happened to Fin if not for an amber cocoon surrounding him the instant before death.

Still, he could not endure the unleashed majesty of the dragon, and darkness claimed him.

Unseen, lines of script emblazoned across the sightless vision of Fin's doppelganger, returning the borrowed Essence to his true body, still held dormant in the wave of Chaos Energy sweeping across the Earth.

***Fabled** Rank of Assessment completed...*

*Calculating Score... Minimum Pass Score of **S** required...*

*You have earned a Score of **F**!*

*Points lost: **-1000%***

You have negative points!

*You are **Cursed**! You shall be a plague upon your world!*

*You are **Damned**!*

*Calculating appropriate **Punishment**... Assessing Grade... Assessing Grade... Assessing Gr-*

Error...

*Candidate is a **Pseudo-Mortal**...*

A Pseudo-Mortal should not have been allowed to enter the previous Assessment...

*The minimum Realm required for the **Battle of Mutara Nebula** Assessment is **Tyrant**...*

Revaluating Score...

Candidate showed fortitude on staying on the path...

Candidate showed idiocy for staying on the path...

*Evaluating the feasibility of awarding the Mythic Title: **Sweet Dumb Idjit**...*

Title found to be inappropriate for Pseudo-Mortal...

Reverting to previous protocol...

     ~*REWARD*~

Evaluating Score...

Aberrant Energy detected...

Appropriate Score cannot be ascertained due to aberrant Energy...

The magical windows popped up one after another, two being deleted before they could even register.

~~Attempting to contact Mortal Administrator...~~

~~All Administrator options suppressed...~~

Initiating secondary protocols...

*Evaluating event of greatest significance during the **Fabled** rank of the Assessment...*

Candidate struck fear in the heart of a Cosmic Dragon...

*For a Pseudo-Mortal this is a quasi-**Legendary** event...*

Assessment complete...

*Candidate will not receive a pass or fail for the **Fabled** rank of the Assessment...*

*The official Assessment ranking will be considered to have stopped at the first rank of the **Saga** Tier.*

All points preserved.

*Due to the quasi-**Legendary** Event, rewards up to the **Mythic** rank allowed...*

*You have earned a Special Reward (**Mythic**) for achieving a **quasi-Legendary** event!*

Your Assessment is complete.

Total Points... 2415!

*For completing the entire **Heroic** Tier, you will be awarded the most suitable rewards for your State of Being in light of your Actions during the Assessment.*

Calculating rewards in line with your Soul, Body and Mind... Optimizing the best combination...

Choices made!

Your Soul has been found to have deep connection to each of the Basic Elements. Searching for the most appropriate Abilities, Skill, Marks...

*The SSS-grade **Elemental Resonance** Ability Tree has been found to have a **100%** resonance with this facet of your Essence and is available.*

ELEMENTAL RESONANCE ABILITY TREE

Elemental Guidance (Scarce)

Intuition shall guide your steps as you interact with the fundamental properties of magic.

Cost: 209 Assessment Points.

Elemental Soul (Rare)

Your soul resonates to the correct path as you interact with the magic of the Basic Elements.

Cost: 513 Assessment Points

Whisper (Epic)

You have a strong connection and innate understanding of the 8 Basic Elements, so much so that they may whisper the secrets of the Labyrinth.

Cost: 1028 Assessment Point

Whisper *has been chosen and is now tied to your **Soul**.*

-1028 Points

*Your **Body** has always been used as a conduit for your desires.*

*The **Mana Connection Skill Tree** will further this end as you interact with the forces of the Labyrinth. This Skill will be provided to you, at the highest rank your rewards allow, at the earliest possible time after your world's induction to the Labyrinth is complete.*

-586 Points

Your **Mind** takes great joy in infuriating other sapient Beings.

The **Violent Delights** Mark will further this end as you interact with the countless beings of the Labyrinth. This Mark will be provided to you at the earliest possible time after your world's induction to the Labyrinth is complete.

-762 Points

Residual Points insufficient for appropriate reward. These points shall lost.

You have earned **2 Special Rewards**!

Determining the most appropriate Special Reward (Epic)...

Reward decided:

Last Words – Your Soul will soon endure great suffering. Rather than be broken by this, you will be allowed to hear the last words of your love.

This will greatly improve the healing of your **Soul** and make it more resilient in the days to come.

Determining the most appropriate Special Reward (**Mythic**)...

Reward decided:

Dragon Mark – You have marked a Dragon and changed its destiny. Such actions cannot go unanswered. You are now Marked in turn.

This Mark will lie dormant until you reach a Realm where you can survive its Power. Be warned, Danger and Reward are close bedfellows.

Assessment complete. Rewards complete.

Protocol initiated for newly inducted worlds...

Memories of Assessment suppressed.

Resuming Time…

Chapter 9: So Normal

EARTH

"Lauren! I'll save you! I'll save you, baby! I'll s-"

"Wait," Fin floated in the void of Chaos. Had something happened? "I think something happened."

The wave passed and, all of a sudden, he was back on Earth.

It was all the same as it had been before the grey wave.

The car, the blue sky… and Lauren!

He heard her speaking softly.

"Oh my god. Oh my god. Oh my god." The words weren't so much spoken as they were breathed.

She was staring straight ahead at the same view they had been watching before the grey wave had washed over them. Her mind was struggling with the same paradox that Fin's own was trying to strangle.

Lauren just couldn't reconcile that the beautiful sky, the white fluffy clouds, and the yellow shining sun were so… normal.

For a moment, she wondered if she'd lost her mind. Had she had a psychotic break? There was no way she'd really seen a wave of grey fire blaze across the world, high as the sky itself, and leave no mark of it passing! That wasn't possible, was it?

Was it?

The fear of insanity compounded the psychological effect of the wave itself, almost forcing her to lose control and just start screaming. She was no shrinking violet, though, she was her father's daughter. She also knew, that despite her fears, there was no doubting one thing.

~REWARD~

When the wave had washed over her, she had felt a resonance. Lauren knew, at the very core of her being, that what she had experienced inside the wave had been real. If that was real, then all of it was. Latching onto that truth, she calmed her breathing. Clutching Fin's fingers, she gave the answer he needed to hear.

"I'm fine."

She searched his face. On it she saw the same fear that she herself felt, but she also saw the iron resolve that she loved in him.

Seeing that she was back with him, Fin asked a simple question, "We both saw the wave, right?"

At her nod, he gave one of his own, "That means it really happened, despite-"

Fin gestured to the normal landscape in front of him. The normality of it all seemed as crazy as the phenomenon they'd just experienced. "I thought it was the end of everything."

"Me too," she responded gazing into the distance.

They looked into one another's eyes intensely before leaning in at the same time and kissing each other frantically.

After they separated, they just stared at each other, deriving comfort from their love.

Looking at Lauren's perfect face, for just a moment, a different image superimposed itself. It was her, but blood was everywhere, and her eyes were open but didn't see anything.

He snapped his eyes shut and shook his head violently.

Looking again, the bloody image was gone, and then even the memory of it faded away completely.

She looked at him urgently, "What just happened?"

Fin shook his head, not knowing how to answer.

Both of them held each other's hands, looking wildly out of the car windows and panting.

It had looked like the wave had swallowed reality.

From their spot on Stone Mountain, they could see for miles. Atlanta sprawled out in front of them about twenty miles away. The landscape was mostly green forest. Even in early October, the browning of the trees was just starting, showing barely any tan spots against the verdant sea.

Their heads swiveled all around, expecting to see utter devastation. Instead, what they saw was almost painfully normal.

Clouds floated in the evening sky. The last vestiges of light illuminated the city in front of them. A gentle wind rustled the leaves on the trees around them and made a few yellow leaves tumble to the ground. A bird warbled from where it perched on a power line before taking wing.

Everything was just so-

Normal.

Fin got out of the car, still looking around wildly. The wave had already moved past the horizon, making him wonder if he'd imagined it all.

Instead of devastation, or any of horrible scenes he'd witnessed while inside the wave, he just saw the typical signs of suburbia. There were orderly rows of trees lining the street behind the car, a mix of elm and maples. Most of the leaves were still green but there was a smattering of yellows and a few reds. Further back from the street on either side were dozens of McMansions.

Looking the other way, he was able to see more houses and streets wending down the mountain. From his high view, he saw the golden arches of a mickee dees standing sentinel across from the stylized red chicken of a chikfila.

The Georgia-Auburn game was that night, so there were barely any cars on the road, but there were a few.   It looked like just a peaceful southern Saturday.

As long as you could ignore the cars that had crashed and the shattered glass that could be seen on the Atlanta skyscrapers in the fading light.

And of course, that was when the screams began.

Almost like it was a consensus, everyone effected by the wave started panicking. From almost every house people began to wail. Some sat there in a daze, but far more found comfort in anger and noise. Gunshot rang out.

Fin and Lauren met each other eyes.

"We should get home," she said with firm conviction.

"Yeah," he agreed nodding. "Yeah, let's get home."

Chapter 10: Collisions

They got back in the car and pulled out fast enough to raise dust under their tires. The lack of other people on the road worked in their favor.

They left the scenic spot and pulled onto I-78. As they drove through neighborhoods, they saw people in various states of distress. Some were speaking animatedly and pointing at the sky, others just sat on their lawns in a stupor.

They saw families anxiously packing their cars to drive somewhere they probably thought was safer. He saw others fighting on the street.

All the different panicked emotions that humans could feel were being processed all at once, and that panic had stripped every one of their illusions. What was left was the raw core of what each person truly was.

Fin kept driving. They left the neighborhoods behind and entered a veritable no man's land of rocky ground.

While he did, he had to blink often.

There was a weird flashing in the corner of his vision. It would go away for a moment, but then come back. He almost asked her to drive, worried that he had a concussion, but he pushed through, and tried to focus on the road.

The blinking also wasn't the only thing that felt off.

Ever since coming back, he'd felt... strange. It was like he'd had too many cups of coffee. He felt energetic. He felt-

Powerful.

It had to be the adrenalin from what they'd just been through.

More important to Fin were the questions running through his head on repeat.

What had just happened? What was that wave?

Lauren had been checking her Link the whole time they'd been driving, but all that was online was other people asking "WTF?" in five thousand different ways.

The Wave with a capital "W," as it was already being called, had spread across the entire world.

Of course, there were already a bunch of crazies blaming everything from terrorists to polluting aliens.

Lauren's Link showed that "#TheWave" was the most popular tag on the Great Link with "#Wave" being the second.

While stopped at a light, Fin looked at Lauren. It had only been a few minutes since they had experienced a phenomena that defied any of the previous experiences, and she was already calm and collected.

It made him love her all the more.

He adored her beauty, but he worshipped her strength. That was the kind of inner power that was not only reliable in a tough moment, but also through a lifetime. Even with people going crazy around them and whatever that grey wave had been, he knew he was a lucky man.

She caught him staring at her and she gave him that slightly crooked smile he knew so well.

"The light's green now, creeper."

"I knew that," Fin retorted, completely playing off that he'd been distracted by her beautiful face.

"Uh huh," she just replied, not fooled for a moment.

Fin's foot pressed on the gas while her hand gently rested on his thigh. They eased forward, only a few miles from home now and almost off the mountain. Her hand suddenly tightened into a death grip on his thigh, strong enough to cut off circulation.

Before he could even register to question why, she screamed, "Kamel!"

He would remember that in the years to come.

Memory was funny that way.

He wouldn't remember the panic in her voice. He wouldn't remember the fear he had when he saw what made her panic. He wouldn't even remember the bruises she left on his thigh. He'd just remember that instead of calling him

Fin, she called him by his pet name. A name that had begun as a joke, but had grown into an eternal pledge of love.

A promise that he would always be her Kamel, her "perfect one."

Before he could open his mouth to respond, one and a half tons of speeding hover truck T-boned their SUV with force equal to forty times gravity. The hit was hard enough to compress Fin's brain inside of his skull, rendering him unconscious in an instant.

*****

Minutes before...

"Sons of bitches. Ungrateful dirty bastards!"

Flecks of spit flew out of Jerini's mouth as he raged alone in his car. He took a deep pull from the bottle of whiskey, one hand casually on the wheel. His truck weaved in and out of his lane, barely missing cars parked along the residential street.

"They'll regret treating me like zis," he slurred to himself.

"I'm worth more than all of them put together! Who cares about some old fucking ritual? What does it matter?

Making a rock glow with your mind? Big deal! What! You've never heard of a light bulb, *dad*?

Old fuck!

I'm just as good.

I'm better. Better than any of them!" he raged.

He took another deep pull from the bottle while he continued to rant at no one. If anyone were to listen, and was actually dumb enough to believe the crap coming out of the young man's mouth, they would think there had never been a greater injustice than the treatment he had suffered. Jerini kept ranting for a full minute before he felt something that he didn't understand.

Even with how drunk he was, his thin Bloodline reacted to the raw power that had just struck Earth. He'd been too deep in the well of self-pity and intoxication to notice the light show of the beam of chaos striking the earth, but as soon as it fully integrated into this reality, he knew something important had happened. Slamming on the brakes, his vehicle came to a sudden and silent halt.

Jerini blinked in confusion and yearning. Before the wave came into view, even before the clouds began to move, he turned to the west. When the wave began to wash across the horizon and rush towards him, he felt fear, but also a deep yearning. With wide and blood injected eyes, he watched as it surged towards him.

The wave washed over Jerini. The power flooded through him, mind, body and soul. After it passed on, he was left with a translucent window in his vision.

Congratulations! Your connection to...

Jerini read the information, his heart thudding with excitement. The old stories. The myths. They were true! Almost everyone in the family, himself included, thought they were just stupid propaganda that the old farts talked about to make themselves sound more important.   But they were right!

With a joyous and vindictive laugh, he started driving again. His foot pushed down hard on pedal. Not only had that wave connected him to the Source, but it had changed him. He could feel it! He had an Ability! His hands began to glow as he accessed it.

Another bout of laughter filled the air. This was so easy! It was nothing like those stupid fucking rituals! He'd get back to the house, and then he'd take that rock and shove it up his sister's ass! She would *pay* for mocking him. The whole family would pay. And then, then, he would take his revenge on his father. Who knows? Maybe the entire Lotus Familia would kneel before him. The entire world!

"Hahaha!"

He took a deep drink from the bottle, and pushed his foot down further. The only regret he had was that he'd already done the emergency bump of coke he kept in the glove box! He laughed at himself a second later.

He was worried about that?

As soon as he got back, he'd be neck deep in coke and pussy, and then, then, he'd start his plan to take over the family!

The hover truck zoomed down the road, moving at over a hundred mph, but still not fast enough for him. His mouth watered he was so hungry to show all who had doubted him how wrong they were. How he was more than worthy.

How he had a destiny!

As he approached an intersection, he looked at the white glow of his hands again with an almost doting love, like a mother for her most precious child. Compared to the beautiful luminosity coming from inside of him, he didn't even take the time to see that the traffic light was red.

He didn't see the SUV easing into the intersection.

He didn't see the moment his hover truck smashed into lives he was about to irrevocably change.

As his truck flipped over, Jerini didn't realize he had triggered a second "wave" that would wash over the world.

***

Fin regained his senses less than a minute after the crash, but the concussion he was suffering didn't let him think about that. The first thing he could register was pain, a diffuse pain all over his body, like waking up the morning after losing a fight.

The next thing was the sound of a constant, blaring car horn. At first, he thought he was leaning on the wheel for some reason, but over the next couple seconds, his addled head realized the horn was a lower pitch than his.

He tried to figure out where it could be coming from, but his vision was blurry.

More than blurry. It was almost like there was a film over his eyes. A blinking film. Were there words?

Irritated and in pain, he waved his hands at it wanting it to go away. Something he did must have worked because the visual disturbance disappeared. At the same time, he was able to think clearly for the first time since waking up.

With a flash, he remembered!

Adrenalin shot through his body. The panic he felt in that moment of realization tore a dagger through his heart, making the aches of his body wash away as if they had never been.

"Lauren!"

Turning his head to right, the world froze for the second time.

Lifeless eyes stared back at him out of a beautiful, blood smeared face.

"Lauren! Lauren!"

Fin tried to lunge and grab her, but his seat belt stopped him short. He scrambled at it, his hands moving rapidly, an animal trying to escape a trap. In the short seconds it took him to find the release of the belt, his mind, trained to always assess, took in and recreated the scene.

They'd been hit by another car on her side.

Whatever had struck them had done so with enough force to cave the passenger side inward. Lauren's body had been crushed by the crumpled metal of the door.

The hit had spun them off the road.

He knew that because her side of the car was now pinned against a tree.

A tree with a low hanging branch.

A branch that had pierced her window and then continued on through her body.

The jagged spear of the wood had stabbed clean through her, but that was the only clean thing about it. Bright red blood coated the four inches of wood that protruded from the back of her seat.

Chapter 11: Better Angels

LIFE

"Lauren! Lauren! No! Lauren!"

Free from the seat belt, he lunged forward again.

Just an inch short, he froze.

Fin wanted to reach out both hands to shake her awake, but he didn't.

He'd seen too much death in his life. He knew she was gone.

It was her eyes.

There was nothing in them.

There was only "lack."

A loss of light.

An extinguished spark that would forever leave the world darker.

The realization broke through his panicked denial and released a far stronger force.

A soul deep reservoir of pain.

Fin started gasping for air. His head dropped and tears fell faster than the blood dripping from the branch.

Even though his eyes were squeezed shut the tears could not be contained.

They flowed so violently his tears threatened to turn into blood themselves.

~REWARD~

Between his shock and loss, he didn't feel any of the bruises forming over his entire body.

The emotional pain could not be ignored, lava burning through him, smothering every joy he had nurtured, consuming every dream he had built.

He almost descended into a place that could have broken him, maimed his heart in a way that could never be healed.

Fin shook, eyes wild, gazing upon love that would never gaze back.

Insanity called, a temptation he would not resist.

Then he heard it, her sweet voice. Somehow, from her still, lifeless face, came a simple message.

'Three promises.'

Those Last Words that she could not have spoken, changed the course of his fate.

Those words saved him from a darkness that would have devoured him.

The next words he heard were like a spell, summoning him to a light he would extinguish.

"Help," came the soft cry. "Christ, is anyone there? Help me!" The sound of a car horn blasted out, two time short, then one long.

The words were soft, barely audible, and easily missed, especially with the concussion Fin was suffering.

He took a last look at the body that was "Not-Lauren," and then finally touched the side of her face. Using his thumb, he rubbed away a single speck of blood from her crimson covered skin.

Fin took a deep breath. With a shaky, pained exhale, he murmured, "Three promises."

He would do his best to keep them.

Looking out of the windows, initially he couldn't see the other car.

Fin's gaze went wide and he searched. His vision was blurry from the head trauma, and the large crack in the windshield didn't make it any easier. He found the source though. There, about thirty yards away, a hover truck was tipped over onto its side, braced against another tree.

The front was half-crumpled, and small flame burned on what was left of the hood.

The hover capabilities must have failed after the collision, because only the back driver's side still remained off the ground, and at a bare six inches at that. From the scrapes all over the truck's body, it looked like it had flipped over, and that the driver was lucky enough to end the tumble with the vehicle upright.

That was who was calling for help.

It took less than three seconds to assess the scene and recreate what had happened.

He did it all with clinical detachment.

When he heard the voice call out again, something inside of Fin shifted with an almost audible click.

The driver was calling for help.

The driver that had hit them was calling for help.

The driver that had killed the love of his life was calling for help.

Fin bared his teeth.

Okay, he thought with venom. I'm coming.

The bottomless pit of pain Fin had been falling into shattered as he was enveloped in a far more familiar emotion.

Rage.

Fin struggled with his car door, his clumsy fingers and addled brain not able to manipulate the latch. Every second he was denied his revenge, his anger flared hotter. Help? The man wanted help?

After taking everything from him, the man dared to ask for help!

"I'll help you ya son of a bitch! Don't you fucking die. I'm coming!"

Fin struggled with the door; the collision having deformed the metal slightly. After slamming his shoulder against it twice though, it popped open and he basically fell through it. The change in position made him dizzy again, but his fury kept him from being sick.

Fin collapsed out of the car and crawled free of the wreck. He barely slowed. Even as his hands ground against shattered glass, he didn't pause. The gashes carved into his palms went unnoticed.

Only one thing mattered and that was "helping" the man in the other car.

Fin got to his feet and promptly vomited. A moment later, he could barely see, a bout of dizziness and blurry vision threatening to take him down.

It even looked like there were words in his field of view, like a hologram. After rubbing his eyes hard though, he focused on just being able to see clearly and the image faded away.

He balled a fist and started walking towards the truck. He imagined slamming his knuckles into the face of the driver. He snarled faintly, imagining the shock on the asshole's face after the first hit, but that expression wouldn't last long. Not after he slammed his fist down again, and again, and again.

There wouldn't be a face left!

This fucker had taken Lauren from him, and he was still squealing and crying like a little bitch!

It was time to put him down.

Just before he marched over to commit murder, he looked inside the SUV again. His gaze fell upon Lauren's face, her beautiful, blood spackled, perfect face.

Then the light of the setting sun caught the diamond ring on her finger, pulling him into a memory. A memory only weeks old. The day she'd agreed to marry him.

He'd been so nervous he'd rambled on for minutes while she just struggled not to laugh at how nervous he was. She knew in her heart how much he loved her and how long he'd been working up the nerve to ask.

She was amazing like that.

She'd never pushed or forced; she'd just loved him for who he was.

She was also a bit of a dick, though.

He'd said once that she was the most wonderful dick in the world. It had been months before she'd stopped torturing about that one.

That day though, she'd just guided the ring to her finger, and then paused.

"I don't ever need you to be perfect, and I know you've done things you regret in the past. I accept you and love you for all of that. And I'll marry you if you just promise me one more thing."

He'd started nodding like a bobblehead, but before he could speak, she placed a single finger on his lips and looked at him seriously.

"Will you promise to do your best to be a good man in the future?"

Sensing the seriousness of her question, and knowing how his anger had governed him too many times in the past, he'd stopped nodding and really thought about her words. With all the truth and love in his heart, he'd answered, "I'll do my best."

She'd slipped the ring on her finger, then kissed him deeply. After several breathless, heaven filled seconds, she'd pulled away and gave him her perfect, crooked smile, "That will always be enough for me."

Then she'd given him a nice light slap, and with more than a bit of snark added, "But that's three promises you owe me now, Evers!"

The memory banked the fire inside him.

His wrath didn't diminish at all, but he regained control of it.

His memory of Lauren and her years of love let him encapsulate that anger. It burned in him now, not through him. With that convenient feeling gone, his pain and loss flooded back to the forefront of his mind, and a sob forced its way out. Tears fell once again, but it was almost like he could hear her voice. She was telling him that someone was suffering, and that they needed his help.

"Okay, baby. I'll do my best."

Grinding a fist across his eyes, he clenched his jaw and started limping towards the truck. Whoever was inside was still calling for help.

"Someone? Someone has to be out there! Please! I can't die like this! Not now!"

Every plea for help fed the anger inside of Fin.

It almost felt like he was going to be burned from within. His jaw was clenched so tight his teeth ached.   Bile tickled the back of his throat, and every breath came out in a strained huff. He wouldn't give in to it though. He would hold to his promise. He would honor Lauren's life by trying to be the man she had loved, not the monster she had saved.

Fin crossed the street in a pain filled stride. After a series of agonizing steps that made him wonder if his ankle was broken or just merely sprained, he reached the truck. The two men caught sight of each other at the same time.

They were about the same age, both in their mid-thirties. That was where the similarities ended. The man in the truck was white, with short cut blond hair so pale it almost matched his skin. The outside and inside of the truck were pitch black and his silk shirt was the same darkness. The kind of black that clothes can only have before they were washed even a single time. A simple gold ring was on the middle finger of his left hand. He wore designer jeans that were bloodied and stylish black leather shoes.

None of that said as much about him as his face.

Green eyes flashed, set in eyes reddened from his pain. To Fin, it looked like they resided within a face that seemed accustomed to arrogance. His nose was sharp, coming to a firm point. High cheekbones hovered above sparse lips and a strong jaw. His face looked too thin, but not in a sickly manner. More the visage of someone with neither fat nor large muscles on their frame. It was also the kind of face that probably got him more than a little attention from the ladies.

If Fin was inclined to be honest and impartial, he'd have said the man was beautiful, but as it was, the refined features just pissed him off.

As Fin stared at the man who had killed his love, the man he had come to save, he was observed in turn.

Cutting off his cries for help, cold emerald eyes stared at his would be rescuer. He saw a black man with light brown skin. Short curls hugged a strong face, with thick lips and a broad nose. Brown, almost amber eyes, stared into his own with a fierce intensity.

He could see anger in them, an emotion he himself was well versed with, but also… pain. The man's face had a cut down one cheek, and bruises forming around both eyes.

The only other thing he could see through the window was the man's bloodied shirt. It was emblazoned with the logo for that game, The Land, and was tight across his broad chest.

In the instant after they took each other in, both arrived at nearly the same conclusion.

They didn't like what they saw.

"Pompous, pretty boy rich shit."

"Musclebound nigger peasant."

Neither said it, but even without the horrific situation they were in, they most likely would have taken an immediate dislike to one another.

The pause only lasted a few seconds, but it was long enough for the man in the car to scream, "Help me!" It came across more as a command than a request.

The fires of anger grew stronger inside Fin, but he didn't it let it break beyond his control. Instead, he took stock of the situation.

The truck had slammed into their SUV, and it had crumpled the front of the vehicle. A small fire was still there on the hood, but it didn't look to be getting larger. If Fin remembered correctly, the fuel cells that powered these hover cars and trucks were much more stable than conventional engines, so there shouldn't be any immediate danger. The downside was that they held more energy than a fuel engine.

The man in the truck was trapped because the steering wheel had bent down enough to trap his legs. The driver's side door was also blocked by the tree the car had rolled into. To get the guy out, Fin would have to go through the passenger door, work him free, then pull him out.

It would take time, but it should be doable. The man was luckier than he knew. Geneva would have automatically called 911 so help was on the way. In the meantime, this asshole had just happened to run into an ER doc.

The man apparently didn't realize his luck, because his next words lacked even the pretense of grace.

"What are you waiting for! I'm hurt and you're just standing like an idiot. Let me make it easy for you. Get me free and my family will reward you. You'll have enough to buy a T-shirt that actually fits. Just help me!"

Gritting his teeth, visions of beating the man to death flashed through Fin's mind, but he controlled it, instead grabbing the door handle.

It was locked.

"I'm trying to help you asshole," he spat. "Unlock the door."

"My name isn't asshole. It's Jerini Lotus," the man spat back as he pushed a button.

The anger flared again in response to Jerini's arrogance. It threatened to even push away Fin's pain, but he wouldn't let it. He'd fulfill his promise. He would save this man's life and honor Lauren's memory.

I'm going to be who she wanted me to be, he thought. I'm going to be a better man. I'm going to-

The door opened and a small item fell onto the street with a clink.

Fin's eyes tracked down to see what had fallen. In that moment, everything changed.

A small, crumpled beer can lay at his feet.

~REWARD~

Looking inside his ruined truck, Fin saw several more and a large bottle of scotch with a crack running down the side.

The man had been drinking.

He'd been drinking when he'd hit their car.

He'd been drinking when he'd killed Lauren.

He'd been drinking when he made the world a darker, colder place.

He'd been drinking when he'd *stolen* the most important thing in the world from Fin.

Fin's reason was consumed by fire.

[BURN!], a voice seemed to whisper in his head, both soft and intense. A voice that was both part and apart from him at once.

The anger that had been a bonfire inside of him suddenly shrank. Not like a dying ember, but instead like an implosion before a nuclear blast. In that moment, he was left cold and empty. In that moment, he finished his last thought, but this time, said it out loud.

"I'm going to kill you."

The words came out with calm certainty. There was no rage in it. No false bravado. It was just the cold inevitability of death.

[BURN!], he heard again. This time, it felt like the voice came from both the anger burning inside of him and the fire burning on the hood.

Yes, he agreed silently, giving in to the voice completely.

The anger he'd been holding back exploded. All the walls he'd struggled to build, all the love Lauren had placed within him, all the promises he'd made, they were consumed in a single glorious release. The air filled with the roar of a newly born predator.

"DIIIIEEEEEEE!"

On a level both lower and higher than conscious thought, Fin accessed his mana for the first time. Following the guidance of the Ability tied to his soul, it poured into the receptable that matched the fury boiling through him.

An interface appeared in his vision, but he barely even noticed when his blue bar bottomed out.

It just felt so good to be free!

Each point of mana that fed into the flame on the hood made the fire grow larger. Not only larger, but hotter. So hot that the fuel cell was compromised, and an explosion enveloped them both.

Jerini had just enough time to see the small, hand-sized, flame turn into a five foot tall bonfire, and the color shift from dark red to orange. Then the cell exploded, releasing a cataclysm of blue hellfire.

Time seemed to slow down. It was like Fin could perceive the ball of flame and force exploding from the hood. He could see Jerini's terrified face as it screamed. He could even see the ripples on the man's face as the impact waves reached it scant milliseconds before the fire melted his face and made the air in his lungs catch fire.

The explosion reached Fin a bare instant later. Though his mind could not register what was happening, much less understand it, he felt something reaching out to him. In this strange state of altered perception, he thought it must be death itself.

A just reward for an oathbreaker.

He welcomed it with all of his being.

The waves of the explosion struck him. While the force remained unabated, the flames themselves were partially consumed when they got within a foot of his body.

What remained was not bone melting white-blue plasma, but instead a simple red-orange fire. Windows appeared in Fin's vision, washed out by the bright light of approaching oblivion. He didn't even register them on a conscious level before the shockwave knocked him out.

The world turned black, and he welcomed death with a smile on his face.

See you soon baby.

Chapter 12: Worse Fate

Sirens blared as a single police car pulled up the road.

"I hate coming into these reclamation zones, Jonesy." Greg looked around at the barren area.

"We all wish the Third War hadn't happened, man. Quit complaining. It ain't like we're being sent to a red zone, and we got a job to do. Trust me, you don't want to piss off someone with enough money to trigger a gold alert. Let's just check it and be done."

"But that Wave man! Some cosmic level shit just happened and we're out there checking on some rich kid that probably just has a blown tire."

Jonesy agreed with his partner, but Greg's bitching didn't change anything.

It just worsened his mood.

His tone went from friendly to commanding. His partner was loyal like a bulldog, but sometimes he only responded to a bark.

"Quit complaining!"

Greg grunted, but snapped his lips shut.

Relenting after a couple minutes, Jonesy tried to take the sting out of it. He was the senior officer, but he didn't like to roll like that if he could avoid it. "Look man. We have no idea what's happening. All we know is that a VIPs car sent out an automated signal. You're probably right, just a spoiled rich kid, and we'll be back in the city in ten. Besides, I heard Marsha responded to a VIP call last month and the guy gave her tickets to the Falcon's game. At the 50!"

Greg looked sullen for a second, but then gave a grin, "That's just because Marsha probably put out."

"As if you wouldn't to get those tickets."

Greg started to retort, but then shrugged. No point when the man was right. Pride had never been high on his list of priorities.

"Besides," Jonesy continued, "whatever that wave was, it's high above our paygrade. Be happy we're out here. People are losing their shit in the city. Not only are the citizens panicking, but every criminal in ATL is taking advantage of the confusion. I hear the governor's already called out the national guard."

"Really?" Greg sounded just a bit too interested for Jonesy's liking. The redneck's family was probably in on the looting.

"Really. So let's just take care of this brat, then we'll drive slow getting back. There's no way they're letting us go at the end of shift, but at least we can stay out here in the country rather than dealing with the shit show in the city."

Greg thought about it before grudgingly admitting, "Good call. Let's go change a rich kid's tire so he doesn't have to risk breaking a nail."

Jonesy drove a couple more minutes before turning a final corner. Both officers' mouths dropped open as they took in the scene.

Greg turned towards him, and lamely observed, "I guess it's more than a flat tire."

What they saw looked like something out of the war. A grey SUV was slammed so hard against a tree that branches had pierced the front of the car like spears. Blood was splattered across the inside of the windshield on the passenger side. As their squad car rolled closer, they saw a dead woman pinned in place. That was the least concerning part about the scene.

On the other side of the street was a crater. It looked like a bomb had gone off. Looking around, it looked like the burning wreckage had been a car of some sort. It was hard to tell because pieces of metal were spread all over the road and grass. Several nearby trees were burning merrily. There weren't any remnants larger than a suitcase. As the wind shifted, Greg could smell burned fuel and scorched trees.

With resigned hope in his voice, Greg asked, "The report you got, was the VIP in the SUV?" If the person they were looking for was in the exploded vehicle-

He'd heard his own stories about cops responding to gold alerts. Not all of them had happy endings for the police involved, especially if they belonged to powerful families. Who knew what a disappointed billionaire would do?

"Nope," Jonesy responded, slowly shaking his head. "The autocall came from a hover truck."

"Crap," Greg cursed softly. "No one could have lived through that. Still thinking it was a good idea to take this call?"

Jonesy glanced at his partner, annoyed, but couldn't rebut the accusation. He had taken the call expecting this to be a simple and convenient way to get out of the city. He wasn't a hero and wanted no part of the panic going down after that grey Wave thing.

Parking the car, he focused.

"Look, we're here now. And we already radioed in to dispatch. They know we're here, so just follow protocol. I'll canvas the area. Even though the city is stretched thin, sooner or later they'll send a higher up for a VIP. Once that happens, it's not our problem anymore. Let's just do everything by the book, and not give whoever shows up a reason to climb up our ass. Plus, there might be a survivor."

"A survivor? Of that?" Greg asked incredulously, gesturing to the explosion site.

"No idiot," Jonesy responded in derision. "The driver of the SUV." He walked up to the vehicle, careful not to touch anything. "Unless you think this lady crawled into the passenger seat to bleed out after the accident."

Annoyed, Greg said, "Maybe the impact threw her over."

"Did the impact buckle her up too?" his partner asked, looking through the shattered window.

"Shut up," Greg muttered, calling the situation in.

It only took a minute to find a body. To both of their surprises, the man was still alive. His clothes were charred, and one leg was twisted at an unnatural angle. His entire front was cooked and covered in blisters, but he was breathing. They stabilized him, running the ABCs, airway, breathing and circulation. There wasn't any major bleeding, and his breath was coming strong. The man was unconscious, but they'd have to wait for the ambulance to arrive to address that. Greg called in the update.

"Must not have been that close when the truck exploded," Jonesy observed. He'd seen his fair share of explosion victims during the war, and hundreds of car accidents on the job. "He's fucked up, but he's one lucky son of a bitch. If he'd been anywhere near a fuel cell explosion we might only find charred bone."

Greg was about to nod, when his phone chirped. Looking down, his mouth suddenly went dry. Elbowing his partner, he showed him the screen, "I- I know who the VIP was."

Reading the name, Jonesy's face paled. He turned back to look at Fin's battered and unconscious face. With a bit of pity, the cop spoke again, "I take it back, buddy. You might be a son of a bitch, but you sure ain't lucky. Not if the Lotus blames you for this."

Chapter 13: Just Another Day

Top Hashtags on the Great Link...

#Wave #ToxicGas #TheReckoning #FireflyReboot

The Great Link itself saw an uptick in activity of nearly 20% in the hours after the event.

"I've been saying it for years and none of you libtards will listen! Toxic gas is being released..."

"I've been saying it for years and you inbreds never listen. The ultrarich have been experimenting on us for..."

"I've been saying it for years and you heathens will burn now that the time of reckoning has come. This is your last chance to call upon..."

"I've been saying it for years...

"I've been..."

"I"

"I"

"I"

The Great Link was filled with conspiracy theories, flame wars and your basic Tuesday night insanity after the Wave. Some said they knew exactly why the "Wave" had happened. Others denied it had happened at all. Many were just there "for the comments."

~REWARD~

***

Inside the ICU of Atlanta General, it was business as usual. If you could trust anyone to be reliable, it was an ICU nurse. In between checking on their patients however, they were glued to the TV in the lounge.

"This is Reagan Watts, with World Confederation News. We are here today to talk about what many are calling the Wave. Approximately six hours ago, a beam of energy descended from outer space and struck the Atlantic Ocean. This created a wave-like phenomenon that spread across the surface of the planet at a speed fast enough to encompass the Earth in less than a minute.

As of now, we are just gathering information, and will continue to keep you updated on this world-shattering story.

Joining me today are three experts.

To my left is Wanda Feder, chief astrophysicist of NASAmazon. Immediately to my right is Darryl Jenkins, press secretary for the president of the Western Confederation. To my far right is Captain Raymond Travers, decorated hero of the Third War. Thank you all for joining me."

A chorus of polite and low volume thank you's echoed around the table.

"Let's dive right in. Darryl, I know you wanted to issue a statement on behalf of the president."

"Yes," came the slightly nasal voice of the president's press secretary. "What is most important to know is that the government is working to keep you all safe. The president has acted swiftly and decisively to bring all of the considerable resources of the Western Confederation to bear, all with the goal of keeping you, the citizens, safe.

Prices have been frozen. Trading on the World Stock Exchange has been frozen. Any lawlessness will with be dealt with fairly, but decisively. We promise complete transparency as we discover more information about the phenomenon that is being called the Wave." With a final caricature of a smile, he added the president's catch phrase, "You are in good hands."

Silence resounded for a solid two seconds as the other members responded to the press secretary's hollow platitudes.

Reagan showed consummate professionalism by not even quivering an eyelid.

Captain Travers' stony face just grew a bit stonier, no stranger to hearing idiocy from on high.

Wanda's face was the most comical, not being dependent on the government at all. While NASA started as a US agency, Amazon's acquisition during the War had placed it squarely in corporate control.

Her expression could best be described as give-me-a-fucking-break-you-penis. She did show some restraint by not saying anything.

"Thank you for that message of hope," Reagan said evenly. If there was any sarcasm in those words, it was either too subtle for Darryl to pick up on or the man was too obtuse to even allow for that option.

The newscaster continued, "Ms Feder, does NASAmazon have any idea as to the nature of the Wave?"

Wanda's face firmed and took on a professional cast, "In the six hours since the event, we have gathered a great deal of information, but are still processing much of it. What we know is that the energy seemed to originate from deep space. Using telemetry from the few remaining orbital platforms that have yet to be decommissioned since the end of the war, we have a rough trajectory of the beam before it impacted Earth."

She steeled her gaze, as if to make sure everyone heard her next words.

"The origin of the beam does not coincide with any celestial body that has been tracked to date. I know that many are concerned that this may have been a type of attack from an extraterrestrial force. As of now, there is no evidence of that being the case."

Captain Perry spoke up, "I would like to second this. The only damage that has been reported throughout the Confederation so far is what we are doing ourselves. The urge to panic is normal, but I urge **you** to remember we are stronger when we work together. We are stronger when stand together."

Somehow, when he said it, though the message was similar, it didn't ring hollow like when the press secretary had spoken.

***

The charge nurse muted the screen before telling everyone to get back to work. The staff scurried off to attend to their duties, no one wanting to incur the wrath of the "ward witch" as she was commonly called.

The matronly woman was extremely kind to her patients and their families, but god help any staff that were seen to be slacking. After seeing one nurse put on fecal disimpaction for a month straight, you learned it was best to stay on the ward witch's good side.

Only one nurse hung back. One with just as much experience, and more importantly, years of friendship with the charge nurse. Though he'd never admit it, he secretly took pleasure in the fact that the nickname he'd come up with years ago had stuck.

"What do *you* think about what happened, Maddie?" Jim asked.

"I think I already said we need to get back to work," she responded waspishly. After getting a long look from one of her few friends, she relented.

In a gentler voice, pitched low enough that no one else could hear and have proof of her kindness, she continued, "What I really think is that the same thing will happen as every time people are given a reason to be afraid."

The next words she whispered as well, but this time, it was out of sorrow, "I think things are going to get bad."

With that pronouncement, she turned back to her work. A new patient had just come in, apparently the sole survivor of an auto accident.

***

"Mmmm. Mmmm."

Fin slowly woke up, completely confused.

Initially, he had no idea what was going on, but when he tried to rub his eyes, he found that he'd been restrained.

Anger flooded him and a bestial panic came with it. Then memory came back. All of it in a rush. Lauren's death. The drunk asshole who'd taken her from him, and the car exploding. After that, everything was black, but he didn't care what he'd missed.

Why wasn't he dead?

"No. No! Why aren't I dead? Lauren! Lauren! I want to be with her!" he screamed. His throat felt like rusty razorblades. He screamed again and again, straining against his bonds, until a doctor rushed into the room. She tried to call his name, but Fin was driven mad by everything that had happened. It didn't help that he was seeing things, like words sprawled across his vision and blinking lights in the corner of his eyes.

A needle jabbed into his thigh, injecting 2 cc's of ativan. When that barely calmed him, it was followed by 5 migs of haldol. His struggles finally quelled. Fin continued to intone Lauren's name, each iteration becoming more garbled until the blessed darkness of sleep claimed him.

The doctor looked at him in pity, having read the police report when he was brought in. The man had somehow survived a fuel cell explosion. Even though the burns covering the front of his body were miraculously only first degree, he was suffering from internal injuries that were much more serious.

The surgeons were honestly stumped how he'd gotten hit with such a hard blast without the burns to match. They'd just shrugged it off though, unknowingly parroting the two police that had found him, calling Fin "lucky sonuvabitch." Shrugging, the surgical team took the win and moved on.

They'd kept the guy breathing, which meant their job was basically done.

Over the next twenty-four hours, Fin went in and out of consciousness, delirious most of the time. When the doctor came back on shift the next day, though, he was laying there calmly, staring up at the ceiling. As she entered the room, he turned his head, ignoring the pain triggered by even that simple movement, and evenly asked, "Will you take these restraints off please?"

He'd woken up several hours before.

Agony, both physical and emotional, radiated through his entire body, but he'd regained enough control to assess his situation. At first, he'd thought he was handcuffed to the bed.

They arrested me for killing that man.

In the next moment, he'd shrugged mentally, and stopped pulling at his restraints. He didn't regret snatching the life out of that bastard. He just wished he could have done it twice.

If a lifetime in jail was the cost, he'd pay it gladly.

Lauren.

The thought of her name had caused a worse pain than any he was already feeling. Tears flowed and he sobbed, unable to even wipe his eyes.

Sometime over the next hour, he'd fallen asleep once more.

The next time he woke, his head had been clearer. Both the emotional fugue and the several rounds of medication that had kept him snowed for the past twenty-four hours, had faded enough for him to better assess his situation.

There was no way he should be under arrest right now. The accident would show the rich prick's hover truck had slammed into them. Even if the cops did know he'd played a role in killing the driver of the other car, they wouldn't have been able to prove that he'd done anything.

Hell, he didn't even understand what he'd done.

He just knew he'd done *something.*

Looking down for the first time, he'd seen that while he was indeed restrained, it was not with shackles of metal. Instead, his bindings were cloth, and his hands were covered by mesh mittens.

He'd seen this plenty of times before, though he'd never worn them himself. This was how hospitals kept AMS, altered mental status, patients from hurting themselves or pulling out IVs. Seeing that had cleared up his situation immensely.

That was why, an hour later, he was taking extra efforts to speak calmly and without emotion. Ranting and demanding restraints come off was a good way to get put on an involuntary psych hold. The best course of action was just to wait for the doctor to come in and ask for his freedom, exuding as much stability as possible.

When he saw the small woman enter with a stethoscope around her neck and a paper mask over her face, he knew his wait was over.

Fin carefully cracked one eye. Now that he was clear headed, he was sure he was suffering from a concussion. Not only was there a constant ringing in his ears, but he could barely tolerate much light.

"Dr Yinying," he spoke aloud to the woman standing by his bedside. "Could I ask you a small favor?"

His initial entreaty didn't garner a response. Carefully shifting his head, he turned his slitted eyes to look up at her face. He saw she was looking down at him, but wasn't speaking. Maybe she was somewhat taken aback by his calm demeanor after a full day of hysterical raving.

"Dr Yinying," Fin tried again, reading her tag. He made his voice as level and moderate as possible. "Would it be possible to turn down the lights? I'm fairly certain I suffered a concussion in the accident."

"Of course," she responded after a moment. Leaning over, she tapped a key on the bed.

The overheads reduced from a bright white glare to a gentle twilight.

Sighing in faint relief, Fin opened his eyes wider. They were both blurry from lack of blinking, but after a few moments, he was able to open them fully without discomfort. Turning his head, he looked at his doctor again, clearly seeing her for the first time.

She was about five-three, had the pale golden skin of an Asian woman with the eyes to match. He couldn't see any more of her face due to the surgical mask she had on. Above however, her straight black hair was pulled back into a tight ponytail.

Not a single strand was out of place, something Fin noted was a bit strange for an overworked ICU doc. Seeing something physically aberrant, his doctor eyes kicked in and he did a more thorough visual exam.

Her skin was smooth and without flaw. Not a wrinkle or her pimple. He'd thought her skin looked smooth because of makeup, but looking closer she wasn't wearing any. Her eyebrows appeared perfectly manicured as well.

For an intensivist to put that much care into her appearance, she must be a real tight ass, Fin thought.

Of course he didn't let any of that show on his face. Instead, he stuck to the plan to achieve his goal.

He continued in a measured tone.

"Would you please remove these restraints? I understand why I had to be tied down, but I'm an ER physician. At the time I was brought in, I believe I was suffering from both physical and emotional trauma. To be more specific, traumatic loss of a loved one coupled with what feels to be a severe concussion. That triggered what any physician would acknowledge to be a normal, physiologic grief reflex. You, and your staff, have my apologies for any untoward behavior I may have exhibited. I completely understand and agree with your decision to restrain me in light of that temporary derangement.

I am now clear headed and calm. I will of course bow to your medical decision making as you are the physician in charge. That being said, I'm fine now and would greatly appreciate the professional courtesy of being released. Please."

She looked at him dispassionately, her clear hazel eyes unblinking. "It's pronounced, 'Yee-ing,'" she corrected after a few moments.

There was no anger or irritation in her voice. He didn't let even a trace cross his face either. One, he guessed people butchering her name was a common occurrence. And two, an offhand comment was just the kind of tricksy trick a doc would pull on a patient to assess their mental state without them knowing.

"Thank you for the correction, Dr Yinying." This time, he used the right inflection.

After several more moments, she responded, "You're welcome, Dr Evers. You do seem clear headed, and what you ask certainly sounds like a reasonable request. If you truly are 'fine' however, then you should be okay with some questions. Would that be alright, Dr Evers?"

Fin took a breath to respond and was rewarded by a painful hacking cough. Once the fit passed, he replied with a slight wheeze, "Of course. But please call me Fin."

"I would rather keep this professional and respectful," she responded in a measured voice. "Please address me as Dr Yinying and I will afford you the same courtesy."

"Whatever you say, Dr Yinying," he responded evenly. Internally he sighed. He'd been right. She was a TAD. Just another Tight Assed Doctor. "I would appreciate keeping the interview short. The ringing in my ears is a bit painful and is exacerbated by sound."

"Of course, Dr Evers. Let us begin."

For the next several minutes she went through standard questions. How do you feel? Does this hurt? What do you remember about the accident? Then they got to the meat of the matter.

"The nurse reported that you said you wanted to die. Is that still the case?"

It was what he'd been waiting for. Staring deep into her eyes, he intoned, "I do not want to harm or kill myself. I am not having suicidal or homicidal ideation. I was suffering from trauma and acute loss. I am not a danger to myself. My fiancé was just killed and that was why, coupled with my head injury and disorientation, I said I wanted to join her. That is not how I truly feel."

"Well," Dr Yinying said in a professionally neutral voice, "that certainly is a complete answer." After staring for a few seconds more, she called out, "Nurse. Help me remove these restraints."

Several minutes later, Fin scratched his nose with a grunt of pure relief, "You have no idea how long I've needed to do that." Immediate concerns done, he asked the two questions that were burning inside of him.

"Where is my fiancé's body?"

She stared at him for a moment, sympathy creasing her eyes above her mask, "She was taken to the morgue. It's only a block away."

A single tear fell from one of his eyes. Fin didn't turn away or feel the need to wipe it. This was his pain. He'd earned it.

Dr. Yinying started to speak again, but he waved her to stop. With a completely different tone, a harsh guttural intonation, he asked his second question, "Were there any other survivors from the crash?"

He knew there couldn't be. He *knew* that he'd seen that green eyed bastard burn. In that strange frozen moment of the explosion, he'd seen blue fire consume the man's perfect, screaming face. Fin remembered clearly the arrogant beauty of those refined features melting, the skin running like liquid wax. He recalled even better how he'd rejoiced while he'd watched it. He didn't know why the fuel cell had exploded, but he *knew* everything else.

But, on the same token, Fin knew there was no way he should be alive either.

While Dr Yinying had been asking him questions before taking off the restraints, she'd mentioned that he was lucky to have been so far from the truck when it exploded. When he'd asked how she knew that, she'd shared that she'd spoken with the EMS who'd brought him to the hospital. Apparently, that was what the cops had said before he'd been picked up at the scene. His unconscious body had been found dozens of yards from the blast.

Fin had been impressed with Dr Yinying when he heard about the extra effort she'd made. Not many doctors outside the ER ever spoke to EMS. Hierarchical arrogance was alive and well in Western medicine.

For obvious reasons he hadn't corrected her assumption that he'd been far from the explosion. He knew that he'd been right at ground zero though. No matter what movies showed, people didn't survive when they were next to an explosion. It just didn't happen in real life.

He'd seen the aftermath of explosives during the War, what they'd done to bodies, turning people into ground chuck.

And he'd seen the aftermath of hundreds of car accidents in the ED.

He should be dead.

More than dead.

He should be in chunks.

There was no "earthly" reason that he should still be here.

Which left only one explanation. Something extraordinary had intervened. Something that had to be related to that grey wave. And if a… supernatural force had saved his life, if the rules and natural laws he'd always believed in now had an asterisk next to them, then he had to consider the possibility that that murderous bastard was still alive as well. If that were the case, the highest priority in Fin's life would be correcting that.

Dr Yinying paused for a few seconds, partly because of the vehemence in Fin's voice, before replying, "I'm not sure it is my place to speak about this."

Fin calmed his voice. Pushing doctors wasn't the way to get what you wanted. You had to appeal to their sympathy and their ego. He looked away before trying again, his voice weak and quavering now, "I know. I get it. It's not right for me to ask. He just took her from me. He kil-"

Fin clipped the last word, selling his pitiable persona.

The simple motion of turning helped him bring the performance home.

Fresh pain shot through him as cracked ribs ground together.

His eyes tightened as a spasm washed through him.

A stressed wheeze passed through his lips.

The pain meds were really starting to wear off. Dr Yinying started to get up from her chair and call for a nurse, but he held up a hand, stopping her. Turning back over brought a fresh wave of suffering, but he was sure the unshed tears he'd summoned would get the job done now. He reached out and grabbed her hand.

Not harshly, but with strength.

She settled back down and he repeated himself.

"It's not right for me to ask, but I'm asking. As a professional courtesy or out of sympathy to an injured man or just out of pity. No matter what reason you need, please. Please tell me if the man that killed the love of my life is dead."

Emotions warred behind her eyes, but after the battle, she leaned towards him and quietly shared, "According to EMS, no one else survived. They heard the police talking. Another person's remains were found charred at the scene. The body was so badly damaged they had to pull the ID from the car. For privacy reasons, they did not share the name of anyone else."

If she had learned the name of the man in the other car, fate would have taken a very different turn.

The name Jerini Lotus was one she would have recognized.

He was a member of a group she was intimately familiar with.

In fact, her Familia and the Lotus tried to have as little to do with one another as possible.

If she'd known about a rival Familia's involvement, she might have given her patient a warning.

She wouldn't have broken her Familia's code of silence of course; but she might still have warned Fin that the other man was part of a "gang."

There was no danger while Fin was in the hospital, it was Shadow territory after all, and no Lotus member would risk war with the Shadow over petty revenge against a civilian.

Once he was discharged though, and beyond the protection of these walls, she'd have had no doubt the Lotus would live up to its vindictive and cruel reputation.

She might even have petitioned her Familia to label Fin off limits, citing the need to protect the "honor and reputation" of the Shadow.

That kind of stupid argument usually was enough to rile the elders up.

Unfortunately, the doctor remained unaware of the storm on the horizon.

She merely watched Fin as he heaved a sigh of contentment.

A faint smile graced his mouth even though the rest of his face was tight with pain. He closed his eyes and thought of his love.

I know you wanted me to be a better man, baby, but I got him. I got the fucker that took you from me! An image of Lauren's face appeared in his mind's eye. She had a faint smile, but when he focused on the curve of her lips, he couldn't shake the feeling that she was looking at him in sadness.

"Dr Evers? Dr Evers? Fin?" Dr Yinying's voice broke his reverie and Lauren's face faded away.

Opening his eyes, Fin focused on his doctor and asked the next pertinent question, "How messed up am I?"

Dr Yinying's head cocked to the side as if to say, "Well…"

Turned out the answer to his question was just shy of FUBAR. Seven cracked ribs, a broken leg, hairline jaw fracture, internal bleeding, acute kidney failure, and the entire front of his body was covered in burns. His recovery would take weeks, maybe months.

After getting the news, he realized none of that mattered.

Lauren was gone, and despite the lies he'd just told this woman, he wasn't sure if he was going to stick around in this life much longer. For now, it was a nonissue. He wasn't in a position to walk, let alone end his life.

He also wasn't an impetuous person.

Fin had survived the war, and somehow, unreasonably, had survived being blown up. If he did decide to go out, it would be on his own terms. Nothing would be left to chance.

There was also… that other thing.

Just as Dr Yinying was about to leave the room, she paused in the doorway before turning back. He was struck by how poised she was. Her posture was perfect, and she moved with a grace he'd only seen in professional dancers. That didn't quite add up with what he knew about ICU docs. They were more the 'married to the job and pale from lack of sunlight' types. Despite that grace, he could pick up on her hesitation. If her mask was down, he had a suspicion he'd see her chewing her lip.

"Dr Evers," she began.

He waved his hand, "Please just call me Fin."

This time, she allowed it for some reason.

"Fin," she repeated, "is there anything else you want to tell me? About the accident?"

She looked at him with an intensity he didn't quite understand. There had to be a dozen other people on her service, and if there was one thing doctors never had enough of it was time. Also, he'd interviewed thousands of patients, and knew that doctors just didn't pay this much attention to someone medically stable. The only thing he could think that would warrant this level of scrutiny was if she knew his true mental state, but he was sure he hadn't given anything away.

Wanting to break the weird intensity of the moment, he asked a question that he was confident would redirect her, "Did you see that grey wave?"

She nodded, her face tightening slightly at the memory, "That's actually what the news is calling it. The Wave. It traveled through the whole world. Everyone saw it, everyone in the world that was awake anyway. There have been reports of it from every country on Earth, but no one knows what it was. And there don't seem to be any long term effects… at least not that anyone has reported."

Her vision sharpened again, "Is there anything you want to tell me about the Wave? That must have been right before your accident."

His eyes flickered ever so slightly to the left, towards the blinking light that seemed on the edge of his vision, before staring back into her dark brown eyes again. Sighing heavily, he closed his eyes and feigned weariness.

"I'm sorry Dr Yinying. I just got tired all of a sudden. Do you mind asking the nurse to bring me a Link? I'd like to touch base with loved ones before I get to sleep."

She paused for a moment, recognizing that he was ending the conversation, but what could she say except, "Of course."

"Thanks doc. Preciate your time."

The way his eye had fluttered had caught her attention and raised her suspicions, but not enough that she could push without revealing the fact that she had an interface of her own. Her lips parted slightly, and a faint exhalation passed through them, but she caught whatever words were going to spill out.

"Call me Sola," she said softly, taking her mask off.

Despite his pain and loss, Fin caught himself staring at her beautiful face. She had Asian features, most likely Japanese he thought. Her face was strangely symmetric, and a dainty nose rested perfectly above full lips that didn't quite fit the rest of features, but didn't ruin her beauty in any way. Instead, they complimented and elevated it.

Fin didn't feel a wisp of arousal or true attraction. Neither his mind nor his body were in a place for that. It was just that her beauty was striking enough that it was impossible not to pause and take note of it. Like someone over seven feet tall or a man with arms more than a foot thick, it just wasn't something you saw very often.

In fact, her beauty not only didn't trigger a positive reaction, it kindled his anger. Her perfect features reminded Fin of the asshole in the truck. Her

Asian attributes were nothing like Jerini's Aryan looks, but both had a quality that seemed not quite normal.

Well, he thought with bloody satisfaction, he's not so pretty anymore.

He didn't let her beauty distract him for more than an instant and he quashed his anger. It didn't serve a purpose right now.

Instead, he responded, "Thank you, Sola. I need to rest now if you don't mind."

"Of course. The physical and occupational therapists will be by later to help with your recovery. And now that you're more aware, we'll be getting you out of the ICU. Should I send the nurse in to give you something for your pain?"

"Please," he replied quietly, closing his eyes. He had held off so he could be clear headed when he met his doctor, but the morphine he'd gotten before was having little effect anymore.

Sola paused at the door, fishing one final time, "Evers. It's such an interesting name. It almost sounds like a made up name."

"All words are made up," he responded evenly and without opening his eyes.

Her head pulled back ever so slightly at the irrefutability of that statement. After thinking a moment, she just left the room, closing the glass door but leaving the curtain open. This man was a mystery, but there were other ways to find the truth if he wouldn't share.

Fin's eyes stayed closed, but he didn't sleep. He was reading. He'd intentionally not done so earlier, choosing instead to face the pain and loss. It would have felt like a betrayal if he'd numbed himself after Lauren's death. That wasn't his way.

Now, a day had passed. He'd sat his shiva. Was that how it worked? He wasn't Jewish and hadn't ever paid that much attention, but he'd liked the idea when he'd heard about it.

Despite the fact that the pain was just as strong, the truth was he was emotionally exhausted. Soon, he'd be rested enough to flay his soul again, but for now, a distraction would be nice.

Besides, his curiosity was rising, and he knew the pain wasn't going anywhere.

     ~REWARD~

He still couldn't quite believe what was happening, but he wasn't some hidebound fool who would deny what was right in front of his face.

Only the truly foolish and truly powerful reimagined facts to fit their views.

Whatever that wave had been, it had changed him. It had changed something inside of him. The words emblazoned across his vision were proof.

Congratulations! Your connection to the Labyrinth has been Enabled!

Chapter 14: Status Page

Fin wondered again if he was going insane, but he knew he wasn't. Junkies saw bugs crawling under their skin. Schizos heard voices telling them to do things. He was well familiar with the presentation of both visual and audio hallucinations. This wasn't that. Also, he hadn't freebased bath salts. And no known mental disorders ramped from zero to a hundred in a single day. It was possible he had traumatic brain damage, but his ability to think clearly argued against that.

Even the pending decision to end his own life was something he was able to think about dispassionately. For others, that might seem like proof of instability, but after living through a World War and witnessing suffering in the hospital, for him, it was just a shitty choice that might be marginally better than other shitty choices.

Also, while there still might be a small chance he could just be off his rocker, having auditory and visual hallucinations at the same time, there was one other big hole in that line of reasoning.

Who the hell would hallucinate a panel of glowing words written in… papyrus font? Only douchebags used that. In fact, anything but Times New Roman 12 font was either doing too much or straight up asinine.

To his surprise, and mild repressed delight, the prompt changed to a more appropriate format.

*Congratulations! Your connection to the **Labyrinth** has been **Enabled**!*

A bolt of pure Chaos has struck your world. Any consequence could and can occur, but the very first is connecting your world to the Labyrinth.

The pathetic Energy null nature of your world makes this a difficult process, but Energy levels will begin to rise.

~REWARD~

Actions to improve your world's Energy levels will be Rewarded.

Danger *and* ***Reward*** *are close bedfellows.*

Connection to the ***Labyrinth*** *has brought a new Age to your world.*

Welcome to the ***Age of Power****!*

He'd lied to the doctor.

If this prompt was telling the truth, then he knew exactly what that tsunami of grey fire, that had apparently washed across the entire world, actually was. It was a wave of Chaos.

Of course, "wave of Chaos" meant absolutely nothing to him. He understood chaos as a concept. Mostly, it was a word journalists added to their headlines.

Just clickbait.

This window hovering in his mind was talking about it like it was a natural phenomenon, like gravity or magnetism. Chaos with a capital "C."

Whatever it meant, things were changing and would be different now. In his experience, a sudden change of the social order meant things would be different with a capital "the-entire-world-is-about-to-get-fucked."

The War had shown that civilization wasn't an immutable truth.

It was more akin to a fragile state that only existed in specific and fragile circumstances. In his opinion, humanity was constantly balancing on a knife's edge with tragedy waiting if it fell to either side. More than three billion had died during the war. Fin was pretty sure the dead would have agreed with him.

Only the living had the luxury of ignorance.

He wasn't alone in his fatalistic feelings. Almost no one had made it through the War without losing a part of their humanity. There was a whole branch of philosophy now that saw humanity as a bunch of lucky apes flipping a coin over and over with heads giving life and tails giving death. Couldn't stay lucky, forever. Maybe this Labyrinth thing was the apocalyptic ending that humanity, in his opinion, was secretly hoping would wipe them all off the face of the planet.

Fin shook his head.

Or maybe he was just dwelling on some maudlin melodramatic crap because he'd just watched the love of his life die.

Yeah, it could be that.

Well, back to distraction, he thought with a sick smile.

There were other concepts in what he'd read that made no sense.

For instance, why was "Labyrinth" capitalized?

And what did "Energy null" mean, and why did it make his world pathetic? Beyond the obvious reasons.

And "Age of Power?" What the hell?

Of course, all of that was secondary to the fact that he was even seeing translucent windows floating in his field of vision!

Was this real?

Had he fallen into an isekai or a VRMMORPG? Like everyone with a Link, he'd played his share of games. He'd also read all the top LitRPGs like most school age children.

And now, he was literally looking at his own notification window.

What was it they normally did when they joined a video game world?

Don't do it, Fin thought to himself. Don't do it. Just be cool.

Gah! I'ma do it.

He swiped an arm up trying to touch the "window."

Naturally his hand just passed through like nothing was there seeing as how this was his own personal interface!

Gah, he thought again, this time in pure excitement. It's really not real!

He chuckled to himself, the joy in his heart warring with the pain in his soul.

The only thing that let him enjoy this moment was that he knew that's what she would have wanted.

And that was the truth. Lauren had had her share of loss, and something she always told him was that joy was a gift not to be squandered or lessened by the inevitability of pain.

For however long it would last, Fin focused on the joy and wonder of a lifelong dream coming true.

With a smile on his face and eyes glistening with suppressed pain, he thought, what should I do first?

In the books, didn't they always check their status window?

Glee filled him again. No small amount of excitement and curiosity bloomed in his heart. Fin deliberately expressed the thought, "Status Page."

For long, looong, seconds he lay there grinning like a fool.

Nothing happened.

Oh, he thought to himself. Dumb mistake.

With an even goofier grin, he exquisitely elocuted, "Status page!"

Nothing.

Happened.

He tried again and again.

And again.

On the twentieth time, each a bit progressively louder, and with complete calm, he finally realized that something was actually happening. While no window describing his stats had appeared, he was picking up on a strange sensation.

He "felt" a slight resistance each time he tried to summon his status page, like his mind was pushing against something. It was a strange feeling, but it kind of reminded him of fighting off sleep paralysis when you woke up in the middle of REM. The mental equivalent of pushing a finger against cellophane.

Somehow, he knew the knowledge was there, he just couldn't reach it. He tried accessing it several more times. Now that he had a path to follow, he no longer questioned if the mental resistance was just in his imagination.

It was real.

He had a status page, but there was something stopping him from accessing it.

Well, as the priest said, just push harder.

Fin's eyes closed. Maybe he just needed the right mindset. He cast his mind back to a somewhat painful memory. It had been of a specialized type of training that had been required of him during the War. He'd had to become something *more* to survive that.

When his eyes reopened, there was something harder, a bit vicious, inside them.

With that frame of mind, he spoke the words "Status Page" again. This time, he willed the universe itself to bend to his wishes. A moment later, and with the mental sensation of a *pop,* two new prompts appeared.

The first gave him basic information about himself. Immediately as he began reading a frown appeared on his face. In response to his strong desire, his name shifted from Japanese to English along with another important alteration.

Reading the prompt again, the alarm he'd felt faded away, allowing him to focus on the information.

FIN EVERS		
Health: LOCKED	**Mana:** 22/22	**Stamina:** LOCKED

The second window was red.

Full Status page locked!

Seeing those few lines and that red window brought a strange rush of emotions.

Body, soul and mind, Lauren's death had wounded him. Her loss had also brought back barely dealt with, and shallowly buried, feelings about… "acts" he committed during the War. Traumas that had cut him deeper than he'd ever imagined possible.

Fin knew he was messed up.

It wasn't in doubt.

He was also battered, bruised, and oh yeah, there was a freaking catheter coming out of his dick. Something he had *not* consented to and, IHHO, needed to be rectified ASAP.

     ~REWARD~

To top it off, like shit sprinkles on a vomit sundae, he was somehow in an old fashioned, sister-banging, backwoods feud with some "Familia." He'd heard the nurses gossiping when they thought he was knocked out. Apparently, the dickhead in the hover truck had deep connections.

He didn't know what a Familia was, but the word just dripped organized crime. Full-on matching track suits and early-onset diabetes. And yet, the guy he'd killed hadn't looked like some goombah.

He'd looked like a Norwegian runway model. Which meant Fin didn't really know what he was up against. He just had another series of questions and most likely some drama waiting for him whenever he got out of the hospital.

All told, he wasn't in a great spot.

That was the bad news.

On the other hand, he had a status page!

Even with the fact that his "full status page" was unavailable, even with the actual numbers of his health and stamina being "locked," he was a player!

And oh yeah, he had mana.

Mana!

Twenty-two points of it. That *had* to be a lot, right?

Years of wish fulfillment were coming true!

With a bittersweet smile, he thought, "Lauren would have loved this."

Shaking his head in disbelief, Fin tried to mentally reach the rest of his status page info. He felt resistance again, but this time it felt more like a smooth wooden wall, lacking even a seam. He couldn't begin to find a place to attack it. After a couple tries, Fin began reading the other prompts awaiting him.

> You are the first Powered to have been attacked by another after your world was inducted into the Labyrinth!
> This has triggered a Quest!
> Quest Grade: Radiant Gold (A)
> Quest Rank: Comm-

He stopped reading again. He'd been given a quest? Right off the bat? He knew he was reading a video game prompt, but did the powers that be really hand out quests left and right?

Everything he read just led to more questions, but it also helped him to understand what came next. His memories after the crash were both hazy in some spots and crystal clear in others.

Fin did remember thinking his vision was blurry from time to time. When he'd replayed events earlier, he'd attributed that blurriness to his head injury, but it appeared the concussion was only partially to blame.

These windows had also been appearing in his gaze. He now knew that they responded to his thoughts and intentions. He must have willed them away without really knowing what he was doing.

Focusing back, he realized the quest prompt had cut off mid-word. It wasn't the only one. The next series of windows were interrupted one after another. It was like a computer glitch, or a processor trying to reconcile contradictory commands.

The "feel" of each prompt was almost stressed.

It finally settled on giving him an upgrade.

Qualifications for Quest upgrade met!

Recalculating Quest!

Chapter 15: Primordial

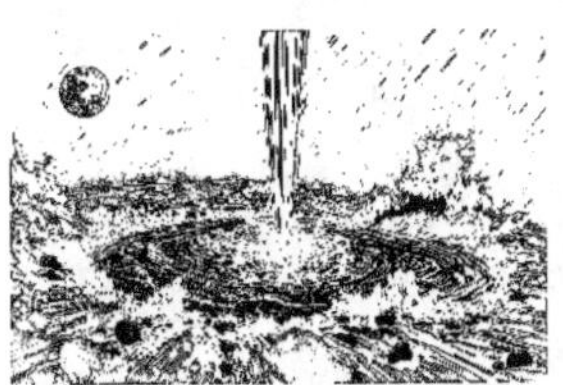

KNOW THIS!

This is one of the first seven Quests generated since your world's connection to the Labyrinth!

Checking other qualifications…

Qualifications met!

You have triggered a **PRIMORDIAL** Quest!

Your Quest difficulty and rewards will be increased dramatically…

KNOW THIS!

The Chaotic nature of your existence forces the creation of a Binary Quest. You shall be given a Choice!

The tone of the information in his head went back to baseline.

You have been attacked by another Powered!

This has triggered a Binary Quest…

WAR or PEACE

Quest Grade: Radiant Gold (A)

Quest Rank: Common

~REWARD~

Quest Type: Transformed PRIMORDIAL

Conflict is an immutable reality. Your response to it is not. This is one of the first seven Quests triggered since the connection of your world to the Labyrinth. Typically, this would trigger a PRIMORDIAL Quest, a challenge that cannot be refused.

So fearsome are PRIMORDIAL Quests, that almost no being in the history of the Labyrinth has ever survived, let alone, completed them.

However, Danger and Reward are close bedfellows.

Those few who do complete PRIMORDIAL Quests have gone on to become emperors, gods and demon kings.

The Chaotic nature of your world coupled with the threadbare connection of the Labyrinth and null Energy levels, have sculpted this Motivation of the Labyrinth into a Binary Quest.

You may now Choose one of two Quest Paths. **War** or **Peace**

Quest Path 1: **PEACE**

The Powered that attacked you is currently helpless. To take this path, help him free from his car.

Success Conditions: The Powered that attacked you must survive until sunset of the next day.

Choosing the **Path of Peace** will close the **Path of War**. The resultant Quest chain can resolve in any number of ways.

Minimum Reward: 250 XP

Penalty for failure of Quest: Choosing the Path of War

Quest Path 2: **WAR**

The Powered that attacked you is currently helpless. To take this path, kill him.

Success Conditions: The Powered that attacked you must die before sunset of the next day.

> Choosing the Path of War will close the Path of Peace. This Quest chain can only end with your destruction or the destruction of your foes.
>
> **Minimum Reward:** 250 XP
>
> **Penalty for failure of Quest**: Choosing the Path of Peace
>
> **NOW CHOOSE!**
>
> This Quest cannot be refused.

Many people would think that forcing someone to "choose" was a fair bit of BS. How was it a choice if you were being forced to make it?

That apparent contradiction didn't faze Fin in the least. Point in fact, the concepts didn't clash.

He'd long ago learned that the world often forced you to make choices. Every choice ever made by anyone was only possible because of previous events that they had no control of and probably wouldn't even understand. Like always, he focused not on the infinite beyond his control, but on the finite that he could affect.

There really wasn't any other way to live.

Of course, none of that highfalutin understanding of universal truths kept him from being royally pissed off.

He hated being forced to do anything. Even though he hadn't known he was being given a magic quest of all things, and even though he still would have made the same choice if he had known, Fin did *not* like being pigeonholed.

He shrugged, setting his irritation aside. It wasn't the first time he'd been screwed by a higher up and surely wouldn't be the last. Of course, this mighta been the highest up that had done it, but done was done.

He forced himself to consider what this quest meant beyond his own irritation.

First, he'd been given a magic quest.

What the fuck.

Really.

What that fuck.

He read back through the prompt a few times. Yup. It was a magic quest.

Fin had a binary choice to make here, and the irony wasn't lost on him.

Either he was going crazy, or he wasn't.

Based on the information he had, he wasn't going crazy. His sensorium was pretty clear, and this just wasn't something he'd hallucinate.

He also had more than a bit of experience with making people question their reality.

This was real.

Now that that was cleared up, he decided to forgo the whole "This can't be happening thing," and stick to what was.

Quest or not, the truth was Fin had known he'd had a choice right after the accident.

He could have done everything possible to save that man.

What's more, he knew that Lauren would have wanted him to do whatever he could to save a life. Not because she would have been overly concerned with the other driver, but because she would have been concerned with him.

If she'd seen the quest, she would have begged him to choose the path of peace. She would have feared what it would cost him to once more walk down a path of war.

He knew all of that.

He'd known it at the time.

It just hadn't mattered.

Fin still vividly remembered the moment after the accident. He recalled looking at her eyes. Once bright and laughing, they'd been transformed into dead and unseeing balls of jelly.

At the moment of choice, when he could have saved that man, he hadn't seen another person.

He'd only seen a "thing" that had stolen from him.

A thing that had extinguished the flickering flame in his heart.

A *thing* that had taken the light from his life.

What else could who do but turn to his old source of light?

The dormant rage gladly answered his call.

Thinking back, the absolute fury hadn't come out of nowhere.

It hadn't manifested and showed him a new side of himself.

It was just finally released.

After years of holding it in check, the tension, the control, the aspirations to be a "good" man all went away.

And he was glad in it.

It hadn't taken much time, perhaps not longer than an instant, but that rage had scoured him. He remembered feeling hollow. The anger hadn't left him once it had flayed him clean of weak emotions like empathy and paltry thoughts like kindness. Instead, that pure, hot anger had filled the now empty vessel of his being.

It had felt…

Wonderful.

Lying in bed now, Fin clenched his teeth so hard that his jaw ached. His fists were so clenched his arms shook. The anger coursed through him again, a salt river through parched lands.

It felt like coming home.

It took minutes for the pain and anger to burn through him once more, leaving more scars on his soul.

Ultimately, his body relaxed, and he collapsed back on his bed.

Reading the quest information now, he wondered if anything would have been different if he'd known what was happening at the time.

Would he have saved the guy if he knew this quest was happening?

He smiled grimly after a moment.

No.

Fin's only regret remained the same. He just wished he could have killed the bastard twice.

He was glad the man was dead.

And no consequences, no quest, no wave of grey fire, nothing, would change that.

What was done was done, either way.

He'd made his choice when he decided to kill that man.

For good or ill, he was, once again, walking the Path of War.

The following prompts agreed. The sound of drums preceded the next window.

Da-dum da-dum!

You have chosen the **Path of War!**

The Path of Peace is now closed.

~REWARD~

Chapter 16: Path of War

LIGHT

Congratulations! You have completed the first step of the PRIMORDIAL Quest: **Path of War**

By killing another Powered in a moment of Choice, you have chosen the **Path of War**. May your enemies breathe their last and may the tears of their children salt their burning flesh!

You have also gone above and beyond in your performance of this Quest. Not only have you killed the man who killed your love, you mutilated the body until it was unrecognizable. Barely anything is left for his family to bury.

This will drive his family to such depths of sorrow that it will mark them indelibly. As their pain burrows deeper, they shall share their rage and sorrow and thus fan the flames of War!

Rage and bloodthirst are encouraged in those who walk the Path of War.

Well done!

Completion Score… **S!**

Do you wish to collect your Rewards?

You have unlocked a new Quest: **Path of War II**

Meet other hidden requirements to access the Quest, Path of War II

The first prompt congratulating him was a bit, shall we say, heavy handed? Indelibly mark them?

Also, he hadn't *meant* to desecrate the body.

Snatching the breath of out that man's lungs would have been enough.

Wouldn't it?

As severe as the words were, Fin just couldn't find it in him to be bothered by what he'd done or even how it was being described. He hoped the man's family did feel, just a fraction of the pain, just a sliver of the loss he was suffering through right now. Again, he mentally shrugged. Two people died every second.

He'd just moved the fucker to the front of the queue.

If he was being honest, what was really bothering him was that a lot of the concepts he was reading about seemed to mirror games he'd played or stories he'd read. While that was still undeniably incredible, how was that possible?

There were also many words that he didn't understand in context.

Primordial?

It was starting to get frustrating. He'd always had an analytical mind so had hated not understanding things. He forced the feeling aside, and focused on the last line.

Curious more than anything else, he focused on the translucent window and the quest completed.

*Know This! To complete a **Mortal** quest at your current **State of Being**, a minimum completion Score of C is required.*

YOU HAVE EARNED

                                 ~REWARD~

C-Grade Reward

- 250 Experience Points
- 50 Magicka

B-Grade Reward

- 375 Experience Points
- 75 Magicka
- 25 Copper Coins

A-Grade Reward

- 750 Experience Points
- 150 Magicka
- 75 Copper Coins
- 1 *Common*, 1st rank, Constitution Orb

S-Grade Reward!

- All lower Grade Rewards Doubled!
- +50 Nobility Points! (50/100 to Noble Title)

Special Reward for Quest Type: Primordial

Title: Primordial of War (Fledgling)

Hmmm.

While it hadn't been his intention to completely mutilate the body, he had to admit, it looked like going full psycho had its benefits.

Jokes aside, knowing there were secret elements to a quest was fascinating. That was in line with some of the better games he'd played before.

That made it clear that not only were quests important, but how he finished them mattered as well. The prompt said the rewards were increased because of his "bloodthirsty" completion of the quest.

At that thought, Lauren's bloodied face came to mind, pain shooting through him with the electricity of a raw nerve. His breathing grew faster, but he forced himself to close his eyes and heave a great exhale.

Later.

He'd deal with it later.

For now, he needed to learn more about this new world.

The levels of accomplishment from the quest, or "score" he supposed the right word was, were based on a letter system, like school for some reason. Maybe that wasn't too strange. He was reading "English" after all. There was obviously some kind of translation… oh hell, might as well call it "magic" going on.

The lowest reward were experience points.

After that, were copper coins.

Some kind of money, he guessed.

The A-grade reward was something called a Constitution orb, and the highest grade reward, the S-grade, seemed to double all the other rewards, which seemed pretty great. It also gave him something called "Nobility Points," and took him halfway to some goal. Focusing on that line didn't give him any more information, so for now, that goal would have to remain a mystery.

Also, something troubling occurred to him.

The initial prompt about the Path of War had said both "rewards and consequences were increased. It had even capitalized "Consequences."

There weren't any consequences mentioned, though.

That was when he noticed the next waiting window was blinking an ominous red.

With a slight furrow he mentally clicked on it.

"Ah, *those* consequences."

Choosing **The Path of War** has Consequences!
Consequence 1
Your relationship has worsened with the House of the Ghost of the Lotus Familia!

-5,000 Relationship Points with the House of the Ghost Lotus!
This has worsened your relationship from Distrust to Anger!
Whereas before members of the House of the Ghost Lotus would merely doubt your words and bemoan your actions, now your mere presence may drive them to true anger!

Hmmm.

Looks like he *did* have to take some, partial, responsibility for his beef with the "Familia." Killing that blond bastard had triggered some kind of cosmic reaction. If he was reading this right, his mere presence would infuriate these people.

But House of the Ghost?

~REWARD~

Emo much?

And triggering spontaneous anger?

Was that even possible? Even with magic?

Fin thought a bit more.

It *was* true that nearly every woman he'd ever dated would get spontaneously angry sooner or later. But that was just because they were hungry, horny or sleepy.

Right?

Certainly not because of anything he'd ever done.

Fin puffed his cheeks.

Hmmm.

Maybe "spontaneous anger" wasn't a crazy reaction to him.

What was more important was his enemies having a name now.

Could this change to Earth, that grey wave, really change the moods of people in real time?

What kind of power was that?

Fin guessed he'd find out.

Maybe just as important, his enemies had a name now.

Lotus.

If killing that dbag had really triggered a war with some mafia family then who cared.

The quest said he'd chosen the "Path of War," so it was kind of in the name. He'd been on the winning side of the last war, and by his chocolate salty balls, he'd win this one too.

Fin circled back to the douchebag "Familia" thing.

He didn't really get down with true crime shows, and he'd never heard about the "Lotus Familia" before.

Just who were they?

Fin shrugged. He'd buried his share of bodies during the War. More than his share.

Hopefully this "Familia" were just a bunch of sister fuckers and uncle daddies. It wouldn't be the first time he'd gone toe to toe with some inbreds in the south.

Chalking the "war" up to a problem for future Fin, he went back to his rewards.

The first one was straight up video game.

You have earned 2,750 XP!

The amount was doubled, just like the S-grade reward had said.

Before he could even check to see if that was enough to "level up," he also got a red prompt.

Leveling locked! All XP banked!

A bit underwhelming, Fin thought, but there was more to come. What happened next made his eyes widen in surprise.

His next two rewards were accompanied by two *pops.*

The noise was caused by a duo of smooth white globes appearing a foot above the bed. They looked like nothing so much as perfect spheres of milk. Their surfaces even looked wet. The pair of spheres slowly rotated above the sheets. They both also had a faint white aura around them, like lamp posts on a foggy night.

With no hesitation, he reached out and touched one.

"It's not like I'm *not* going to touch it."

The milk ball disappeared with another barely audible *pop* and two golf ball sized orbs dropped into his hand. Fin stared at them in surprise. It wasn't just that these objects had materialized in front of him. It was that both were larger than the original white sphere.

It was like Time Lord technology.

"It's smaller on the outside," he muttered to himself.

These new orbs were warm to the touch, and they looked like they were made of clear crystal with an undulating, ameboid glow in the center, the color of a golden rising sun. Something in the light seemed to call to him, almost like the light was reaching out, trying to connect with him.

Not fully understanding what he was doing, and without moving, something inside of him reached back. He almost thought he could see a nearly transparent blue tendril reach from his hand into both spheres.

The light in the crystal orbs flared in sync. The clear outer shells sublimated into vapor, leaving the golden centers in his palm. A moment later, those began to flow like water, melting before his eyes. The liquid didn't fall through his fingers. Instead, it was absorbed through his skin.

In just two seconds, barely a breath, both were gone.

A great warmth, almost bordering on heat, spread down his arm and into his chest. His whole body began tingling, a faint vibration that transitioned to an intense alertness that felt like he'd free based opium.

A prompt, the same bright red color as a stop sign appeared.

Warning!

*Over the next **4-8 hours** your body will be changed by the Energy being absorbed.*

*The Power available in both this world and your body are far too low to accommodate adding these **2 Constitution Orbs**.*

*Your Constitution will gradually be increased, and your body will undergo severe strain until the process is complete. It is recommended that you choose a safe place to rest. Without sufficient resources, there is a high chance of **swoon** and **death**.*

Good luck!

Fin didn't complain.

After everything he'd been through, a simple and resigned thought shot through his head.

"If it ain't one thing, it's another."

The tingling turned into pain. The pain descended into agony.

It was an anguish as bad as anything he'd ever physically endured.

It was exponentially worse than all of his current injuries put together.

His arteries coursed with lava and his veins were frozen into ice. Fin bared his teeth like a wounded animal. His eyes widened to their max, blood vessels standing stark against his white sclerae, until one burst, spilling scarlet across the landscape.

His jaws clenched so hard that he couldn't scream. With his hands locked into claws, Fin began seizing on the bed, his motions so hard that even his smart mattress couldn't keep up and the back of the bed began knocking against the wall.

The machine checking his vitals began beeping like crazy as his heart rate skyrocketed to 188 beats per minute. His EKG danced the lambada set to a rapid, high pitched beep. The pain was too much, as unknown magic forcibly injected into every cell of his body.

The equivalent of a large lake poured onto desert sands that had never seen a drop of rain.

The magic of the Constitution Orbs forced his body to improve at a rate previously unknown to mankind. Something that would normally take years of daily, dedicated exercise and perfect diet, would happen over the next several hours. It just wasn't something either his body or mind was prepared to handle.

Even more importantly, the changes being forced upon him, while mystical, were not without logic or consequence. In civilized areas of the Labyrinth, no mortal would try to increase their Attributes without sufficient Energy or resources at hand.

As Fin had neither, his life was in jeopardy, and he brushed against the gates of death. If he was not in a hospital, this would have been the end of his story.

Instead, due to pure luck, his fate was changed.

Your first interaction with an item of the Labyrinth could have brought death or delight.

You have balanced on the edge of fate, avoided Danger and found Reward!

+1 Luck...

Error!

***Pseudo-Mortal** status detected...*

Full Status Page Locked...

Assessing...

*Assessment complete. A **Judgment** has been made.*

Memory and evidence of this increase shall be purged.

*Your **Status Page** shall remain locked as the necessary requirements have not been met.*

*The increase to the **Luck** Attribute shall be maintained however, and Luck is now functionally unlocked.*

As the windows erased themselves from his view, his mind was altered as well. From his perspective in the days to come, these series of prompts would have no impact upon him, but as had been said, in the land of the blind, the one eyed man is king.

In an established world of the Labyrinth, one point of Luck might not even be enough to win a single coin while playing tavern dice, but on an Energy null world, merely having the Attribute functionally unlocked gave Fin access to metaphysics of the Labyrinth.

His mere presence began to warp the threads of fate.

Humans without their own connection to the Labyrinth could only be woven into his tapestry.

Fin, of course, knew none of this, and wouldn't have understood it if he did.

Instead, he lost consciousness, an evolutionary defense mechanism to trauma, and his unconscious body sighed in relief.

His seizures stopped, but his limbs continued to jerk periodically due to the forced advancement of his body. In just seconds, those involuntary motions began to ease even further.

After passing out, his subconscious mind stopped instinctively resisting the changes occurring and his vitals stabilized. Heart rate and breathing normalized by the time the crash team arrived in the room. His body continued to change, but to all outward appearances Fin just appeared to be a sleeper with a bit of restless leg syndrome. When his nurse leaned over the bed to better assess him, her body passed through the remaining white sphere hovering above his bed. It remained invisible and intangible to her while it floated above Fin's body.

The members of the crash team looked at each other in confusion. They'd expected a patient at the edge of death, not a man breathing peacefully in his bed. The four of them turned to his nurse.

"What should we do?"

Like all true and smart nurses, she made a judgement call. Wake up a peacefully sleeping doctor of unknown personality type with stable vitals-

Or not?

In almost any other situation, the nurse would have risked a doctor's wrath, but Fin's Luck came into play.

Of the infinite branches of Probability that would stem from the nurse's binary choice, leaving him to sleep had a higher chance of playing out better in Fin's favor than paging the ICU doc on call.

On the Energy null Earth, there were not any other sculptors of fate close enough and strong enough to push Probability away from the path that would benefit the sleeping man.

That was why the Labyrinth automatically and casually stimulated a specific synapse in the nurse's brain, providing her with what she thought was her own original thought.

"We follow protocol. Patient is stable. Vitals are normal. We will closely monitor Doctor Ever's condition q1 for the next four hours and respond accordingly."

All four rapid responders heard her slight stress on the word "doctor" and nodded knowingly. This wasn't their first rodeo. There wasn't a basic bitch among the lot of them.

Waking up the on call doc could always bring an irate baby with a medical license down on their heads. Having the patient be a doctor too meant double the potential for trouble.

Those that knew the charge nurse better were bit surprised that such a stickler for the rules was going to let this slide, but hey, it meant more down time for them.

First rule of every hospital was if you got to go sit down, you sat your ass down.

Quietly easing out of the room with the stealth of ninja parents wanting a well-earned glass of wine, they filed out, even picking up the crash cart slightly to not catch the lip of the door frame.

None of them had been Enabled by the Labyrinth, so not a single one of them saw the white sphere hovering above Fin's bed.

Just outside of the room, the charge nurse continued to observe her patient.

Though she'd said they wouldn't notify the on call doctor, her own professional nature was rebelling at the manipulation triggered by Fin's unlocked Luck stat.

Standing there, she began to second guess her earlier decision about not calling Dr Yinying. She was just about to do so, but then Fin let out a small snore.

It was actually more of a snort.

For some "reason," the noise reminded the nurse of an old girlfriend she'd never fully gotten over.

Valerie used to do that all the time.

That happy memory changed the course of history.

No need to call Dr Yinying, she thought. After all, I can watch the patient just as well as she can.

She checked the patient's vitals again.

"Not like there's anything really to see here," the nurse murmured, her shoulder passing through the floating white ball like it didn't exist, which for her and everyone else not connected to the Labyrinth, was true.

After checking to ensure the autodoc was connected and would provide whatever food and sustenance her patient might need, she just shook her head fondly, still lost in the memory Fin's Luck had manifested in her head.

She closed the door, thinking about whether she should muster up the courage to call Val, and left her patient lying in the golden rays of the setting sun while magic forged him into something new.

Chapter 17: Lotus

FIRE

In a mansion near the heart of Atlanta, a man sat at a table with his wife. His posture was straight, almost rigid. The black sweater he wore contoured his well-built frame. The sleeves bulged over the large muscles of his arms, but rather than looking tacky and boastful, he exuded a powerful, nearly regal energy.

Just as austere and immaculate, the woman's black dress also hugged her slim form in just the right way to exude femininity and power. Both of them had pale skin, refined features, and hair so blonde it was nearly white.

Silver lotuses encircled by a three-pointed silver crown were stitched around the cuff of his sleeves. The same was stitched along the hem of her bodice, showing they were the matriarch and patriarch of their region, specifically the eastern half of the United States and the Caribbean.

All Lotus business in those areas, legitimate and otherwise, fell under their purview.

Everything in the room spoke to wealth and opulence, from the crystal chandelier to the Italian marble of the table and Bohemia crystal glasses, even this simple dining room was a testament to the wealth and power of the family that dined within it. The two leaders of the House of the Ghost Lotus ate quietly, the only sound being the *click* and *clink* of their utensils tapping porcelain.

Most people would never notice, but beneath their austere demeanors, both of their minds were working furiously.

The Wave had changed everything.

Both of them had formed a connection with the Labyrinth. No one in the family knew what that was, outside of a few mumbled words from the House's historian about paths between worlds, but it brought a new age to the Familia.

It had taken a few minutes, but by force of will and power of self, the man had discovered how to unlock his status page. Not long after, his mana

122

strengthened mind broke through a strange resistance, revealing his full status page.

He'd enjoyed the process, rarely finding a challenge for his prodigious mind.

His wife had followed his achievement less than a minute after. The two had disseminated the knowledge to the rest of the family and many other members of the Lotus Familia had similarly unlocked their pages.

Both rulers had gained Abilities, and they were not alone. Most members of the family had also been connected to the Labyrinth and a good number had been granted abilities as well. They also learned that not all abilities were created equally.

His own was *rare.* Through reports from other Lotuses in their region, it seemed he was the only one that had gained an ability of that rank. Via the same method, other ranks had been discovered. *Common* seemed to be the most prevalent rank. After that it went *uncommon, limited,* and then *scarce.* If there was a rank higher than *rare,* they hadn't discovered it yet.

His wife was one of three people in the House who had a fourth rank, *scarce*, ability. This discovery hadn't been overly surprising. The two of them had become the leaders of their region due to their ability to garner power from the old rituals. It was also why they were married.

It was a common practice to pair those of greater strength in the hopes of keeping the old blood as concentrated as possible. Their Family had been carefully interbreeding for centuries to preserve their gifts. Bringing in new blood was also necessary to avoid mutation, of course, making some dilution was inevitable, but the bloodline was always the priority.

The Lotus Family also had a long-standing practice of using any flawed children as ritual sacrifices, which was very effective in reducing the threat of mutation, so inbreeding had far more benefits than detractions.

In the day after the Wave, the various Houses of the Lotus Familia had engaged in a furious series of phone calls and video conferences. By sharing information from around the world, it had been made clear that the vast majority of humanity had not been connected to the Labyrinth.

That information was not shocking in and of itself, but it was also found that nearly everyone in the Familia could now see "The Interface."

Scattered reports from their spies in other Familias seemed to indicate the same held true for their counterparts.

The Wave had changed everything.

The old stories were found to be true. Rituals that had been conducted with no success for millennia were now showing signs of revival. If even one of the faded magics could be mastered, it would herald a new golden age for their faded Familia. Nothing was more important. Every Lotus was being mustered.

Fortunes were being spent to purchase resources that the day before had no practical use, but today, according to old scrolls and moldy books pulled from storage, were vital.

The fact that every other Familia was scrambling to obtain the same resources heralded the beginnings of a trade war. From the patriarch's point of view, actual war between the Familias was inevitable as they fought over resources in a mad scramble for more magic. It was only a question of when.

He did not care about the potential loss of life.

He was the patriarch of the House of the Ghost Lotus, and he would pay any price to see his people once more take their rightful place at the top of the world.

Every member of the Familia felt the same.

Cries of joy echoed in Lotus households around the world. At least for those who had been connected to this "Labyrinth."

Some had received Abilities and were calling themselves the Powered.

Others focused on the first line text that everyone connected had received.

*Congratulations! Your connection to the **Labyrinth** has been **Enabled**!*

Over the last day, it had already become vogue for those who had connected to the Labyrinth to call themselves the Abled, or Able. The implication being that anyone without the connection was then DISabled.

The patriarch did not deign to police the verbiage nor the elitism of his subordinates. If they were strong enough to back up their words, then they had the right to speak them. And if those without a connection were too weak to compete, then they deserved to be relegated to a lower rung of society.

At the very least.

He did find it mildly amusing that within the family compound, "Able" Family members were already splitting into groups, and those without a connection were conspicuously silent.

The groups were being further stratified between those that had manifested Abilities and those who hadn't.

The Patriarch had much larger concerns, and had immediately begun making decrees after the Wave had passed over the Earth.

He still couldn't quite wrap his mind around the sheer might that had been embodied in the silver tide.

There were few beings on the planet that could match his level of power, and none that he truly considered his equal.

Yet, that Wave-

That Wave had not shown him to be a frog at the bottom of a well. It had revealed he was a speck of dust in a hurricane.

While other, lesser men, would find themselves crushed in the face of such majesty, he saw the Wave for what it truly was, a path to power. A path that he would tread no matter how much blood was required to be shed. He would stand upon a mountain of bones if that was required to reach the heights that were owed to him!

The eyes of the patriarch widened ever so slightly in a nearly religious zeal, lost in his aspirations to attain the powers of a god, before his iron will reasserted itself. In the next moment, his face regained its steely impassivity, and he took another bite of his lunch.

He mentally reviewed the orders he'd given minutes after the Wave had passed.

The first was to make every member of the Familia under his purview report in. It had taken him less than five minutes of experimentation with the interface to discover that not only could he see the transparent windows, but they could be shared with others who had been connected to the Labyrinth.

With that knowledge, each family member was forced to show all windows they had received. Some would most likely have hidden information had they more time to think, but as he was in all things, the Patriarch had been swift and ruthless.

What he had found had been illuminating. Of the many men and women under his rule, more than a thousand had been connected to the Labyrinth. In fact, almost everyone who had been able to light the Trial Stone had received the notification.

Even side branch members.

He'd also given orders to interview non-Family members that his subordinates commanded. His people were given wide latitude to threaten, coerce or bribe to gain more information after the Wave.

Though only the first reports were now coming in, a pattern was already emerging. It seemed most lesser humans had not been Enabled. After more than ten thousand had been interviewed, less than a dozen Enabled had been found and none with abilities.

If these reports could be trusted, which he was sure they could not fully, then his Familia was hundreds if not thousands of times more likely to gain the interface as the herds of humanity.

It had also become clear that gaining abilities was a rare variant of connecting to the Labyrinth. Not all abilities were also ranked equally. So far, it seemed that those who had a greater affinity with rituals had received more rare abilities.

This made logical sense to the patriarch, as their mana measurement devices had long ago shown the correlation that men and women with a higher mana concentration were better able to perform rituals. It also seemed like higher ranked abilities were more powerful. His own ability was certainly fearsome, though he could currently only use it twice without needing time to recover.

There had been a few cases of those who had not been able to do even the most basic ritual, not even possessing the ability to sense mana, let alone light the trial stone, who were able to access the Interface.

These were Family members who had been dismissed as near useless, and who were thought to lack even the barest trace of the old blood. And it was true that most of those without ritual affinity had shown no change after the Wave. A few however, *Alter Adel* or not, had gained abilities.

One, had even gained a *limited* rank ability, and they had identified less than two dozen other such individuals so far.

That all made the patriarch think of his youngest son.

The jackass.

The spendthrift.

The disappointment.

It had been all he could do not to beat the boy bloody after the latest round of shit the entitled brat had stirred up. All because the man-child been embarrassed over failing to light the Trial Stone.

The patriarch was positive that if the lazy git had adequately prepared, then he would have passed. In addition to having poor magical talent however, the little shit was as lazy as the day was long. His brothers and sisters were saints and geniuses in comparison. The head of the Lotus sighed heavily, the first show of blanket emotion he'd revealed since sitting down.

Annoying jackass or not, Jerini was his son.   And he was currently missing. Normally that would not have been worth noting, but after the Wave, every single other member of the Family had reported in. It was nearly a day later now, and they had seen neither hide nor hair of his youngest.

Part of the patriarch hoped that his son was a member of the rarest group to become Powered. Even when being angry enough to beat the boy bloody, he'd always felt Jerini had potential. It was not just a father's love that made him feel that way.

Light knew there was little love in the patriarch's heart for anyone, let alone a disappointing son. That certainty in Jerini's potential came from the same place as his magic. Something inside of the boy resonated with him.

If Jerini had become Powered, then it was entirely possible that his son was neck deep in whores, cocaine and sadism. It would be completely in line with his youngest's personality to play with his new ability while he worked up the nerve to come back to the family compound and attempt an ill thought out coup.

His son was an idiot, and a cruel, spoiled one at that. The patriarch had little love in his heart for the fool, but that didn't mean he didn't take his responsibilities towards him seriously. And if Jerini had indeed gained an ability, and a higher ranked one at that, then the boy was precious resource. A vital soldier in the conflict the patriarch was sure would come, most likely sooner rather than later.

Despite his hope that Jerini would stumble home, reeking of cheap perfume and misplaced self-importance, a dark doubt had been growing in the patriarch's mind. Something, a new sense that he was still coming to terms with, was telling him that trouble was coming. It was the rumble of thunder in the distance. The feeling was why despite having so many other important issues to consider, the famously unreadable man found himself disgruntled.

The two heads of the Lotus Family continued their meal when, minutes later, a servant entered the room. The patriarch recognized her as a member of the intelligence division, Emmeline Ringer. Not a Family member, but a lesser bloodline that had served the Lotus for generations.

Her unease was obvious.

Placing his fork face down on the edge of the plate, he gestured towards Emmeline with his knife, "Speak."

The command in his voice could no more be denied than the baleful green-eyed glare he directed at her.

Taking a step closer, Emmeline placed the folder she was holding on the table.

Opening it, the matriarch saw a picture of an explosion, pieces of truck scattered around. She shuffled through more pictures, showing closeups of the scene until her heart stopped. The matriarch started shaking her head in denial.

The picture in front of her showed a silver necklace with a silver lotus.

It couldn't be. It wasn't. It wasn't! Her son wasn't-

Emmeline spoke, bringing her worst fears to life.

"We know why Jerini has not checked in, my lord. There was an accident shortly after the Wave. It appears the fuel cell of his truck exploded. The police arrived at the scene a short time later, but with the havoc yesterday in the city, it took some time for our informant..."

Her voice faded to a drone in the patriarch's mind, though his subordinate continued her thorough report at a normal tone. He processed what she was saying while simultaneously reading through the prepared dossier, his sharp mind filtering the information faster than Emmeline could speak.

In less than a minute, he'd processed, categorized and memorized the relevant information.

There was one simple conclusion to the report.

His son was dead.

He stepped away from the table and looked out the window, watching the last rays of light disappearing over the trees.

Behind him, a low pitched keening competed with Emmeline's measured voice. His wife was rapidly shuttling through the photos, desperate to find a way to refute what her mind had grasped, but her heart rebelled against.

She rapidly shuttled through them, snapping at their servant to shut up and stop telling lies. After not seeing her beloved son's face, she asked a question filled with anger, irritation and vain hope.

"How do you know? I don't see his body here, so how do you know my son is dead? How dare you say such horrible lies when you have no proof!"

Slowly, Emmeline related the facts that were obvious in the file. Obvious to anyone that was not but a mother that did not want to face the truth of her youngest child's death.

"The remains were not recognizable, my lady. That is why it took so long for us to report this horrible tragedy."

"But you don't know! You haven't personally seen the body, have you? Have you!"

The response was slow and careful again, "No, my lady. But the DNA was checked three times. I am so sorry, but there is no doubt that-"

The woman's report was cut off by the sound of keening again, this time, much higher pitched. It continued to grow in volume until it was beyond what a human should be able to create. Another woman's screams joined the matriarch's misery.

The screams sounded human, but were filled with unbearable pain.

The patriarch turned around in alarm. What he saw would forever be etched in his mind.

His wife was staring at Emmeline. Her mouth was opened twice as large as any person could humanly manage. It looked like her jaw had unhinged like a boa constrictor. Pale blue light shot out of her eyes and mouth bathing Emmeline in their beautiful glow.

The light was anything but benign.

Blood poured out of Emmeline's eyes, ears, nose and mouth. The intelligence officer was clawing at her own skin in panic and pain. In the bare seconds it took the patriarch to recover from the shock of what he was seeing, she had dug bleeding furrows down her own face. Ruby red blood flowed in small rivers onto her clothes, staining them crimson. Whatever his wife's light was doing, it was clearly agonizing and had driven the poor woman mad.

With yet another heavy sigh, the patriarch raised one arm, forming his hand into a knife blade strike. White light surrounded it, and then he brought it down sharply.

Shhtt!

Emmeline's screams cut off, and her body fell to the ground in two pieces. The energy had sliced across her torso and through her rib cage which steamed slightly, both sides cauterized. The keening from his wife faltered, looking at the dead body, before rising in pitch again and turning towards him.

"Gisela!" he warned sharply.

His glowing hand was already raised again.

He knew his wife and what her response would most likely be when he stole her kill.

He knew he could not show a moment of weakness or he would fall next.

In response to his threat and strength, her keening faltered.

Soon after, the light coming from his wife's mouth eyes and mouth flickered.

Within seconds, it winked out completely.

Her mouth returned to its normal shape, and she crumpled to the ground, wrapping her arms around herself. Sobbing she just repeated, "My baby. My baby," over and over.

Jaw tight, the patriarch lowered his hand, and the glow faded.

He walked back over to the table, not to comfort his wife, but to look at the file again. Guards had run into the room, drawn by the worrying sounds. Seeing the bisected body, one leader sobbing uncontrollably and the other glaring at them, they stopped cold, unsure what to do.

"Take that away," he commanded with a dismissive flick at the body, "and then leave us."

Without question, the guards rushed forward to remove the offending mess and shut the door behind them. No one in service to the Lotus was a stranger to violence or gore.

After reading through the file again, slower this time, he tapped on the smart paper included with the photos and reports.

Fuel cells did not just randomly explode.

That was the whole reason they had bought Jerini the truck. He'd wrecked his last three sport cars, and his mother was sure he'd wind up dead if they bought him another. That truck wasn't just an expensive toy. It was a finely tuned hover tank.

All cars had built in cameras now. It was Federation law.

Normally, only police or high-level government officials could access the feeds, but that wasn't a problem for a Familia.

The patriarch watched the time leading up to the explosion from the POV of both the truck and the SUV. Unfortunately, neither camera showed much of anything.

The SUV camera was not pointed at the truck and the truck's cam was badly damaged during the initial collision.

It was clear that Jerini was at fault. There was also a tox screen that showed his son had been heavily inebriated. The "official" toxicology screen given to the police would show no abnormalities of course, but the patriarch knew that his son's stupidity had been the primary cause of death.

None of that mattered.

The only thing that did matter was what he heard on his third listen. The audio was distorted by the fire and damage, but he heard it. He then listened several more times to be sure. Each time, it echoed in his mind, stirring his anger.

He pulled another photo out of the file.

It was the license picture of the SUV driver, a smiling black man with a strong jaw. The man that had threatened his injured son.

With a tap of his finger, the patriarch looped the last words his son had ever heard.

I'm going to kill you. I'm going to kill you. I'm going to kill you. I'm going to kill you.

Staring at the picture, rage slowly twisted the patriarch's aristocratic features. It was the first time in more than a decade that he had been moved to such an undisciplined show of emotion. His feelings were further manipulated by the magic of the Labyrinth in response to Fin choosing the Path of War.

With his wife sobbing at his feet, bile in his throat and Fin's words echoing in his ears, he clenched the picture tight enough for his hand to shake. With firm promise, he looked into Fin's laughing eyes and made a vow.

"I'm going to bury what is left of my son. I am going to learn everything I can about you, and I will make you, and those you love, feel the same pain my wife is feeling. And after I render your life to ashes-"

The patriarch let Fin's own voice finish his oath.

"I'm going to kill you."

~REWARD~

Chapter 18: Long Live the Confederation

Fin and the rest of the world remained unaware of the Lotus patriarch's vendetta. He actually remained in the deepest sleep of his life. While he slumbered, the world panicked.

Suicides and impregnations skyrocketed. Religious attendance surged, and scientists struggled to find explanations for what had happened. Criminals took advantage of the chaos, humanity causing far more immediate damage than the Wave itself.

And half the world didn't believe it had happened at all. As more people, keyboard warriors and armchair "experts" took to the Great Link to share their "truth," even more people began to doubt that the Wave had even occurred.

Governments around the world panicked and started checking defenses; theirs, their enemies and especially their "friends." It was the special Olympics of world-wide governmental overreaction. Predictably, it accomplished nothing but pain and confusion.

Any government members with an Interface that were dumb enough to admit it online or out loud were black bagged faster than you could say "secret police."

It didn't matter if it was in the Eastern Hegemony or the Western Confederation. Any government member smart enough to trust no one with knowledge of their new normal, either started making plans of their own, ranging from hiding to world domination and all seven sins in between.

"Experts" on every topic imaginable flooded the Link with everything from conspiracy theories to thousand-year-old predictions about cheese that history buffs manipulated until they could explain a thousand foot high wave of grey fire encircling the world and leaving no trace of its passing.

Every officially recognized news channel in the world was filled with people shouting at one another, and leaving just enough breath to say that everyone else was crazy. The less reputable ones weren't even worth

~REWARD~

addressing. Alien invasion, hallucinogen solar wing, scientologist terrorists, and mass hypnosis were among the most popular theories.

Surprisingly, one college student named Doug Forcett, completely baked on Afghani Kush and flying on Golden Teachers, came up with a theory that a beam of energy, probably comprised of the building blocks of creation itself, had been traveling through time and space for aeons. During its passage it had changed, shed and collected potential and been refined until slamming into the Earth, the end of its journey and yet somehow, also the beginning.

He was on the cusp of being awarded a Unique, *Legendary* Title, *Knowledge of All*. Unfortunately, an essential part of Doug's anatomy was eaten by a mimic posing as a gloryhole outside of a Krispy Kreme only minutes later, in a tragic monster-munchies accident that could have happened to anyone.

He died shortly after.

***

Leaders around the world spoke platitudes to try to calm their citizens. The speech from the President of the Western Confederation was played on a loop.

Citizens of Confederation. We have shared an unprecedented experience. Scientists around the globe have confirmed that the energy wave originated from deep space, and impacted approximately 2,000 kilometers from the US coastline on the 37th parallel.

Waves radiated out from the point of impact in all directions. In less than a minute, it encircled the globe. The waves disappeared as quickly as they came. I am here to tell you that there was no long term damage from the phenomenon.

Let me say again. You are in no danger. Our Federation remains strong, and will protect you.

We are looking for answers, and I promise you, as soon as we know anything definitive, I will personally let you, my valued citizens, know. As of now, we believe this Wave was the result of a seldom seen "Super Massive Solar Flare." As I said, however, there is nothing to be concerned about. I promise, you are in good hands.

With a patented smile on her face, Susan Sahara, the number one politician of the world's greatest superpower finished strong.

You can trust in your government.

You can trust in Sahara.

Long live the Confederation!

***

In a sealed room that doubled as a faraday cage, Susan Sahara looked at her closest advisors.

The practiced smile she'd shared with the world was nowhere to be seen. In its place, was a snarl under eyes that blazed fire.

"You incompetent fools! I looked like a damn idiot up there. Something just happened that changed reality, and you still don't have answers!"

"Madam President," began her Secretary of Defense.

"Shut your mouth," she shrieked at him. "I don't want to hear your excuses. The eggheads tell me every mana sensor we possess was burned out because the event possessed more raw power than we thought was possible.

All they can tell me is that our most powerful sensor registered such a high reading that compared to the highest concentration we ever recorded before, the event would be like a nuclear explosion compared to a fucking candle!"

"Madam president," this time it was Dr Wu, her chief science advisor who spoke up. "We are being shackled by the administration's position to keep mana a secret from the world. I cannot even assign more than a handful of scientists to truly investigate the matter. If we could just let the people know-"

Susan's voice, dripped venom, her words clipped, "Be silent, you child."

She closed her eyes, praying for the strength to endure idiots. This stupid fuck was trying to get them all killed.

When she opened them again, she leaned on the table with her fists. Her glare encompassed every man and woman there. Every person there possessed great political, economic and even military power, but not a single one had the audacity to stand up to the president.

None had the same societal level that she had. It would cost her, but she could order any of their deaths if they angered her enough.

Susan hadn't become president of the Confederation by being kind.

She stared at each of them in turn before speaking her next words.

"What do you think the World AI will do if anyone in the Eastern Hegemony harnesses this power before we do?"

The silence that followed was filled with fear of more than just her.

***

It wasn't until around ten am that Fin woke up. Blinking, out of the dark pit of unconsciousness, he immediately tensed the moment he became fully aware.

What the?

How the fuck?

What *was* that pain?

Fin was no stranger to torture after his experiences during the War, but what had just happened was something beyond his understanding.

It had felt like his body was being torn apart from the inside.

An involuntary shudder ran through his body, followed by an even more horrific thought. What if it wasn't done?

He tensed again in anticipation of a return to that painscape until several long seconds passed. Once the event horizon of apprehension had been passed, he realized he felt… better!

Not only was the sheer and utter agony he'd experienced all night now gone, but he also felt better than he had since waking up in the hospital.

All signs of his concussion were gone. His eyes tolerated the light, his hearing was clear, and when he took a deep breath, his ribs no longer dug into his lungs on inhalation.

Over the last several hours, he'd been healed nearly back to normal.

Hell. He felt better than had in years. "Normal" might be an understatement.

Fin did a self-examination and found that while he was definitely still injured, his body was in better condition than it should be. In fact, it felt like he'd been recovering for weeks rather than just a single night.

He also felt energetic, like he'd slammed several cups of coffee.

Moving around in the bed a bit made it clear he was still injured, but there was no denying the energy he felt coursing through him.

A blinking in the corner of his vision showed him he had new prompts. He couldn't help but wonder, yet again, at how crazy it was that he had a video game style interface. Even crazier was how quickly he'd come to accept that fact.

Sadness seized him.

Lauren would have loved this.

It would have literally been a dream come true for her.

"Oh baby," he murmured sadly.

Fin gave himself a full ten seconds to process his grief, before he willed it to the side for later. He'd lost loved ones and friends before. More than he wanted to think about during the War. Anyone who said it got easier was a fool, but if you were strong enough, you learned strategies to manage it.

After the ten count, he took a deep breath and sat up. His pain smoldered inside of him like a well banked coal, burning every second but no longer threatening to burn through him.

Fin was about to check his new prompts, eager to see just what the Constitution orbs had done, but those windows took back seat to the smooth white ball hovering in front of his face!

Fin blinked in surprise, but then he remembered that there was more "loot" to claim from finishing his quest.

I hope this ball doesn't trigger another round of pain and sleepy time, a thought that was followed by a heavy sigh.

It was one of life's great injustices that you couldn't "that's what she said" yourself.

Shaking his head he reached out and poked the white ball. With a faint *pop* the sphere disappeared, and two silver coins fell onto the bed. Both were the size of silver dollars.

The coins had a maze like design on one side. The other held an embossed depiction of the planet Earth. It looked like the Pacific Ocean was centered on the coin, North and South America were on the right, Western Europe and Africa stood in stark relief on the left.

Thinking back to his quest rewards, he recalled that the rewards had been twenty-five and seventy-five coppers. His "S" score for the quest had doubled the rewards.

"I guess a hundred coppers makes a silver," he murmured. "Nice of them to convert it for me."

Anyone who had ever held a hundred old-world pennies at once would know how annoying that was. Not only would you inevitably drop some, but your hands would smell like prom night.

He had no idea if two silvers were a large or small amount of money, but the bigger question was, why had nobody freaked out when they saw a milk ball floating in midair over his bed?

A quick check of the wall clock showed he'd been passed out for more than twelve hours. He was in the ICU. There was no way a nurse hadn't come by and checked on him. He could buy them not waking him up seeing as how the autodoc would warn them if there was a problem, but they would have definitely freaked out if they'd seen a levitating white sphere.

Fin shook his head. That mystery would have to wait.

What truly mattered was that he had to piss like a racehorse!

He'd only been awake for about a minute, and he'd been distracted initially. Now that he was fully alert, natural needs were making themselves known and loudly. With a curse, he realized there was a real chance that he was going to make a mess.

There was a bed pan nearby, but he'd be damned if he asked his nurse to wipe his ass.

After disconnecting his IV from the autodoc, it took a full minute to cross the 10 feet to the bathroom. Thankfully, it looked like they'd take his catheter out while he was passed out.

     ~REWARD~

Kinda glad I slept through that, he thought.

His broken leg didn't make it easy, but Fin was determined. And it was actually far less painful than he'd thought. If he didn't know better, he'd have thought he'd just injured his leg rather than having snapped a bone.

With a series of awkward hops, he finally positioned himself over the bowl. With a bit of panic fumbling at the end, he lifted his gown and let fly. He was sweating by that time, and a small squirt might have sneaked out before the fabric was fully clear, but he'd take the truth of that to the grave.

What's a little dribbling between friends?

His vision nearly went black again, but this time from sheer relief. He braced one hand against the wall and just enjoyed the familiar sound of a fire hose shooting down a well.

"Oh. Oh, thank god."

A full fifty-three seconds later, he finally finished, washed his hands, and hobbled back to the bed. As he did, he shook his head at how much better he felt since waking up. Without mother nature screaming in his ear, he was better able to take stock of his body. There was no doubt about it. His injuries were partly healed.

He'd actually been partially healed by those magical orbs.

Now if only he had his Link-

Fin's eyes went to the bedside table. There, hidden behind the bedpan, was a familiar bracelet. It was only half an inch wide and barely an eighth of an inch thick. The band was clear, but had an opalescent sheen. He knew from experience that the material could be pliable as putty or stiff as high density plastic. The whole thing was made out of smart rubber that could mold onto his arm like a second skin.

After sitting back on the edge of the bed, he snapped it over his right wrist. The subcutaneous bioimplant there, no larger than a grain of sand, connected to his Link and confirmed his identity via several hundred genetic markers in an instant.

The implant was free to every citizen of the Federation. It was a bioorganic seed that the body recognized as a renewable artificial organ linked to a person's central nervous system. Even if a person's hand was chopped off, the body would regrow the implant on the stub. Lost your whole arm? It grew on the other side. Both arms blown off? It would grow under the forehead and could be linked to a headband.

Head cut off?

Well, then you were dead, weren't you, so who cared?

The clear bracelet, or Link, was the other half of the tech, and was also made available and for free for every person on Earth. Together, they provided access to the Great Link, which was hailed as the greatest invention to come out of the War.

The Great Link had replaced the internet and deep web. The plastic wristband had replaced smart phones. Governed by the World AI, a benevolent intelligence that oversaw the entire planet and was independent of any government or human influence, the Great Link gave each person access to every song, video, and book ever uploaded.

Originally, created to improve morale during the War, it was also completely unhackable. A yearly contest was held with an ever increasing jackpot if anyone managed it. For more than a decade, it had remained unclaimed, and the prize was now more than two trillion credits.

It took less than a single second for the Link to recognize him and personalize his settings. The clear band turned opaque black. Gold letters reading "Gnomes Rule" appeared across the top.

"Geneva," he called out.

"Yes, Fin," came the feminine response, slightly amused and very kind. A holographic window projected across his palm from the bracelet. A small red headed face floated on the window, smiling at him.

Hearing its mocking tone brought a sense of familiarity and solidity that he hadn't known he craved. It was like being home. It was like being with Lauren.

Fin felt his throat tighten, but he clamped down on the emotion, going cold inside instead.

"It's good to see you, G. Can you order me some clothes? Just some jeans, a T and underwear? Oh, and I'll probably need some new cross trainers and socks as well."

"Happy to help," came the pleasing voice. "I've put the order in to the Zon. I chose the washed option, so they should arrive in the next few hours. Oh, one more thing. Lauren has an appointment tomorrow. Would you like me to send a reminder to her Link?"

That casual question threatened his emotional stronghold again, but through will and effort, his face remained stoic. "No, G," was his measured response. "And don't mention Lauren again until I give permission."

"Okay, Fin. Whatever you say." After a short, one second, pause, an eternity for an AI, it added, "I'm here for you."

The pause was atypical, something that shouldn't happen, but Fin's mind was already on other things.

Namely, he was doing a thorough self-exam.

He activated the mirror function on his Link and a small, holographic image appeared above his wrist. Turning it this way and that, he whistled softly in amazement. While he'd been unconscious, his burns had drastically improved.

Pink skin stood vivid next to his normal cocoa goodness. The demarcations were as stark as lines of a map. While it would have been obvious to anyone that he'd suffered extensive injuries, the lighter patches of skin were the color of healthy granulation tissue, missing the shininess of permanent burn scars.

Based on what he was seeing, when he was finally fully healed, he should be back to his normal sexy self with no permanent scarring.

That should not be possible considering the first degree burns he'd had less than a day before.

The orbs hadn't just healed him faster than he otherwise would.

He was healing faster than human beings *could.*

Of course, after the explosion, waking up at all had been a surprise.

He still didn't know how he had survived.

Standing next to an exploding fuel cell, the damage should have been… total.

Not only was he alive, when he'd woken up, his wounds had not been nearly as severe as they should have been.

Still, he could have explained that away by some fluke of physics though. Maybe he'd been thrown clear of the blast somehow. Perhaps a compression wave had radiated outward, flinging him back and away from the kinetic component of the explosion.

It was utter bullshit, but, on the other hand, just before the collision, a tsunami of grey fire stretching high enough to reach outer space, had swept over the world leaving no trace that it had ever happened.

He'd have been willing to roll with it and chalk it up to "ish happens."

The healing he was observing now was something different. He knew the human body. He'd trained for a decade to be able to rightfully call himself an expert in medical matters. In the War, he'd had other training, no less extensive.

Fin knew how exactly how resilient the body could be, and he knew exactly how fragile.

You just didn't heal this much after a night's sleep.

The signs of his improved health were obvious and numerous. His breathing was no longer pained, and his broken ribs, which should have been making him wince with every breath, were barely sore.

He'd also suffered a concussion, and now he only had a faint headache. He should still have some photophobia or at least some dizziness, but his sensorium was clear. That wasn't even mentioning his burns. It just didn't add up.

Fin wished he could see that red prompt that had popped up before he'd passed out. To his surprise, a window appeared in his vision offering to let him see old prompts. Not only that, but it had a separate section for his "combat log."

I'm definitely diving more into that later. For the moment, he focused on retrieving the prompts he'd gained just before blacking out.

Warning! Over the next 4-8 hours your body will be changed by the energy being absorbed. Your Power and available Energy are far too low to accommodate adding these 2 Constitution orbs. Your Constitution will gradually be increased, and your body will undergo severe strain until the process is complete. It is recommended that you choose a safe place to rest. Without sufficient resources, there is a high chance of swoon and or death.

Good luck!

He'd seen that part before he blacked out. The next line made him roll his eyes and mutter about captain obvious.

*You have **swooned**.*

*Warning! The strain upon your body has placed you into a state of **Starvation**!*

-2% HP/hr. -5% SP/hr. Stamina regeneration halted.

*Congratulations! You have received sustenance. **Starvation** debuff removed.*

*Warning! The strain upon your body has place you into a state of **Dehydration**!*

-5% HP/hr. Mana and Health regeneration halted.

*Congratulations! You have received fluids. **Dehydration** debuff removed.*

*Warning! The strain upon your body has placed you into a state of **Starvation**!*

-2% HP/hr. -5% SP/hr. Stamina regeneration halted.

There were a lot of repeat messages. He'd gotten the *Starvation* debuff eleven times and the *Dehydration* debuff more than twenty. For a moment, he wondered if his interface was glitching somehow.

That happy thought started him down a "bad thoughts" spiral that lasted about five seconds, or two eternities, depending on how you understood the time space continuum.

What if his Interface *did* glitch?

What if windows kept popping up, over and over, and not disappearing until they blocked all of his vision and he was effectively blinded?

Chapter 19: Broken

EARTH

F in strangled that panic in its crib.

Just like he was processing Lauren's loss, he centered himself. He would not deny his feelings, but he would not be controlled by them either. If there was a problem, then he'd fix it. After several deep breaths, he was under control again and forced himself to think critically.

Maybe he wasn't broken. Maybe there was another explanation for the repeat screens. He turned his head to look at the autodoc. The device looked like nothing more than a small box attached to the wall with an electronic display with tubing coming out of it. In actuality, it was a highly sophisticated piece of machinery that measured dozens of blood levels at once, provided IV medication and continuously monitored a patient's vitals. It was able to respond nearly instantaneously to any number of parameters, providing instant care twenty-four hours a day.

It was another piece of technology that came out of the War. Older docs talked about how they had to draw blood on a daily basis and worry about toxicity levels from medications. Even giving IV fluids could cause harm if not properly monitored. The autodoc streamlined all those processes.

The electric interface was intentionally a bit convoluted to navigate, mostly to keep patients from playing with it, but for Fin, checking its data log was a cinch. All Fin had to do was cycle back through the logs. When he did, his mouth dropped open in shock.

In the past twelve hours his body had consumed more than 14,000 kcal of nutrition and 35 liters of fluids! That amount of intake should have killed him by itself. The calories were the equivalent of a week's worth of meals, and the fluids should have made him swell up like a balloon. That wasn't exaggeration. During the war, he'd seen a patient bloat like a corpse because a sleep deprived doctor had written for ten times as much IV fluid as the patient should have gotten. Seeing how much fluid he'd taken in explained why he'd

144

had to pee so bad, but with that amount of fluid put into him, he should have been pissing for an hour! It just didn't make any sense!

Fin considered himself a scientist. He placed his faith in reason and verifiable facts. In that, he never forgot that the pursuit of knowledge was endless, the wealth of truth was infinite.

He had enough respect for the expansive possibility of the Universe to understand mankind had only scratched the surface of what was possible. Put another way-

"There are more things under heaven and Earth, Horatio, than are dreamt of in your philosophy," he murmured to himself.

Those were words he'd always taken to heart. Unlike many educated people, his training and increasing understanding of the world didn't make him arrogant. Instead, it served as a reminder of how much more he had to learn. When the grey wave had appeared, he'd accepted that maybe it was a weapon he'd never seen before, maybe even an astrological phenomenon. Both explanations still fell under the purview of "things that existed but he just hadn't known about before."

His healing body though, resided under a different category. Injury and healing were two things he was well familiar with. He had seen thousands of patients come through his ER. The human body wasn't nearly the mystery most people thought it was. Very often in fact, it followed a simple "If A, then B" model. What he was seeing now, from his faster healing, to the sheer amount of food and drink he'd been able to absorb, was more like, "If A, then watch this one eyed, no armed ewok speed run Super Mario Bros in under four minutes."

It just wasn't possible.

The only way he could have survived consuming so many calories and fluids was if his body was burning it up at the same rate that the autodoc had poured them in. Which was exactly what his prompts were saying, but it still just didn't seem possible for a human to not only reach, but maintain, such a heightened metabolic state for a full twelve hours.

Though, he touched his sodden bedding, it might explain why it felt like he was laying on a used tampon.

Heaving a deep sigh, he realized he might have to throw out everything he knew about the world he lived in… along with these sheets. That world was turning out to be a lot larger than he'd ever imagined.

With the info he had now, he was pretty sure he knew what had happened while he was unconscious. It looked like those Constitution orbs had increased his metabolic processes to an insane level. In layman's terms, whatever the orbs had done, it had been so taxing on his body that it had continually forced him into a state of starvation and dehydration. The autodoc had saved his life.

Fin was still feeling ravenous, but he wasn't in any danger and his vitals were stable. He realized how lucky he'd been to be in the hospital when this had happened. He might have died if he'd just collapsed at home. That realization shot cold water through his veins. If even getting stronger could take his life-

Would this happen anytime one of his attributes increased? And what would have happened if the orbs had been a higher rank than *common*?

There was so much he didn't know about his new normal.

He read back through the red prompt. It said that he'd had an adverse effect because he didn't have enough "Power" or "Energy."

Did this tie back into the whole "null" world thing? Maybe if he or the world had more Energy, then he'd be able to tolerate the increase stats better?

If that was true, then all he had to do was figure out how to increase his Power level… and learn just what the hell Energy was. No problem.

"Fuck," he murmured.

Did it mean magic? He shook his head and went back to reading.

*Congratulations! You have absorbed a **Common** rank **Constitution** orb. Your Constitution will be increased by 3-5…*

CON increased by +3

*Congratulations! Your **Constitution** has increased from 16 to 19!*

*Congratulations! You have unlocked a Primary Attribute: **Constitution***

***Constitution** (CON) – This Primary Attribute determines your Health Points and improves Stamina regeneration. It will also increase your resistance to disease, poison and other negative conditions. Other unknown effects.*

"Oh my god," Fin breathed out. Then for good measure added, "Shit."

His brain was having a hard time reconciling the horrid pain he'd just lived through and the amazing feeling he had now. His body felt-

Alive.

He knew how dumb that sounded, but that was what it felt like.

He felt invigorated, tingling and more alive than he'd ever felt before. It was amazing.

Fin smiled and spent the next several minutes running his hands over every inch of his skin. Anyone else would have thought he was rolling on some exceptional E, but he was just marveling at the health that was filling him. That was why he didn't catch a very important part of the last prompt for far, far too long.

"I absorbed 'an' orb?"

As in singular?

If he still had to absorb the second orb, was he going to go through another bout of pain? Was he going to pass out again?

Thankfully not.

Increasing your Primary Attributes through this method has provided a miniscule surge of Energy. While this amount is paltry in concern to the greater Labyrinth, compared to your Energy starved nature, the surge was enough to let you remain conscious while the remaining Constitution orb is added over the next 4-8 hours.

Your body will continue to undergo various types of stress. It is advised that you avoid strenuous activity.

Apparently, adding the first orb had changed him enough that he was able to better tolerate the second. He went over what he knew now, or at least what he suspected.

The increase to his Constitution explained why he felt better than he should. It explained his healing. He still felt achy and tired, but undoubtedly stronger than before.

The next prompt showed that he was quantifiably "healthier" than before.

Congratulations! You have unlocked your second Stat: **Health**

Health *is a measure of the physical damage your body has and can endure. This does Stat does not make you immune to the previous reality of your existence, but your connection to the Labyrinth now allows its rules to supersede the previous natural laws of your world.*

Unlocked my second stat?

I was able to see my Mana Points before, but when did I unlock it?

Those questions were eclipsed by something much more pertinent and awesome.

I have health points?

Fin couldn't get the thought out fast enough.

Status page!

<table>
<tr><td colspan="3" align="center">FIN EVERS</td></tr>
<tr><td>Health: 18/30 (23*)</td><td>Mana: 22/22</td><td>Stamina: LOCKED</td></tr>
</table>

As promised, his health stat was now there for his viewing pleasure.

Honestly, it didn't look great. Nearly half of his health was gone.

That wasn't so surprising based on having survived a car explosion.

He was alive so he decided not to complain.

What was the last number, though? The twenty-three?

And what was the asterisk?

Concentrating on it, didn't give any info, but the next windows made Fin think he knew what the answer was.

*Healing energy floods your body. Your **Severe Injury** status has improved to* **Moderate Injury!**

          ~REWARD~

This time, focusing on the words did give an explanation.

Severe Injuries *– You have endured physical injuries classified as **Severe** for more than 24 hours. -50% to max HP and SP. -50% to physical abilities.*

Moderate Injuries *– You have endured physical injuries classified as **Moderate** for more than 24 hours.*

-25% to max HP and SP.

-25% to physical abilities.

The increase in his Constitution hadn't just given him more health points, it had also healed him overall. It looked like whatever governed his Health Stat could be given a lower max value if he suffered major injuries.

Again, that made logical sense, but he had a feeling there was more to these "injuries" than just 'getting hurt.' There always seemed to be specific meaning with the capital letter words in these prompts.

He did some quick math.

If his max Health, or HP, might as well really lean into this game frame of mind, was thirty, then his *Moderate Injuries* status would decrease that by 25%. Which would be about twenty-three if you rounded up.

That was just his maximum allowable health though. His actual wounds had still knocked his health down another five points, leaving him at eighteen.

This was trippy.

Shifting around, he found that his pain had significantly improved as well. Fin continued his inspection.

He still felt like his body was a giant bruise, but he wasn't in dilaudid level pain, which was remarkable after what he'd been through.

He kept up his exam.

The physical trauma made it tough to tell if the points of Constitution had changed his physical form. Was his chest a bit more expansive? Were his shoulder's a bit broader? Maybe he'd be able to tell better after the second orb was fully added.

Fin turned his attention back to his interface.

Two more prompts were waiting for him. The first actually showed him something in his combat log. After reading it, he finally understood how he'd survived the fuel cell explosion.

These prompts were some of the first he'd received. They showed what had happened right before, and immediately after, the explosion. As he read, he was shocked yet again.

Memories of the moments before the truck blew had started coming back, but they were fragmented. If he tried to focus on any one of them, he got a headache. With a bit of gallows humor, he realized that was probably the brain damage.

From those fragments, he'd pieced together a reasonable guess of what had happened. The conclusion he'd finally come to made him think his memory was flawed. That what he'd "remembered" had actually been just a mix of truth and a pretty bad concussion.

This whole time though, he'd been subconsciously thinking that there was no way what his mind remembered had, in fact, really happened.

Turns out, it had.

Chapter 20: Remembrance

Right after he'd, oh so eloquently, passed judgement on the driver of the other car with a softly spoken, "DIIIIEEEEEEE!" there had been an avalanche of prompts.

*Warning! Recent exposure to raw Chaos has temporarily increased your Power drastically: **+1000 Power***

*Your **State of Being** has progressed drastically!*

*Warning! Your **Pseudo-Mortal** nature cannot tolerate this Power!*

Safety Protocols triggered! Aberrant Power will be rerouted!

*Epic Ability, **Whisper**, detected!*

Funneling excess Power into your Ability.

Your Whisper Ability is overcharged!

*Your overcharged Ability has detected a miniscule source of **Fire Element** in your immediate vicinity.*

*Your overcharged Ability is attempting to connect to the **Fire** Element.*

*Congratulations! Your overcharged Ability has forcibly taught you a **Skill**!*

*This **Skill** requires access to a locked **Stat**!*

*Congratulations! You have unlocked your first Stat: **Mana***

***Mana** is a measure of the magical energy held within your **State of Being**.*

That answers why it was on my status page earlier. A deluge of windows waited.

~REWARD~

You have learned the Skill: **Mana Sense** *(Common). You can now sense nearby sources of mana.*

+10 Magicka for learning your first **Common** *(Low rank Mortal Tier) Skill*

As you are the first person on your world to obtain the **Mana Sense** *Skill tree, +100% chance for this Skill to* **Advance** *or* **Evolve***!*

Know This! Synergy detected between your **Whisper** *Ability and the* **Mana Sense** *Skill!*

Your overcharged Ability is attempting to forcibly **Advance** *your Skill...*

Beginning Assessment... Aberrant Power has bypassed the **Assessment***!*

Your Skill has been forcibly **Advanced** *from* **Common** *to* **Uncommon***!*

Maximum Advancement Perk awarded!

Uncommon Perk: **Mana Efficiency**

You have learned the Skill: **Mana Connection** *(Uncommon). You can feel and connect to nearby sources of mana.*

+20 Magicka for learning your first **Uncommon** *(Mid rank Mortal Tier) Skill*

Know This! Synergy detected between your **Whisper** *Ability and the* **Mana Connection** *Skill!*

Your overcharged Ability is attempting to forcibly **Advance** *your Skill...*

Beginning Assessment... Aberrant Power has bypassed the Assessment!

This Skill has been forcibly **Advanced** *from* **Uncommon** *to* **Limited***!*

Maximum Advancement Perk awarded!

Limited Perk: **Mana Stability**

You have learned the Skill: **Mana Manipulation** *(Limited). You can feel and manipulate nearby sources of mana.*

+50 Magicka for learning your first **Limited** *(High rank Mortal Tier) Skill*

Know This! Synergy detected between your **Whisper** *Ability and the* **Mana Manipulation** *Skill!*

Your overcharged Ability is attempting to forcibly **Advance** *your Skill...*

     ~REWARD~

Beginning Assessment… Aberrant Power has bypassed the Assessment!

*This Skill has been forcibly **Advanced** from **Limited** to **Scarce**!*

Maximum Advancement Perk awarded!

Scarce** Perk: **Mana Penetration

*You have learned the Skill: **Mana Control** (Scarce). You can feel and control nearby sources of mana.*

*+**100 Magicka** for learning your first **Scarce** (Low rank Heroic Tier) Skill*

*By reaching the **Scarce** rank in the **Mana Sense** Skill tree, a **Branch of Evolution** is possible.*

*Your overcharged Ability is attempting to forcibly **Evolve** your Skill…*

*Checking for **Catalyst**…*

Unknown rank Catalyst provided by unknown Higher Energy and aberrant Power!

Evolution Successful!

*Your Mana Sense Skill Tree has **Branched**!*

All previous bonuses maintained.

***Mana Control** (Scarce) has Evolved into **Mana Threads** (Scarce). By expending MP, you may create immaterial threads to increase your connection to sources of mana*

*Evolution Bonus: **Mana Penetration Perk** has evolved into **Mana Invasion Perk***

*+**250 Magicka** for Evolving your first Heroic Skill*

*As a **Scarce** Skill, Mana Control consumes **30 Energy***

*As this is a Heroic Skill your current Realm cannot support a Skill of such grandeur. Extra Energy is required. +50% Energy required for using a **Scarce** Skill.*

***45 Energy** Sequestered!*

Total Energy Remaining: 5

The Aberrant Power has bonded this Skill tree to your soul!

Fin stopped reading, feeling completely overwhelmed.

After a few moments, he read it again.

And again.

And then again.

He basically got what had happened, but his mind was recoiling from concepts that it had never had to deal with in the "old world."

If he was following, he had some sort of ability called "Whisper." It must have come from the Wave? Maybe it was one of the things locked away on his full status page?

Whatever the case, it looked like the ability had given him a "skill."

No, that wasn't right.

It had given him a "Skill," with a capital "S," the same way Whisper had a capital "W" and was an Ability with a pointy "A."

He read back once more, not seeing anything to explain the difference between Abilities and Skills, except that the Skill took Energy.

As he didn't even know what "Energy" was yet, it wasn't exactly helpful.

What was more clear, was that his Whisper ability had upgraded his Skill somehow from *Mana Sense* to *Mana Control.*

The Skill had Advanced, again with a capital "A" three times, from "common" rank up to "scarce." Once more, there was no explanation about what those rankings meant, or even what a ranking was, but presumably higher rank was better?

A fourth progression had been called an Evolution. It looked like it made the Skill a super version of itself.

All of it led to countless questions.

The word "magicka" had also been mentioned several times.

No idea what that was either.

Unfortunately, focusing his attention on the specific words didn't bring up any explanation or dictionary. All it did was show him his total.

~REWARD~

*Total Magicka: **1080***

And last, but not least, there was the whole "bonded to his soul" thing.

Fin visually scanned his body, but if a 'soul bond' did anything in the material world, he couldn't tell.

He read the rest of the combat log entry. Everything up until now had been the warm up.

What came next was the main course.

*Congratulations! Due to a Blessing of your world, **Lucid Abilities**, you may actively cultivate your Ability!*

*You have unlocked your first **Ability** Aspect: **Flux** – Create a conduit between yourself and external Elements*

*+100 **Magicka** for unlocking an Aspect for the first time.*

***Mana Threads** has allowed you to trigger the **Flux Aspect** of your **Whisper** ability for the first time!*

*Your **Whisper** Ability has forced a connection with a source of Fire Element through your **Mana Threads** Skill.*

*You have invested 100 Mana Points into a nearby source of **Fire** Element. The **Miniscule** Fire Element source has increased to **Moderate**!*

As a result, a small flame has greatly increased in size!

The enlarged flame has triggered an explosion!

***Mana Threads** has triggered an instinctual activation of the **Flux Aspect** of your **Whisper** ability!*

Forcibly connecting to the Fire Element.

Absorbing the Fire Element.

*You have collected 8 motes of **Fire Element**.*

You have absorbed all Element from this source.

The flames of a nearby explosion have been drastically reduced.

Warning! You have emptied your mana pool!

You have gained a Debuff: **Mana Depletion** *– You are at great risk of losing consciousness!*

You have lost consciousness.

Warning! Absorbing such a great amount of Fire Element so quickly has overwhelmed your Energy null body.

You have gained a Debuff: **Ability Deprivation** *– Your Whisper Ability is locked for a natural day of your current planet.*

Another prompt followed those.

1 day has passed.

Debuffs removed.

All abilities have reverted back to normal levels.

That was the last message.

He didn't need any more.

Reading the prompt had jogged his memory.

He remembered it all.

He remembered hearing the voice say "burn," and he remembered agreeing.

Then he'd felt something drain out of him. That must have been his "mana" pouring his into the flame that had been on the hood of the truck. That had made the small fire turn into a massive blaze. That in turn was why the fuel cell had exploded.

Fin stopped for a moment.

He really *had* killed that guy.

Reading about the "Path of War" earlier hadn't really made it clear.

The car explosion hadn't been a fluke accident.

He'd taken a life.

Again.

This whole time, he hadn't actually thought he was directly responsible for the man's death.

Reading the combat log, he realized that he was.

He'd deliberately chosen to end a life. Once more, he was the sole reason another person had stopped breathing.

Fin let that truth wash over him. He'd fought in the War, and he'd killed. Many soldiers had. What he'd done in service of the Nexus, had been even… worse.

The mental traumas of that time still plagued billions, himself included. The evaluators had said his psychological profile meant he had an easier time than most, but he hadn't been part of the select group of humanity who wasn't affected at all by the atrocities.

For which he was extremely thankful.

He'd gladly take the nightmares and midnight awakenings soaked in sweat rather than be one of *them*.

He'd sublimated that pain into a desire to do good. It had driven him to pursue medicine after the war.

When the new era began, he'd dedicated his life to saving people. It had taken years, but he'd become a doctor, and had positively impacted thousands of lives.

He'd never allowed himself the lie that he'd balanced the scales, but he knew he'd done some good.

Now that he'd taken another life, the life of a man who had selfishly taken everything from him, he searched his feelings for just what that meant to him.

What did it mean, that he'd actually added more red to his ledger? That he'd killed the man who'd killed Lauren? That he might have even triggered a war?

As the moments passed, he didn't even try to keep the smile off his face.

Chapter 21: Overachiever

LIfe

rey Stone Cemetery, Portland Oregon, 2 days after the Wave

"I'm telling you, Joe. There is something off with the trees."

"Ugh, not this again!"

"Keep your voice down," Paul scolded in complete seriousness. "They'll hear you."

Joe rolled his eyes and attempted to explain it for the thousandth time, "The trees can't hear man."

"There's a person buried under every tree here. How do you know they can't hear?"

"Because they're dead man!"

"And each tree grew out of an organic burial pod. Each tree grew out of a body and now they are living again."

"But trees don't have ears!"

"Corn does," came Paul's reply.

Joe glared at his fellow custodian. After months of working together, he still wasn't sure if the man was a nutter butter, or if the guy was fucking with him. The vacant expression on Paul's face argued for the first, but he might just be a diabolical genius.

Giving up, Joe pointed at the tree he was talking about, "Just look man! I walked by this tree the other day, and I'm telling you it didn't look like this. It's got a face!"

Paul squinted. He did indeed see what could be a face in the wrinkled bark. He also was guilty of fucking with Joe as often as possible. It was the

~DANGER~

only amusement he had in this otherwise boring job. He wasn't about to let a prime opportunity like this pass him by, even the pattern in the bark was a little weird.

"I don't see it."

"What? It's right there. Right there!"

"Ummmm, I wish I could help you man, but it just looks like a tree to me. Are you stressed?"

"I don't believe you. Look! These are the eyes, this is the mouth, and there's even a nose." He drew his hands along the tree trunk while he made his points.

"And you think there might be a face because the trees grew out of dead bodies?" Paul asked.

"Well… I didn't say that."

"But," Paul pressed, scrunching his face meaningfully, "you're thinking that aren't ya?"

Joe's lips thinned and he basically shook before admitting, "Fine! Yes! It occurred to me."

"It's okay," Paul reassured him understandably. "It's completely normal that you would feel a bit creeped out and see things that aren't there."

Joe opened his mouth, feeling aggrieved, but Paul cut him, with a very professorial tone, "Apophenia."

"What?"

"A-po-phe-nia," Paul repeated, emphasizing each syllable. "It's the psychological tendency to make connections between unrelated things. You see a face in the bark of a tree and now you think dead people are coming back to life."

"I didn't say-"

"Apophenia is a hallmark of schizophrenia. Are you feeling stressed?"

"What! What are you talking about? I was just saying-"

"Whoa, whoa, no need to yell buddy. I'm on your side," Paul consoled him with a voice *just* short of being patronizing. "Can we just agree that it's crazy to think that the trees are growing new people. We can agree on that right?"

Joe looked mad enough to chew nails, but he muttered, "Right."

"What?" Paul asked, cocking his head to hear better.

"Right," Joe said a bit louder.

"What?" Paul repeated, with one hand cupped to his ear.

"Right!" Joe screamed.

"Whoa. Keep your voice down. The trees can hear you," Paul admonished, walking off.

"That makes no sense you son of a-"

"You know shouting is a sign of schizophrenia too."

Joe kept arguing, getting madder by the minute while Paul died with laughter on the inside.

Behind them, the newly born monster stirred. Though still slumbering, its eyes opened staring at the prey foolish enough to come near. Pupils and irises of dark brown wood stared at the two food bags. It wasn't strong enough to be fully aware, let alone act, but it looked at the men in hunger.

The eyes closed and it fell deeper into sleep while the men continued their argument, unaware that they were marked for death.

***

There were more prompts waiting for Fin to read. Evidently, gaining skills and upgrading them had earned him something called "Achievements."

*Congratulations! You have met hidden conditions and have been recognized by the Labyrinth. You have been awarded **Achievements**! All Achievements are limited in number.*

*Congratulations! For at least some of the following **Achievements**, you are the first to gain them on your world.*

*This has improved the **Achievements** to **True Achievements,** increasing the reward!*

           ~REWARD~

*Congratulations! You are the **First** being of your world to **Advance** a Skill within the Mortal Tier (i.e. Common, Uncommon, Limited).*

*You have been awarded the **Limited** rank **True** Achievement: **First Mortal Advancer***

*True Achievement Reward: **+50%** Advancement Points gained during Skill Assessments of any Mortal or Heroic tier skill*

Achievement increased from only dealing with Mortal Skills due to being a True Achievement

This Achievement can only be claimed 1,000 times.

*+200 Magicka for your first **Limited Achievement** (Reward doubled as this is a Mortal True Achievement)*

Fin had kind of gotten that the Labyrinth had some sort of classification system called ranks. He'd also pieced together that ranks were further divided into tiers, but the first True Achievement made it abundantly clear. It looked like the first three ranks, *common, uncommon* and *limited* were in something called the "Mortal Tier."

This Achievement must have come from his *Mana Sense* skill Advancing to *Mana Connection* and then *Mana Manipulation.*

He still didn't really get why that mattered, but Fin assumed it was a good thing.

The reward itself gave him more points during a "Skill Assessment."

He remembered from reading the prompts about Advancing and Evolving his Skill that the Assessments had been "bypassed."

If Skill Assessments were how Skills became stronger, maybe this Achievement would help him with that in the future.

Unfortunately, focusing on the words didn't bring any more information so he went on to the next prompt. There was a method to the madness of this new world.

He needed to find out what that was ASAP.

Fin turned his attention to the next prompt hoping for more insight into these new natural laws.

The second Achievement apparently came from improving a skill beyond the Mortal Tier, into something called "Heroic."

*Congratulations! You are the **First** being of your world to **Evolve** a Heroic Skill*

*You have been awarded the **Epic** rank True Achievement: **First Heroic Evolver***

*True Achievement Reward: **Heroic Fast Learner Token (Epic)** – Use this on any Skill, with rank **Epic** or below, to improve the speed the Skill levels by a factor of 5*

Achievement increased from Heroic Fast Learner Token (Limited rank with factor of 2 bonus) due to being a True Achievement

*This Achievement can only be claimed **100** times.*

*+**750 Magicka** for your first **Epic Achievement** (Reward tripled as this is a Heroic True Achievement)*

He'd just learned three more ranks and the name of the next tier, Heroic. If he was reading it right, looked like this Achievement let him… level-up a Skill faster? Did the world really work like a game now?

He could see this "token" coming in handy.

His *Mana Threads* had already saved his life the moment he gained it. It would obviously grow stronger as it leveled up. This token being able to make the skill grow five times as fast, yeah, that could definitely be useful he thought, nodding to himself.

Before reading on, Fin considered how he'd gained these True Achievements.

They were due to his Whisper Ability, an advantage he'd been given by the Wave.

No matter how he got the Achievements, he'd happily take these bonuses.

That didn't mean he'd relinquish all reason.

There was a lesson to be learned about this changing world.

Without his Whisper Ability, a power he'd been given without doing a thing to earn it, he'd never have gained the initial skill *Mana Sense*. Without his Ability, he'd also never have Advanced and Evolved it, something he still had no idea how to do.

That initial "gift" from the Wave had both kept him alive in an explosion that should have torn him to chunks and was now giving him even more advantages.

That was the lesson of this newly changing world.

A lesson he wouldn't forget.

A lesson that was no different from an iron clad truth he'd learned long before that wave of grey fire had swept over him.

Success today always made future success easier.

Having power made it easier to accumulate more power.

Having money made it easier to gain more.

If there was one common thread that wove all throughout history, it was that those with money and power generally did better.

He resolved to gain more of both as quickly as possible.

Fin's eyes hardened, and he'd fuck up anyone that tried to stop him.

He turned his attention back to the rest of his prompts.

There were two more Achievements.

Unlike the first ones that he'd gained because of his new ability, these came because of the person he'd been before the Wave.

These, he had earned.

Congratulations! Upon facing what you believed to be certain death, you did not shy away or show fear. Instead, you accepted death as a consequence of achieving a higher goal.

*You have been awarded the **Rare** rank True Achievement: **Unflinching***

True Achievement Reward: **New Trait – Unflinching**

Achievement increased from **+5 to Fear Resistance** *due to being a True Achievement*

This Achievement can only be claimed **250** *times.*

New Trait Revealed: **Unflinching (Rare)** *– This Trait provides* **Fear Immunity (Rare)**

You now have complete immunity to Fear effects from any sources at your Power Level at or below the Rare rank. **+100% Fear resistance** *against Fear sources one Power Level above you at or below Rare rank. Resistance drops sharply at higher Power and rank differentials.*

Know This! Traits cannot be granted, they can only be revealed. Without the requisite inner strength, this reward could not have been provided.

Know This! Traits reveal the depths of your existing Power

+450 Magicka *for your first* **Rare Achievement** *(Reward tripled as this is a Heroic True Achievement)*

Fin remembered the feeling of acceptance right before the fuel cell had exploded. He would have traded his life to kill the man who had killed Lauren. It also wasn't the first time he'd faced death. You never knew how you would react. Fin didn't judge anyone who feared death or violence. That indicated only that they were still sane.

For himself, there were definite things that he feared, but after what he had been through, death was not included in that list. It wasn't because he was a hero. It was just that he knew, beyond a doubt, that there were things worse than your own life ending.

He'd definitely take these bonuses as well. In games, "fear" wasn't just being scared, it was an actual magical attack. In some games, it was as debilitating as putting someone to sleep. If he came up against this kind of attack in the future, he'd be glad he had this new "Trait."

The last Achievement brought a savage smile to his face. Even more than his *Unflinching* Trait, this Achievement fit him like a glove.

*You have used your **Ability** to take the life of another **Powered**. Not only that, you did so while not in combat and before a single day had passed since your planet was Assimilated into the Labyrinth. Most important, you did so with absolute joy.*

Truly, savagery lives rent free in your heart.

*You have been awarded the **Limited** rank True Achievement: **Violent Delights***

*Upgraded Reward: **Mark: Violent Delights** – You may now designate an opponent as a **Hated Enemy**. Any attacks against a Hated Enemy deliver +20% damage. A Hated Enemy's disposition towards you will drop to Hatred. You can only designate 3 Hated Enemies at once and this status can only be removed by death. Only those who already possess a negative disposition towards you may be designated as a Hated Enemy.*

*This Mark consumes **15 Energy***

Warning! You do not have enough free Energy to sustain this Mark. It shall be placed but will remain dormant!

*+**30 Magicka** for your **Limited Achievement** (Reward doubled as this is a Mortal True Achievement)*

While it was a *limited* rank achievement, it wasn't his first. That looked like it had reduced the base reward from fifty to fifteen. That suggested that the amount of magicka he earned wouldn't always come in such large amounts. A good thing to remember if he ever figured out how to use it.

Any thought of magicka, or anything else for that matter, fled as Fin felt a searing pain on the inside of his left forearm.

Chapter 22: Fledgling

"What the f-, aaarg!"

Fin almost fell to his knees. It felt like someone had put a red-hot iron on his skin. Thankfully, the feeling faded in seconds, and he kept his feet.

Looking down in amazement, he saw a tattoo!

This son of a bitch branded me!

It looked like liquid grey metal had been inserted under his skin. It was a single line, shaped like a lower case "n," but with the ends angled inward until they were almost a triangle. Three irregular drops, like blood droplet splatters, were in the center of the figure.   As he watched, they faded from view.

Fin knew on an intrinsic level that he could summon the tattoo back at any time, but also knew he could not use it.

He didn't have enough Energy.

Fin shook his head. Now he had a tattoo made of blood that could disappear at will?

What was he turning into?

Once again, the same answer came to his mind, final as the grave.

Whatever I need to be.

A single prompt remained dealing with his Achievements, bringing reverberations through his body.

+50 Magicka *for your first* **Limited** *Mark*

Achievement notifications finished; Fin claimed the final rewards from his Path of War quest.

The next was a Title.

He was starting to see a pattern. "A"chievements, "A"bilities, "S"kills, "M"arks, and now capital "T"itle.

"These words have "M"eaning," he murmured.

Congratulations! You have been awarded a Common Title: **Primordial of War (Fledgling)**

Not many Paths are as dangerous or rewarding as that of a **Primordial**. *By taking the first step, you have embraced Power. As such, you will be rewarded.*

Effect: +5% Noble Points, +1 Title Slot

This Title is **Upgradable**

+10 Energy *for obtaining a* **Common** *rank Title (Energy doubled for first Title)*

This **Title** *must be equipped.*

+10 Magicka *for earning your first* **Common** *Title.*

Once again, he felt a faint thrill go through his body. Checking his status page, he saw that his Energy had indeed increased again. Flexing both hands into fists, Fin couldn't really tell if he was any stronger. Really, the best word was that he felt faintly more "energized."

What the hell was Energy exactly?

Whatever it was, he felt it moving inside of him, flowing directly into his forearm.

Before his eyes, his Mark reappeared. This time it was flooded with color. The three blood droplets became crimson, and the metal symbol turned the color of bronze with a faint blue sheen atop it.

You may now use your Mark: **Violent Delights**

Free Energy Remaining: 0

The Energy he'd gained from the Title was immediately put to good use. He didn't have any left, but he didn't really have another use for it anyway.

At his mental flexion, the tattoo disappeared again.

Amazing.

Fin turned his attention back to his Title. Thinking about it brought up a new screen.

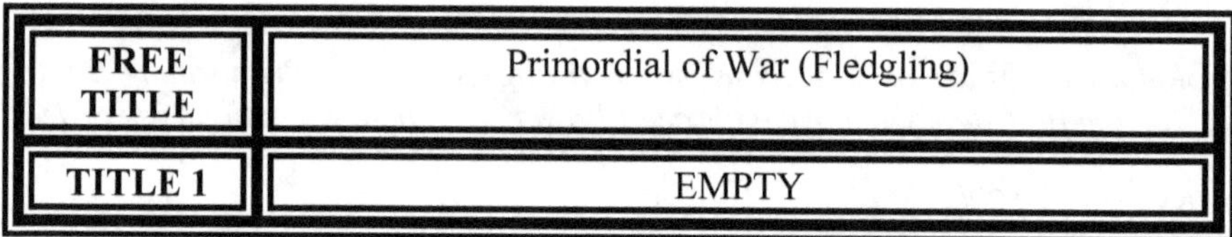

FREE TITLE	Primordial of War (Fledgling)
TITLE 1	EMPTY

As advertised, it had given him another slot to have Titles. In effect, *Path of the Primordial,* was a "free" title. Which was great, because so far, he couldn't tell that it did anything.

He didn't feel any different after getting a five percent boost to his Noble Points.

In fact, Fin wasn't sure he liked the idea of a nobility at all, especially not with a capital "N."

No matter what the effect of Nobility Points were, he was happy to see the next prompt.

Congratulations! You have earned Magicka. Do you wish to claim it now?

Fin had gotten several prompts saying he'd earned magicka just now. There had also been several mentions of it from when he'd been reading about his *Mana Threads* skill, but he still didn't know what it was or even what it looked like.

Eager to know, Fin thought "yes."

This time the reward didn't come with a lactosey ball.

                         ~*REWARD*~

It did coincide with an interesting sensation, however.

Rather than the full body tingling of increasing his Energy, this time, pulses of warm vibrations began to suffuse Fin's entire body. In quick succession he received several waves of magicka, the first was almost subtle while the second was twice as strong. The intensity increased after that.

Soon his entire body was buzzing. It was the most incredible sensation.

None of them were painful. Instead, they felt revitalizing, like the first few seconds after drinking espresso.

Barely had he thought that, then a flood of warmth hit him. If the previous ones felt like increasingly stronger pulses, then this felt like freebasing sound waves.

Again, there was no pain, but the vibrations were nearly overwhelming. It was a strange feeling. He'd never felt a tremor this strong without an accompanying discomfort.

Fin's mind felt clearer than it ever had before.

More waves descended on him. The bonus for unlocking the *Flux* Aspect of his Whisper Ability, then another that was twice as strong for his *limited* Achievement, *First Mortal Advancer.*

Finn nearly lost consciousness when he drowned in the vibrations of his *epic* True Achievement.

For a few seconds, he was very close to a sensation almost never experienced by living beings on Earth.

It was the feeling of evolution.

More waves passed through him, and Fin lost all time as his very core was set in tune with the music of the Universe.

Then, it was over.

As quickly as the sensation came, it faded. To his primal sorrow, Fin felt like half the vibrations in him drained away. The loss happened so fast that it was more a suggestion of a feeling rather than a fully formed experience. He did not want to let go of the warmth, but he could not stop it.

The remaining vibrations concentrated just below his throat.

In a few moments, even that quickly dissipated.

All that was left was a prompt.

Total Magicka: *2170*

"What the fuck was that?" he breathed; eyes wild as an addict's.

~REWARD~

Chapter 23: Capitals

DEATH

*I*n a mansion several miles away...

A blond woman approached her patriarch with a black leather dossier in hand.

"What have you found, Mila?" he asked in a light voice.

Some might hear his voice and think it belonged to someone easygoing and unbothered. The woman did not make that mistake. The patriarch was a man of extreme control and brutality.

Weakness and failures were sins in the House of the Ghost Lotus.

She had also heard what had happened to the last woman to bring him bad news.

Mila was extremely happy to see the matriarch was not in the room.

It would have felt like she was standing on plastic.

The woman's German accent was a bit heavier than her leader's, "The target, Fin Evers, does not have many friends and no family. The initial reports show he spent most of his younger years in a series of orphanages.

He was adopted three times over the years. In each instance, he was returned within three months. The reason provided always dealt with anger and violence. In the last case, he broke his foster father's jaw and the foster mother's wrist. He was not prosecuted however, as it soon came to light that the couple had been sexually abusing their wards for years."

The patriarch did not register any response so far, and the woman wisely continued so as not to waste his time.

"He emancipated at the age of sixteen, and chose voluntary service during the Third War. At that point, his records become spotty. I believe the records have been obfuscated. We are in the process of discovering why.

After the War, he went to medical school. Excelled and finished with a 4.02 GPA and finished his training in Emergency Medicine.

He was married to the woman who died in the crash, a Lauren Evers. They had just come from a dinner party with their friends. The intelligence department has classified these people as second or third degree social bonds.

Unfortunately, these are the only social links we have been able to discover for either of them. The woman's family were all killed during the War."

Mila finished her report, and stood sharply, her boot heels clicking together while she awaited her patriarch's pleasure.

For long seconds, he simply continued to stare out of the window, looking at his wife gathering roses from their garden to lay on their son's body.

"This is all you have found?"

His voice remained light, but a bead of sweat formed at the woman's temple.

"This is only the preliminary report, my Lord. Commandant Reinhard wanted you updated and promises we will find out everything about this mongrel."

Silence reigned again, until he turned to her, his pale green eyes boring into her own.

"Fine.   Second degree bonds or not, my wife needs to grieve. Even if the ingredients are subpar, the meal must still be prepared. Have everyone that was at that party collected and placed in cells. Have all of their first-degree social links that are within one hundred miles brought as well. This must happen within the next twenty-four hours.

Put out contracts on any first-degree links that are too far to be brought here within the time frame. Anyone beyond this distance should be killed within two days. All assassinations must be recorded and more will be paid if the target suffers first."

The woman nodded sharply, "Commandant Reinhard anticipated your needs, my lord. The capture orders have already been issued for one hundred fifty miles and our people are en route now. He has promised punishment if they are not all detained in the manor within eighteen hours.

~REWARD~

He also thought you might want the final count. The tally will be thirty-two men, forty-six women and fifty-three children under the age of fourteen."

The patriarch's only response was to walk back to the window and watch his wife.

Such trivial details were beneath his notice.

***

Fin had no idea of the horrors about to descend on his friends and their families.

His entire focus was on the word "Magicka," and the amazing sensation he'd just experienced receiving it. Unfortunately, concentrating on the word didn't provide any more information.

Fin paused, feeling frustrated.

The series of vibrations he'd just savored were the kind of thing that some people would chase for the rest of their life. Yet now it was gone like it had never happened.

He'd also just gotten a lot of information, but it was just enough to raise more questions.

Fin was being shown glimpses of a greater universe, but only glimpses.

It wasn't enough!

He needed more info than just these scraps.

If he had really gotten some "super" primordial quest, then it also made sense that he'd gotten "super" rewards.

The Constitution orbs had healed his body a great deal, there was no denying that, and the magicka made him feel like he'd just done absinthe while having a threesome.

Once you'd done that a couple times though, it was only kinda interesting.

What he was really having a problem with was what was the point of the other rewards?

In every game he'd ever played, experience points could help him level, but leveling was locked for some unknown reason.

The coins he'd gained didn't seem to have any utility right now either.

He was sure he could sell them to a pawn shop, but he wasn't an idiot that would sell magic coins for a couple of credits.

Also, he was already a doctor.

And seeing as how he'd bucked the stereotype of most of his profession, namely that he wasn't hooked on pills, coke or hookers, he had plenty of credits in the bank. Which all meant the coins weren't doing squat for him right now.

Even his Title, *Primordial of War*, while sounding infinitely cool, didn't seem to do jack.

Gah! It was so frustrating!

He felt like he was in the middle ages and had been given all the pieces to build a car, but he hadn't ever seen one before and had no idea how to put them together.

Fin was sure there was something he could do with all of this.

He just didn't have enough information.

Hell! If he could just see his full status page, that would be a win.

It might give him a hint or two on how to proceed. In a fit of consternation, he pulled it up again.

<table>
<tr><td colspan="3" align="center">FIN EVERS</td></tr>
<tr><td>Health: 18/30 (23*)</td><td>Mana: 22/22</td><td>Stamina: LOCKED</td></tr>
</table>

The abbreviated version appeared, but as soon as he thought about getting more information, he felt that strange sensation of mental resistance, like he was trying to remember someone's name that he'd definitely met before.

In irritation, he tried pushing against that mental barrier again.

Nada.

~REWARD~

The resistance felt nearly as strong and smooth as before. His efforts just seemed to slide off. It was perhaps a bit more pliable, but barely.

He might have even been imagining the change.

Just when he was about to let the matter drop, he felt a vibration beneath his throat. It was the same spot that the reverberations had coalesced at when he'd absorbed the magicka. He couldn't explain it, but something was telling him to try to unlock his status page one more time.

Frowning slightly in thought, Fin focused on the vibration while keeping in mind his goal of unlocking his full status page.

To his surprise, there was a reaction. Not just in his body, but from the interface!

He heard a sound like perfect crystal bell.

Ting!

*Your **Magicka**, **Actions** and **Essence** have yielded a **Random Opportunity**!*

*Would you like to unlock this **Common** Opportunity for **10 Magicka**?*

There wasn't any more information, but that didn't matter.

Seeing as how he had thousands of magicka and nowhere else to spend it, it wasn't a hard choice.

Fin sent a mental "yes" and that spot beneath his throat grew warm. Right after, he noticed a faint drain, a mere trickle, from the same location and spread through his body and into the air.

*Barrier to full Status Page reduced by **91%** for the next **91** minutes.*

Frowning slightly, he tried pushing at that mental resistance again, keeping the thought of a status page in his mind.

To Fin's delight, this time, the resistance lasted for less than a moment. That energy combined with his will to pierce the barrier with an inaudible *pop*.

Congratulations! You have unlocked your Full Status Page!

A new window appeared in his vision.

FIN EVERS		
Level: 0 (LOCKED) 2,750 XP Banked	**Magicka:** 2160	**Total Energy:** 105
Grade: Pseudo-Mortal	**Power:** 50 *Power Level:* 0	**Free Energy:** 0
STATS		
Health: 18/30 (23*)	**Mana:** 22/22	**Stamina: LOCKED**
ATTRIBUTES		
LOCKED	**CON:** 16 > 19 *Threshold: 1*	**LOCKED**
LOCKED	**LOCKED**	**LOCKED**
LOCKED	**LOCKED**	**LUCK:** 14 *Threshold: 1*
ABILITIES		
Whisper (Epic, Upgradable, Unique): You have a strong connection and innate understanding of the 8 Basic Elements, so much so that they may whisper the secrets of the Labyrinth		
TITLES		

<table>
<tr><td align="center">(1/2 Slots Taken)</td></tr>
<tr><td>Primordial of War (Fledgling): +5% Noble Points</td></tr>
<tr><td align="center">MARKS</td></tr>
<tr><td>Violent Delights: Assign up to 3 Hated Enemies</td></tr>
</table>

"My god. The world really has become an MMORPG."

This was a status page. An honest to god status page. He'd spent far too many hours playing games and watching anime on his Link for him not to make the connection.

Unfortunately, even though he'd unlocked the status page itself, it looked like most of the info was still behind yet another firewall.

Fin examined what he could see.

As he'd already seen, he had three Stats. Health and Mana were visible, but Stamina was still locked.

For the Attributes, it looked like there were nine of them, but only two were shown, Constitution and Luck.

He got why he could see the first, but why could he see his Luck? Could everyone who unlocked their full status page see it? There was no way to tell.

Staring at the word did give him some information.

Luck – This Primary Attribute will affect you in a million different ways… or not. But as the man said, "I'd rather be lucky than dead."

"Some" might have been a bit generous.

He didn't even know if a Luck of fourteen was good or not.

His Constitution was higher, but neither really gave him any frame of reference. Were these numbers exceptional?

Good?

Normal?

They couldn't be subpar.

Right?

Jokes aside, Fin was pretty sure his Attributes weren't bad.

Not to blow his own horn, pause, but he was a pretty tough guy, and his head wasn't just a hat rack. He'd read deep books like Unbearable Lightness of Being and Love in the Time of Cholera, and he was pretty sure he'd understood them.

They were about chicks, right?

Point was, he'd come across thousands, maybe millions of people in his life. Based on what he'd seen, he wouldn't describe himself as "middling." He didn't think he was the end all that be all, but he knew he wasn't just some shlub either. Using himself as a reference, he assumed most people would have stats similar to his own or lower.

If that were true though, what was this "Pseudo-Mortal" all about? Was it saying he wasn't even a person?

He felt a bit better when he focused on the word "Grade" and more information popped up.

Pseudo-Mortal – *Lesser Mortal is the lowest **Powered Grade** of the **Mortal Realm**. While you are technically a Lesser Mortal, due to having a Power Level less than 1, you are considered a Pseudo-Mortal.*

*Pseudo-Mortal is the average **Grade** of everyone on your planet.*

Reading the explanation made him feel a bit better. It wasn't that he was personally failing, it was that the interface apparently judged the whole human race as "meh."

Hmm, he thought grimly, just made you feel all warm and fuzzy inside.

Fin's face grew serious.

In the end, what was on his status page just wasn't as important as the fact that he had a status page at all.

However he stacked up against the rest of the world, what was clear was the Wave had changed things. It had given him an interface, something that no one else would see, or rather, something that not everyone could see.

What other hidden changes had the Wave wrought?

He'd served in the War, and he knew how to fight. He'd killed. More than once. And done worse. He knew the inexplicable heaviness that arrived when a living body turned into dead weight.

All that was to say, he knew how to handle himself. He was six feet and two hundred and thirty pounds of big bad nasty boy. And if all of his attributes were in the mid-teens, then what would it mean if he went up against someone with numbers in the twenties or thirties?

Hopefully he wouldn't have to find out.

More interesting than anything else was that he had an ability.

Whisper *(Epic, Upgradable, Unique): You have a strong connection and innate understanding of the 8 Basic Elements, so much so that they may whisper the secrets of the Labyrinth*

Reading the description once again led to more questions. This ability, though, was apparently why he was alive. Why standing next to an exploding fuel cell hadn't been a death sentence. According to the prompts he'd read about the accident, the Wave had apparently supercharged his ability, so he wouldn't be repeating the occurrence, but he was eager to see what it could do now.

The whole "innate understanding" sounded like bullshit though. He had no idea what the "8 Basic Elements" were.

There was one last line that gave a peek at how this system might all work.

Your *Epic Ability provides **+50 Power***

He'd seen Energy and Power mentioned several times in the prompts he'd received. Even his primordial quest had said he was the first "Powered" to be attacked by another. If his Ability was the whole reason he had any "Power," did that mean that piece of shit in the other truck had an Ability too?

How common was that after the Wave?

After playing around with the page a bit more, Fin couldn't glean any more information. With his curiosity now at least partly assuaged, Fin closed his eyes and leaned back in the bed. Both his body and his heart were still injured after all, the latter suffering the most grievous wounds. In fact, a wave of exhaustion swept through him after he'd focused on his prompts so much.

Yeah, I still need to heal, he thought.

Fin dozed off and on for the rest of the day.

His increasing Constitution didn't make him pass out. Instead, he just indulged in restorative sleep. He was actually awoken by the need to use the bathroom and hunger more often than not.

Dr Yinying came and checked on him, but he told her he was tired and would just like to rest. While she was there, he made sure to keep the blanket over his healing scars. If she saw his fast healing, it would trigger a lot of tests and even more problems. He planned to just sign out AMA once he was done absorbing the second Constitution orb.

He might have already left, but having the autodoc fill his sustenance and hydration needs was just too useful. Without knowing it, Dr Yinying agreed with his plan. She informed him that he was strong enough to be transferred out of the ICU soon.

Fin was eager to get home. There were things to take care of. Namely, he had to see Lauren's funeral. Neither of them had any other family to speak of, but they had some friends that probably didn't know she was gone. After that, he'd decide what to do with the rest of his life.

And he'd decide how long that life would last…

Chapter 24: Threshold

DARK

Just before sundown, his ability and skill came off of its twenty-four hour freeze. Throughout the day he'd alternated between sadness and fascination. Lauren was never far from his thoughts, but being able to pull up his status and windows was more than interesting.

A couple hours before his ability and skills unfroze, the second Constitution orb had integrated into him. The effect had been… drastic.

*Congratulations! You have absorbed a **Common** rank **Constitution** orb. Your Constitution will be increased by 3-5…*

CON increased by +5!

*Current Constitution: **24***

*Healing energy floods your body. **Moderate Injury** status improved to **Mild Injury**!*

Healing energy floods your body.

Mild Injury *status removed!*

You are no longer Injured!

*Congratulations! Your Constitution has risen above **20**.*

You have passed a Minor Threshold!

*Constitution is now at **Threshold 2**!*

Reaching a Threshold provides not only a quantitative increase, but also a qualitative change.

*CON:HP ratio improved from **1:2** to **1:3**!*

Stamina consumption is marginally decreased. Increased resistance to physical ailments.

*Energy from Constitution Attribute increased from **+5** to **+10**!*

*Free Energy: **5***

If the first Constitution orb had made him feel a lot better, this one made him feel like vitality was surging though his body, nearly overflowing.

Was this the healthiest he'd ever felt?

Fin felt like he'd felt in high school. Like he wanted to jump out of bed and sprint a hundred yards just because he could.

He could feel literal Power coursing through his body!

Before he could marvel in his new vitality, a new prompt appeared.

*Hidden injuries of the rank **Common** and below will now be removed.*

A laundry list of more than a hundred items ran down his visions like the closing credits of a movie. Reading just a few of them made Fin curse softly.

Hidden Injuries removed...

Weakness – Left Knee

Scar Tissue – Right Shoulder, Left Shoulder, Lower Back, Left Knee, Right Hand...

Alveolar Scarring – Bilateral Lungs

Cancerous Lesions x 5

Precancerous Lesions x 139

Epidermal and Dermal Radiation Damage (Mild)

Dormant Infections (Varicella-Zoster, Human Pap...)

Chronic Kidney Disease I

Liver Steatosis

...

The cavalcade of horrors continued, more than a few of the hidden injuries serious enough that they could have killed him in the next few years.

All over his body, Fin felt series of strange sensations.

One spot was his left knee. He'd had it operated on after taking some shrapnel during the War.

As he watched in amazement, a tiny hole opened on the lateral side with a small amount of blood. Before he could even begin to "WTF" about that, a bloody object pushed out of the hole before falling on the bedside.

A second later, the hole closed, only a small trickle of blood showing it had ever been there.

Blinking in amazement, Fin picked up the fallen object. Wiping the blood off, he confirmed what it was. It was the surgical pin that had been used to put his knee back together. Not giving him any time, his jaw opened against his will. The same strange sensation filled his mouth, and a second later, he felt several small objects on his tongue.

Spitting them into this hand, once again his guess was proved right.

Fillings. His body had just ejected his dental fillings from his teeth.

Whatever a Threshold was, it seemed like it had pushed him back to a state of health he never thought he'd reach again!

Changes kept sweeping though him, filling his body with strange sensations. It never advanced to actual pain, but there was more than some discomfort. He could literally feel his muscles shifting and smoothing in places. His abdomen was filled with strange twists and turns and faint popping noises came from his joints.

This lasted for about six or seven minutes, until a whole body sensation overtook him. It felt like he was vibrating slightly, from his head to his toes. After a few seconds of this, he started noticing a strange film on his skin. A moment later, he started sneezing. It felt like he'd breathed in pepper and was expelling it from his lungs.

When it ended, he ran a finger along his skin. The film came off easily. In fact, just shaking his arm made it fall. Not understanding what had happened, he scanned back through the hidden injuries. There, at the bottom, was the answer.

4.8 g of Microplastics removed.

Fin blinked. Had this change to his Constitution really removed even the artificial contaminants that every human had tucked away amongst their cells?

Thank god I don't have a penis pump, he thought with an amazed chuckle. Not that I'd need it because…

He lifted the blanket to check. Yup. Hard wood.

Whatever had been in those magical balls, had made him harder than a diamond in an ice storm.   He couldn't wait to put more in him!

He was also thankful that his circumcision hadn't been considered a "Hidden Injury." Canadian bacon wasn't his thing.

That revealing thought aside, he checked over his body. With wonder he saw that even his scars were gone. The acid burn on his left thigh from when he'd been captured during the War was gone.

His body was also missing the myriad number of marks normally accumulated through childhood and that nearly everyone who had survived the War had to live with.

Fin continued his physical exam and his jaw dropped.

All the bruises and cuts were gone. Checking all over showed only smooth, light brown skin. There wasn't even a trace of pink healing flesh.

Fin blinked in astonishment.

He was better.

Broken legs, cracked ribs, concussion, extensive burns, they were all gone!

His skin was smooth.

Using the mirror function on his Link, he actually stopped and stared.

He looked younger.

Instead of his forty-three years of age, he looked like he was in his thirties. His early thirties. There was no denying that black don't crack, but this was ridiculous!

He looked good!

His joy immediately dampened.

Why should he be celebrating when Lauren was lying cold in some morgue drawer?

Fin grabbed hold of that guilt and didn't let it grow. Lauren was gone. He was still here. That was the reality.

If he decided to change the second part of that later... then that's what would happen.

Right now, spiraling down into guilt was a waste of energy.

His emotions back under control, he looked back in the mirror. Assessing himself clinically. He did indeed look younger. The bags under his eyes were lighter and the few wrinkles he had looked a bit more smoothed. Fin only had a few strands of grey in his black curls before. While he could still see a couple, there hadn't been enough to really notice a difference if there was one. One question did pop out at him.

Had he actually been this handsome when he was younger?

For anyone else, that would have been cocky, but he'd always been realistic about his looks. He wasn't a heart throb, but he'd never lacked for company. What he was seeing now was a man who would definitely turn heads. He still looked like himself, but maybe just a better version of himself.

Maybe that was the healing?

Healthy was sexy after all, at least that's what the ads said.

If nothing else, the changes in his appearance made it even more necessary to get out of this hospital. If people noticed the change in his appearance, it would raise red flags. Fin quit his self-inspection and went back to the prompt. Specifically, he was looking at the part that mentioned "hidden injuries."

Going through the long and exhaustive list, he was able to trace many of the injuries to specific wounds he's suffered. Right shoulder was a bullet wound. Left shoulder had been a hammer blow during hand to hand combat during an op that'd gone FUBAR. Low back, embarrassingly, had been an ill-advised foray into tantric sex. Right wrist had been a fight with the Tijuana pimp right after.

He also laser focused in on the cancerous lesions that he'd apparently been living with. The list did not tell him where they were and his doctor mind couldn't help, but start going through horrible scenarios. The literal dozens of precancerous lesions he'd had didn't help either.

"Stop it," he told himself quietly.

That was the problem with having too much medical knowledge. You couldn't look at mole without worrying, and you couldn't see a hot chick without worrying she had a transmissible reason for a low grade fever.

Giving the list one last look, he noticed it mentioned healing radiation damage from the sun. If his new state of health really had removed sun damage, that could definitely explain why he looked younger.

Fin focused back on the second part of the prompt. The one telling him about the qualitative change in his CON attribute now that he'd passed a threshold.

Pulling up his status page he was able to see exactly how much that had changed things. It was *not* a small shift!

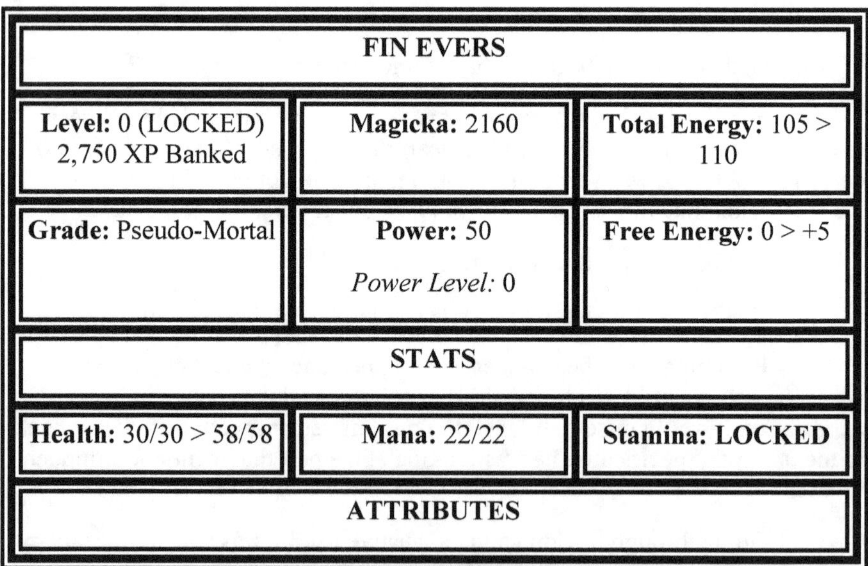

FIN EVERS		
Level: 0 (LOCKED) 2,750 XP Banked	**Magicka:** 2160	**Total Energy:** 105 > 110
Grade: Pseudo-Mortal	**Power:** 50 *Power Level:* 0	**Free Energy:** 0 > +5
STATS		
Health: 30/30 > 58/58	**Mana:** 22/22	**Stamina: LOCKED**
ATTRIBUTES		

~REWARD~

LOCKED	CON: 19 > 24 *Threshold: 1 > 2*	LOCKED
LOCKED	LOCKED	LOCKED
LOCKED	LOCKED	LUCK: 14 *Threshold: 1*

ABILITIES
Whisper (Epic, Upgradable, Unique): You have a strong connection and innate understanding of the 8 Basic Elements, so much so that they may whisper the secrets of the Labyrinth

TITLES **(1/2 Slots Taken)**
Primordial of War (Fledgling): +5% Noble Points

MARKS
Violent Delights: Assign up to 3 Hated Enemies

The first thing he saw was that his Energy had increased by five points, the boost coming from crossing the threshold in Constitution.

That was good to see. He was starting to pick up that the "magic" of the Labyrinth ran on Energy.

His Power was the same, but he didn't waste much time on that. He still didn't know what the point of Power was overall. From an earlier prompt, he knew it had something to do with his grade and why he, and apparently most of the people on Earth, were considered "pseudo-mortal" rather than "lesser mortal."

Fin didn't even know how much Power he'd need advance from level zero to level one.

In that moment he couldn't care less. What was way more important was the increase in his health points!

Before the Constitution orbs had been fully integrated into his body, his total health had been thirty without his Injuries. Now it was almost double!

With his Injuries gone and his Constitution increased, his health points had increased from eighteen to fifty-eight!

That was amazing!

According to the notifications, the boost to his health hadn't just come from adding eight points of Constitution, or CON, to his attributes.

It was because there had been a qualitative change as well as quantitative.

Each point of CON was now worth three Health Points now rather than two.

In games, his higher health pool would mean he could take twice as much damage. Real life couldn't work exactly like that, but Fin was sure there must be hidden mysteries in his increased health.

Just what could he survive now?

Would the explosion have even knocked him out? Could he take a bullet?

That was when his trained mind noticed a discrepancy.

He reread the earlier prompt.

If he got three points of health for every point of Constitution now, he should have seventy-two points, not fifty-eight. Fin ran the numbers in his head real quick.

"I'm getting, what, eighty percent of that?"

Frowning slightly, he checked the prompts again, but he couldn't figure out a reason for it.

What he did know was that his status page said his health was full now. Fin decided to think about the number discrepancy later.

Was he actually completely healed?

With wonder, he swung his legs over the side of the bed. Bracing, he stood again, and was shocked to find that he could stand without help. After taking a few steps, he found that his leg was fine, and he could walk normally!

~REWARD~

In fact, it was better than fine.

Ever since his surgery during the War, there'd always been a slight twinge if he twisted his knee a certain way. That discomfort had fled his body with the surgical pin apparently. He'd effectively had years of bad decisions removed all at once, he realized with a grin.

After consuming the first orb, he'd only been able to hobble to the bathroom with much difficulty. Now, he didn't have so much as a charley horse. Fin shook his head, and couldn't keep a smile off of his face.

This was amazing.

He'd gained a new prompt after his body had finished absorbing the second orb.

*Congratulations! You have improved a **Primary Attribute** by a **Minor Threshold** for the first time!*

*You have earned **50 Magicka**!*

Total Magicka: *2210*

Once again, was suffused with warm vibration. Paying more attention this time, he was now sure that half of that energy flowed out of his body before the rest settled beneath his throat.

Fin breathed out appreciatively. He didn't think he'd ever get tired of that feeling.

Even more than how good it felt, he now knew magicka could help him discover things about the Interface and this new world.

The "Opportunity" had reduced the strength of the mental barrier keeping him from his full status page.

Which begged the question, what else could he do with magicka?

And why did it feel like he lost half of the magicka he gained?

Where did that energy go?

Fin put those questions aside and took stock.

He had over two thousand magicka, but couldn't seem to do anything else with it despite concentrating on that spot beneath his throat for several minutes.

He also had several hundred experience points, got the same red prompt about his leveling being locked.

Fin was starting to hate those red prompts like the blue screen of death.

He also spent some time playing with the two silver coins. Occasionally he felt like his fingers lightly tingled when he held them, but whenever he focused on the feeling it disappeared, so he wasn't sure. Examining either face didn't reveal anything new.

Next, he focused on the eight points of Fire Element he'd gained.

Frustratingly, whenever he examined it before, it said the points were locked until his Whisper ability was off cooldown.

Now that it was, new prompts greeted him.

Chapter 25: Cultivator

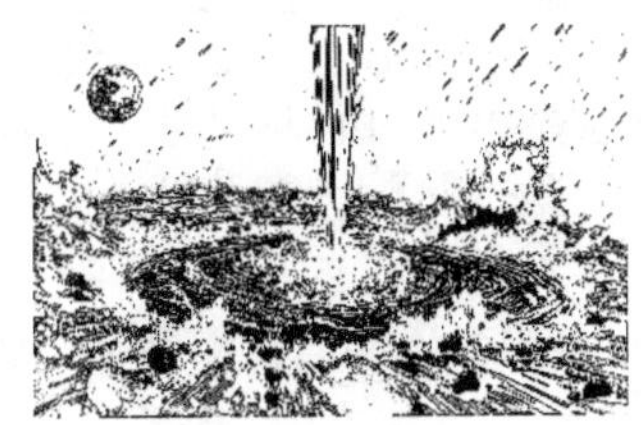

*You have absorbed **8 motes of Fire Element**.*

By absorbing raw Elemental Energy, you have two paths open to you to augment yourself.

1)   *Elemental Empowerment – A **Rare** Boon gained by your world (LOCKED. Requirement: Power Level 1)*
2)   *Whisper – Your Ability*

Fin blinked, looking at the prompt like it was crazy.

The first Constitution orb he'd absorbed had beat him like a red headed stepchild. If he hadn't been connected to the autodoc, there was a good chance he would have died.

While assimilating the second hadn't nearly been as bad, it had still taken a major toll on his body.

And now he was now he was supposed to absorb fire?

The same fire that he'd absorbed from a power cell explosion that had thrown him dozens of yards through the air and had turned the other guy into lil' charred chunks?

Yeaaah.

Maybe some other time.

With that rejection, the window disappeared, and he found himself looking out the window. It was pretty close to sundown. Now that he was healed, he was more than ready to leave the hospital. Fin debated for a bit, but decided to just leave first thing in the morning. He should be getting transferred out of the ICU soon to a regular floor.

And a change in hospital acuity meant a change in doctors.

It'd be way easier leaving AMA or even getting medically discharged with a new doctor that hadn't seen how banged up he'd been before. There'd be questions sure, but contrary to every medical show ever, doctors just didn't have the time to investigate mysteries, not when they were already working a hundred hours a week.

In real life, if you couldn't bill for it, most didn't care.

That decided, he closed all the prompts, and then closed his eyes.

His last thoughts were, "I wonder what I can do with that *Mana Threads* skill?"

***

Fin woke with the dawn.

As expected, with his improved health and stable vitals, they wheeled him out of the ICU less than an hour later. He'd just needed to keep the covers up until the night shift nurses gave way to the day.

There were some questions about how his overall health didn't seem to fit what his chart said, but overworked nurses had even less time for mysteries than docs.

He was on his way within the hour.

It was standard protocol after all.

Unit beds were always in demand.

Even more important, ICU rooms cost the hospital way more to operate than beds on lower acuity floors. A hospital might be a place of healing, but whether you were selling bullets or band-aids, it was still a business, and the all-mighty credit was king.

As they rolled Fin's hospital bed through the halls, he got his speech ready for the doctor he'd meet on the new floor.

'Yeah doc, I guess I wasn't as banged up as I thought I was. I know the chart said I was covered in bruises and now I look great, but maybe it was that Wave thing?'

With his own status as an ER doc, it shouldn't be hard to get discharged.

He'd be out of here before lunch.

Maybe he'd even swipe a jello cup on the way out.

As long as it wasn't orange or green.

As he was transported past the cancer ward however, the Labyrinth changed his fate once more.

It began with a whisper.

<Grow. Grow. Grow.>

Then the speed that he got the notifications was almost an assault.

*You have discovered a **Miniscule** source of the **Life Element**!*

*You have discovered a **Miniscule** source of the **Life Element**!*

...

*You have discovered a **Small** source of the **Life Element**!*

More than a dozen of those lines of text assaulted Fin's gaze.

Then another window appeared.

The border of the notification was thicker, and the font felt almost demanding.

You have uncovered a Quest!

Chapter 26: Horror

LIGHT

Fin was so shocked that the vitals monitor on the bed showed a spike in his heart rate. The team transporting him stopped in concern.

"Dr Evers, are you alright?" the nurse asked urgently. "Do you think you need to go back to the unit?"

"I'm fine, I'm fine," he assured them. He rubbed his stomach, and put on a rueful expression, "Even though this hospital food is tearing me up something awful."

His vitals normalized quickly so they started moving again. While they did, one of the orderlies looked down with phantom pain on his face. He whispered loud enough for everyone to hear, "This food is responsible for the worst weekend of my life, man. I hear ya."

No one else confirmed, but a mix of grimaces and chuckles was shared all around.

Fin gave a faint smile, and then closed his eyes. He wasn't resting of course, he was reading his new quest prompt. It occurred to him that his HUD was the ultimate tool for an introvert.

You have been offered a Quest: **Life Crop**
Quest Grade: Dull Bronze (F)
Quest Rank: Common
Quest Type: Personal Growth
Your Whisper ability has detected a cluster of the Life Element. Discover the source of this energy and perhaps learn more about your ability.
Success Conditions: Discover the source of the Life Element
Minimum Reward: 50 XP
Penalty for failure of Quest: None

Do you wish to accept: Yes or No?

Fin guessed that the experience reward was lower because of the grade of the quest, seeing as how Path of War quest was *common* ranked as well. Or it could have been the quest type.

A "Primordial" quest certainly sounded more impressive than "Personal Growth."

Though the type of this quest made his Scooby sense tingle. Somehow, he didn't see the Labyrinth placing a premium on self-help and spiritual awareness.

He immediately accepted it, despite the reward offering far less XP than his first quest. Not that the amount of XP mattered seeing as how leveling was locked.

Hell, even without the quest, he still would have hustled his butt back up here. How could his curiosity allow for anything else? Fin wanted to know as much about this new reality as he could. It looked like this quest's purpose was to encourage him to do exactly that.

He still wasn't sure what he wanted to do with his life now that Lauren was gone, but until he made a definitive decision, he wouldn't deny his fascination with the changes he'd undergone since the Wave.

Seeing that his heart rate was calming, the transport team resumed wheeling him to his new room. While he lay there, Fin started to wonder at his eagerness to accept the quest. While he'd always been inquisitive, he'd rarely been impulsive.

So why couldn't he wait to sneak back to the cancer ward and find out where the Life Element was? After all, he'd already nearly died once just by using an orb to increase his Constitution. Something that basically doubled how much health he had in his body had nearly killed him.

Obviously, danger could blindside him from any direction now.

Who knew where the next threat would come from?

So why was he willing to dive right back into experimenting with more magic?

As interested as he was in discovering more about his new nature, his analytical mind could not help but think about what the price of all this would be. And not just for him, but for the world.

What nightmares would arise to balance out the wonder?

Then again, could he afford not to learn more, no matter what the final price was?

He was sure other people were already gathering all the info they could about this new world.

Fin didn't think he was overly special.

Sure, he'd accomplished some things in his life.

He'd survived the Third War when so many of his brothers and sisters in arms hadn't. When *billions* had lost their lives.

Afterward, he'd been able to become a physician, something that took a decade of effort, in a vain attempt to balance out the scales of his life.

While he was proud of himself and what he'd achieved, billions of others had also survived the war.

And there were about a million doctors in the former US.

All of which meant he doubted he was the only one that had been changed by the Wave.

Some of the news stations had even mentioned reports of people seeing boxes in their vision. Which begged a bunch of questions.

How many other people had gotten this HUD?

How many others had been given abilities?

Whisper had let him absorb a fuel cell explosion less than a yard from his own face.

What were other people capable of now?

What were they going to do with that power?

What would they do to gain more?

Which brought him back to his original question.

Why was he so eager to grab more of this power himself?

Even after he'd almost died several times, he felt almost compelled to learn about where the Life Element was.

And why-

Why wasn't he thinking about Lauren more?

She was never far from his thoughts, and god knew he could be a cold bastard, but he'd loved her.

He still loved her.

Yet while his heart was aching, shouldn't it be worse than this?

Was he being manipulated somehow? Were his very thoughts and emotions being manipulated?

Fin had no way to know, but he smelled fuckery.

And if the HUD, interface, Labyrinth or whatever this all was, could manipulate who he was, what was it doing to the rest of the world?

Even if it wasn't direct manipulation, and was just indirect encouragement to grow and get stronger through these quests, how quickly would the world change?

Would it change for the better?

No matter how the Wave had changed the Earth's natural laws, people were still the same as far as he could see, and he knew people. Some men and women were devoted to the common good, but most operated from self-interest.

Plain and simple.

While some might call him pessimistic, he considered himself a realist. Watching out for yourself didn't make you evil. It was what you were willing to do to achieve your goals that determined your worth.

There was a large difference between speeding on the drive to work, and being willing to push someone onto the tracks so you didn't miss your train. Most people wouldn't do acts that would be considered "evil" unless they were placed in extraordinary circumstances.

There was another category of people, though. Those who would do anything to achieve their goals. Those who believed the highest cause was always their own, no matter how many men, women and children suffered to achieve their desires.

And they still weren't the worst.

There were also the people who were just downright awful.

As a great man once said, "some men just wanted to see the world burn."

***

Kyle's breath came faster. He couldn't help it. They were so close!

So wet!

So glistening!

So many pussies and nipples and titties!

Kyle's tongue stuck slightly past his panting lips.

The girls' voices competed with the sounds of the shower. Practice had let out a few minutes before and the entire squad was cleaning the sweat off. They joked and teased each other while they soaped up and rinsed off. All their bodies…

His breath sped out even faster.

Watching his fantasy come to life, Kyle was shocked by the things they said.

Women had never been kind to him. They'd mocked him and called him "creep." No matter where he went, he saw them laughing at him. Laughing because they knew about his… "problem."

That all meant he had no real experience with women. They were just creatures that taunted him in his dreams. Objects of desire that he didn't understand. When he heard them saying such *filthy* things about men and sex, he was appalled. Then he was excited. Then ashamed of himself. Which led to anger, which led to excitement, which led to shame, whichledto-

His entire body was camouflaged to match the white tiles. Even his eyes and open, panting mouth, were white squares with whiter lines between. In the past days, he learned that if he didn't move too quickly, then he was nearly invisible. When he moved his hand down to his privates, he did it slowly. His breath came faster as he stared and stroked himself. He couldn't help it! Watching them soap their supple bodies, rubbing between their crevices-

One thought played through his mind. Each time it did, it seemed to be building in strength.

Whores. Whores! WHORES!

***

A young man ran into his superior's office, placing both hands together under his chin and bowing slightly.

"Doctor Gamage! Doctor Gamage! There is an emergency in the central province."

The elderly woman looked up from her desk, sighing slightly. The younger generation was always so excitable. Had she ever been so impetuous?

"The entire world is in a state of emergency after the event," she responded calmly.

"The Wave," he corrected her nodding. He was in so much distress, he did not even realize he had corrected the woman who was in charge of the health of all of Sri Lanka.

That made her focus, not in anger, but in concern. Romesh might be excitable, but he was always respectful. Something must truly be wrong.

"Take a breath, mulli, and tell me," she spoke in her same calm voice.

He did as directed, blowing the air deliberately out through his nose, "There is a lice outbreak."

She frowned slightly. There had to be more than that.

"Initially it did not register on our radar. There was a large uptick in violence after the Wave, after all. I was sent pictures, however." His hands shook, but he tapped his Link and sent a series of images to her smart desk.

Her eyes widened in alarm.

"This is not lice."

She was looking at a series of bloody scalps and weeping children. She flicked her finger once, twice and then in larger sweeps, each movement showing more children, all with the same horrible presentation.

There were hundreds of them.

"We did not think it was lice either, Doctor Gamage, but we have recovered countless mites during autopsies."

"Autopsies?" she repeated sharply.

"Yes, Doctor Gamage. To date, 6% of the cases have been found to be fatal."

He sent another image.

It was indeed a head louse.

"Why is it so bad?"

"We don't know. This outbreak came out of nowhere and spread so quickly. We do know it is resistant to chemical treatments. Only removal of the individual insects has proven successful. That brought another… finding."

He tapped on his Link, zooming in on the picture of the head louse.

Doctor Gamage blinked in confusion. It had been a long time since she had looked at a picture of a louse, but she didn't remember their skin looking like that.

"What is wrong with its skin? Why is it that color?"

"That is the problem," he responded gravely. "We have found that the individual insects can endure pressures up to five times greater than is usually required to kill them. That is why their skin is a different color than normal.

Microscopic analysis has been done dozens of times to reach a single conclusion. Their bodies are sheathed in a thin layer of metal."

"What?" she responded blinking.

"Yes Doctor Gamage. There is an infestation of metal insects in our country. And they are eating our children."

***

Around the world, fantastic and astounding events were taking place.

Some were stories of hope and beauty, but they were drowned in seas of violence and horror.

Chapter 27: Glyphs

As soon as Fin was in his new room, he called for crutches. His leg was healed, but he didn't want to raise any suspicion. The earlier plan of immediately leaving was put on hold. All he could think about was getting back to the oncology ward.

It took about half an hour for them to be brought, but once he got his crutches, he was able to move relatively freely around the hospital. He wasted no time leaving his room and made his way back to the cancer zone. When no one was watching, he'd pick up the crutches and walked as quickly as he could. Thankfully, it was the middle of the night now and few people were roaming the halls. In minutes he was back.

As soon as he got close enough, he got the prompt again.

*You have discovered a **Miniscule** source of the Life Element!*

As soon as he saw the notification, he stopped walking and reversed.

Taking a step forward again, he got the same notice.

A theory began forming in his mind.

He quickly reviewed the notifications he'd gotten from right before the hover truck had exploded.

His Whisper Ability had detected a small source of Fire Element, and then after the fuel cell had exploded, it had detected a larger source.

That begged the question.

Did the amount of Element increase just because an explosion was a bigger fire is bigger than a small flame or, had there been something else at play?

Fin stood still in the hallway, his unneeded crutches held out to the side, and closed his eyes. The night shift was working, and foot traffic was at a minimum.

No one would disturb a patient just minding their own business.

He took a deep breath, breathing in the antiseptic smell and listening to the hum of the long bulb lights overhead. The air was a bit cool, and he could feel it play over his skin, not from wind, but from the ducts.

Breath after breath, he centered himself and opened his senses. This was something he'd been taught to do decades ago, and had practiced many times since.

Not dutifully enough to satisfy his old master he was sure, but it had always helped him focus his mind.

Fin deliberately opened himself to every sensation, even the faint red glow through his eyelids. He didn't focus on any one sense or stimulation. Instead, he let them all wash over them equally. By doing so, he was able to catalog them. Then dampen his awareness of them one by one.

Minutes later, the outside world began to fall away.

It was hard to explain really.

It wasn't like he was actually shutting his senses off, so much as turning them down. Hunters had used this trick for thousands of years. When you were in tune with the song of the forest, you could more easily detect anything that didn't fit.

It would twang like an off key note.

When he'd first gotten the prompts about the Life Element, Fin felt like he'd detected something in himself. Now that he was back in the same place, he was trying to find that feeling again.

With eyes closed, he searched for that "note."

In that state of calm, he took steps back and forth, getting within range of the Life Element prompt over and over. To anyone else, he'd look like a guy slowly waltzing back and forth on crutches. Strange to say the least. Fin didn't mind how he looked. It even served his purposes in a slow waltz.

On the night shift, no one wanted any part of "that" guy.

~*REWARD*~

After a minute of internal searching, he felt the resonance again.

There.

Getting in range of the Life Element gave him a warm feeling. It was very faint, similar to when the sun is revealed for just a moment on a cloudy autumn day.

He triggered the sensation several more times and realized it wasn't just warmth he was feeling. It was more. In fact, he could smell it, taste it. It was beautiful. On a deep level, he knew it was… Life.

He also knew that he wanted it!

Fin focused further trying to pinpoint the location, but it was just a diffuse feeling. Walking up and down the hallway didn't help him localize it. Once again, the lack of information was maddening.

He felt like a starving wolf who had caught the scent of blood on a swirling wind.

Fin cast about, doing his best not to look too creepy. That would draw attention to him. Thankfully, a childhood in an orphanage had taught him how to look just the right amount of pitiful. If you struck the right balance, it would make people feel sorry enough to leave you alone but not concerned enough to check on you.

It took another twenty minutes, but then something miraculous happened. After trying different techniques, his mind "pulled" at something inside of him. He stopped. It felt similar to the resistance of unlocking his full status page, but also distinctly different.

He was on to something.

It took another ten minutes to find the resistance again. He realized it happened when he really focused on "seeing" the mana he was looking for. This time, Fin intentionally held onto the feeling of resistance and simultaneously thought about his magicka, about the feeling of vibrations just south of his throat.

Focusing hard on two things, to put it plainly, didn't work out at first.

Fin immediately lost the feeling of resistance when he tried to split his focus.

Resisting the urge to just start swearing, he instead took a deep breath.

It took about fifteen minutes, but he was ultimately able to focus on the resistance and access that feeling of vibrations. The trick, he found, was actively pushing his determined mind against the barrier he could feel while, paradoxically, releasing any active hold on the magicka.

He heard the crystalline bell.

Ting!

*Your Magicka, Actions and Essence have yielded a **Random Opportunity**!*

*Would you like to unlock this **Uncommon Opportunity** for 20 Magicka?*

With a faint grin, Fin agreed.

Concentrate your mana in your eyes to obtain what you need. Your Magicka has reduced the amount of time needed to focus 74% for the next 64 minutes.

Vibrations flowed from the spot beneath his throat, but this time didn't spread through his body. Instead, seeming to know how to do this better than he did, the reverberations flowed up and localized on his eyes.

The vibrations stayed in that location, bouncing off of one another. They didn't grow stronger, or weaker. It didn't hurt though it was a bit strange feeling his eyes vibrate.

Looking around, it didn't shake his vision, which definitely didn't seem right, and made him wonder. Were the vibrations he was feeling even physical?

A countdown appeared in the corner of his vision showing that this Opportunity wouldn't last forever.

He read the prompt again.

'Concentrate his mana.'

How the hell was he supposed to do that?

Then it hit him, and he smiled.

He had a Skill for that.

For the first time, he consciously used *Mana Threads*.

With instinctive knowledge, he reached for his Skill.

  ~REWARD~

Fin realized that a shape, no, a glyph, was starting to form in his mind's eye.

The word "glyph" came from the same foreign lore that had come with his Skill. He just knew that word was correct.

His mind, his Skill, was forming a glyph that he could see without seeing. If pushed, Fin didn't think he could draw it on a piece of paper. He knew it intimately, but on such a deep level, it went beyond the conscious.

When it fully formed, he felt an odd draining, different from the vibrations of magicka. This felt like it came from his entire body. Again, knowledge came to him unbidden and he knew that it was his mana pool that was decreasing.

It was being channeled through the glyph.

And something miraculous happened.

He felt a faint pull on his right hand. Opening his eyes, Fin saw an ethereal blue tendril, no larger than a hair, extend from his middle finger.

It was a brilliant azure, yet could be seen through as if it were a ghost. It extended from his finger about six inches, hanging towards the ground. With a mental strain, Fin thought about the thread moving. To his delight, it obeyed his whim.

The thread could disappear and then reappear on another finger. He could also make it appear on his other hand, but couldn't make two threads appear at once.

What he could do was shorten the thread, which increased the glow it provided and made it easier to bend to his will.

He moved it left, right, up and down.

No baby elephant had ever had as much fun as he was having right now.

Fin quickly found that manipulating the thread was increasing the drain on his mana however, and he'd already lost four Mana Points.

He had just burned five minutes of his Opportunity.

Not wanting to lose this chance, Fin held the thread up before his eyes. Hoping he wasn't about to blind himself; he slowly pushed the blue tendril into his skin.

Nothing happened.

It passed into his body. Yet he felt nothing, not even a tingle.

Fin tried both eyes and his forehead, but there was no reaction.

He stopped and forced himself to think.

The prompt had said he needed to focus his mana. It hadn't mentioned his *Mana Threads* Skill at all. That was his own interpretation.

Which didn't mean his initial impulse was wrong. Maybe he just needed to change his approach.

Fin dismissed his thread, and then summoned it again. He did that several more times.

He activated his Skill, the glyph formed, his mana was mobilized, it poured through the glyph, and the thread appeared. The process was fairly quick, but not instantaneous.

That was what led Fin to victory.

If this had happened all at once, he might not have been able to figure it out, but the fact that it took several seconds to activate let him parse the various links in the chain of events.

He focused on the third step, the mana mobilization.

His ability to differentiate such a process showed his genius.

Fin sat in a nearby chair and emptied his mind again, focusing on the feeling his mana moving evoked in him.

For the first ten minutes, he wasn't able to feel a thing.

For the next twenty, he tried different visualization techniques until he finally felt that particular pulling again.

It was like the mana was flowing through him, a closed underground river. He wasn't able to change the course of the river, but he could slow it down so it started to build up in one spot.

Fin was only able to do that for a single moment, but it was something.

At first, he was only able to trigger that sensation in his chest. Anywhere else made it feel like the river was slipping though his fingers immediately. As time passed, he grew more accustomed to the sensation, however, and the "blockage" was moved further and further north.

Finally, he felt it focus around his eyes.

He couldn't split the block, so it was more like there was a buildup of mana in the top half of his skull.

As soon as he was able to keep that going for a full second, Fin felt the sensation of resistance again, but much stronger this time.

That was all the vibrations of his magicka needed.

Fin pushed against the barrier with his mind while keeping his mana pooled in one second increments.

He started getting a headache.

The mental resistance started vibrating in sync with the reverberations from his magicka and the pain ratcheted up quickly.

A bead of sweat formed on his forehead, but he kept at it. One single second at a time, he pooled his mana at the top of his head, and pushed against the feeling of resistance.

The pain in his head continued to build. He didn't let it stop him. After what he'd lived through, this kind of pain was just a nice hello from an old friend.

Fin pushed and pushed until finally, he mentally felt a "pop."

He couldn't describe it better than that.

The vibrations in his eyes died out, and his view of the world came alive!

*Congratulations! You have created a new **Uncommon** Skill: **Mana Sight***

Expend MP to see concentrations of Mana. Level this skill to improve detection, distance and specificity.

*As you are the first person on your world to create the Skill, **Mana Sight**, if accepted, **+100%** chance for this skill to **Advance** or **Evolve**!*

*This **Uncommon** skill will require **10 Energy***

*Warning! You have entered an Energy deficit! Total Energy: **0 (-5)***

*Warning! You do not have enough **Energy** to properly use this **Skill**. It will remain nascent.*

Warning! **Skills** *without sufficient* **Energy** *may not function, and always have a drastic reduction in Skill leveling, effectiveness and other attributes.*

Warning! Using Skills without sufficient Energy can have **deleterious** *effects.*

Fin blinked. He'd just created a magic skill.

He took the time to think about that again, and this time gave the proper emphasis to mimic the prompt.

He'd just created… a magic… Skill.

When he'd gained his first Skill, *Mana Sense,* he hadn't been in his right mind. His bloodlust and anger had overwhelmed him.

After losing Lauren, the only thing that had mattered was killing the man that had taken her from him. That was why it had been so easy to accept his own death in trade.

From Fin's perspective, gaining that Skill, and definitely the Advancements and Evolution of it, was all lumped together with the insanity of the wave, Lauren's death, the explosion and his feud with those pale headed bastards.

Emotionally, all of those events just blended together.

This felt different.

Through his own actions and intent, he'd just tapped into what was, in effect, a new natural law. The world really *did* operate like game now.

He whistled softly.

Fin had played some truly dark and disturbing games in the past.

He shook it off, refusing to waste any more time down that rabbit hole.

Whatever came, he'd be ready.

Nothing would stop him from learning about this new world. If need be, he'd bend it to his will. During the War, Fin had spent a decade bringing pain and death to others. After, he'd devoted the next chapter of his life to learning how to heal and preserve life.

This next phase?

Well seeing the universe itself respond to his will in the form of this new skill, a seed began to grow. Perhaps this next phase wouldn't only be about life or death. Maybe it wouldn't be about other people at all. Perhaps the moment had finally come for him to live for himself.

Fin focused back on the here and now. He'd created a new Skill, and the prompt was waiting for him to claim it. He didn't see a downside, except that he didn't have enough Energy to fully use it.

Thankfully, it looked like he'd be able to utilize it with a handicap.

He wasn't excited about those red prompts warning about "deleterious" effects, but he knew himself.

"This might hurt" was basically a love song to him.

And he *needed* to find those sources of Life Element now. It almost felt like a compulsion.

He accepted the Skill.

In retrospect, he should have expected the migraine that came after.

The headache started immediately. It centered on his temples, but thankfully didn't last too long. Instinctive knowledge about how to use the Skill poured into his mind.

Not seeing a reason to wait, he activated *Mana Sight*.

Dismissing the window, Fin focused on what was happening.

A new glyph began to form in his mind's eye.

Once again, he couldn't fully describe it if he needed to, but Fin knew without a doubt it was different than the glyph for *Mana Threads*.

In the hour he'd been learning to affect his internal mana, his MP had fully restored. Fin hadn't been paying enough attention to really get how quickly it replenished, and he made a mental note to figure that out later.

At that particular moment, he just examined the new glyph as much as possible.

It formed fully over the next few seconds, but seemed to lack the luster that his *Mana Threads* Skill had. It also seemed less intricate.

It completed and his mana flowed through it.

In seconds, the figure was filled, and Fin's view of the world changed forever!

Chapter 28: Three Promises

*For obtaining an **Uncommon** Skill, you gain **10 magicka***

Vibrations spread in Fin's body before half concentrated beneath his throat and the other half bled away.

While he enjoyed the sensation, a clinical part of his mind still grabbed ahold of something.

He'd just gained magicka for getting an *uncommon* rank Skill, but he'd spent twice as much to even be allowed the chance.

The *uncommon* Random Opportunity had cost him twenty.

That meant spent magicka was a diminishing return. It only paid out at all because he'd succeeded.

He didn't spare much that much thought.

Not when his entire view of the world had just changed.

Fin's lips parted and the ghost of a gasp escaped.

Everywhere he looked, there were glowing constellations of blue.

Everything he saw was superimposed with these series of blue lines. It was like every edge, of every surface, was glowing slightly.

In contrast, the inside of nearly everything he saw, the walls, the floor, the lights, and the cart full of medical supplies sitting in the hallway, all seemed… empty. He didn't know how else to describe it.

It was all a bit confusing.

His new sight was also extremely limited. Looking around, while his normal vision was uninterrupted, the glowing lines grew hazy after about two feet and disappeared after five feet.   All of these analytical observations barely registered.

The skill had triggered an unexpected emotional response.

Looking through these "new eyes" made him feel strange. It was like he'd been living in squalor all his life, but it had never bothered him because he didn't know there was another option. Now, it felt like his eyes were finally open and everything around him made him feel dirty, almost ashamed.

This was not how things were supposed to be!

While the blue lines were unmistakably beautiful, he feel, deep within himself, that everything around him should have more light than just the paltry amount he could see at the edges.

Everything around him, his very world, was… hollow.

The lack of light, the lack of mana, disgusted him.

There were two exceptions. Holding his own hand up, he saw a faint glowing radiance. The beauty of it far outweighed the emptiness he saw around him.

For the first time since Lauren's death, he experienced a moment of pure joy.

His hand, his entire body, was glowing softly. The light slowly pulsed and shifted like an azure kaleidoscope. In the center of his hand was a faint brighter line that tracked up his arm.

Looking down, he saw that it split at his shoulder, one branch continuing across his chest and the other down his side. The horizontal line reached his other shoulder and split again, one going down the opposite arm and the second tracking down that side of his body. The two vertical lines split at his waist, both horizontal lines joining to form a box that outlined his torso and the remaining lines going down either leg.

Put together, the glowing lines made a box like stick figure inside of him.

Did he have a line going up to his head? Fin wasted no time triggering the mirror on his Link. To his surprise, the holographic image didn't show any mana at all.

Blinking in thought for a moment, he walked into an empty room and looked in the mirror. Thankfully, that did the trick.

A single stripe traced up from the middle of the line at the top of his chest. The line ended in the center of his head, narrowing to nothing like a cut string.

The bands created the most simplistic of figures, but it was beautiful. Fin just watched the lines for several minutes, the quest momentarily forgotten. As he continued to examine himself, he realized while the diffuse blue light that made up his body undulated like a slow moving ocean, without appreciable pattern, the brighter lines were actually flowing in a trackable cadence.

The light moved in both directions down each line. There wasn't a clear demarcation like a highway, where half went one way and the other side the opposite direction. When he focused on one particular point, he could only see it flowing one way, despite watching for several seconds. If he looked away and turned back though, it might be flowing in the same direction or the opposite.

He wasn't able to actually see when and where it switched orientation, but looking at his body as a whole, it definitely flowed bilaterally along each bright line.

He was so taken with what he was seeing that he failed to notice when the glyph of his Skill throbbed slightly and developed a faint crack.

Fin watched it in wonder, mesmerized, seeing nearly every shade of blue, ranging from almost a rich black to a pale white. The lights also varied in intensity. A rich glowing sapphire outshone a dull periwinkle before the colors and luminescence shifted in a pattern too complex for Fin to follow.

Fin caught himself.

The wonder faded and was replaced with shame.

How dare he? How dare he get wrapped up in the beauty of this new world when it had already cost him everything? When he had been the one driving and if he had only-

Fin shook himself hard and his jaw clenched.

This wasn't the first time he'd had to fight off thoughts like that since the accident. It was like his mind would ambush him with pain, sorrow or guilt at any time. Intellectually, he knew he was just processing the trauma and loss.

Emotionally, it was a stab in the heart every time.

He closed his eyes and focused on his breathing. He wouldn't be crippled by sentiment. Whatever he did, it would be a path of his choosing.

"Three promises," he murmured.

After several long breaths, he was able to force his thoughts into a more clinical direction.

He recalled the mirror function on his Link again, confirming that it did not show mana. Maybe tech and these new skills didn't mix? That would be worth knowing.

Fin turned off his Link and turned his head towards the other source of light that had appeared in his *Mana Sight.*

He had a quest to finish. A quest that just might give him more answers.

He peeked his head into the next room. There, he saw a light that shone like the sun. It was an odd shape, with tendrils extending in all directions. The ameboid form might be repulsive in any other context, but there, in that moment, Fin found it beautiful.

Though he was seeing it with *Mana Sight,* Fin knew he wasn't just looking at mana. This was more. It was power more pure in every way imaginable.

It was Element.

It glowed, beckoning to him, looking like the first peak of a rising sun over the horizon. Liquid lapis swirled in a strange shape.

Fin deactivated his Skill, seeing how even that short time of activation had drained about a quarter of the blue line in the corner of his vision. When the Skill deactivated, the glyph disappeared, taking the unseen crack with it.

He remained blissfully unaware of how close he'd come.

It was just that he'd been using *Mana Sight* for a bit and had noticed his mana bar was down by about 25%. It wasn't a major drain, but he still didn't know how long it took to replenish.

Walking into the room confirmed what Fin had seen through the wall. A man was lying in the bed. He was the only one there. No matter what happened next, Fin knew he wouldn't be getting any answers from the guy.

The patient was emaciated. His limbs were locked in a twisted position and multiple tubes were coming out of him. A bipap mask was fitted over his face helping him breathe. The body was cachectic, limbs thin from lack of nourishment.

Discolored bruises dotted his pale skin, ugly eggplant blotches, and his arteries and veins stood in stark relief.

Fin tapped on the screen at the end of the bed. Reading the medications the autodoc was administering, he saw that without them the man would have already passed on.

Three pressors and an unstainable amount of fluids, and even with the support, the man's vitals were borderline.

Fin had been around enough patients to know this man wasn't long for this world.

With a slight frown, he hobbled closer. He thought for sure his new skill was misleading him. The prompt had clearly said "Life Element" but how could this poor soul so near death be an example of "life?"

Not understanding, he turned his *Mana Sight* on again.

The glyph reappeared, completely whole.

His eyes began to glow a pale blue in the faint light of the hospital room. Now that he was closer and without the wall between them, what he saw was a lot clearer. It left only one horrible, but insane, conclusion.

With *Mana Sight* activated, every object became pseudo-transparent again. Everything except for three things had that horrible hollowness, his body, the patient's and the liquid blue shape inside the man.

In the light of his Skill, the patient's twisted form gained a measure of beauty. It contained the same undulating blue luminescence as Fin's but to a much lesser degree. If his was a painting with vivid colors, the man's would be a stained glass window at night.

The Element source was *inside* of the patient's body. It had an odd shape. Two large blobs were on either side of the man's chest, branching like coral. There were smaller specks scattered through the man's body, and one bright spot in the patient's head. Seeing the pattern, and knowing where they were, there was no doubt in Fin's mind.

The faint whisper he heard confirmed it.

[spread. grow. spread. Grow.]

The source of the Life Element was cancer.

Chapter 29: Evil

EARTH

A notification appeared, but he immediately willed it away without reading it.

Was this some sort of sick joke?

Was Life Element evil?

A parasite that would kill them all?

What did that mean about him and his *Whisper* ability? It was supposed to give him an innate connection to the stuff. What did it mean that the Life Element he could see looked beautiful?

Was mana something that corrupted?

Just what had that Wave changed inside of him?

What had it taken from him!

Countless questions pinged inside of him like shrapnel, tearing down his walls of careful control.

That was the moment.

That was the moment his brittle armor of curiosity and false honesty shattered. All the coping mechanisms he'd tricked himself into believing just so that he could make it another hour, another minute, even a second, were stripped away.

While he had cried cups full of tears, for the first time in days, Fin truly grieved.

The weight of everything that had happened over the past few days finally, and truly, crashed down on him.

His guilt over surviving, the intense, soul-scarring wound he'd suffered when he lost Lauren, even the stress of trying to ignore the insanity of a grey tsunami washing over him, it all landed at once.

He finally was forced to bow to the Universe as he proved too weak to hold it back by will alone.

Fin's hands started shaking and his breath stuttered fast and short.

He collapsed into a nearby chair.

His emotions ran rampant and swelled until they grew so large his body could no longer contain them.

Once that threshold had been breached, his mind, body and soul could no longer bear it.

They wept.

Tears flowed down his face. Each second, they flowed faster, harder.

The tears took away his ability to see. He wrapped his arms around himself, still vainly attempting to contain the emotions avalanching through him.

His breaths were sharp, but soft, as he forced himself to be as quiet as possible.

Fin's shoulders heaved with every tight exhale, a sharp one second staccato.

Seconds turned to minutes, and he continued to grieve, his eyes a hellish red. The pain flowed out of him like pus from a wound.

Two men shared that space and time, both equally trapped by their own silent pain.

Slowly, Fin regained control of himself. His breathing started to ease.

After more than an hour, his breath grew regular. Subconsciously, he matched it to the artificial wheeze of the ventilator. Each inhale was a counterpoint to the machine keeping the other man alive.

After more time had passed than he could say, Fin let out one last shuddering exhale with his eyes closed.

When he opened them, nothing had changed.

Yet everything was different.

Sitting in the shadows of the patient's room, the only light coming from the autodoc and the fluorescents in the hallway, it was no surprise that he'd remained undiscovered. He heaved another nearly silent, but heavy, breath. He felt hollowed out, too emotionally exhausted to grieve any further, at least for the moment.

There was no doubt in his mind that the pain would come again.

That was okay.

Pain was the shadow of time.

It wasn't to be feared, only accepted, survived and used.

What mattered now was that he'd done what he'd been too afraid to do. He'd truly and deeply accepted Lauren's loss. Fin had admitted to himself that he was in pain, and it wasn't the fault of Labyrinth or anyone that he hadn't faced it before.

Even for him, some pains could reach so deep, that only time would let them see light.

Rather than dwelling on his loss any longer, he decided to focus on what he could control.

First and foremost, there was that light blinking in the corner of his vision.

He'd finished the quest.

Congratulations! You have completed the Quest: **Life Crop**
Though it cost you more pain than you realized you already possessed, you persevered.
You have discovered that the Life Element can manifest in many unexpected ways.
Completion Score… C
Do you wish to collect your Rewards?

A quick yes earned another prompt.

YOU HAVE EARNED

C grade Reward:
- 50 XP
- 5 Magicka

Special Reward for Quest Type: Personal Growth
- Unlocked Ability Aspect: Cave of Whispers

The initial rewards seemed sparse. There was still nothing he could do with the XP. He already had more than 2K of the stuff sitting, useless, on his status page under his locked level. And five magicka was nothing compared to thousands he'd already accumulated.

The last reward though, came with a prompt of its own.

*Congratulations! Your quest has unlocked the 2nd Aspect of your **Whisper Ability: Cave of Whispers***

Cave of Whispers – Visualize your Power

+50 Magicka for unlocking an Aspect.

The vibrations spread through him from his magicka reward,

That was it. "Visualize your Power."

Once again, the prompts weren't so great at sharing the information.

Valiantly, Fin fought the impulse for one and a half long seconds, before his curiosity got the better of him.

"How do I even access this cave of wond-aaholy shit!"

Fin was suddenly completely surrounded by blackness.

"What the fuck!"

He shifted down into a fighter's stance, ready for anything.

His foot shifted backward a bit, leaving a small circle of light surrounding him. Just like that, a split second later, he was back in the hospital.

"What?"

Furrowing his brow, rubbed his hands together. The sensation felt real. He checked his other senses, and nothing indicated that he was hallucinating.

Had he really just instantly transported to another place and then zapped right back?

Fin took a couple breaths.

No denying that suddenly being somewhere else had been discombobulating, but his rational mind reasserted itself.

That dark place must have been the "Cave of Whispers."

He reread the previous description.

Visualize your Power.

Visualize.

Maybe he hadn't teleported? Maybe his mind had just shifted to another... reality? Another state of being? Dimension?

Or was this cave some kind of mental construct?

Fin closed his eyes and focused.

Even though he'd only been in that place for a moment, his trained mind had taken in details.

Taste? The air had felt a bit stale, like it hadn't been ventilated in a while.

Smell? Nothing.

Sound? Candles? He faintly remembered hearing the flicker of a flame.

Feel? Nothing again.

He finally arrived at sight.

An old instructor had taught Fin to review this sense. What you saw was usually what people trusted the most. Strangely, science had shown that it was the least reliable sense in regards to memory.

Recalling the scene, to the front of him he only remembered a pure impenetrable darkness.

Yet, somehow, there had also been light?

He knew that because he remembered seeing his own body in his peripheral vision. Had there been a spotlight overhead?

And that was it.

Searching his memory for a few more seconds didn't bring anything else to mind.

Fin opened his eyes.

Time to get more info.

Focusing again, he thought about returning to the cave.

For the second time, with no pause or sensation of movement, he was seamlessly transported to the dark space.

This time, he kept his body still, remembering it was when he dropped into a boxer's stance that his perception had shifted back to the hospital.

Panning around with his eyes, he took better stock of his surroundings.

While almost all of the cave was shrouded in an impenetrable darkness, he could see his own body. Slowly tilting his head up, all he saw was more darkness, yet his body was clearly lit.

The light didn't have a source. It just was.

Looking down, he saw the light also illuminated the ground, about an inch past his feet. He was standing on what looked and felt like black stone, so smooth it might have been glass, but it didn't reflect. There wasn't a single granule of gravel underfoot.

It took Fin a second, but he realized there was something strange about the boundary between the light and the dark.

It was too abrupt.

Light always gradually gave way to dark as the energy fell below a person's ability to perceive what was being revealed.

This was more like a wall of black forbid the white light from going any further.

The demarcation was a perfect circle.

That was a powerful message in and of itself.

"Light and dark," Fin murmured. "Duality."

Was that the trick?

Curious, he extended a hand. The moment his fingers left the circle of light, he was back in the hospital again.

There wasn't any pain or disorientation, but it looked like he'd just learned a new rule of his Cave of Whispers.

Don't break the seal.

Focusing, he transported back to the cave for a third time.

He thought about leaving and was back in the hospital.

Leaving the light or just thinking about it will bring me back to reality, he thought.

Fin did this about a dozen more times, all in the name of scientific research, of course.

Definitely not because he was initially freaked out and then because he was playing with it.

He did find that if he focused, he could still feel tactile sensations from his "real" body in the hospital room even when he was in the visualized space of the Cave of Whispers.

Back in the cave, Fin slowly turned his body, making sure not to pierce the circle of light. Once he'd done a one-eighty, he found out what was making the dry sound that he'd thought were flickering candles.

Off in the darkness were eight points of orange red light. Each looked just like the dancing flame of a candle. They all hovered together in one section of the dark.

The flickering flames were arrayed like bowling pins with a single flame in the middle of the fourth row.

Fin knew without being told that he was looking at the Fire Element he'd absorbed from the truck explosion. The glow around each flickering orange light illuminated the far cavern walls just a bit, but not enough to make out any details.

Even though he couldn't see anything else in the impenetrable darkness, it felt like the lights might be about ten feet away. Of course, without knowing how large the lights were, he couldn't know, but that amount of distance felt right.

Even if they were a foot away though, that was the same as a mile seeing as how he couldn't move from the spot he was standing in.

Focusing, he thought about pulling one of the lights closer.

As soon as he did, a familiar prompt appeared.

Do you wish to augment yourself with Fire mana? If yes, pick a Path.

1)   *Elemental Empowerment – A **Rare** Boon gained by your world (LOCKED. Requirement: Power Level 1)*
2)   *Whisper – Your Ability*

Chapter 30: Backlash

AIR

Fin dismissed the notification and left the cave.

The idea of absorbing the energy from an explosion still didn't sit right with him.

Instead, he got up from the chair and walked back over to the patient's bed. There was no real change in the man's situation.

Sadly, he'd seen men and women stuck in this state of half-life for years.

As much as medical professionals knew, there was so much more they didn't.

With the same set of circumstances, some patients might pass on in minutes while others might linger for months to years.

If he just looked at the emaciated man, there was no indication that the body contained magic.

Activating *Mana Sight*, he was once again able to see beyond the veil of the world he'd grown up in. Fin's eyes glowed a pale blue, and the swirling sapphire mass appeared inside the patient's body again.

Even though he'd seen it before, he was still taken aback by how beautiful it was.

Unlike before, this time seeing it didn't trigger a mental shutdown.

Looking at the sapphire light, Fin knew that it didn't look beautiful just because of some aesthetic appreciation.

No.

Something about what he was seeing resonated with him somehow.

With his emotions now lanced, Fin's thinking was clearer.

He didn't have any answers to the questions that had flashed through his mind before, but he also wasn't leaping to panicked conclusions.

The Elements could indeed be some malevolent force, but there was no inherent proof of that. Without that proof, there was no reason to think the Wave had corrupted him somehow.

No reason to think he was "chaotic" evil, he thought with a rueful smile.

Lauren would have rolled her eyes if he'd said that to her.

With a fleeting "I love you baby" drifting through his mind, he focused back on the dying man.

Fin could objectively say that, for some unknown reason, the glowing mass inside of the comatose man was as beautiful as any sunrise he'd ever seen.

He could also admit that he craved that light.

The mana, Element, or whatever the hell it was, felt like something he needed.

And now that he was thinking more clearly, Fin thought he might have an explanation for the Life Element appearing in the oncology ward.

Cancer could take many forms and came in many types.

At the end of the day though, cancers were basically cells that didn't follow the rules.

All cells replicated. They were living creatures after all.

Cancer cells could be likened to mutations of normal cells.

The problem with the little fuckers was that they replicated and replicated until they compromised surrounding structures and threatened the life of the person they grew in.

Thinking back to med school, Fin realized there was an even deeper potential connection to life.

Some cancer cells survived much longer than similar cells that hadn't mutated.

There were scientists who posited that cancer could be the secret to extending the human lifespan.

The HeLa cell line, for instance, was still dividing with no signs of degradation, more than a century later.

Unfortunately, the racist and unethical actions of the doctors that had collected those cells were also why little research had been conducted along that specific scientific branch.

Humanistic ideals aside, from a purely abstract standpoint, an ever growing, immortal biomass just might be the perfect example of life.

Even the fact that cancers caused death just made them more like every other lifeform on Earth.

Fin leaned over the patient's bed, staring at the bright glow, both mesmerized by its beauty and disgusted by its nature for long minutes.

Then, without any previous indication, he did more than just look.

If someone had asked what he was doing, Fin wouldn't have been able to say. It was an impulse, nearly a compulsion that made him touch the man.

Once his hand connected though, he knew.

Somehow, without ever being told, he knew how to connect with the Life Element in front of him.

Mana Threads activated and a tendril of turquoise energy touched the brilliant sapphire of the Life Element.

Through his *Mana Sight*, he saw a thread of turquoise energy flow out of his hand. His mana pool fell by a point, fueling the line burrowing into the other man.

Physically, what Fin was doing had no effect, not even dimpling the patient's skin, but the instant the tendril made contact with the cancer, the energy flow of the tether reversed.

To his *Mana Sight,* light flowed from the mass and into him. The moment it entered Fin's body, a wonderfully warm sensation filled him.

Fin wanted and craved more of the feeling immediately. He tried to pull the energy into himself faster. As wondrous as the sensation was of absorbing the Life Element, now that he'd experienced it, it felt like a drop of water hitting the throat of a man dying of thirst.

Unnoticed, the glyph for his *Mana Sight* skill developed a hairline crack.

At that moment, Fin wouldn't have cared if he'd known.

He was in the thrall of something powerful.

He desperately tried to pull harder on the mass of Life, but the mana thread began to shake and stretch.

The doc could tell there was more "water" for him to consume, but the tether he'd created was like trying to drink through a swizzle straw.

No matter how hard he tried, he just couldn't increase the flow. He kept trying until his thread snapped.

That felt like he'd been slapped in the forehead hard enough to literally hear a ringing sound.

It wasn't a horrible pain, but Fin learned his lesson.

Thankfully, he was able to reestablish his Skill right after.

He did try other things to increase the speed of the flow.

Putting a second hand on the patient didn't make a second connection and he didn't truly understand how'd made the first one. The glyph in his mind's eye just did its thing.

Sighing to himself, he settled in to stand there as long as it took.

After a few minutes, Fin started having a headache. Annoyed at anything that would distract from this great sensation, he ignored it. The pain worsened over the next half a minute until it felt like a full grown migraine. Unable to ignore it any longer, he took his hand off of the man's body and grabbed the top of his head, wincing hard.

It felt like his head was on fire!

His first thought was that absorbing the energy was having negative side effects. As he gritted his teeth against the pain and closed his eyes, he finally noticed a faint blue flashing in the upper right corner of his eyes.

Pulling up his HUD, he saw the problem. The blue bar of his mana pool was almost empty.

His eyes shot open in surprise.

Fin hastily went to deactivate *Mana Sight.*

Focusing on the glyph let him register the large number of cracks in it before it shattered like rapidly cooled glass.

Blood ran from both of his eyes like rivers and Fin fell to his knees.

~*REWARD*~

*You have suffered a **Backlash** from a failed **Skill: Mana Sight***

-2 HP

Skill usage may be hampered for a period of time.

      His mouth opened in a scream he was just barely able to keep silent. His teeth bared and the muscles in his neck stood stark as he did all he could not to let out his pain.

      Fin collapsed to the ground, unconscious, hitting his head on the side of the patient's bed as he did.

Chapter 31: Double Dip

LIFE

"What the fuuuck," Fin groaned.

He looked around blearily, and then touched his face. It came away sticky and red.

"What the fuck, man."

His Skill had "Backlashed?"

That was possible?

He needed a damn instruction manual.

A distant voice, that sounded surprisingly like Lauren, told him there had been a very clear, very red, warning label about using Skills that didn't have enough Energy.

"That's not the point," he snap-mumbled to no one, before muttering, "sorry baby."

He lay on the ground, just praying away the stabbing pain in his head.

It didn't vanish, but it did start to get better after about ten minutes.

Fin exhaled in relief when the pain truly vanished.

Checking his Link, he saw that about an hour had passed.

Fin sat up, the steady beep of the patient's autodoc keeping time.

When he could think again, he decided to look on the bright side.

The time he'd been lying on the ground with his eyes bleeding had at least let his mana pool refill.

And at least the headache that had come before his Skill failed wasn't because his Whisper ability was self-harming.

It was the MP cost from using two Skills at once.

Now that he was stopping to think about it, that'd been dumb. Both *Mana Sight* and *Mana Threads* had clearly stated they consumed mana.

He'd been double dipping.

Come to think of it, an old girlfriend had told him that was a bad idea.

He'd ended up with unconscious with blood on his face that time too…

Meh, probably just coincidence.

"Well at least now I know what happens if my mana gets too low."

Feeling like the pain was definitely worse on the left than the right, he triggered the mirror function on his Link.

"That's not great," he admitted.

When his Skill had backlashed, it had apparently triggered physical injury. He already knew that seeing as how he'd bled out of his eyes. What he hadn't expected was that he'd burst blood vessels on the left and that the entire globe would be blood red.

These Skills were dangerous.

After taking a few more deep breaths, the headache faded to manageable levels.

Fin went over to the sink and scrubbed his face vigorously.

Getting dried blood off skin wasn't that easy.

He wished he'd had some lube.

Fun fact, KY was good at loosening up blood.

It was that kind of info that made med school worthwhile.

Once he was cleaned up, Fin looked at the comatose man and decided to get right back on the horse.

So to speak.

He stood over the bed, not sure if he could absorb the Life Element without placing his hand back on the man's chest, he cautiously started to activate *Mana Sight*. He was only going to use it for second to locate the Element.

He thought that the cracks in the Skill glyph he'd seen were probably an early warning sign of backlash. Maybe if he just used it for a second and watched out for fractures, it would be fine.

The headache started roaring back as soon as the glyph started forming.

"Nope. Nope," he relented with a wince. "Let's not choose violence."

It took a few minutes for the pain to fade to manageable levels.

To be safe, he gave it another five mikes.

Pain free, he stood back at the bedside, the heart monitor beep piercing the night silence.

Fin attempted to create another thread of his mana.

No pain.

At least it wasn't both of his Skills that were screwed.

Thankfully, it worked. He placed the thread where he remembered the mass was and it connected!

When he felt the flow of Life energy resume, he smiled without realizing it. It had only been a few minutes, but he, like every other denizen of the Labyrinth, was becoming addicted to the power.

After about fifteen minutes, he was rewarded with a prompt.

*You have absorbed 1 mote of **Life** Element.*

The flow of energy cut off and Fin was left feeling both very satisfied and yearning for more. He knew there was more Life Element nearby, but the craving wasn't enough for him to start running down the halls like a junkie.

Instead, it just felt like he'd had a satisfying meal.

Focusing, he found himself in the Cave of Whispers.

With a smile, he saw that there was a new light in the darkness.

A golden sphere bobbed slowly in midair. The surface was like molten sunlight, yet the light it emitted was soft and pleasing.

                    ~REWARD~

It was about the same size as the red flames that hovered in another part of the cave. A large gap of darkness separated the gold and red lights, and the two types of Elements didn't seem to react to each other.

He turned his attention to a familiar prompt.

Do you wish to augment yourself with Life Element? If yes, pick a path.

1) *Elemental Empowerment – A **Rare** World Boon. (LOCKED. Requirement: Power Level 1)*
2) *Whisper – Your Ability*

Fin stared at the glowing translucent window for a full minute. He'd avoided augmenting himself with Fire Element before because he'd learned a healthy caution about playing with magical powers, extremely recent events notwithstanding.

The Constitution orbs had knocked him on his ass.

There was also the whole "you shouldn't play with fire" thing. That kind of wisdom was right up there with "don't run with scissors" or "never beat your meat on Sunday or you'll burn in hell for all eternity."

Which, in a way, brought you right back to "don't play with fire."

Basically, just good common sense.

Now though, riding the high of absorbing the Element, he decided it was worth the risk. If he passed out, he'd just have to explain to the nursing staff why he was half naked in a hospital robe and collapsed over on an unconscious man.

Not his first rodeo.

Besides it was Life Element, not Fire.

What was the worst that could happen?

He chose to augment himself with the path provided by his Whisper ability. He had no idea what Elemental Empowerment was and even less of an idea about why it was a "World Boon."

What was a "World Boon?"

And a boon from whom?

Besides, it was locked like what felt like every other damn thing he came across.

And so far, Whisper had done right by him. He'd stick with that.

The very moment he mentally chose the second path of augmentation, the window disappeared, and a strange feeling filled his body.

It was at that *very* second that another thought occurred to him.

"Oh shit! Please don't give me cancer!"

~REWARD~

Chapter 32: Brent Roth

Fin's vision shifted to his Cave of Whispers. The eight motes of Fire Element still floated in one part of the cavern, looking like flickering candles. The floor and walls around them were still too poorly lit for him to see.

Just like last time, he was sure there was a pattern that he just wasn't able to observe yet. No matter how he strained however, he couldn't make it out.

There was something new that he could see this time.

In a section of the cavern separate from where the Fire motes were dwelt, there now hung a softly glowing gold light. It bobbed up and down slightly, but more or less stayed in the same position. Just behind it was a much smaller, flickering golden light. It phased in and out of view like it was struggling somehow.

Curious, Fin focused on the smaller one.

Three-tenths of a mote of Life Element.

It looked like the cancer had given him enough for more than just one Life mote. There was some left over, but not enough to make another full measure.

No matter, there was more Life Element he'd grab once he learned what this cultivation thing was all about.

Choose a mote to begin augmentation.

~DANGER~

"No going back now," Fin murmured and then focused on the one full mote of golden energy.

In wonder, he watched a slight bulge form on one side of the mote. In seconds, it lengthened to a thin string of metallic gold light. The glowing chain was made of a light so dim it was barely able to be seen. It was also finer than a single strand of hair.

The radiant string waved slowly in the air like a fishing line shifting in a stream. If he'd been out in sunshine rather than in a dark chamber, he doubted he would even be able to see it. It continued to stretch towards him until, in a moment without time, it pierced the circle of light and they became one.

The effect it had inside of him was impossible to miss. The now familiar warmth he associated with Life Element bloomed in center of his chest. With it came knowledge. It didn't come in the form or words or a prompt. It was more like he was being given a fundamental understanding of a basic truth.

To call the sensation "confusing" was an understatement.

As he stood in his Cave of Whispers, his ability taught him how he could use the captured Life Element. By pulling it into himself, it would connect to the Life Element already inside of him.

That was when he learned, to his shock, that this Element he'd been absorbing was not a new phenomenon. It had been in him before the Wave. It had always been in him. In fact, Fin blinked as his understanding of the Universe widened. Life Element was in everyone. It was in everything alive.

He blinked and then turned to look at the Fire Element, golden tether still connected to his chest.

Did that mean-?

Fin shook his head, at least he thought he did, it was hard to know seeing as how he was floating in some metaphysical space about to absorb a fundamental element of nature.

Point being, he had more important things to do than wonder about the secrets of the Universe.

Namely, eating one of those secrets.

The golden tether was anchored to his torso about two inches below his sternum. The energy seemed to be waiting somehow. Fin's mind continued to process the information his Ability was giving him.

The knowledge went beyond words, beyond even feelings. It was more like instinct. The same kind of pull that made birds weave nests.

His body, or whatever this representation of his body really was, just needed to pull on the Element and make it part of himself.

Taking a deep breath, he rubbed his eyes.

What the hell was thinking?

Was he being brainwashed?

Was this "knowledge" pouring into him giving him a psychotic break?

And then there was the fact that he'd been magically transported into some dark cavern with magical lighting. As he rubbed his eyes again, he wondered, are these even my eyes? Is this even a real place? Am I hallucinating or having some kind of waking dream?

There were always more questions. Despite that, he couldn't bring himself to doubt the knowledge, the understanding, his Ability was giving him. It just rang true on a core level. He couldn't have proven that he loved Lauren, but he had and still did. This new knowledge felt like that. It wasn't just something that he knew. It was something that he *was*.

He very well might be going crazy. Maybe this was his mind's way of dealing with Lauren's loss. Maybe he didn't have any magic powers and he was just drooling on himself strapped to a bed.

It just didn't matter though.

He had to operate by the information he had. And in this moment, all the information he had was telling him this was real. He really was in some "Cave of Whispers," and he really was attached to a ball of Life he'd stolen from the body of a comatose man.

Yeah, he thought with a rueful chuckle.

When you put it like that, who would think they were crazy?

Of course, if you could wonder if you were crazy, you couldn't be that fucking crazy.

He began to absorb Life itself.

Golden light coursed down the tether, the golden sphere getting marginally smaller. Energy of the same color began to shine in his eyes.

As it did, he relived moments of his own life. Times that he'd thought he'd forgotten.

He was seven, waking up in a warm bed with the sun on his face. It was his birthday. He could smell someone making blueberry muffins downstairs, his favorite.

In the next moment, adrenalin coursed through his veins. He'd just shot the winning basket in the championship game.

A week later at the dance, Nadine Richie whispered, "My parents won't be home til Monday."

A week after that, her friend Florence walked up behind him, bit his ear and whispered, "Sprinkles are for winners." Then she'd placed a wet finger on his tongue, filling his mouth with a sweet, tangy flavor.

"This is what sprinkles taste like."

More images and memories replayed in his mind, deepening his connection to his own life and Life as a whole.

Fin focused on the tether and willed the energy to flow into him.

He quickly learned that he had to actively focus for the process to occur. Early on, he'd experimented and had stopped willing the golden light to flow out of the darkness just to see what would happen.

The tether immediately began to vibrate and whip around. He'd hurriedly resumed the transfer. Fin was almost sure that if he'd taken even another second to start back, the cord would have broken.

Somehow, Fin didn't think that would be a good thing.

The process continued on for a good long while.

Once again, he found he could not hurry the flow of energy. No matter how hard he concentrated and "pulled," the golden Element wouldn't come any faster.

What did change was that longer the process went on, the harder it became.

He didn't notice at first, but over what felt like the next ten minutes, Fin definitely picked up on that he was having to concentrate harder to maintain the flow. It was barely an increase, but it was there. If the initial mental strain was similar to tapping two fingers on a beat, then the increase felt like leaving a pause after every third two count.

It wasn't hard, but it was harder.

As the minutes passed and the Element flowed. The mote of Life grew smaller. It dwindled over the next ten minutes, and without too much effort, he finished absorbing it all and the golden sphere disappeared.

The light faded from his eyes.

Fin looked around his cavern.

The full mote of Life Element was gone.

New windows appeared and told him what he had earned for his efforts.

*Congratulations! You have successfully cultivated the **Life Element**! This has increased the amount of Life in your body and its effects.*

There was an entire cascade of prompts, but rather than reading them, Fin did something much more important.

He immediately blinked out of the cave and back into the hospital.

Then, Fin clinically examined every inch of his body, paying extra attention to the jewels, and not neglecting the crevices.

After a few minutes, he heaved a sigh of relief.

No tumors.

Fin's smile froze.

At least no external tumors.

No external tumors that immediately presented and didn't grow larger over time.

After frowning over those thoughts for a bit, he just shrugged, and adopted another smile.

Meh, let's just say no tumors.

Though he'd joked it off, using a magical substance he'd absorbed from someone else's cancer had made him feel a bit edgy.

He also hadn't forgotten an earlier prompt. Specifically, one dealing with his "hidden injuries" that had included five!

One-two-three-fo'-five cancerous lesions!

Little hidden bastards that he'd apparently just been walking around with and hadn't known about until his Constitution crossed the Threshold.

That wasn't even counting the more than three *dozen* precancerous lesions.

Can't forget those little guys!

The next concern that popped into his mind made him check his Link.

When he saw that only a little over twenty minutes had passed since he'd started cultivating, he breathed out a sigh of relief.

Some of his favorite stories were LitRPG and Wuxia.

Dragon's Wrath was still one of his go to's, and not just because the author's son had finished the books decades later.

These kinds of stories abounded with people losing time while they cultivated.

When he was younger, he'd always thought it sounded implausible that someone could sit in a cave for years on end.

Ridiculous, that years could pass in the blink of an eye.

Now, it only sounded cuckoo if you didn't also acknowledge that a tsunami of grey fire had given him a status page.

But it had all worked out.

He'd actually cultivated magical energy like a mystical samurai, and it had made him stronger!

*Congratulations! By increasing the amount of Life Element in your body you have improved a **Hidden Attribute**!*

*You have unlocked the tributary Attribute, **Natural Healing**!*

+1 to Natural Healing

***Natural Healing** – a measure of the speed and extent of your body's ability to correct ailments*

~REWARD~

Fin blinked.

Hidden Attributes what now?

Chapter 33: Heal Thyself

Fin pulled up his status page. At first, he didn't see any difference, but then he noticed a distinctive detail.

FIN EVERS		
Level: 0 (LOCKED) 2,750 XP Banked	**Magicka:** 2250	**Total Energy:** 110
Grade: Pseudo-Mortal	**Power:** 50 *Power Level:* 0	**Free Energy:** -5
STATS		
Health: 56/58	**Mana:** 22/22	**Stamina:** LOCKED
ATTRIBUTES		
LOCKED	**CON:** 24 *Threshold:* 2 **Natural Healing:** 12 *Threshold:* 1	**LOCKED**
LOCKED	**LOCKED**	**LOCKED**
LOCKED	**LOCKED**	**LUCK:** 14 *Threshold:* 1

<table>
<tr><td colspan="1" align="center">ABILITIES</td></tr>
</table>

Whisper (Epic, Upgradable, Unique): You have a strong connection and innate understanding of the 8 Basic Elements, so much so that they may whisper the secrets of the Labyrinth

<table>
<tr><td align="center">TITLES

(1/2 Slots Taken)</td></tr>
</table>

Primordial of War (Fledgling): +5% Noble Points

<table>
<tr><td align="center">MARKS</td></tr>
</table>

Violent Delights: Assign up to 3 Hated Enemies

Under his Attributes was where he noticed the change. None of the "locked tiles" had changed, but beneath Constitution there was a new entry.

The next prompts explained why Natural Healing had appeared there.

Congratulations! You have revealed a tributary Attribute for the first time!

Know This! Primary Attributes can possess tributary Attributes if certain conditions are met.

Natural Healing** is a tributary Attribute of the Primary Attribute, **Constitution

A thrill shot through Fin's heart. He was about to discover another tidbit about this new Universe.

Know This! The baseline Value of tributary Attributes for a human Pseudo-Mortal is 10

*Your devotion to physical fitness, lifestyle choice and insights have already formed a faint connection with the Basic Element of **Life**.*

*This has resulted in you possessing a higher than normal **Natural Healing** value of 11.*

*Cultivating a mote of Life Element for the first time has provided **+1** to tributary Attribute **Natural Healing***

Total Natural Healing: 12

For unlocking a tributary Attribute for the first time, you have earned +50 Magicka!

Total Magicka: 2300

He hadn't just learned about this new world. He'd learned about the old one.

Through cultivating the Life Element he'd already learned that he'd already had some in his own body. And not just him. Life was in almost everything apparently.

Which led him back to his own Ability.

Whisper *(Epic, Upgradable, Unique): You have a strong connection and innate understanding of the 8 Basic Elements, so much so that they may whisper the secrets of the Labyrinth*

His ability said that he had a strong connection with Basic Elements. All eight of 'em. If the name wasn't randomly chosen, then these eight Elements, of which it looked like Life and Fire were two, then maybe they were "basic" because they made up other things.

Maybe not just things.

     ~*REWARD*~

Maybe him.

Maybe everyone.

No matter what the Elements made up, there was now no doubt that his body contained at least Life. And it said the way he'd lived his life had increased his connection with that Element. Unless it meant just the last few days, the Life Element had been part of him since before the Wave.

Had been inside of him years?

Deep inside, Fin knew the answer was longer.

This Element he'd siphoned from a dying man, had been within him from the beginning.

He couldn't be a hundred percent, but he was sure as he could.

The Life Element he'd collected wasn't some new phenomenon.

The Wave was just revealing something that had been part of the world long before it had swept across the planet.

Which raised a whole host of other questions, but one pinged Fin's trained mind more than the others.

Was he really the first person on the entire planet that had gained this information?

If Life Element, and maybe the other seven, had been part of the world for years or centuries, did it make any rational sense that no one else knew about it?

Or was the info just not widespread?

After all, every ancient culture had stories of demons, magic and gods.

Were they not just stories?

Were there people on Earth now that knew more about the Wave?

Maybe even actively suppressing the information?

Fin grimaced.

Questions. Always more questions.

Not knowing these things made his asshole itch, but there was nothing for it.

Despite always finding new things to wonder about, he had gained some answers after absorbing the Life Element.

He now knew there were more than just the nine "Primary" Attributes on his status page.

Uncovering his tributary Attribute, *Natural Healing,* confirmed that the information he'd gained so far only scratched the surface of what the Wave had either changed or revealed.

In addition to his new knowledge, there was the boost to *Natural Healing* itself.

He reread the prompt, but didn't get anything deeper about it. It basically looked like it sped up how fast he healed.

Faster recovery from wounds was always something he could use. After all, it wasn't adamantium that had made Wolverine a truly bad mofo.

It was his healing factor.

The Constitution orbs had healed him from his injuries, including the ones with a capital "I," after the truck explosion, but now he was all out of magic healing balls.

Fin didn't think he was lucky enough to keep stumbling into them. In fact, thanks to his status page, he now knew his Luck was nothing special.

If there was one thing Fin was willing to bet on, Luck or no, it was that he'd probably need more healing, and sooner rather than later.

The Wave had given him magical powers.

The power to see the unseen and survive an explosion point blank.

If the Wave had changed him that way, he sincerely doubted he was the only one the global event had altered.

Whether the Wave had truly shifted natural laws or just revealed hidden ones, he had zero doubt things were going to change, and on a world-wide scale.

The Third War had taught him about change.

Some change brought good things, some brought bad, but all change brought one thing, and that, was blood.

~REWARD~

Chapter 34: Appreciation

DARK

All of which meant faster healing would definitely come in handy. He focused back on what had just happened.

He'd just absorbed Life itself. Fin needed to better understand what that meant.

The prompt said people's tributary attributes were usually only set at a ten. His own was a bit higher, for some reason, maybe because he ate his veggies and took care of his health.

The value hadn't been much higher though, only 10%, after a lifetime of making the "right" choices.

Now, after absorbing only a single mote of Life Element, that difference had almost doubled.

A lifetime of effort had just been replicated by an hour of cultivation.

Like everyone who had ever taken the slow path, he got pissed off learning about a shortcut.

Like everyone who got on the fast path, he intended to sprint his butt off.

A grin crossed Fin's face.

And he just so happened to know where there was more Element waiting for him.

Before he went on a shopping spree though, he took one last look at the comatose man.

A quick tap on the auto doc showed that the patient's vitals had gone up a bit.

~REWARD~

It looked like the man had actually had his condition at least partially corrected after-

Fin stopped short.

What the hell had he just done?

In that moment, and far too late, Fin felt remorse.

It occurred to him only now, when it all said and done, that he'd basically experimented on another human being.

He'd risked the life of a very sick man, using powers that he *knew* were dangerous.

And he'd done it without hesitation or thought.

Fin's hands started to shake.

He knew himself, and he knew what he'd done in the past.

During the War, he'd done… horrible things.

He'd taken life more than once.

Given the right circumstances, he might even enjoy it…

He'd definitely enjoyed it in the past.

But this?

The fact that he'd used his new power on a helpless person without even pausing-

Why had he done that?

Fin searched his memory with self-directed brutality.

He'd been standing at the man's side, just like he was doing now.

He remembered feeling a resonance between himself and the Life Element in the patient. Then-

His body had just reacted.

It was like he *needed* to consume the energy that he'd found.

Part of his mind started to argue that this guy was on his way out anyway, but Fin ruthlessly strangled that coward's rationalization.

He'd never hid from the truth even if it made him look bad, and he wouldn't start now.

The truth was, he'd taken something he'd wanted, and had not given a single solitary thought about the consequences to another human being.

Fin stood back from the bedside and really thought about that.

For the next ten minutes, he thought about what had happened and also observed the patient. He felt some relief that the man's vitals stayed strong. The pallor of the unconscious man's cheeks even improved a bit, though you'd have to be looking to notice it in the pale fluorescents.

Checking the autodoc, Fin also saw that the man was actually requiring less support than before. The patient's BMR was increasing, and nutritional intake was also increasing. By all measures, the man's health was continuing to improve by the minute.

That didn't change what he'd done.

When Fin had first found that the Life Element was a cancerous mass, he'd worried his new power was evil. After connecting with the energy, that worry had been removed. That feeling of warmth and connection, it just could not be evil.

A lack of evil didn't mean a lack of danger. And it didn't mean he couldn't do evil with his new power.

Thankfully the patient was improving, but it could have gone the other way.

Fin's eyes hardened, and the man behind his eyes stared out for the first time in a while.

He would do better.

With that soul resolution, he decided to let go of any more guilt or recrimination. Those feelings had served their purpose. Now they would only be distractions.

Fin wasn't one to dwell and wring his hands.

He would have the courage to accept his sins.

There was just one thing he felt compelled to do first.

He activated *Mana Sight.*

The pain came back, but it was less than before. Fin paid close attention, but the glyph formed in his mind's eye without any cracks. He wasted no time examining the patient.

In delight and relief, he saw the changes in the man's condition.

The bright blue radiance had almost disappeared completely.

In fact, looking at the mana in the patient's body, the blue ripples seemed a bit brighter and the pulses of light on the brighter lines, what he'd come to think of as "mana pathways," were flowing with greater regularity. The change was marginal, and it could have been his imagination, but he didn't think so.

Fin quickly turned off *Mana Sight*, not wanting to risk another backlash.

Whatever absorbing the Life Element had done, it looked like the man was better off.

Fin didn't think that absolved him from what he'd done, but it did make his future road easier.

He resolved to absorb all the Life Element he could find in the cancer ward. He'd do it slowly and watch the patients closely, but he was going to do it.

If he was a cowardly man, he'd lie to himself and say it was only to help the people around him.

Whatever his sins, he was no coward.

If he was a weaker man, he'd feel shame about doing something involving others that would benefit himself.

Whatever his sins, he was not weak.

And he would not hesitate or half-step once he made a decision.

He was ready to get back to work.

There was time to do one more important thing first, however.

He checked the patient's autodoc, reviewed the patient's vitals a final time, and then spoke aloud for the first time since coming to the room.

"Mr Stanczyk. I don't know what road I've started walking down, but you've helped me get there. Thank you."

The only response was the slow wheeze of the bipap machine.

 ~*REWARD*~

After making sure there weren't any nosy nurses walking down the hall who would ask why he was in another patient's room, he ghosted across the hallway. He'd activate *Mana Sight* for a single second in each room to see if there was any Life Element, then quickly shut it off.

Hopefully that would let him avoid a backlash.

If it didn't, what was a bit more blood loss from the eyes?

He healed faster now anyway, right?

With a cocky smile, he continued walking the Path of Power.

Behind him, Mr Stanczyk remained unconscious and motionless.

At least externally.

Inside the man, there was an entirely different story.

The primary sites of Mr Stanczyk's cancer began to shrink over the next hour until they were only half their original size. Almost all of the smaller metastases were completely obliterated.

Tendrils of Life Element that had been too small for Fin to see with *Mana Sight,* too small even for his Whisper ability to detect, had been drained of all energy. The cancer the Life Element had been feeding, turning it into the most aggressive of masses, now withered, unable to exist without the higher grade Energy it had already become reliant upon.

The power that had fed it, made it strong, was now something it could not exist without.

Such was a Truth of the Path of Power.

That was something Fin was fated to learn another day.

For now, he had already homed in on his next source of Life Element.

This time it was a brain mass.

Inoperable.

The woman lying on the bed was a bit younger, sixty perhaps, and was on life support just like Mr Stanczyk.

Her body was cachectic just like his.

Checking her chart, Fin saw she'd been in a coma for more than a year.

Checking the prompt that appeared, Fin saw the Element source was even larger.

*You have discovered a **Small** source of **Life Element**!*

He walked to the bedside and placed a hand on her head. As soon as he did, he felt the same eagerness that had been there last time. Knowing what to expect this time, Fin was able to control the impulse. It wasn't easy, but he managed it.

There was no doubt in his mind now that his ability could be addictive.

That risk was not enough to stop him. He'd walked with danger more times than he could count.

What was important was that he was in charge of his power, not the other way around.

He turned his attention back to the patient and activated *Mana Threads*.

He'd seen that her head was the site of the largest blue mass, though there were three more, one in each lung and another on right lobe of her liver. Looking at where the mass was in her head, it was probably a glioblastoma. He wasn't a neurosurgeon but between the location and size, it was clear why it hadn't been removed.

Fin took a moment to marvel at his skill. He'd become a human PET scan. What other wonders would his new powers bring?

The Element spoke to him, barely louder than the lightest breeze.

<Grow. Spread. Grow. Spread.>

"You're growing days are done."

Not wasting time, he used *Whisper*.

The same warmth as before filled him as he began absorbing the Life Element. This time, he kept a watch on the patient's vitals. They remained stable the entire time. Minutes later, he'd absorbed the available Element from each of the lesions.

He also risked triggering *Mana Sight* periodically. Thankfully, the glyph formed each time without cracks, and the headache was decreasing in severity.

250   *~REWARD~*

Watching the patient's vitals, Fin had no doubt he was improving her condition.

Her mana pathways grew brighter as the masses grew more dim.

That was when he realized the cancers were siphoning energy from the rest of her. That was no surprise biologically, but it was fascinating to see that it also held true magically.

After about ten minutes, he'd received another pleasant surprise.

+1/2 **Mana Threads** *Skill Progression Point.*

And that was how he learned to level up his Skills.

Fin continued siphoning Life Element with enthusiasm.

Once he was done, he'd collected several more motes of Life Element.

The "small" source he'd just collected had given him three motes of mana unlike the "miniscule" source from Mr Stanczyk that had given him one.

He watched the patient's vital continue to improve over the next few minutes, now convinced he'd helped.

Fin decided to forgo cultivating until he'd collected more mana. He didn't want to get caught crouching in someone's room.

He walked out into the hall and looked at the long line of doors in the cancer ward.

There's gold in them there hills, he thought with a chuckle.

Before he moved on, tried one last thing.

Mana Sight had shown him that everything, the walls, floor, even the patient's blanket, contained mana. He still wasn't sure what the relationship between mana and Elements were, but if he could absorb the mana in random objects, he'd have a never ending supply.

That idea withered immediately.

Focusing on one wall, he tried to absorb the mana inside it.

Nothing happened.

He couldn't even feel the mana in the wall with his Ability. When he'd absorbed the Life Element from the tumor, it had looked like the mana had grown dim and flowed into him. His thread had seemed to attract it.

There was no response from the faint specks of mana in the wall at all.

Absorbing the cancer's energy had felt like drinking a milkshake through a swizzle straw. It was frustratingly slow, but at least it was something. Trying to access the wall's mana was more like standing on the damp sidewalk and trying to drink the water by inhaling really hard.

Compared to the energy in mass he'd just drained, it was like comparing water vapor in a desert to compressed ice. Actually, it was worse than that. It was like drinking a few molecules of water floating in out space.

Fin gave up on the experiment and went on to the next room.

While he absorbed Life Element for the next several hours, the world was changing.

All across the planet, the fates of men, women and beasts were shifting like flooding rivers carving new channels in fate.

Energy coursed through the world in response to the wave of Chaos.

In many broken homes and shadowed alleys already filled with sadness, misery bloomed as those who no longer believed in happiness used their newfound powers in the only way that made sense to them.

Yet in some of the deepest slums and most forgotten corners of the world, hope was kindled for the first time in decades. Some beauty shone through even the thickest filth.

And in the oncology ward of Atlanta General Hospital, lives that were slated to end in hours, continued on for far longer. Instead of taking his last breath in two days, Fin's first patient, Mr Stanczyk, would wake up in three.

Hours later, his family would rush to his bedside.

His granddaughter would weep tears of joy, her faith in miracles so firmly planted that it would last her the rest of her long life. What effect that would have on her life and the world at large was too complicated for even gods to measure, but there was no doubting the ripples that came from Fin's actions that night.

The Powered man himself, going from room to room, had no idea of the currents he was creating. Threads that were meant to be cut, continued on and wove new tapestries, for both good and ill.

     ~REWARD~

He just continued on his way, partially or fully curing the about a dozen men and women of their cancers.

Not every patient on the ward had malignancy that contained Life Element. Wanting to help if he could, he still tried to cure a woman whose chart said she had bilateral lung cancer. Sadly, without the Element present, his mana thread had nothing to siphon away.

With regret, he had to leave her room and move on to the next source of energy.

And that's what he did. He went from room to room, until he learned a few facets of his ability.

It had a limitation.

Fin found he couldn't hold more than eight motes of a specific type of Element at a time. Trying to absorb more made him feel like a wall had appeared between himself and his *Whisper* ability.

When he maxed out at eight, that didn't mean he couldn't siphon more Life Element. It just meant he had to make space first.

To do so, he cultivated.

A chapel on the same floor made that very easy. No one would disturb someone praying in a hospital gown.

Chapter 35: Level Up

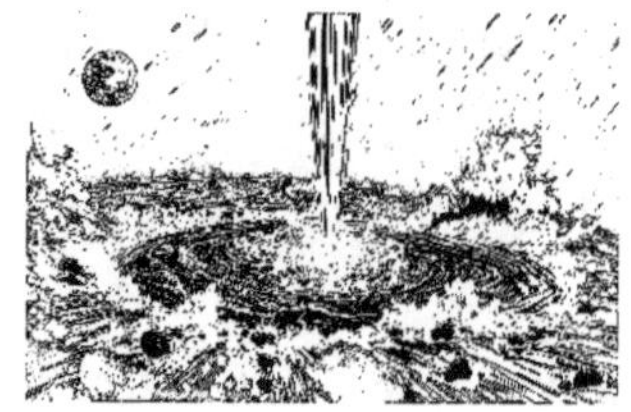

In an ornate temple at the top of a skyscraper in Atlanta...

"My Lord, our best ritualists have gathered," the man bowed before his patriarch, while his Lady wept over the body of her youngest child.

"Begin," came the powerful man's reply.

Bowing again, the other man gave a signal.

Forty-nine men and women that had been flown in on private jets for this ritual began to summon glyphs. Each stood at a different point around the room under a large lens.

The cost had been astronomical, but the House of the Ghost Lotus had constructed this building with a specific goal in mind, to collect Light Element. The skyscraper had been heralded as "bold," "innovative," and "ahead of its time."

There was no hiding the large crystal structure that topped the edifice and so the Lotus Familia had not even tried. They had merely hidden its intent.

The massive "jewel" that sat atop the seventy story building was not made of glass. It was constructed from materials that had only existed after the Third War. Harder than titanium, lighter than plastic, only the World AI could have computed the complex equations to make the wondrous resin.

It took the sum of the Earth's progress to infuse mana into the materials and make it possible.

The cost had been enough to bankrupt countries. Measured in the hundreds of millions of credits, it had drained nearly half of the coffers from the House of the Ghost Lotus.

For that price however, they had created a small wonder of the world.

The crystalline resin did not simply capture Light Element, it attracted and stored it.

The resin drew in the scant amount of mana that existed in the surrounding atmosphere. It then used that to create an attractive force for any and all Light Element in the vicinity.

The ability of the House to cultivate and create magical items had skyrocketed.

It had also earned the envy and enmity of other Familias around the world. Even within the Lotus, the other Houses were now scrambling to repeat the feat.

How could they not?

The power this building offered the patriarch's House could not be challenged. On a good month, and with a full complement of ritualists like they had tonight, they could collect a full ten motes of Light every thirty days. That was a full mote every three days.

Such wealth was literally priceless.

Standing next to his sobbing wife, and gazing upon the body of his youngest son, the cold visage of the patriarch finally cracked. The emotion he showed was small, but it was there.

As the ritualists began to gather small iotas of Light from the stars above, the left corner of the patriarch's mouth twitched upward a fraction of an inch.

None could challenge the power of his House.

***

Only a few miles away, in a small chapel outside of the oncology ward of Atlanta General Hospital, Fin knew nothing about the ritual being enacted or the foolish pride of his, as yet, unknown enemy.

Instead, he was flushed with light of Life.

Every success grew that wonderfully warm feeling inside of him.

Each absorbed golden sphere had also strengthened his *Natural Healing* Attribute. It was intoxicating to actually know in real time that you were getting stronger.

He couldn't get enough of it!

Which didn't mean the process had been seamless.

Fin discovered that with each success, the next attempt would become fractionally harder.

The increased difficulty was barely noticeable initially, but it had added up.

On his first two attempts, he easily walked the Element into his core. Each time, a dimple would form on the side of the mote he focused on. Next, a tether of energy would stretch to the column of light.

Once it reached the lit pillar, it was his. The golden energy would connect to his body, and he would begin to feast.

*You have cultivated 1 Life Element. +1 to tributary Attribute **Natural Healing***

The trick was getting it into the light.

If his first attempt had felt like he was pushing against a light breeze, his third had felt like her was leaning into a stiff wind.

It was nothing he couldn't handle, but it was potentially distracting.

*You have cultivated 1 Life Element. +1 to tributary Attribute **Natural Healing***

That was how he found out that if he failed to fully convey a mote into his avatar, then there would be consequences.

On his fourth attempt, he lost focus.

It was just for a moment, but that was all it took.

The Life Energy he'd been pulling into his avatar, which is what he'd started calling his body in the Cave of Whispers, had snapped back into the darkness all at once.

He'd felt like a piece of himself had been ripped away, and an electric shock had been left in its place.

The Labyrinth had punished him with a red screen of death.

~REWARD~

*You have **failed** to successfully cultivate Life Element! Cultivation **frozen** for 5 minutes!*

*You have **failed** to successfully cultivate Life Element! You have lost **1 HP**!*

The red prompt had been accompanied by severe headache. After feeling some wetness on his lip, he'd looked in the mirror and saw a bright red streak of blood coming from his nose.

That was three health he'd lost so far trying to increase his power. With his Constitution at Threshold two, it wasn't that bad, but if this had been before, he'd have lost 10% of his total life.

That setback hadn't stopped him, but it did underly the fact that there were consequences to what he was doing.

Potentially deadly consequences.

Despite the game like elements, this was still real life. He was in a real human body with all the frailties that came with it. He couldn't forget that he was channeling an unknown energy that was bound to have unknown effects.

He resolved to keep that in mind.

Resolved or not, he resumed absorbing more Life Element the moment his cultivation had unfrozen. While he did, he'd pondered on that word.

Cultivation.

In the games he'd played, getting stronger was almost always a central theme. There were several categories that normally fell into. There was the classic LitRPG style of leveling up, but there was also the cousin style of wuxia.

In wuxia stories, characters grew more powerful by pondering the mysteries of the universe, absorbing divine energies or both. He already knew for a fact that leveling was possible, even though it was currently locked.

His status page made that clear.

Now it appeared the Wave had made cultivation possible as well.

Was there a relationship between the approaches?

He was sure he'd find out in time.

Another thing he'd pondered was his initial value in *Natural Healing*.

If humanity's baseline was ten with tributary Attributes, then he'd only been 10% above that mark before he'd absorbed his first Life Element.

The prompt had given him a loose reason, referencing "good decisions," but that was hardly helpful.

Doctors had also known for decades that making healthy life choices made it easier to fight off disease and recover from injury. Despite the occasional keg stand in his youth and what some might call a "generous" appreciation for good scotch and better women, he'd mostly made healthy choices.

Exercise had never stopped being part of his life, even after the War, and he cooked most nights. He wasn't above grabbing some fries from the golden arches, but he made sure to eat gross, boring salad at least a few times a week as well.

That was what was bugging him a bit.

According to his initial *Natural Healing* score, all of that, all that effort, had only resulted in a marginal gain. While that was a bit of a kick in the nads, it also made what was happening now even more remarkable.

In just the last hours, his *Natural Healing* number had skyrocketed. Between his speed of absorbing Life Element, the time it took to cultivate it, and the time he needed to refill his own MP from using *Mana Threads,* it took a little over half an hour to collect and cultivate a single point of energy.

That meant a single hour of cultivation was superior to a lifetime of good choices.

That knowledge was both exciting and fearsome.

His training during the War didn't let his mind look through rose colored glasses. He couldn't just see the benefits of this kind of progression. His mind immediately went to the other side of the coin.

If he was able to make this kind of gain, what were other people, the wrong kind of people, learning to do after the Wave?

A life full of painfully learned harsh truths had proven to him that power did not discriminate and did not judge. It simply was.

If he could gain this kind of power, others probably could as well. The type of people that didn't just belong in jail, they deserved to be buried under it.

He shrugged off those maudlin thoughts as he'd continued to absorb energy.

~REWARD~

One, there was nothing he could do to control what other people would do, and two, collecting Element and cultivating with it just felt too damn satisfying!

*You have cultivated 1 Life Element. +1 to tributary Attribute **Natural Healing***

When he tried to cultivate the fifth golden sphere, Fin ran into his next stumbling block.

He'd worried about the increased difficulty in drawing the Element out of the dark. What if whatever mental muscle he was using to do so wasn't strong enough to overcome the resistance?

And that was exactly what happened.

The tether of gold extending from the fifth mote stopped a full two inches before the circle of light. No matter how hard he strained, Fin wasn't able to force it any closer. He mentally pushed until his injured eye spasmed. He began to be sure he'd do himself damage if he kept trying to force it, and that it still wouldn't be enough.

He just wasn't powerful enough.

That thought contrasted heavily with the smile that had formed on Fin's face.

He might not be strong enough, but he was Skilled.

He was pretty sure he muttered something like "Please no backlash," as he manifested a Skill inside of his Cave of Whispers for the first time.

The glyph formed and a blue mana thread emerged from his hand. He held his breath as it left the circle of light.

Thankfully, his Skill pierced the column, and he remained in the cave.

It looked like the rules governing the column of light were different than when his avatar entered the darkness.

As soon as his thread touched the golden sphere, the transfer of energy began.

Once more, he siphoned raw Element.

Molten gold had flowed down the thread and into him and Fin's eyes glowed like a setting sun.

Not only did that let him continue cultivating, but it seemed like using his Skill in that way had earned him progression points faster than just using it to siphon from the cancer patients.

*You have cultivated 1 Life Element. +1 to tributary Attribute **Natural Healing***

*You have cultivated 1 Life Element. +1 to tributary Attribute **Natural Healing***

*+2/2 **Mana Threads** Skill Progression Point*

After Fin got his second progression point, his Skill advanced to level two.

*Congratulations! **Mana Threads** has advanced to **Level 2**! Your ability to control and sense mana has increased. The stability of your mana thread has increased.*

The increased stability had somehow increased the speed he could siphon energy from the golden spheres. It also decreased the mental strain required as he did not need to pull the motes quite so close to the column of light.

The more he used his Skill, the faster it progressed, which made it easier to use and brought more Life Element into him.

It was like putting lube on lightning.

Both Life and Skill progression points flooded him!

*You have cultivated 1 Life Element. +1 to tributary Attribute **Natural Healing***

*+1/4 **Mana Threads** Skill Progression Point*

*You have cultivated 1 Life Element. +1 to tributary Attribute **Natural Healing***

*+2/4 **Mana Threads** Skill Progression Point*

…

~REWARD~

4/4 *Mana Threads* *Skill Progression Point*

*Congratulations! **Mana Threads** has advanced to **Level 3**! Your ability to control and sense mana has increased. The stability of your mana thread has increased.*

It took four Skill progression points for him to reach level three.

Each Skill level increased his control over his thread. The maximum distance now extended beyond two feet.

The only downside was his limited mana pool.

Lengthening it that much increased the mana drain, but also increased the speed he siphoned the Element.

Fin spent some time trying to find the right balance.

To that end, when his pool got close to bottoming out again, he didn't push past the headache that flared up. Instead, he snapped out of the Cave of Whispers, and set a timer on his Link.

Each time he regenerated his MP, he noted it. After the third one regen'd, he was sure. His mana came back at almost one point a minute. It was a bit shy of that, but one to one was close enough for government work.

Once his pool was full again, he went back to cultivating.

Fin consumed golden sphere after golden sphere. After each, the difficulty of pulling the energy towards the column increased.

After the seventh round, about a foot and a half remained between the light and the golden tether. After the eighth it was nearly two feet.

The ninth, the mote that would take his *Natural Healing* score from nineteen to twenty, was almost beyond the max length of his thread. It still took about a minute to control the thread to latch onto the golden tether that whipped back and forth.

If not for reaching level three in his Skill, he wouldn't have been able to do it but, at long last, Fin absorbed a ninth golden sphere and crossed the second Threshold of *Natural Healing*.

Chapter 36: Light

In the temple of the Ghost Lotus…

"My Lord, the dawn approaches."

The patriarch of the House of the Ghost Lotus had remained standing like a statue through the long night. Above the body of his dead son, hung a clear disc. Inside the table size device, a liquid version of the resin that made up the jewel atop the skyscraper was contained.

Throughout the night, the forty-nine exhausted ritualists had poured all of the Light they had collected from the stars overnight into this disc. The culmination of their efforts hung in the center of the colloidal gel, a light of the purest white.

It had been a good night. They had collected nearly a twentieth of a mote!

The ritual was almost ready. Though each looked like they could drop, they knew the most pivotal moment was about to arrive.

Each sunrise there was a surge of Light Element that passed over the Earth. All their efforts in the past hours had been to capture as much Light as possible during the split second it passed over them.

"Do not fail me," the patriarch intoned. His tone was soft, but the threat held within those German syllables was clear.

"On my life," his subordinate responded. The man knew those were not idle words.

As the sun peaked over the eastern horizon, the beams of light that each ritualist bathed in intensified.

More than one cried out in pain, but none allowed themselves the weakness of failure.

Inside the disc, the white light grew brighter.

***

Miles away, Fin was on the precipice of his own success after a night of trials.

The light that shone upon him was shining gold rather than blinding white.

Time would show which would prevail.

All that mattered to Fin at that moment was that after a long night of exhausting effort, it had finally happened!

*Your tributary Attribute, **Natural Healing,** has increased from **19** to **20***

*Congratulations! Your **Natural healing** has risen above **20**. You have passed a **Minor Threshold**!*

He let out a, "Woot!" as soon as he saw the word 'Threshold.'

If this Threshold offered anywhere near the boon that he'd gotten from improving his Constitution past Threshold two, then this would be a game changer.

HP, at least from how he understood it, was a measure of the punishment he could take before kicking the bucket. Having passed the second Threshold in CON had nearly doubled the damage he could take.

Fin read the prompts he'd just earned with eager anticipation!

*Natural Healing is now at **Threshold 2**!*

*HP regeneration has increased from **0.2%** per point of Natural Healing every **12 hours** to **0.3%** every **12 hours**.*

Recovery from poison, disease and other physical ailments marginally improved.

Marginally greater chance of resolving Injuries.

Marginally greater speed of resolving Injuries.

Reading the prompt, he'd found his understanding of the human body being upended once again.

According to the numbers listed, even before he'd improved his tributary Attribute, he'd have healed any wound in less than a month. Even being maimed.

That was insane.

It also wasn't how the human body worked.

A simple car accident might have someone in traction for months. Other injuries required more than a year to simply walk again.

Athletes, men and women at the peak of physical conditioning, might need physical therapy for the rest of their life after something as simple as a ground level fall.

Health was precious and far too fragile.

At least, that had been the case before the Wave.

From what he now understood, a person that had unlocked Constitution didn't just get access to their health points, they also gained access to accelerated healing. It wasn't anything that would snap a broken bone back into place, but it was amazing nonetheless.

He now knew that before he'd started cultivating the Life Element, he'd had a *Natural Healing* score of eleven. That meant he would have restored 2.2% of his health every twelve hours. As long as he still breathed, he could have recovered from any wound in less than two months.

As a physician, that was nothing less than astounding.

Even with advancements in medical science, the world was still full of men and women that had injuries that would never heal.

Infections that never fully resolved, leaving open wounds that still hadn't fully healed years later.

Fin's mind had only let him celebrate for a short minute before his rational, slash party-pooper side had asserted itself.

There was no way it was that easy.

He'd reread the prompt and realized his excitement had let him gloss over a salient point.

Specifically, injuries with a capital "I."

His own status page had shown debuffs dealing with Injuries after the explosion.

First *Serious Injuries* and then *Moderate Injuries* and finally *Mild.* There'd also been the fact that his health had been capped lower than his previous maximum in light of the debuffs. Taking that into consideration, it probably meant that his *Natural Healing* wouldn't be able to fix everything, at least not quickly.

It was still possible for him to get hurt so badly that he might never heal past a certain point.

It was just that the "point" had moved.

That dose of realism didn't decrease his excitement.

The human race had just gotten a serious upgrade!

Advancing *Natural Healing* also fixed another problem.

Your Energy has increased!

*+5 **Energy** from having a tributary and Primary Attribute both reach Threshold 2.*

*Free Energy: **0***

Energy deficit resolved!

A thrill of Energy had filled him, and he "felt" it immediately drain into *Mana Sight.* The Energy was gone as soon as he gained it, but it let him use his Skill without risk.

He'd wasted no time triggering *Mana Sight* and watched for a couple minutes. With a smile he saw that it remained completely stable.

More prompts had appeared after he crossed the threshold.

*Congratulations! You have improved a **tributary Attribute** by a Minor Grade for the first time!*

*You have earned **+50 Magicka**!*

Total Magicka: 2300

There was no way Fin would have been satisfied to stop there, but after reaching Threshold two, he came across a divide he couldn't bridge.

The difficulty of cultivating even one more mote of Life Element had ratcheted up dramatically.

The Elemental mote he'd needed to cultivate before reaching twenty in *Natural Healing* had stretched into it came within about two feet of the column of light.

The difficulty of wrangling the next one had increased so much that he couldn't get it within three feet.

His mana thread just didn't stretch that far.

Until he somehow was able to force sphere tendrils further out of the dark or leveled his thread to reach further, his days of cultivating Life were on pause.

That was how he'd ended up with two golden spheres remaining in his cave.

On the plus side, with his *Mana Sight* glyph now fully energized, he was able to use it to completely scour the oncology ward. By doing so, he found a few more sources of Life.

It took another hour of work, but after a full night of work, Fin ultimately came across eleven sources of Life Element.

Nine were sources that the interface termed *miniscule* and three were coined *small*.

There hadn't seemed to be any rhyme or reason as to type of cancer or location in the body, but it did seem like sicker patients were more likely to have malignancies that contained Life Element.

~REWARD~

It wasn't always the case though, as there were several patients on palliative comfort measures that his Whisper ability didn't react to at all. *Mana Sight* showed nothing in these men and women no matter how long he looked.

Each of the *miniscule* sources had disappeared after he'd absorbed a single point of golden Element. The 'smalls' though, seemed to offer between one to three points. Ultimately, he'd been able to absorb fifteen points of Life Element.

Six golden spheres, and a partial, still hovered in his Cave of Whispers when he left the oncology ward.

He'd also gained another progression point.

*+1/2 **Mana Sight** Skill Progression Point.*

Fin couldn't help but let a faint smile grow on his face with each power up. There was something so satisfying about literally being able to mark your progression.

He could get used to this!

But for now, he needed sleep.

The sky was lightening when he finally stumbled out of the cancer ward. All he wanted was to crash on his bed and sleep for a thousand years!

To his surprise, after his first step out of the ward, a new quest icon had appeared in the corner of his vision.

Even more surprising, he'd actually already finished it!

*Congratulations! You have finished a **Secret Quest**.*

Chapter 37: Many Paths

Know This! Secret Quests are tied to existing quest lines and can only be triggered if specific conditions are met.

Congratulations! You have completed a Secret Quest of the Life Crop
Quest Chain: **Embrace Your Power**
Quest Grade: Dull Bronze (F)
Quest Rank: Common
Quest Type: Personal Improvement

Completion Score… A
You not only discovered the source of the Life Element, but you also claimed the opportunity before you!
Your Whisper ability has great potential, but will only bring power if it is nurtured. By cultivating to past a Threshold with one of the Basic Elements within a week of your world's induction into the Labyrinth, you have completed a secret quest!
Continue to explore your new powers to gain control of them!
Power and Danger are close bedfellows!
Do you wish to collect your Rewards?

That was an easy choice.

YOU HAVE EARNED

C-Grade Reward
- 50 Experience Points
- 5 Magicka

B-Grade Reward
- 63 Experience Points
- 10 Magicka
- 5 Copper Coins

A-Grade Reward
- 75 Experience Points
- 15 Magicka
- 7 Copper Coins and 50 Iron Chits
- 1 Healing Herb (common)

Special Reward for Quest Type: Secret Personal Growth
Cultivation Technique: Elemental Splinter Technique (Epic)

Material Rewards will be available for the next 7 days

Having finished a secret quest taught Fin something important. It looked like there was more to quests than just what was written down in the prompts.

If he'd just done the bare minimum of the *Life Crop* quest, i.e. discovering the link between the cancers and Life Element, then he'd have gotten the XP, but he'd have missed out on this secret quest and even bigger prizes.

That meant he couldn't take these prompts at face value, not that he'd ever thought it was a good idea to blindly trust floating colored boxes that only he could see. If whatever sent these boxes was intelligent, and there were strong indications it was, then that was dangerous.

Where there is intelligence there is will and where there is will there is ambition.

At best, these windows were a guide, and even then, he had no idea where they would lead.

If Fin really wanted to understand this new world, then he'd have to push boundaries and question everything.

Based on the secret quest he'd just completed; it looked like the interface rewarded initiative. That might be a good or bad thing depending on the person involved. He could just envision unscrupulous individuals causing havoc at the chance of a reward.

The War had been full of stories like that.

Concerns like that were for the future.

Right now, he'd gotten a windfall!

The XP still didn't excite him, but learning more about his ability did. He turned in the quest and experience had flowed into him along with something much more interesting.

The moment he turned in the quest, information flowed into his mind.

It was a glyph, and unlike the ones dealing with his Skills, he could fully describe the simple figure.

It looked like a cylinder filled with lines of light. Eight indentation marked it at regular intervals.

The glowing lines that comprised its inner workings undulated slowly.

Watching the movement, Fin felt like he was getting a glimpse at a truth that hinted at a hidden pattern connecting all things.

His eyes widened and he KNEW!

*Congratulations! You have learned a new **Unique**, **Epic** Cultivation Technique:* ***Elemental Splinter Formation***

*The Elemental motes you have collected are only in their most raw form. By arranging these motes into a particular pattern, you may further harness the power of they contain. Only someone with the **Whisper** Ability can use this Technique.*

*+**250 Magicka** for obtaining your first **Epic** Cultivation Technique!*

     ~REWARD~

Knowledge and vibrations poured into him for long minutes. Not only how to begin the process of creating an Elemental Splinter, but also looser knowledge of what these Splinters could do.

The formation began with the linear glyph.

Along this line of power, there were eight nodes. Each node could hold a single mote of absorbed Element.

Once he'd filled each slot, the lattice of energy would contort, allowing the supplied energy to interact. Bonds of energy would form between the motes and the splinter would form.

Despite having experienced it several times at that point, he was still filled with wonder.

It was like that vintage movie that President Reeves had been in.

Out of all the things he'd experienced in the past few days, this instant knowledge remained the weirdest.

After all, Fin had spent decades in school.

He knew exactly how painstaking and long of a process it was to truly learn and internalize knowledge.

Except, apparently, that was no longer true.

Now, he just *knew*.

And he didn't just know this new information. He comprehended it in depth.

The knowledge was as familiar to him as his steamed pancake technique, or the exact amount of pressure needed to crush a man's testicle.

And when you'd watched the pounds of pressure increased incrementally over an hour, and heard the screams of the man who was experiencing it, you never forgot that 110 was the magic number.

Point was, this new learning wasn't something he could forget if he tried.

There was just one thing he didn't understand about the Elemental Splinter Technique.

When successfully made, the Splinter would allow the collected Elemental motes to manifest as a physical object, but also it wouldn't?

Somehow, the splinter was both real and not real.

Fin frowned, trying to reconcile the paradox.

After a bit, he realized that the problem wasn't the information he'd been provided. The knowledge wasn't incomplete or flawed.

It was more like he was being presented with a concept that he'd never heard about before. Like the knowledge was describing the color hazel to someone who'd never seen green or brown.

His lack of understanding didn't bother him for once. It had only been a few days since the Wave, and he'd already come across two of the eight Elements.

He'd find the others soon enough.

There was also the fact that he was almost falling over.

He was exhausted.

Even though he hadn't physically exerted himself, it turned out that cultivating took a toll on him even without requiring movement.

It was like comforting someone. It wasn't physically draining, but you still needed rest after doing it for a while.

He'd been exhausted by the time he'd crossed the Threshold for *Natural Healing*. That was why when he stumbled back to his room he crashed into a dreamless sleep.

Fin slept through both breakfast and lunch, having no idea of the forces being arrayed against him.

He blissfully slumbered with a smile on his face.

The doc that showed up that day got sign out that an ER doc had wound up on his service. After taking a quick look at his smiling patient, and seeing that Fin's vitals were stable, he just said, "Let the man sleep. He looks great for having survived a car wreck. Just make sure he doesn't drop a dangler."

Like that, the greater part of a day passed.

It was said in the Labyrinth that "Many are the Paths of Potential."

In another version of reality, he would have left the hospital much earlier. The lives of the cancer victims he'd saved would have been snuffed out in a matter of days.

Yet, by staying, he triggered a future that would be drowned in death.

~REWARD~

Chapter 38: Sealed Hate

In the temple of the Ghost Lotus…

"**M**y lord, the sun will soon pass its apex. I believe this is all the Light we will be able to collect."

The Patriarch looked upward at the clear disc and the shining white light held within.

His people had done well. More than a full mote had been collected.

He raised his hand in permission, and the forty-nine men and women collapsed after more than twelve hours of constant strain. Servants that were also fully trained EMT carried them away expeditiously.

The ritualists would be of no use for at least the next week.

This kind of active siphoning of Element was not with cost.

Such costs did not matter to the patriarch. The only thing relevant was the pristine white Light hovering above his son's dead body.

All through the night, his wife, his matriarch had wept, clinging to the corpse of her youngest. He pulled her away now, the ritual needing to be completed.

She shrieked, her heart breaking anew, but followed his lead, clutching onto her love. The patriarch gestured imperiously with two fingers, and the ritual was triggered.

~DANGER~

Blinding light filled the temple. To anyone watching from the street below, it looked like a second, pale sun appeared in the sky.

Many inside the temple wore protective eyewear, the dark goggles being the only thing that preserved their eyesight.

The patriarch of the House of the Ghost Lotus stared unencumbered.

To the uninitiated, the Light was dangerous. To one such as him, who had been born in the Light, molded by it, the Light would never be blinding.

He watched as the body of his youngest son be consumed by a beam of incandescent white.

The boy may have been a failure and disgrace, but he was his blood.

Nothing less than a Pyre of Alfr would suffice.

This was the culmination of an entire night's worth of effort by dozens of the most powerful members of his House.

Beside him, his wife sobbed quietly.

Blood thirsty and sadistic were words that described his matriarch, but she was also a woman who loved her children above all.

Once the body of his son was completely consumed by the light of ritual, the light winked out. The smell of burnt ozone filled the temple.

An elderly man, so old his sparse hair was truly white, walked forward. His hand reached out from the sleeve of his snow colored robe, and he plucked a small gem, no larger than a thumbnail, out of the ashes.

Inside the jewel throbbed a pure white light, much less brilliant than the mote of Light that had powered the ritual.

It was the sum total of Light Jerini had collected during his disappointing and short life. With such a pathetic amount, it would take years before tonight's investment was paid back.

As the gem was handed to the patriarch, he felt his first emotion in hours.

Shame.

Shame over having produced such an unworthy progeny.

His face did not betray his inner thoughts with so much as an unplanned blink.

The patriarch dropped the jewel back in the hand of elder dismissively. Paltry or not, the jewel would be interred in the primary cultivation chamber of the House, aiding the cultivation of future generations.

The patriarch walked out of the temple with his wife holding his arm for support. Not a single emotion ruined the stony perfection of his face.

The proper forms had been observed.

Respect had been paid and the ritual was complete.

Enough energy had been wasted upon past failures.

The time of spilt blood had come.

It was only a short drive from the temple back to their estate. A convoy of armored vehicles took the leaders of the Ghost Lotus House from the funeral site back to their home. The patriarch walked with grace and poise, his eyes matching his demeanor and power, the image marred only by Lauren's red rimmed eyes.

Upon entering his study, several subordinates and servants bowed deeply in greeting.

As was only proper.

"It is time to seize the mongrel that killed my son," the patriarch enunciated in clipped tones of command.

"Have him stripped, bathed and conduct a full assessment of his health.

If he dies too quickly due to your negligence, all of you," he swept a pale manicured finger over his assembled minions, "Will take his place in the Red Room. The wergild has already been paid to the Shadow. Send two squads. Go now."

Every man and woman in the room shared the same features as their patriarch, sharp facial lines, striking eyes the color of glacier ice and hair so blond it was almost white. Each bowed immediately, and were already leaving the room when the matriarch spoke for the first time.

"More!" she commanded; voice full of death. "Send an emergency signal to the Charlamagnes. I want every member of our subordinate gang at the hospital immediately. In addition, send eight squads. Take a Powered to support each."

The patriarch slowly turned his head to look at his wife, thinking the same thing as everyone else. Mustering one of their subordinate gangs in totality was a bit extravagant. The price that would have to be paid to the World

AI for circumventing the local laws would be steep, even for higher level Citizens like themselves.

The hospital was also the domain of another Familia, and the Shadow would definitely increase the price of the wergild for such a large incursion.

Yet to bring his wife succor in her time of pain, he would pay that price gladly.

Even sending eight squads of their elites to capture a single man, the definition of overkill, did not give him pause.

Sending so many with abilities, however… there was not a word for that level of reaction.

While every main and core branch family member had been Enabled to use an interface after the Wave, strikingly few were Powered with Abilities. In their entire House, there were less than one hundred.

Right now, every Familia, every House, was treating their Powered as strategic resources.

In any other situation, the patriarch may have overridden his matriarch, yet his absolute will was affected by the same unknown, and undetected, energy as his wife.

They were united in their hatred of the man that had witnessed the death of their son.

Instead of chiding her for being emotional, he walked to a small chest resting on a nearby shelf. Opening it, he extracted eight shining coins.

If looked at closely, the words "Gnomus Imperare" could be seen engraved on one side.

Seeing any form of physical currency in the age of credits was odd. Seeing coins made out of actual gold was doubly so.

Though well trained to school their countenances, his subordinates' eyes widened slightly upon being given the coins.

This was not because of the value of gold. It was because of what these coins represented.

Entire bloodlines had been scoured from the face of the Earth for less largess than had just been casually allotted to them.

Indeed, professionals around the world would kill four or five people for a single golden coin.

~REWARD~

That was the current going rate.

The fact that their patriarch would invest such wealth to seize a simple man who was not even a Citizen was shocking.

Any random member of the Familia was more than a match for a peasant. To spend so many coins…

The patriarch saw their reaction, but was not in the habit of explaining himself to his lessers. He simply spoke in command, "You heard your Lady's orders. Ride swift and bring our judgement."

His subordinates saluted and quick marched out of the room. The patriarch turned to look at his wife, expecting to see her seething. Instead, she had a smile on her face that did not reach her eyes. Those were filled with bloodthirst.

Looking up, she saw the unspoken question on her husband's face, she tapped a final command into the virtual interface of her Link.

"I'm just giving the strike team a video. They'll send it to that mongrel right before they grab him."

The patriarch immediately thought back to her recent time in the Red Room, of her walking back into the house with a white dress splattered in scarlet and a pair of dripping black scissors in her hand, and knew exactly what she had just done.

No matter what came of this day, their enmity with Fin Evers was forever sealed.

Chapter 39: Killers

EARTH

A convoy of armored black vehicles drove through the streets of Atlanta. Inside one, a group of men and women sat, all wearing bespoke black suits that contrasted with their pale skin and nearly white-blond hair.

"I can't believe the patriarch sent all of us for one ape," a man laughed with a heavy German accent.

"Yes," a woman rejoined with the same enunciation pattern. "We could have just sent a zookeeper."

"De mund halten!" commanded a man in the passenger seat.

The previous speakers glared at him from the back. His features were a bit less refined than everyone else in the car, and his hair a bit more golden.

"Jürgen, you're too serious. If you were a true member of the Familia, you would understand better."

Heat filled the man's face, but his voice was ice cold as he looked in the rearview mirror.

"You would question the will of the matriarch? The patriarch! I bet you would not be nearly so bold if you knew they called the Photographer."

Silence reigned.

"The Fotograf?" one woman asked with a whisper.

"That animal?" another echoed at the same volume.

Everyone in the House knew about their Lady's old mentor. The man was a sadist, only called to deal out the harshest punishments.

~DANGER~

"Ja," Jürgen replied smugly. "Unless you would like to meet him yourself, I suggest you focus on our mission."

It was quiet for the rest of the ride, and more than one member of the car actually felt pity for the man they were about to abduct.

***

Five large, black SUVs pulled up in front of St Francis Hospital. Three more took up positions at the other main exits. Each vehicle was equipped with ballistic glass windows and solid rubber tires. The frames were reinforced titanium.

When the doors slammed shut, they made a dull *thunk,* rather than a *thud,* due to the heavy armor plating. These were tanks disguised as luxury vehicles. Just like the people being transported, the cars were examples of hidden strength. A large stylized "L" was on each hood, black ink on black paint.

Each car discharged four blond men and women dressed in well-cut black suits.

A man wearing jeans and a black t-shirt approached the cars. A quick glance around the hospital would show several dozen other people dressed similarly ringing the building.

The approaching man was muscular, had a rough look about him, and large scarred hands. The type of man most didn't want to meet in a bar, but in the face of the well-manicured blonds, he wore an obsequious expression.

He looked back and forth at the twenty suited men and women, not sure who to address.

Jürgen took lead, beckoning the man closer, "Report."

The black shirted man angled his right hand completely flat while keeping it at waist level, a surreptitious salute before speaking.

"Sir. My name is Hector. I'm the leader of the Charlamagnes."

Jürgen showed his impatience and utter lack of being impressed by the accomplishments of Hector's life.

The gang leader picked up on the other man's oh so subtle disdain. While inside, he railed, he hadn't made it to the top of a Familia's subordinate gang just because of his scarred fists. Without allowing his anger to show on his face, he continued to report.

"The entire gang was mustered as soon as we received the emergency signal. We had eleven members on the scene within ten minutes and currently have thirty-seven members watching everyone that comes and goes.

The other twenty-three will be here within the hour. My apologies, but they were outside of the city when the call came and-"

The blond man waved him to silence, not interested in gibberings of an inferior. He personally thought his Lady was just mad with grief and wasting all of their time by sending so many to bring in a simple peasant, despite what he'd said in the car.

Not that he was fool enough to speak those thoughts out loud.

"You didn't enter the building, did you Jesus?" the blond asked.

Completely ignoring being called the wrong name, Hector answered with a shake of his head.

"No sir, we would not dare to intrude on any Familia's territory without permission."

The blond nodded, staring up at the tall white building. While the Shadow was undoubtedly a subpar Familia filled with slant eyes, it was still good that peasant showed the proper respect to their betters.

Making an "L" with his left hand, a holographic display appeared between Jürgen's thumb and forefinger. Tapping on it, the suited man sent a signal to each of the black shirted men and women.

Hector, lacking the funds for a holographic upgrade on his Link, pulled a small clear circle from his pocket that promptly showed Fin's face. All around the hospital, other members of the Charlamagne gang did the same.

"This is our quarry. Enter the hospital and begin searching. When you spot him, notify us immediately. If you capture him, you will be well rewarded. What is most important is that you take him alive. The Lady herself has made it clear that she will show our target special attention."

Affixing Hector with a glare, the blond continued, "Or the one responsible for letting him go free will take his place."

The hardened criminal kept his face impassive, but couldn't stop a slow, dry swallow. Everyone in the know knew about the "Red Room."

Smiling, Jürgen leaned forward, "Yes. And I promise you Jaime. The Red Room is worse than you can possibly imagine."

Done with his joke, the suited man stood tall and snapped his fingers. "You have permission to enter Shadow territory in pursuit of this goal. The building schematics show six exits at street level. One on the north side of the building. Two to the south, east and the last to the west. Dispatch three of your subordinates to each exit to ensure he doesn't escape. Report and coordinate with the strike teams on each side of the hospital.

Take another five of your people and go to the subbasement. There is a tunnel that leads to a neighboring building. Make sure he doesn't get out that way. Send the rest of your gang inside. Now move!"

After internally strangling even more anger at being spoken down to, Hector made another salute and began giving orders to his people through the smartglass rectangle of his Link.

As the man walked away, one of the blond, suited women glared after him with almost a snarl on her face. With an easily heard German accent, she spat out, "Mongrel. I don't know how you can bear speaking to such as him Jürgen."

Jürgen smiled, but still gently admonished her.

"Your prejudice betrays you, Olga. Despite being inferior, these lessers have their uses, just as cows or horses can be of use. Currently, they are our hounds who will flush our fox out into the open."

Speaking again, but with a commanding clip in his voice, he gave his team orders.

"You four, guard the exit." He turned to the next squad leader, "Split your team. Two of you go to the main security office. Our Lord and Lady have parlayed with the Shadow Familia for our entrance and access to their systems. Still, be prepared to take control of their surveillance system by force. I don't trust shades."

"The other half of your team should go to the target's room. The Shadow said he should be on the fifth floor, room 5C-16. Wait for me to arrive before engaging."

The four entered the hospital, splitting into pairs.

Now that the hospital was secured and their quarry could not escape, Jürgen sent a video to their prey. It had been specially curated and edited by their matriarch. A faint beep showed the file was delivered with the customary protocols used for such incendiary material.

"The rest of you," Jürgen smiled and straightened his shirt cuffs under his suit coat, "let's go bag an untermensch."

Smiling, twelve killers entered the hospital.

Chapter 40: Trespass

AIR

Dr Yinying's Link chirped.

The tired doc stifled a groan. She was finally trying to grab just a few minutes of sleep, and her head was resting on her arms.

No one looking at her would know how bone weary she was. Even after a twenty-hour shift, her hair remained perfectly in place.

Of course, she was still a doctor. Her attention to personal appearance didn't stop her from abandoning all pretense when the chance for a nap presented itself.

Every ICU doc learned quickly what the number one rule was.

If you have a chance to grab even a few minutes of sleep, you cherished it.

Which was why when her Link went off, she grunted in irritation, not even bothering to crack a single eyelid.

The last thing she wanted was one more nurse telling her about one more whining patient.

The hospital had been even crazier than usual today.

Mostly due to the reporters that had descended on Atlanta General like a pack of locusts.

When more than a dozen cancer patients went into remission overnight, the news would definitely get out.

That, and the Wave, were the top stories on the local Link services so far today.

~DANGER~

On one hand, Sola didn't blame the reporters. It was a noteworthy story. Even patients that had been at death's door were now sitting up and smiling. She herself was curious about what had happened.

On the other hand…

Fuck all that noise, she wanted to sleep!

Thankfully, oncology wasn't her specialty, so she'd been spared the questions of both the reporters and lookie-loos that had come to investigate. It hadn't spared her from having to submit a full report to her own Familia.

A report that could be summed up with an "I don't know."

Of course, her family hadn't just accepted that. Instead, she'd needed to waste hours being asked endless questions that she couldn't answer. After all of that, she was five hours after her end of shift, was worn thin and was more than a little irritable.

All of that anger was about to be unloaded on whatever unlucky soul had decided to contact her.

The prick.

Not even having the inclination to pick her head up, she flexed her pinky twice and triggered the tactile function of her Link.

Tactile messaging was an upgrade that only came with military grade Links. Civilians didn't even know the tech was real, thinking it was just something you saw in holomovies. It was only because of her family's connections that she had this and other upgrades.

The messaging technology had been inspired by braille. Rather than reading a message, her Link stimulated the skin on her arm to contract in specific patterns. Without special training, the tactile function would just feel like a strange itching on her arm. Knowing how to interpret it though, opened up interesting possibilities.

Currently, it allowed her to read a simple, but serious message without even needing to open her eyes.

What she read banished all exhaustion.

Weariness was supplanted by anger.

The message was from a security guard on her personal payroll. She shot up from her chair and held her hand flat, a series of holographic images appearing in midair.

They were real time video feeds from the hospital's security cameras. They showed groups of rough looking men and women wearing black t-shirts and jeans.

The sight of them made her start running even as she spat a single word.

"Charlamagnes."

Immediately after, she was sent another video. This one showed of a group of white men and women wearing perfectly tailored suits. They were as refined as the t-shirted men and women were not.

"Lotus!"

The second word had far more venom than the first.

While she ran, she had her AI dial several numbers, cursing each time she got a recorded message. When it finally connected, she just spoke urgently into her Link, "Trouble with Lotus Familia at my location. Major incursion. At least a dozen Lotus. They've sent their dogs inside as well. Recommend mobilizing the Savage Huns."

Her Link chirped again, a message from her security guard, making the skin on her arm contract once more.

"The main group is walking to Ward 5C. The smaller groups are spreading through the hospital."

The man was doing just what she'd told him to do, even though this was the first time he'd actually been in this situation. She made a mental note to give him a raise, even as she cursed and picked up her pace. She'd already been running towards 5C, because that was where a specific patient of hers had been transferred.

Something about Fin Evers had been tickling the back of her mind ever since she'd met him. Despite the fact that it was impossible, he'd felt like a member of a Familia. He'd felt important. More than that, he'd felt-

Powerful.

She'd come to trust her instincts. Some members of her Familia even thought her intuition might be some kind of hidden power. She wasn't psychic, but her insight had always been on point.

Those instincts had told her one definitive thing about Fin Evers.

He was going to be a problem.

Problem or not, this hospital belonged to her Familia, not that the official tax record would ever reveal that.

Those in the know, knew it well, and that included the Lotus members brazenly walking through her hospital. While that could be a simple breach of protocol, there was no way that the *dozens* of black shirted Charlamagnes surging though the buildings corridors were anything other than a full martial exercise.

Even as she ran, she couldn't help but wonder what could possibly necessitate a show of force of this magnitude.

The Familias did not brawl in the street and sunlight.

That's what their gangs were for. Even then, it was an unwritten law, strong as steel, that the public was kept in the dark as much as possible.

Even with her suspicion that Fin Evers was special somehow, this was like mobilizing a full SWAT team because some kid snatched a woman's purse.

"Vash!" she called out to her AI.

"How can I be of service?" came the response from her Link, the AI adopting a gruff American, pack a day, man's voice

"The Lotus are invading the hospital in force. Coordinate with surveillance and give me updates on their movements. Prioritize the Lotus, but keep an eye on their subordinates as well."

"No problem. I'm on it," her AI assured her in a low rumble.

"Also, find out everything you can about a patient named Fin Evers. I think they might be here for him. And send this message."

After she finished dictating, without ever stopping her sprint or losing her breath for a moment, she focused on the upcoming confrontation.

It didn't matter if they were here for Dr Evers. It didn't matter to her if they had all simultaneously gotten sick and would die without immediate help.

They were Lotus.

They were filth.

And they'd trespassed on the grounds of her Familia.

They had trespassed in *her* hospital.

They would pay for such disrespect.

Chapter 41: Wergild

LIFE

Before turning the final corner, she stopped and collected herself.

Sola hurriedly began a breathing exercise passed down through the years in her family. Her heart rate slowed back to normal much faster than should have been possible. Sweat glands closed and her already regular breathing became even more fluid.

All in a matter of seconds.

Looking in a nearby window, she checked her faint reflection in the glass, putting errant hairs back in place. These bastards would not see her frazzled. Calmed, she typed one last quick message into her Link.

Taking a final look in the window, she turned the corner, the soft soles of her sneakers contrasting with the clipped sounds of hard leather insoles of the ten men and women in suits walking towards her.

Outnumbered, she still did not back down and showed no hesitation.

Her left hand rose to her chest and moved through a particular gesture of greeting. Her right formed the symbol of Shadow, her Familia. She said nothing, her expression cold and implacable.

For a moment, it looked like the group of Lotus would walk into her, but with only three feet separating her from the leader, they all stopped. The man in charge mirrored her first gesture with his own left hand, and then formed the symbol for the Lotus with the other.

"Why are you here?" she demanded, despite the forms not being fully completed.

The leader's eye twitched at the disrespect, but he could not afford failure, so he kept to the forms, "I am Jürgen Blüte-"

~DANGER~

"Side branch of the family, huh?" Sola asked smugly. She didn't really care if the man was core, main or side, but she knew these blonde bastards were wound tight.

With an audible grunt, and more aggression this time, he began again, "I am Jürgen Blüte, and represent the local domo of the Lotus Familia. We are here to fulfill a directive from our patriarch. We need-"

"You need," she interrupted, "to get your powder asses out of my hospital. This is Shadow territory."

All twelve of the pale skinned blonds bristled at her insult this time.

Their wan features and blond hair were an easy way to identify them. Among other Familias, jokes were rampant that they achieved their complexions by powdering each other regularly.

The jokes weren't limited to them powdering their faces… or using powder.

Before his subordinates could react, the leader held up a clenched fist, quieting them down. He leaned in until Sola could feel the heat from his breath on her face and smell the boiled chicken he'd had for lunch.

"Listen, little tint," his voice was thick with superiority and hate, "I have been given a directive from my patriarch to retrieve a package. That is exactly what I am going to do. Do you plan on stopping us?"

Even though he was more than a foot taller, and had to outweigh her by a good seventy pounds, she looked back at him without a trace of fear. Without the faintest tightening of her eyes. All she did was shift her breathing pattern and prepare for a fight.

One of her hands remained behind her back and a faint blue aura surrounded it. Her other hand hung straight down. It would take only a moment for her to release the stiletto hidden up the sleeve of her white coat.

Some might take exception of a doctor so willing to break the Hippocratic Oath by spilling blood. No one really took that seriously though.

Besides, she was bound by oaths of actual power.

That was why, as she stood there, a five foot three woman in scrubs facing down a dozen blond Vikings in black suits, her expression was deadly serious.

Jürgen's Link chirped and he brought it to his chin. Sola couldn't hear what was said, but the tactile function on her own triggered at nearly the same time. A hospital guard had sent another message.

"A pair of those blondes in suits looked in a room on 5C before they came back out looking pissed."

The fact that they were looking in 5C was the final confirmation she needed.

They were definitely looking for Fin.

She still just didn't know why.

Which didn't keep her from enjoying the show unfolding in front of her.

Jürgen had clearly just gotten a message from his subordinates that they hadn't found Fin.

It was all Sola could do to not openly laugh at seeing Jürgen's face contort in anger. She settled for a faint smirk.

Seeing that riled him up all the more. He leaned perilously close to her again, and for a moment she thought he might actually attack her.

In a way, that would be the best result.

It would free her to take his life without risking retaliation from his Familia.

Jürgen stared at her intensely for a few more seconds, but then his expression shifted like a switch was flipped. He laughed in her face, before straightening up and raising a hand.

"Settle down little tint," Jürgen mocked. "You want to play games. We can play."

A holographic display appeared on his arm, and he tapped something out.

With a dismissive flick, he swiped the information towards her.

A series of vibrations ran down Sola's arm, and her eyes widened in both surprise and betrayal.

While she stood there in shock, Jürgen gave his people curt orders.

"Teams two, three and four, split into twos and begin a systematic search of every room in this hospital. Have the Charlamagnes spread out to all major junctions and camp there to limit the target's movements.

We will go floor by floor. With the elevators locked down, he won't get by us."

This time, Sola didn't say a word in protest. She just glared at him, thin lips sealed by fury and family.

Seeing her impotent anger, Jürgen laughed out loud again, making the scent of unseasoned chicken fill her nostrils a second time.

"What? No more smart mouth, little tint? The wergild has already been paid, both for the intrusion and the civilian." With a cruel glint in his eye, he added, "Not to worry. Even in a building this size, we'll find him before too long."

Raising her own left arm, she double checked what her tactile interface had already told her. A hologram appeared showing two images. The first was a black coin. It had copper edges and rotated slowly. The crest of her Familia was on one side and the other showed the symbol of the Lotus.

The second image was a 3D model of Fin Ever's face.

It took less than a second to send the data to her family's AI and then receive a response. The prickling skin on her arm confirmed what Jürgen had said.

It was real.

The Shadow had accepted the payment for the Lotus Familia's intrusion. That meant they tacitly agreed with the other family's actions. There was nothing she could do.

Echoing her own thoughts, he mocked her, "There is nothing you can do, unless you intend to attack us."

Unknowingly, he echoed back what had been her plan.

With numbers firmly on his side, he'd like nothing more than for her to lose control. If that happened, he'd be well within his rights to kill. Not even her own Familia would seek retribution.

There were unwritten rules that would still protect her in many cases, but with her current status in Shadow-

"Kind of strange they didn't tell you though, huh?" the leader asked, his shit eating grin eating more shit. "Are you in the scheisse with your people for some reason?"

His faint German accent just made the mocking worse somehow.

While the threat of bloodshed didn't faze her in the least, the thought of her own Familia triggered an involuntary tightening around her eyes.

That didn't escape Jürgen's notice.

With true pleasure, he laughed in her face a third time, this time, a bit of spit flecked onto her pristine white coat, "I guess so. Now, unless you plan to go against your own Familia, or have a reason to contest the wergild," his tone turned rough and aggressive, "get the fuck out of our way."

Sola stared back at him and the other blond men and women who were glaring angrily at her, while her mind raced. He was right. The deal had been struck and there was nothing she could do.

There was something about Fin Evers that made her think he was important. She trusted her gut. It had saved her life more than once, but that wouldn't be enough for her Familia. If only she had some concrete proof that he was more than a regular civilian. If she could even prove that he'd been Enabled by the Wave, that might be enough.

She hadn't seen anything like that though, and without that proof, the Shadow would not take her word.

To put it mildly, she wasn't in her family's good graces, and not only because she'd ignored the order to gather after the Wave. She didn't fear these powders, but her the Shadow… yes, they had taught her fear.

If she went against her Familia now, it might be the last bad decision she ever made.

At least, if she did it openly.

With a false smile, she stepped back and swept one out to the side as if in magnanimous welcome, "I will of course comply with the wishes of my Familia. In fact, it will be my pleasure to escort you to find your target. If he is not in his room, and it looks like he wasn't?"

Her mocking question tightened the skin around Jürgen's eyes. Her false smile became real, and she continued, "Well then, I'm afraid we will just have to search room by room. I wish I could be of more help."

Jürgen glared at her with not a small amount of distaste, annoyed both that his gambit had failed and that he couldn't keep her from chaperoning him.

"Fine," he spat. "In accordance with the terms of the wergild, I demand you shut down the elevators, seal the exits and provide my team with access to the security feeds. I have a strike team waiting outside the security office. Now do as you're told, little girl, if you can handle it."

As he spoke, he'd pointed his Link at her, a holographic camera appearing above his wrist. The hologram wasn't necessary to record things, but it made the threat unambiguous.

Sola got the message.

Basically, that Jürgen was a bitch of a snitch, and he was planning to tell his daddy if she didn't play nice.

Smiling, she responded with a simple, "Of course."

Tapping her Link, she gave an order. "This is Dr Sola Yinying giving an administrative order. Clearance code ZX78-95. Place the hospital on lockdown. Stop all elevator traffic and post guards at the doors. Four security specialists are waiting outside of the security office. Give them entrance and extend every courtesy to help them."

Sola rarely asserted her authority as the top administrator in the hospital, preferring to focus on patient care, but all knew that her word was law. With zero pushback, the head of security immediately assented with a, "Yes, ma'am," and carried out her instructions.

Jürgen held his Link to his jaw, the device using bone conduction to silently relay information to his inner ear.

As Sola watched, his eyes rose in smug triumph.

Which made it all the more satisfying when they plunged into despair for just a second before fury stole across his face.

"Your people triggered a security update! All of the camera feeds are down!"

Sola opened her mouth in mock horror, "Is this the fourteenth? There *was* a regularly scheduled security update for today. It's weird how bad your luck is." She stuck out her bottom lip in commiseration, "Ooooh. Poo!"

"It's," Jürgen chewed the words with his German accent, "the eleventh!"

"Oh!" Sola's unlidded eyes widened comically, and she looked up to either side as if seeing an answer in the corners of the hallway. "Then that's *really* weird."

She snapped her fingers in epiphany, "Wait. Wait! I know what happened! When I was trying to help you before, I told them to use code ZX78-95. I shoooould have told them to use code ZX78 ninety-six! Ninety-*five*, as we all now know, triggers a security update."

Sola exhaled heavily before nodding at Jürgen in mutual commiseration, "Women, am I right? I guess I *couldn't* handle it."

Exaggeratedly looking around, she whispered in a very loud voice, "I think I'm on my period."

Chapter 42: War Protocol

She finished her performance by holding up her hands in mock frustration, "And the update can't be stopped. Sadly, the feeds will be down for the next few hours."

"How many 'hours'?"

"Don't remember," came her smiling reply. "Gah! If only I had known *before* that you'd need the cameras. I could have done something."

Her bottom lip stuck out in true sadness, and she stared directly into the holographic camera above Jürgen's wrist.

She hoped his pale assed superiors enjoyed watching that later.

Jürgen's clenched fists literally shook with rage.

Sola looked back nonplussed, "Should we start looking?" she suggested in a helpful voice.

The shaking got worse. She really thought he might lose it.

While she looked at him doe eyed, Sola's AI sent her a message through her tactile interface, "Before the surveillance cameras went down, I placed Fin Evers on the eight floor."

Showing no indication that she now knew where Fin was, she turned away from the quivering man and walked up to a hospital map on the wall. Pointing, she tapped 5E, "Now that I think of it, there's almost no one in this section. The guy you're looking for could be hiding there. I don't think it'd be a good idea to leave this section unsearched. There are only about fifty rooms."

~DANGER~

Jürgen glared incredulously, his arm still raised toward her, though it seemed like he'd forgotten he was making a recording. For good measure she pursed her lips coquettishly, "Of course, I'm happy to follow wherever a strong man like you wants to lead."

Just in case she wasn't laying it on thick enough, she gave him an overly exaggerated wink.

"You'll regret this," he growled. Then he raised his Link and started to give an order. There was no response. In confusion, he tapped it. Then tapped it again.

Realization dawned on him. As it did, his anger grew so great that he literally heard the sound of blood rushing in his ears like river rapids.

Seeing that, Sola delivered her final fuk-u.

She snapped her fingers in false realization.

"Oh yeah. Code ZX78-95 is a war time security update protocol. Which means any strike teams that aren't already in the building won't be coming in. And all internal communications are down as well, including Links. I guess you won't be able to coordinate with the other strike teams or your pet gang members."

"You dare!" he started to splutter.

"Dare? Me? I'm just doing what my Familia agreed to do."

"Let the rest of my teams into the hospital. Now!"

"I'd be happy to lift the lockdown if that's what you really want." Sola replied with a smile.

Before Jürgen could respond in the affirmative, one of the other men grabbed his arm, "Don't. It's a trick. The agreement with her Familia was for a single lockdown. If we ask her to lift it, she won't be obligated to reestablish it once our people are inside."

Sola put on an anime level pout, "Oh, you must be the smart one. Poo."

She smiled at Jürgen again, praying internally that he'd be angry enough to attack her and let her retaliate, "Soooo, I guess we'll have to start looking for him ourselves. It shouldn't take too long, there's only a few dozen rooms per floor and twelve floors with three distinct wings. And I locked the elevators down, like *you* asked, so I hope you're ready to get your steps in!"

Jürgen eyes almost sparked in rage, and his white face was now noticeably redder, but ultimately barked, "Let's go!"

The other suited men and women glared daggers at her as they followed their leader.

As they began moving down the corridor, her AI sent her another message, "I think I know why they are so interested in Dr Evers. Two people died in the car crash that injured him. The first was his fiancé. The second was-"

She almost stumbled when her tactile interface revealed that a scion of the House of the Ghost Lotus had died.

No wonder they had paid what must have been an astronomical amount to her House for this intrusion. Not to mention the cost of purchasing a wergild from the Great Link.

Sola moved along with them thinking, "I've helped you as much as I could Dr Evers. I hope you can find a way out. And if you can't, I hope you fight to the death. Anything would be better than letting them take you alive."

For the next half hour, Jürgen's people started to clear the hospital floor by floor.

To his consternation, and Sola's silent, but obviously smug delight, nearly half of his kill squads were locked outside the hospital, along with most of the Charlamagnes.

Unfortunately, Jürgen wasn't wholly incompetent.

He'd immediately peeled off nearly everyone in his team to coordinate with the forces he did have inside the hospital. The gang members were all brought down to the ground floor. Half were positioned at the stairwells. A quarter were made to search the rooms on that floor, and the rest of them were used as runners to coordinate messages and progress. Like that, they searched the first floor with clinical precision.

Her own security teams were coopted as well, something she couldn't go against by the terms of the wergild. They didn't actively search for Fin, but they did keep the patients, who were not happy about being restricted to their rooms or having their Link access removed, more or less under control.

The Third War had brought many changes to society, and one of them, for good or ill, was people not giving a lot of push back to armed and official looking groups. Too many horrible things had happened during the War for the public consciousness to place liberty over safety.

When her security team told the patients that "a dangerous fugitive had taken refuge in the hospital and they needed to stay in their rooms for their own safety" no one believed it, but few wanted to push the line either, not when they were promised it would be over "soon."

Patients and their families complained about being forced to stay in their rooms, but one look at the cold eyes of the Lotus quelled most complaints.

Not a single signal was allowed out of the hospital either. There would be no news vans screeching up.

The Great Link itself suppressed any police or governmental intervention. The wergild could only be purchased by higher level Citizens. The cost was higher than most families made in a year, but it let those more valued by the world literally get away with murder.

Most people did not even know that Citizens or social levels existed, and that was by design. As some, less delicate, Citizens suggested, there was no point in letting the cows know their pasture was a holding pen.

All that meant the patients were forced to endure the disrespect of being detained and swallow the "police lockdown" bullshit story they were told.

Of course, not everyone complied.

That was when the Charlamagnes stepped in.

Each time a patient's irate family member got a punch to the face, Jürgen smirked, knowing he was making a large problem for Sola and the Shadow family. Even better, he would be able to argue that such brutality had only been necessary because Sola herself had triggered a war protocol.

Which was something that occurred to her as well. She was not looking forward to the 'talk" with her family later.

She stood by her decision, however.

She'd bought Fin time and had thoroughly shit on Jürgen's sundae.

Even in a smaller hospital, checking room by room could take hours and this was not a small hospital.

It just didn't buy as much time as she'd hoped.

With the manpower at his disposal, Jürgen was able to clear a floor in about ten minutes and then move upward.

Sola tried to delay them as much as possible, but Jürgen never stopped recording and she could not actively oppose him. Doing so would mean opposing her own Familia. That was something she wouldn't survive.

Instead, she continued her quiet defiance.

The primary source of that was thanks to a simple lie Jürgen had been too dumb to challenge. Her "war protocol" wasn't a true triggering of war time footing. There were a few key differences, namely that a sublayer of comms was still active between her and her paid guard who was camped in an auxiliary security office.

She'd always thought her uncle was a crazy old coot for making a second, hidden security office for just a hospital, but she'd kiss the top of his wrinkled bald head the next time she saw him.

Meanwhile, her security guard had sent a tactile message that he was pretty sure Fin was somewhere on 8B.

He'd gone into a room there that didn't have cameras and there was no sign he'd left.

As time passed and they cleared floor by floor, Sola kept waiting for an update that Fin had kept moving, but it never came.

That was why as exited the stairway separating the seventh and eighth floor, Sola stepped in front of in front of Jürgen, actively impeding him for the first time since the search began.

Naturally, she didn't present it like that.

"Maybe if you told me why you wanted him, I could help more. Understand his motivations. Predict him maybe."

She had a helpful look on her face, but Jürgen was far past the mood for games.

"Bitch! Are you going to move, or do I need to move you?"

The smile melted from her face like ice on hot metal, leaving only steel behind. The two stared at each other, dislike bordering on hate in both of their eyes, all subterfuge stripped away. Anything might have happened if one of the other Lotus hadn't shouted, "Jürgen, there he is!"

They all looked up and saw Fin at the end of the hallway, wearing only a hospital gown, and delivering a heavy punch to a Charlemagne. He struck the man in the face, knocking the guy out cold.

Blood decorated his face, and it looked like he was bleeding from a wound in his back.

At the Lotus member's shout, Fin looked up and stared at them all. A cavalcade of emotions shot across his face as he saw the blond men and women, making a mental connection to the man in the hover truck immediately.

Finally, his eyes locked onto Sola for just a moment before he took off in the opposite direction.

The men and women with Jürgen took off in immediate pursuit. Jürgen himself grinned at Sola in triumph. She smiled back, only one hand visible. The other one was glowing with glacial blue energy, a gift from the Wave, and was behind her back, hidden from Jürgen's holocam.

Looking completely innocent, she triggered her new power.

Chapter 43: New Attribute

DEATH

An hour before Sola released her Power...

Fin woke up feeling like he'd had his best night's sleep in years. He stretched happily, enjoying the feeling of the sunlight streaming through the window.

"Whoa. I slept late."

Checking his Link showed it was late afternoon, even later than he'd thought.

Fin chuckled. It looked like it had been a beautiful day.

And it ain't over yet, he thought with a hopeful smile.

He felt great!

There was zero doubt in his mind as to the reason.

He'd cultivated Life Element more than a dozen times throughout the night.

Cultivating was just *satisfying*.

There were some repetitive actions that felt like torture. Others could occupy a person's attention for days and not feel like a chore.

Cultivating felt like something he could do for years.

Now that he was awake though, he was eager to get back at it.

Somewhere in the night, he'd gotten over his reservations about using the Fire Element he'd collected.

~REWARD~

Even with his enthusiasm though, he'd known it would have been the height of foolish to try cultivating when he was exhausted.

The first time he'd failed in cultivating it had cost him a health point.

Speaking of which…

Fin pulled up his stats, and a truly shit eating grin spread across his face.

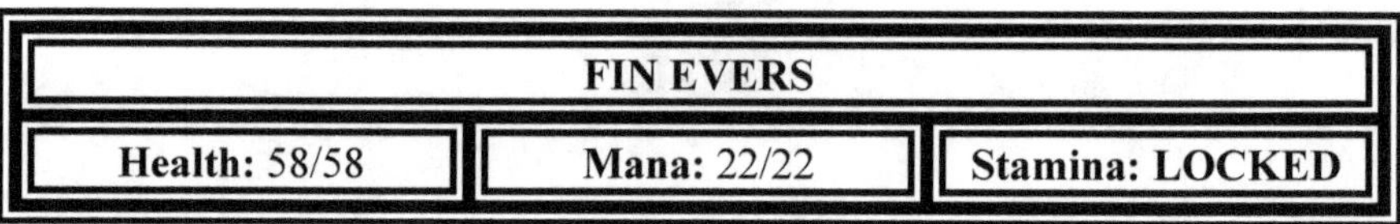

A little bit more than twelve hours had passed since he'd lost those two points of health from his *Mana Sight* backlash.

Thanks to his natural healing, he recovered over three HP every twelve hours.

Which meant, his health pool was full again!

Fin triggered his Link's mirror, and stared at his two perfect, not bloody eyes in the reflection.

He started chuckling to himself.

This was really, really happening.

A pang of sorrow shot through him as he thought about Lauren.

"I miss you baby. I know you would have loved this."

The pain was still there, and raw, but he no longer hid from it.

By accepting his sorrow, it had lost power over him.

Which was why he was able to focus and dive right back into his Cave of Whispers.

As had been the case each time, the transition was seamless.

He stood in the middle of the circle of light and stared at the eight orange-red flames flickering in the dark.

 ~REWARD~

Crossing his fingers, Fin murmured to himself, "Big money, no whammies, no chunkies, let's go!"

He drew the first flame towards him.

To his surprise and dismay, the difficulty was much higher than the first time he'd cultivated Life.

Just as with the golden spheres, a dimple was formed on the side of the mote of Fire. It then lengthened in a long, thin line, stretching from the darkness of the cavern towards him. Focusing, Fin was able to pull the Element almost all the way to the avatar, but it fell about a foot and half short.

To cross the final span, he needed to use *Mana Threads*.

The blue mana string connected to the tether of orange-red Fire, and the connection was established.

The energy flowed into him as his eyes glowed the color of flame. Less than ten minutes later, the mote of Fire disappeared, and he increased the Fire within him.

A slew of notifications appeared, but Fin did a self-check again, just like when he'd cultivated Life for the first time.

This time, he wasn't checking for tumors, just that none of his bits were feeling "explodey."

After a good sixty-count, Fin smiled.

"I wasn't scared," he remarked to himself convincingly.

With his first success, he claimed more power and learned the name of a new Attribute.

Chapter 44: Apologies

DARK

Congratulations! You have unlocked your second tributary Attribute: **Reaction**!

Reaction – Your ability to respond to surprise stimuli and a measure of the speed of beginning actions.

He also learned why he'd had a bit of trouble cultivating the first mote of Fire.

*Your Machiavellian training, anger and insights have already formed a faint connection with the Basic Element of **Fire**.*

*This has resulted in you possessing a higher than normal **Reaction** value of 16*

*Cultivating a mote of Fire Element for the first time has provided **+1** to the tributary Attribute **Reaction***

Total Reaction: 17

Seeing his initial starting value was also a relief.

~DANGER~

For a moment, he was worried that cultivating one Element had increased the difficulty in cultivating another. If that was the case, by the third or fourth he came across, he might not be able to move the motes anywhere near the column of light.

Thankfully, that wasn't the case. The difficulty of advancing *Reaction* from seventeen to eighteen didn't feel any harder than doing the same for *Natural Healing*.

It was just that *Reaction* had started from a more advanced point than *Natural Healing*.

In one way, that made a lot of sense. He'd spent decades training his body. Not only normal calisthenics, but hand to hand combat. Unlike an ability to heal, a person's reaction speed could literally be improved by diligence and years of training.

The only problem with that theory was the prompt said his higher reaction was due to him having a "connection" to the Fire Element.

The question was, what did that mean?

Anger had always been one of his go-to emotions. He'd needed to work for years to gain control over it. The prompt had clearly referenced the emotion.

Was that why his connection to Fire was higher? Or did his higher connection with Fire lead him to be angry?

Were all of the Elements connected to different emotions, or was he completely on the wrong track?

Was he even scratching the surface with any of these theories?

None of those questions were as interesting as continuing to cultivate.

He only needed to do it twice more to get his tributary Attribute to twenty.

First, he cleared a couple more notifications.

There was one more benefit to him braving the risk of cultivating with Fire.

Unlocking *Reaction* had also revealed a "locked" tile on his status page.

Reaction *is a tributary Attribute of the Primary Attribute,* **Agility**

By unlocking the tributary Attribute, you have unlocked the Primary Attribute Agility.

    A thrill shot through Fin's heart. He immediately brought up his status page. Frowning at the flood of information, he idly thought that he only wanted to see his Attributes. To his surprise, the page curated itself to present only the desired information

FIN EVERS		
STATS		
Health: 58/58	Mana: 22/22	Stamina: LOCKED
ATTRIBUTES		
LOCKED	**CONSTITUTION:** 24 *Threshold: 2* **Natural Healing:** 20 *Threshold: 2*	LOCKED
LOCKED	**AGILITY:** 15 *Threshold: 1* **Reaction:** 17 *Threshold: 1*	LOCKED
LOCKED	LOCKED	**LUCK:** 14 *Threshold: 1*

    He'd just discovered another Primary Attribute, Agility.

*Congratulations! You have unlocked a Primary Attribute: **Agility***

Agility *(AGI) – This Primary Attribute determines your movement speed and affects your ability to dodge attacks. Also improves your melee attack. Other unknown effects.*

His Agility was fifteen, whatever that meant.

Unfortunately, it didn't look like this was the Attribute which would unlock his Stamina Stat. In fact, right now, he didn't gain anything immediate that he could see from having his Agility revealed.

That didn't matter much though, not when there was mo' Fire to eat!

He mentally reached for another Fire mote.

Ten minutes later, he'd earned two prompts.

You have cultivated 1 Fire Element. +1 to tributary Attribute **Reaction**

+1/8 ***Mana Threads*** *Skill Progression Point*

Another round of cultivation consumed one more Fire Element and brought him to a *Reaction* of 19!

He was about to cultivate what would hopefully be the last round before crossing another Threshold, when he felt a strong buzzing on his wrist.

Just a moment before, Jürgen had sent a video file before entering the hospital.

Looking down, Fin was initially confused. There was nothing on his wrist that would explain the strong buzzing he was feeling.

Then it clicked.

Only his avatar's wrist was empty.

In the real world, that was the wrist he kept his Link on.

Blinking back over to the hospital, he tapped on the band of smart rubber.

His AI's red headed face appeared above it as a hologram. Fin was immediately on his guard because he saw apprehension in its expression.

The AI could not actually experience an emotion like that, but Geneva was smart enough to mimic human looks in order to facilitate easier communication.

"What happened?" he asked.

"Fin, I'm sorry. I have to show you something… disturbing."

Chapter 45: Need

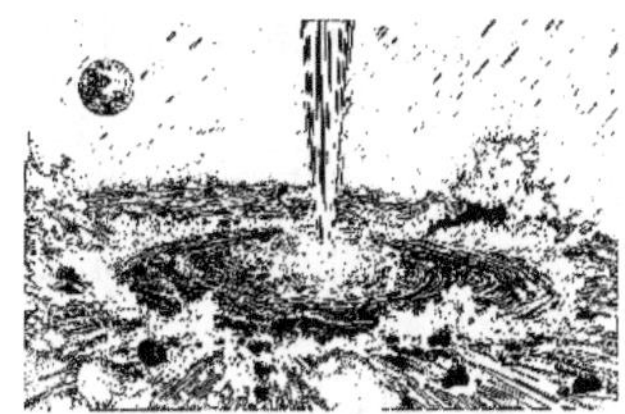

"I am going to decrease the volume by 93.6%. That should allow you to hear what is happening without the sounds spreading into the hallway. I have also modulated the video file so that only you will be able to see it."

He nodded, foreboding growing within him.

G's face was replaced by a new image.

He was now looking at what appeared to be a room lined in wall to wall red tile and filled with furniture completely upholstered in red leather. As soon as the image resolved, screams reached his ears. The camera quickly panned to a face he knew well.

It was Ashley. One of the few friends he had in his new life. The same friend he and Lauren had shared a meal with right before the Wave. Right before she died.

Fin's heart grew cold as a sunken stone as he watched a pair of ornate black scissors slice her ear off.

Ashley screamed even harder as blood spurted and tears ran down her face.

"Why?" she screamed. "Why are you doing this to us?"

Fin's heart hardened further at the last word.

Us?

Whomever was making the snuff film answered his question all too soon. The image panned around and he saw more than a dozen people chained to varies devices, all bloodied and bearing signs of torture.

He knew each and every one of them.

These were his friends. It was everyone that had been at the dinner party with him and Lauren before the Wave.

And their families.

Children and elderly people were strapped to various devices, all crying out in pain and fear.

The camera panned back to Ashley who was slumped down and weeping in her bonds. Off screen, he heard a woman's voice ask in a heavy German accent.

"Do you want me to stop?"

"Yes," Ashley whimpered.

"I cannot hear you."

"I said yes!" Ashley cried louder, a bit of defiance still inside of her.

Fin's heart warmed with the heat of a single ember upon seeing that, but it froze over completely after what came next.

"Then say 'Help me Fin.'"

At first, Ashley didn't comply, but within a minute of the torturer using her razor sharp scissors again, a now noseless Ashley screamed out, "Help me Fin!"

True to her word, the camera operator stopped cutting her. The scissors were applied to her child next until same words were screamed.

"Help me Fin!"

What came next was a highlight reel of sadism.

The torturer would cut a piece off of each person in the room until they screamed out, "Help me Fin!"

If the person screamed out before having something sliced off, they would lose an eye, and then, something else would be removed. Until each paid with at least an ounce of flesh, and then screamed the magic words, the pain didn't end.

His friends, their husbands, wives, parents and even their children were tortured to death before his eyes.

The entire video lasted only three minutes, which did not mean the torture of more than a dozen people had been limited to that amount of time. In fact, due to a time stamp in the bottom left corner of the video, he knew that the torture of most of the people he cared for on Earth had taken long, long hours.

It was just that whoever had sent him this had decided to create a highlight reel of their sadism. The torturer had made sure he not only heard each person scream in agony, but also their pained pleas of "Help me Fin!"

The entire video was a chorus of the damned.

"Help me Fin," sobbed a man as he cringed away from the approaching scissors.

"Help me Fin!" screamed a woman, her voice high pitched as a finger was severed one knuckle at a time.

"Help me Fin!" shrieked a child who looked no older than eight, next to her screaming, lipless brother.

The cries echoed in the room and over the stone of Fin's heart.

He did not turn away. He would not dishonor the pain of these innocents by not baring this small iota of it himself.

Maybe whoever had done this had thought to hurt him by showing him the pain of his loved ones.

Whoever they were, they did not truly know pain.

Maybe they were trying to torture him by showing him what they were capable of doing.

Whoever they were, they did not understand torture.

Maybe they even wanted to just let him know they planned to take revenge.

They did *not*, understand, revenge.

But they would.

His hands began to shake.

Not out of fear. Not out of distress.

Out of need.

He needed to bathe them in blood. He needed to find whoever this was and share his gift with them. The gift he'd spent so long burying, deep within himself after the War. So far down, he never planned to let it see the light again.

It was time to let it out.

Another person, any other person, would have stopped watching.

A normal man would have shed tears, would have sworn in anger and vengeance. A person who was not broken inside would have felt sick.

Fin felt… hungry.

He fed every cry, every tear of skin and muscle, every spray of crimson blood to the thing waiting behind his eyes, deep in the most twisted pit of his soul. It ate the horror of the video eagerly, lapping at the bars of the cage he'd forced it into after the War, wanting every drop as it screamed in joy and fury at the appetizer he'd allowed it.

Fury because it had been denied so long.

Joy as it knew it would feast again soon.

The video ended, finally showing the face of his enemy. Until that point, all he'd seen of the torturer was a well-manicured white hand holding the dagger like scissors.

The sadist had no intention of hiding any longer.

A blond woman, with hair so light it was almost white, stood in a white evening gown. A white lace mask covered the top of her face. It was so delicate and ornate; it did nothing to hide her identity.

Instead, the mask was ornamental, the kind of thing you wore to a party or in celebration.

The dress she wore was so covered in blood that it was sodden through. The wet material was plastered to her body, revealing her erect nipples.

In one hand, she held a dripping pair of ornate scissors. The other was raised to her full pink lips, a single bloody finger resting against them as she softly breathed, "Shhh," as if comforting a troubled child.

"This will be your fate. This will be the fate of everyone you love."

The video disappeared.

Geneva's voice echoed out from his Link, "Fin, the video self-deleted, and the sender completely masked their identity. I don't even have log of receiving any message. It's like the video never existed."

None of that should be possible, not with Great Link technology.

The World AI had great power and seldom ever used it. It subtly guided humanity as a whole towards what would hopefully be a brighter future.

One of times it had asserted itself, however, was to remove the possibility of anonymity when communicating with another person.

It did this to encourage personal accountability. There were no hidden IP addresses like in the past, no fake IDs that keyboard warriors could hide behind as they spewed filth and bile into the world.

If you said something hateful about a group or person, the World AI would not punish you, but it would not let you hide behind anonymity.

That simple change had led to a 99% reduction in cyber bullying, online hate speech and digital abuse overnight.

There was still plenty of privacy, even more than before the War as the World AI guarded personal information better than any firewall from the old world. That privacy only extended to the point that you did not choose to engage another person, however.

It was possible to circumvent that rule, but the only people Fin had heard of doing so were highly ranked government officials, and that was only because the World AI allowed there to be different rules for those placed in positions of power.

The fact that a random person could send the video anonymously and also erase their tracks, was not something that should be possible.

In that moment, Fin could not care less.

After having watched the agony of those men and women, he had come to a simple, Labyrinth shaking resolution.

He would destroy the woman who had tortured his friends and their loved ones. He would make her own words a self-fulfilling prophecy.

He had sworn to never again be the man he had been during the War.

That was a promise he would break, and any price that came with that shattered vow, he would pay gladly.

Fin would wage war in the only way he knew how.

Without hesitation.

Without reserve.

Without mercy.

The time of peace was over.

It was time to finish cultivating Fire.

He was about to blink back into his Cave of Whispers to do just that, but his Link buzzed again.

He might have ignored it, not needing to see another video of misery and pain, Geneva told him the message was a simple text message that had been flagged "urgent."

Giving his assent, a holographic sentence scrawled down his arm.

It began with a single bold word.

Run!

Chapter 46: Run!

Run! *The man who died in the accident belonged to a powerful family. They are here to kidnap and then torture you to death. Run!*

Fin's stone heart thudded excitedly.

Vengeance had come to him!

Before his eyes, the message autodeleted.

That simple observation saved his life.

It startled him enough to let his trained mind wrestle his savage heart into submission.

First an anonymous self-deleting video, and less than a minute later, a second secret message that could do the same?

Whoever these people were, they were not simple, which meant they were dangerous.

While he wanted nothing more than to immediately claim his own pound of flesh, Fin had spent decades learning to control the thing inside him. Mostly by promising it a better meal later if it would follow his lead now.

There would be blood, rivers of it, but ideally, it wouldn't be his.

Fin forced himself to think critically.

Messages didn't self-delete from your Link.

That didn't happen.

No one could reach into someone else's Link.

~DANGER~

Personal ownership was one of the sacrosanct laws coded into the digital DNA of the World AI.

It was one of the fundamental tenets of the Great Link, and the Great Link was the foundation of modern society.

The World AI assured complete privacy for each personal artificial intelligence on Earth. Not even during the War, with his high level Nexus access, had Fin been able to invade another person's Link.

That faith, that truth, was what made the whole system work.

Not trusting your AI was like not trusting your own eyes.

Which meant that the message must have come with a self-erasing program attached. That was something most people thought only existed in bad spy dramas.

Fin knew for a fact that the technology was real.

He'd used it himself during the War, but only because he worked for the Nexus.

No civilian should have access to that kind of program.

Who the hell had sent the message, and how did they have access to high grade military tech?

A second later, Fin admonished himself for wasting time on the wrong question.

Why were these people coming to kill him? Who was the guy in the truck? What kind of monster would torture *children* just to send him a message?

He knew he lived in the South, but was some red neck, white haired, yokel family really coming to "git him?"

It didn't even fully make sense that they blamed him for the other guy's death.

Fin was to blame, he knew that now, but he'd used a *magic* power to trigger the explosion.

There was no way they could know that.

At worst, they should think he was a survivor of an accident that the police report should have pinned on the asshole in the truck.

In spite of all of that, his friends had been tortured to death and the guy's family was coming to settle the score?

~REWARD~

In a hospital?

In broad daylight?

Disbelief or not, he was a black man in Georgia. Things were a lot better than they'd been in his granddad's time, but there were still some rules you followed.

If someone told you to run, you ran.

Hell, even if you just saw people running for some unknown reason, you ran!

Questions could come later.

The thing inside of him snarled in rebuttal, wanting nothing more than to choke these people and break their bones, but that would come later, at a time and place of his choosing. Not when all he had on was an open backed hospital gown that let his ass fly in the wind.

The good news was that after his night of cultivation, he was quite possibly literally in the best shape of his life.

Walking about last night, he'd moved and stretched in every way he could think to do so. Breaking through the Constitution threshold had fundamentally changed his body.

He'd even gone a bit masochistic in testing that theory.

His full health bar confirmed what the prompts had told him.

With his *Natural Healing* past the second Threshold, he regened 0.3% of his total health pool every twelve hours for each point he had in the Attribute. That was 6% each half-day.

Wanting to know how it worked, he'd grabbed a scalpel and had given himself a small nick on the back of his arm. That hadn't budged his health pool, but he had gotten a damage notification.

You have suffered 0 damage.*

An hour later, the small cut was gone like it had never been there. From a medical standpoint, it was amazing. From a battle standpoint, it meant he was much harder to kill.

The experiment had also helped him understand something.

By focusing on the asterisk, a small bit of knowledge had flooded into his mind.

Not all damage he took would decrease his health pool unless it passed a certain minimum amount. It would accumulate over time though. If he'd kept nicking himself, soon or later he'd have lost an HP.

If he didn't though, the damage he took would disappear once his *Natural Healing* was given enough time that he'd have regenerated a Health Point.

Understanding that made certain interesting ideas start to swirl in Fin's head.

Last night he hadn't had a chance to test any of them.

He had a feeling he was about to be given the chance.

He sprung out of bed and prepared to grab his clothes.

First order of business was to leave this room.

Thankfully, hospitals were mazes, and he was a doctor.

He didn't work at Atlanta General, but he'd been here before. With his knowledge of medical buildings, he might be able to sneak past these bastards.

And if he did run into them, well, then he did.

Fin wasn't afraid of that white-haired ahole's cousins. If they wanted a fight, then he was going to make the god damn chimichangas!

A moment later, the sound of drums filled his ears.

He'd heard them before. This time, they sounded more insistent and closer.

They were the drums of War.

Chapter 47: The Drums

FIRE

Da-da-da-da-da-da-da Dum-dum!

The drums. The drums. The drums beat of War!

The second chain in the Quest, Path of War, has been triggered!

Quest Grade: Radiant Gold

Quest Rank: Uncommon

Quest Type: Transformed PRIMORDIAL

You have begun the Quest: Second step on the Path of War

Due to your previous decisions, battle has found you once more. Once more your path will leave footsteps of blood. No matter your future choices, this Path will end in Death.

The House of the Ghost Lotus has come to capture, torture and kill you.

Escape their pursuit and show them the perils of trifling with the War Primordial!

Success Conditions: Evade capture or complete annihilation of your enemies

Rewards: Variable based on performance

Penalty for failure of Quest: Death, Testicular torture, further unknown consequences

This quest cannot be refused!

The first thing Fin noticed was the color of the window. It was a rich green rather than the white he'd seen on other quest windows. He had to assume it was because of the higher rank. The others had been *common* while this was *uncommon*.

That probably didn't bode well for his survival chances.

He read through the prompt focusing on words like "blood," "death," and "annihilation." He'd being lying if he said "testicular torture" didn't grab the lion's share of his attention.

Yeah.

Somehow he doubted his medical knowledge would let him slip out of the hospital.

Dammit!

Fin grabbed a pillowcase out of the closet and threw his meager belongings into it, including the Labyrinth coins. There was also a cardboard box he didn't recognize sitting on a shelf by the door.

It had his name on it though and it was from the Zon.

After a second, he realized what it was. A faint grin bushed across his face, and he threw it into another pillowcase.

He then faced a choice.

~REWARD~

He was only one cultivation round away from reaching twenty in his *Reaction* attribute. Increasing his Constitution and *Natural Healing* had both greatly increased his survivability. If *Reaction* did the same when he crossed the Threshold, it could really help him survive this quest.

The problem was, did he have time? Would he be better off just making a run for an exit?

Fin spent precious seconds making a decision. Ultimately, one thing swayed him more than anything else.

The quest.

The first step on the Path of War had put him in a coma.

He didn't think the danger of the second would be any less.

The quest had ranked up from *common* to *uncommon,* almost assuring that this was more dangerous.

He couldn't hope for a quick solution to pay off.

Fin needed all the strength he could get.

The initial plan was still the same. He needed to get out of this room.

Poking his head out into the hall, he didn't see anything amiss. Walking quickly down the hall, he got into a stairwell and began sprinting up. After three flights, he was barely winded, his new body showing it value once again.

It felt like he was twenty years younger.

He exited on the eighth floor.

It had most of the imaging equipment in the hospital.

That meant greater shielding in the walls than anywhere else.

That didn't help him with the security cameras in the hospital, but if they had access to the feeds, he was screwed no matter what.

Leaving the stairs, he went down a hallway and found an empty room. Going into the bathroom, he locked the door and sat down on the pot, bare cheeks on plastic.

"Gee," he called out softly.

A smiling red head's face appeared above his Link.

"How can I help you Fin?"

"Foxfire," he intoned before placing the band to his jaw.

His AI's face flashed out of existence; a preset battle protocol triggered by his key word. The faint luminescence of his Link winked off as well. To anyone looking, it would appear inert. Her voice carried into his ear, no longer audible to anyone else, but instead conducted through his jaw to trigger reverberations in his ear canal.

"Situation?" Geneva asked, all playful banter gone from her voice.

"Active pursuit by hostiles. Unknown number and capabilities. Assume deadly. Need escape route and monitoring of my position. Will be ready to move in ten mikes. Pain protocol allowed for communication. Issue warning to all allies. Forward all relevant information without filter."

"Understood," she conducted through his jaw.

Nothing else was said, but he knew she had already sent info packets to anyone still living in his close sphere of relationships.

It wasn't a long list.

She would also be scanning all social media and accessible data, including the public records for this building. By the time he was ready to move, she'd have compiled the information for him and discovered whatever she could on his pursuers.

Now he just needed to get out of dodge and let the cops deal with whoever was coming after him.

Speaking of which, "G, call the cops."

A holographic screen appeared above his wrist. It started connecting to the local law enforcement channel, but then the screen switched to only grey static.

Of everything that had happened in the last couple days, this was somehow one of the most surprising. More than messages didn't self-delete, the Great Link was always, always accessible.

Static just didn't happen.

"Geneva?"

"Sorry Fin, my connection to the Great Link is blocked."

Who, the fuck, were these people?

The Great Link blanketed the entire world.

Every inch, without exception.

It even worked if you were a mile underground.

"How?"

"Fin, someone triggered something similar to a war protocol for the hospital. All surveillance is down, and all local access to the Great Link has been severed. The doors to patients' rooms are being closed and secured as well."

His teeth clenched. No one should be able to do that!

There was no way it was a coincidence. The people that were coming after him had shut down hundreds of people's access to the Great Link just to capture him.

The Third War had changed everything.

The destroyed infrastructure and civilian casualties had been so devastating to the human race's potential that the World AI had decreed all rebuilds of strategic significance be built with safeguards against attack.

A major hospital certainly counted.

In fact, dozens of buildings in the city probably had war protocol capabilities, but nobody knew for sure because they were only triggered in the most dire of emergencies.

How did they think they were going to get away with this?

Fin had barely even heard of a war protocol being triggered in the Western Confederation in the last decade. Except for the occasional test…

He cursed silently.

His abduction was about to become a "random test."

People would complain, but no one would even remember a week later once the latest song dropped or the next big game was broadcast.

After they'd had a chance to massage the story, they might even spin this to blame him.

All the public needed to hear was about how some "hacker" had triggered the hospital's defenses, and they'd cheer the people that were coming to take him away.

"How are you talking to me?" Fin murmured.

If access to the Great Link was being blocked, his AI shouldn't be able to function either.

The response reverberated through his jaw.

"I was given a limited passkey to use the internal war protocol network. The key allows localized function, but I cannot connect to the Great Link.

Along with the key I was given a text message.

The message is as follows, 'I will help you if I can. If you can evade them long enough, the authorities should investigate why the war protocol was enacted.'

The sender did not include their name. The message self-deleted just like the first warning."

Fin's mind raced. While his pursuers had what seemed like Illuminati level connections, he had his own secret helper. Whoever it was, had sent him the initial message to run and was still trying to help, but seemed limited in the aid they could offer.

He'd take what he could get.

Besides, Fin had never planned to rely on someone else to save him.

His ass was his responsibility.

If he was going to make it out of this, he needed to be stronger.

That was why sitting with is balls dangling over an open toilet, he reentered his Cave of Whispers.

As soon as the cavern replaced his view of the bathroom, an exhilarated thrill shot through him.

Except for his sense of touch, he was cut off from the outside world.

While he was being hunted, he couldn't watch to see them coming.

It made no logical sense, but a savage smile crossed his face.

People could respond to stress and violence in any number of ways.

Personally, Fin never really felt so alive as when he put everything on the line!

He took a quick breath, settling himself. It wouldn't do to let his excitement distract him. So far, every successful step in cultivation had made the next one harder.

~REWARD~

If he lost his focus, not only would he waste time, but he might get another debuff locking his ability. He didn't want any handicaps seeing as how a bunch of angry Aryan hillbillies were coming to get him.

Fin focused and pulled on a mote of Fire Element from the darkness. A blazing tether undulated out of the dark. Just like with his last cultivation round with the golden Life sphere, he couldn't force it any closer than two feet away.

His thread shot out, and with practiced focus, he latched onto the tether after a few attempts.

Liquid fire flowed down his mana thread and entered his chest, filling him with heat. His eyes glowed the color of flame.

After what felt like an eternity, but was closer to ten minutes, the last of the mote drained into him. He waited for an impatient split second for the prompt to tell him the result.

A smile bloomed on Fin's face.

*You have cultivated **1 Fire** Element. +1 to tributary Attribute **Reaction***

*Your tributary Attribute, **Reaction,** has increased from **19** to **20***

*Congratulations! Your **Reaction** has risen above **20**. You have passed a **Minor Threshold**!*

*Reaction is now at **Threshold 2**!*

*+25% to the speed effects of **DEX** and **AGI** during the first 0.1 seconds of movement*

To those who didn't understand, the bonus from reaching the second Threshold might not seem like much. And a tenth of a second was no time at all.

To a student of combat and the human body, however, the bonus was nothing short of astounding.

King cobras carried neurotoxic venom that could kill an adult man in less than an hour. They also attacked at a speed that could be measured in hundredths of a second. That kind of speed was why humans had feared snakes for millennia.

Again and again, however, deadly cobras would lose to cats or mongoose. The deciding factor was speed. A mongoose could react just a few hundredths of a second faster. That discrepancy, less time than it took for a single heartbeat, was the difference between life and death.

A tenth of a second magnified that difference by a factor of ten.

It was the kind of difference that could make someone a world fighting champion!

With a savage grin, Fin felt much better about surviving this latest link in his quest.

Chapter 48: Charlamagnes

There was a secondary benefit from passing the Threshold. He'd unlocked a new Primary Attribute!

*By crossing the 2nd Threshold of Reaction, you have unlocked a new Primary Attribute: **Dexterity***

It looked like Dexterity, or Dex, had been unlocked because *Reaction's* Threshold bonus affected it. Fin wasted no time bringing up his abbreviated status page.

FIN EVERS		
STATS		
Health: 58/58	**Mana:** 22/22	**Stamina:** LOCKED
ATTRIBUTES		
LOCKED	**CONSTITUTION:** 24 *Threshold: 2* **Natural Healing:** 20 *Threshold: 2*	**LOCKED**

LOCKED	**AGILITY:** 15 *Threshold: 1* **Reaction:** 20 *Threshold: 2*	**DEXTERITY:** 14 *Threshold: 1*
LOCKED	LOCKED	**LUCK:** 14 *Threshold: 1*

His DEX was just slightly lower than his Agility. From the definition, it looked like it affected how his body moved as well.

__Dexterity (DEX)__ – This Primary Attribute determines your attack speed and affects your ability to dodge attacks. Also improves your ranged attack. Other unknown effects.

The differences in the AGI and DEX were subtle, but from what Fin could get, the first seemed to deal with large body movements and the second finer muscle control.

The line "other unknown effects" showed he was probably barely scratching the surface.

Finally, there was a slight bump to one of his Skills and his magicka creeped up again.

+2/8 __Mana Threads__ Skill Progression Point

+10 Magicka for improving a __tributary Attribute__ by a Minor Grade

Total Magicka: 2560

Fin didn't have time to fully process the Threshold reward or his Skill progression before he felt a strange pain on his wrist.

He immediately knew what it was.

Pain protocol.

~REWARD~

It was walking the line of what the World AI allowed, but Link settings could be pushed to the max to cause an unpleasant situation if a user instructed their personal AI to allow it.

Fin hadn't wanted to rely on simple vibrations, not with him being hunted.

Geneva must have something urgent to tell him. She wouldn't have disturbed him otherwise.

Dismissing the Cave of Whispers, he found himself back in the hospital bathroom, the door still blessedly closed. He brought his wrist up to his jaw and the pain stopped. Geneva's voice conducted through his jawbone again.

"Our unknown benefactor has been updating me on the movements of one of the groups hunting you. They have made it clear that this group is to be avoided at all costs.

The benefactor conveyed that the people hunting you have been searching the hospital floor by floor. They are about to reach the eighth. The recommendation is to ascend to a higher floor if you cannot evade detection or escape in some other way."

Fin nodded to himself.

He'd been planning on changing location now anyway.

The Threshold bonus was just as good as he'd hoped.

His current plan was to make his way to the most distant stairwell. With comms down, the people hunting him wouldn't be able to coordinate well. If he could fight his way past whatever group was blocking that stairwell, maybe he could race ahead of the rest of them and make his way out onto the street.

After searching eight floors they had to be spread out by now.

It was time to fight back.

Fin shot up to his feet, full of conviction, and promptly almost fell.

With a curse, he realized what had just happened.

His body had accelerated upward faster than he'd been expecting causing him to be slightly off balance.

It was his new *Reaction* speed.

He'd expected to have to make some adjustments, but it made enough of a difference that even standing up was different?

He shook his head. He'd figure it out on the fly.

Geneva didn't exaggerate, at least not when battle protocol was enacted. If she said he had less than a minute, then he needed to move.

Poking his head out of his doorway, he saw the hallway was empty. A couple patients peeked out of the windows of a neighboring room.

Fin turned right, heading for the stairwell he'd picked out. He turned left, then right again. He was only a dozen yards away.

Walking was strange, but only when he started his stride. Once he got going, there was no difference from any other time he'd walked in his life.

Fin peeked around the last corner and, seeing the hallway empty, jogged towards the stairway door, and hopefully his freedom.

That was the very moment that six men and women wearing black t-shirts turned the far corner and saw him. All of them were holding weapons. Two had hammers, three retractable batons and one had a bat.

They all grinned simultaneously and started rushing towards him.

He didn't think it was to be friends.

Six isn't so bad, he thought.

Which was when four more black shirts shouted from the *other* end of the hallway and started running towards him too.

Fin brought both fists up and cracked his neck with a sharp twist.

"Let's go."

Chapter 49: Oh Boy

Fin ran at the first six he'd seen. They were closer to the stairwell, and he needed to thin them out before the other four got to him. Seeing as how they were all making a crazy racket, he might have more company in minutes.

The distance closed between them in what felt like an instant.

For the first time in years, he fully released his control over his emotions.

For love, he'd restrained what he was.

Now, he was ready to let it all go.

If this was his last day, he would rage.

The leading man swung his hammer at chin level, looking to knock Fin down with a single, iron haymaker.

In that moment, Fin experienced what it meant to have a *Reaction* time twice what average men and women would ever harness.

The hammer flew at Fin's face almost faster than could be tracked with the naked eye right up until he started to react. Then, for a split second, exactly 0.1 seconds in fact, time seemed to slow. He was able to react faster than ever before, and his body obeyed.

With only a faint exertion, Fin ducked under the hammer swing and threw a straight right cross into the throat of the woman behind his attacker.

She flew back into the people behind her, and Fin used the recoil to begin a new action. Planting his right foot, he threw his elbow backwards. It connected just as the hammer wielder was turning.

As effective as a battering ram, his elbow slammed into the chin of the man that had targeted his.

The guy dropped like a sack of potatoes.

Five seconds in, two down.

He couldn't see how this could go wrong!

Of course, the next ten goons that piled out stairwell might do it.

Dammit!

Fin kicked the man he'd just knocked out, because he could, and then got back into the fight. The choking woman had been thrown to the side of the hall by her compadres and all three ran at him at once. Fin ducked a baton swing, blocked a fist from the second man, but the third kicked him in the side.

You have suffered 0 damage.*

Oh yeah baby.

He threw an uppercut at his first attacker, and his fist accelerated before the guy could respond. He was lifted off his feet and tossed back a full foot.

Fin had already thrown two jabs at the second man, getting him in the chest and nose. Blood splattered and Fin went low, slamming a fist into the thigh of the third man.

Cries of pain filled the air.

The four men from behind reached him all at once. One tackled him, taking Fin down to the ground. Before they landed, Fin slammed an elbow down on the guy's shoulder, shattering his clavicle. He released his grip with a cry, but the other three were there raining down blows.

You have suffered 0 damage.*

You have suffered 0 damage.*

Damage has accumulated! -1 HP

The other ten arrived and began kicking him on the ground.

~REWARD~

He took the punishment for long seconds. Even an increased *Reaction* time didn't help when there was a pile on. They kicked and hit him on the ground as the damage began to accumulate.

You have suffered 0 damage.*

You have suffered 0 damage.*

Damage has accumulated! -1 HP

You have suffered 0 damage.*

Damage has accumulated! -1 HP

Damage has accumulated! -1 HP

The worst was when one the fuckers stabbed him in the back!

-3 HP from piercing damage

The blade wasn't huge, but as prison taught, even one inch could be too much.

Fin let out a shout and they all pulled back a bit, leaving the blade sticking out of him.

Seeing a guy stabbed could have that kind of impact on a fight.

That's when they made a mistake.

They checked to see if he was dead.

One woman grabbed handful of his fro. Before she could yank his head up, he reared back and launched a meaty fist right into her pussy!

She let out a sound that was half wolf howl, half dying sheep, and then collapsed to the ground, clutching her swelling genitalia.

Fin had already grabbed another man's leg and then bit the shit out of him.

"Oh my god! He's biting me!"

The Charlamagnes learned something that day.

~DANGER~

Fin fought dirty.

With blood in his mouth, he clawed his way up the man he'd just bit, while the guy screamed like a bitch. Fin took two shots to the kidney as he did.

Damage has accumulated! -1 HP

A low kick to his attacker's ankle snapped the bone inward with a crunch.

One more down.

The guy Fin was man handling slammed a hammer into his side. It hurt but the angle wasn't enough to break a rib. He lost another health point though, proving he wasn't a superhero.

-1 HP from blunt damage

A quick check of his total health still brought a shark's smirk to Fin's face.

Health: 41/58

After fighting more than a dozen armed dickhead and dickettes, taking out a half dozen of them, fighting his way out of an LA style beatdown, *and* getting stabbed in the back, he still had more than 70% of his health.

Not a superhero, but close enough!

Fin wrapped his fingers around the man's throat and put his back to the wall. He spun his dance partner around until the guy was cheeks to meat and used him as a human shield.

Digging his fingers into the guy's larynx made him panic enough that stripping away the hammer was easy.

Fin swung the hammer back and forth wildly to keep the others at bay. When they pulled back just a bit, he spat some blood at them then slammed the

~REWARD~

hammer into his hostage's hip. The black shirted douche gave a choked howl, mainly because Fin was still choking him.

The doc turned terminator released his grip on the man's larynx and proceeded to unheal the shit out of him. Three hammer blows fell on the man's shoulder, back and neck.

Each time the hammer fell, Fin felt meat compressing and tearing under his tender ministrations.

The gang members pulled back in alarm.

It wasn't just the ferocity or savagery. These were men and women of violence. It wasn't even the wild joy on Fin's blood face as he rained down hammer blows.

It was the speed.

From their perspective, Fin's arm was raised in the air, there was a blur, then it was embedded in the body of their unfortunate friend. Another blur, and the hammer was primed again.

Blood blossomed under each hit.

Leaving the man sobbing in his own piss, Fin looked at all of them, relishing the fear in their eyes.

He slowly and deliberately reached back and pulled the knife out of his own back.

-1 HP from piercing damage

Holding the blade in one hand and the hammer in the other, he took a deep, loud breath, before smiling again, blood coating every tooth.

"I hope you bitches aren't getting tired."

Chapter 50: Sucker Punch

AIR

One, two, three stiff jabs and the last black shirted bastard was laid out. Seriously, where did these guys shop?

Fin was panting at this point. His hospital gown was splashed with a dozen people's blood. And his health was down to half.

Behind him, a sum total of twenty-two people, all from a gang called the Charlamagnes for some reason, a couple of them had kept shouting that, were laid out in states ranging from unconscious to FUBAR.

Twenty-three if you counted the one he'd just put down.

Right when Fin had thought he was in the clear, three more goons had piled out of the stairwell.

This last thug had been a bit tougher.

One of the others had called him Hector before Fin slashed that thug's throat open, leaving him choking in his own blood.

At the end, it was just Hector and Fin still standing, and their fight had ranged the entire length of the hallway.

Hector had known how to throw down, and he'd used a brutal mix of street brawling and Krav Maga. Honestly, there were times over the minutes long back and forth where Fin thought he might not win, but he seemed to avoid hits faster than even his increased *Reaction* time should have allowed.

What neither man knew was that having unlocked both Agility and Dexterity had allowed Fin's Actions and Essence to tap into the new metalaws of Earth. The Labyrinth itself helped him dodge certain attacks and improved the speed he launched his own.

Without a connection to the Labyrinth, Hector never stood a real chance.

336

At long last, even with blood running down his body in more places than he could count, Fin was the only one still on his feet.

Now all he had to do was make it back to the stairs.

"Bitch! Are you going to move, or do I need to move you?"

That shout made Fin peek around the corner.

At the far end of the neighboring hall stood his ICU doc, Dr Yinying, staring down several tall men and women in suits.

They all had blond hair so pale it was almost white.

Fin remembered that cocky crispy critter had the same features before the explosion. Unless there was a Norwegian convention in town, the pale blonds that were leaning over her were the ones looking for him.

"Guess my redneck theory wasn't too far off," he huffed. "They've got to be sister fuckers to all come out looking the same."

Part of him wanted to beat the ever-loving crap out of the people coming for him, anything to let out more of his pent up anger and pain, but his trained mind overcame his bloody nature.

Life wasn't a movie.

He was knocked all to hell. Fin was the last one standing, but it had cost him. If his stamina had been unlocked, he was pretty sure it would have to be low. And that was with none of those black shirted jokers having a gun. All he could think was that they'd been given orders to take him alive.

The rules might be different for the boy band crew yelling at Sola.

He'd watched enough kung-fu movies to know the elite squad when he saw it.

It was time for a strategic retreat. The stairway had to be more or less clear at this point. He just needed to get to it. Even if he ran into more black shirts, as long as he could blow past them, he'd be home free.

Yup, time to get out of here.

Keep it calm, he thought. Keep it cool. They don't even know I'm here. I just need to tip toe away. I'm just one more patient, no different from any other.

The cynical part of his mind chimed in that all the other patients were in their rooms due to the alert.

Then it added that he was a bleeding black man without pants standing over the bodies of what had to be their henchmen.

Don't think about that, he chided that part of himself.

Be positive.

They hadn't seen you yet.

All I need to do is turn around and make it to the st-

That was when one of the black shirts, that he'd thought was down for the count, made his move.

The guy had just been playing possum.

He dove at Fin, pushing them both out into the hallway intersection.

Fin immediately landed a heavy punch. He hit the guy so hard, that his skull bounced off the linoleum floor.

Sadly, the damage was done.

"Jürgen, there he is!"

Fin craned his head to the right and muttered, "Shit."

Chapter 51: Intro: Klaus

With a pissed off grimace, Fin started running.

The moment he moved, he felt that strange acceleration again, but after the fight he was more used to it. Rather than stumble, it let him move a yard almost immediately. He didn't slow down. Instead, he poured on the speed while his fists tightened.

Turning the corner, he looked over his shoulder at his pursuers again.

My god, did they manufacture these people from an Aryan blueprint?

It really did look like they were a bunch of extras from the village of the damned.

They started chasing him.

Let them come. Once he was done with them, they'd-

Fall over like they were drunk?

"What the deuce?"

In the space of a second, the men and women coming after him had all wiped out.

Some fell. Others flat out faceplanted. One almost did a backflip, his patent leather shoes flying up above his head before slamming into the ground.

Fin was so shocked at the ridiculousness of what he was seeing, a bunch of Aryans wearing black suits straight out of a Yakuza movie, falling over each other like a Bennie Hill routine, that he watched them fall, refall and curse for a couple seconds.

~DANGER~

As he did, Fin was finally able to understand what was happening. The floor beneath them was strangely shiny. On a hunch, he switched his gaze to *Mana Sight* and, lo and behold, there was something on the ground that glowed with blue light.

Switching his sight off, he stared again.

Was that a thin sheet of ice?

Whatever it was, it had made the ground almost frictionless.

As he watched, he saw Sola stand off to the side, a barely concealed grin on her face. The man that had screamed at her was still standing next to her.

That guy was *not* smiling.

Fin was about to take off again, leaving his pursuers to their slapstick predicament, when it happened. The hilarity, and the falls, came to an end when one man glowed white for a moment before his body swelled to twice its previous size.

The discount Hulk raised one basketball sized fist before slamming it into the ground. The ice, and the ground beneath, shattered. An impact crater formed, a full two feet in diameter.

Fin didn't need to see anything else. He took off running again, hearing something that sounded like, "I am Klaus," echo behind him.

***

The cracks in the ice spread down the hall, turning the thin sheet of ice into countless shards, fixing the slipping problem. One of the men looked towards Sola in anger, but she just raised her hands in innocence, and asked in mock concern, "Are you alright?"

Jürgen bared his teeth. He was sure Sola was the cause of the ice but had no way to prove it. The Wave had blessed him with his own Ability, which was why he'd been given charge of this operation, but that didn't help him prove she'd broken the terms of the wergild.

Focusing on what he could control, he grabbed one of his men, "You, you and you. Run down through the halls and tell everyone that the target has been sighted on the eighth floor."

~REWARD~

He pointed to another pair, "You two stay with me. Everyone else, pursue. On my authority, the rules of engagement have changed. Weapons free. Powers free. Injury allowed. Must be taken alive."

The men and women of his strike team smiled vindictively. Three ran down the stairs behind them to gather the rest of their people. Almost everyone else ran off in pursuit of Fin leaving only a pair to stay behind.

Jürgen turned to Sola. Any frustration or consideration in his voice had withered, leaving behind only barely controlled rage and deadly intent, "Get in my way again, and I swear by the Lotus, I will kill you."

Staring up at his pale blond face, Sola wasn't impressed, "Maybe you should focus on completing your mission and not blaming an innocent woman. If all of your kill squads can't catch one injured civilian, or even keep from falling over," Sola smiled broadly, "well, I wouldn't want to be you later. How does your patriarch deal with failure?"

Jürgen couldn't help it. He swallowed hard at the thought, his mouth suddenly dry.

With pure spite, Jürgen tapped a code into his Link. The holocam reappeared. The tone in his voice turned completely respectful, "Sir, we are on site, but the local Shadow, Sola Yinying, is not being helpful. In fact, I believe she is actively helping our quarry escape. She may have even used an ability to obstruct us. Could you speak with her superior? There is a high probability that she has gone rogue. I am sending a video file of her crimes now."

Jürgen flicked his finger towards one of his subordinates whose own Link pinged.

"Go down to the ground floor and send that video to one of our teams outside. Make sure it gets forwarded to the patriarch immediately."

This time, it was Sola's face who dropped, much to Jürgen's delight. War protocol might block access to the Great Link, but line of sight data transfers were still possible.

The hologram above this Link winked out and he turned back to Sola with an expression that could only be smarmy.

"Why don't we just wait here?" he suggested without it being an actual suggestion. He stepped between her and the hallway Fin had fled down. "We can keep one another company until our superiors let us know what they would like to do."

"I go where I like," Sola retorted, "especially in my own territory." A blue glow surrounded her left hand again, and this time, she didn't try to hide it.

"I'm afraid," he replied, undaunted, "I have to insist."

An orange glow kindled in the center of his pupils, like a glimpse of hellfire at the end of a poorly spent life.

***

Fin ran as quickly as he could towards the elevators. Not for the first time, he thanked whoever might be listening that his Constitution had passed the second Threshold.

If he still had the injuries from the crash and explosion, he'd have only managed half this speed. As it was, he was pretty sure he was 20% faster than he'd been at what he'd thought was peak health only a week ago.

Even with the injuries he'd suffered just now with the Charlamagnes, he was almost flying down the halls.

This was the first time he'd really opened up with his new body.

Crossing the Constitution threshold had changed him on a fundamental level.

As he sprinted down the hall, he realized there hadn't been anything in the Threshold prompt that said he'd run faster or increase his physical capabilities. Which meant that the amazing increased output was due to the hidden injuries that had been healed. Damage that didn't even qualify as *common* ranked Injuries.

Winning with health, he thought with a grin as he ran from the cast of Schindler's List.

He still wanted to bash all their faces in, but after seeing that guy shatter the floor with a single punch, he knew he couldn't take them all down.

That guy had *transformed* and had busted through his clothes like the hulk!

Fin clearly wasn't the only one changed by the Wave.

And unless he missed his guess, Sola had been given an Ability as well.

Both her ice, and discount Kevin Sorbo, seemed a lot more suited to direct combat than his own Whisper ability, *epic* ranked or not.

And if both of them had powers, then how did he know everyone chasing him didn't?

For now, there was no question about what needed to happen.

It was time to get out of dodge.

He came to a stairwell and threw the door open. There he was confronted with a binary option, up or down.

"Had to be on the eighth floor," he cursed.

With gritted teeth he started running up. There was no way he'd make it all the way to the ground floor ahead of his pursuit. Maybe he could lose them on a higher floor and double back down another stairwell.

He climbed up a flight, pulling hard on the handrail to accelerate himself up.

Interestingly, his improved *Reaction* seemed to kick in with every step. Fin could basically hear the wind whistle by him as he climbed.

Which also winded him faster than before, but his improved health seemed to help with that as well. At a faster pace than he could have sprinted up the stairs a week ago, but with only half the exhaustion, he reached the tenth-floor landing and ran out onto the floor.

He quickly pulled the door closed behind him, slowing it at the last moment to muffle the sound. The door closed just before he heard the stairwell door on the eighth slam open. A split second after, the door to the ninth banged open as well, showing he'd been lucky not to exit there.

Shouted voices filled the stairwell.

Fin ran.

Behind him, half of the strike team found themselves on the stairs, trying to figure out which floor he'd gotten off on. Cursing, they split up, excluding the floors they'd just left. Three of the suited men and women chose the tenth floor. One ran to the right and the other two chose the left.

Fin ran as fast as he could, leaving a series of patients staring at him from their rooms.

One thing he found was that his extra acceleration didn't kick in during a sustained flight. It was only when he first performed an action that it manifested. That was actually good news. He doubted he'd be able to run if he was constantly fighting against a lifetime of instincts.

He moved past the elevators, hitting the down button. A second later, he banged his fist into the button again.

"Worth a try," he muttered.

Even knowing about the War Protocol, he'd hoped they hadn't shut down all the shafts.

Once again, he had to ask, who were these guys?

They were in the middle of Atlanta in the middle of the day.

They had to realize there was a chance they wouldn't get away with performing a manhunt in a busy hospital.

He started running once more. Maybe a service elevator would still be working. If not, he'd try the stairs again. Hell, he'd jump down a laundry chute. If he slowed his descent, maybe he'd hobble away with just a broken leg.

It was better than the testicular torture his quest had mentioned.

Meanwhile, a faint smile was graced his face without even him realizing it, enjoying the challenge and once again walking on the edge.

I can do this, he thought to himself. All I need is a little luck.

"There he is!"

"Fuck you luck!"

Fin looked behind him and saw a man and woman in black suits. The woman was pointing at him. He threw up his own finger in response, but he went with the middle one.

Both took off in pursuit, the man shouting urgently into his Link. Comms were down, local functions still worked. In this case, as a megaphone.

"He's on the tenth floor. The tenth floor!"

The broadcasted sound was so loud it echoed, more than enough to reach any Lotus on the stairs.

Everyone who heard the message used their own megaphones as well, bringing all the Lotus, and any still conscious Charlamagnes, to Fin's location. Once they got to the tenth floor, they spread out, cutting off all avenues of escape.

Jürgen and Sola ended their stalemate as well, rushing towards the stairs.

The man and woman chasing Fin grinned at each other as they ran. They worked together often and shared a love of violence. More than once, they'd spent wonderful afternoons making small cut after small cut on their victims, treasuring the scarlet and pain.

They were main branch members of the Lotus and had benefitted from strengthening rituals before even their birth.

Neither had ever been sick and both had grown up stronger, healthier and smarter than the average person because of their advantages. These innate benefits had been compounded by Spartanesque training from an early age. Added together, it meant, at least in their minds, that they were superior in every way to the sheep that thought themselves people.

The fact that the Wave had Enabled them had only cemented their feelings of manifest destiny.

The fact that the patriarch had sent so many squads to grab one civilian was ludicrous to them both, but they certainly weren't stupid enough to voice that out loud. Besides, Jürgen had given them permission to test their new powers out, something they were both dying to do. The two of them, and the Lotus Familia as a whole, believed in strength and one law above all others.

The weak were meat, and the strong do eat.

The two raced down the hall, and the man jested, "Fifty credits to whoever bags him."

"Ha. You already owe me twenty!"

"You know I'm good for it."

"I know I'll take it out of your ass if you don't pay."

"Promises. Promises."

The sound of their laughter echoed through the hallway as they turned the corner.

That made it all the more satisfying for Fin when that laughter turned to curses and moans. Once he'd been spotted again, Fin had no illusions about being able to outrun his two pursuers. They had surely called in his location and others must be on their way to even now.

If he ran, they'd drive him into the waiting arms of their buddies, fish in a net. That made his next course of action easy. If he couldn't run, he'd have to fight. His only hope was to take these two out fast, then he could hide and hopefully slip the net while they searched.

Right after turning the corner, he'd grabbed an IV stand and waited on his knees. Hearing them joke about taking his freedom made anger surge in his heart, but he steadied his breathing.

His timing had to be perfect.

Ignoring the stares from the nearby nurses and patients peeking their heads out of their rooms, Fin listened to the two bastards get closer, their steps growing louder. At the exact right moment, before they'd even rounded the corner, he shoved the pole out and succeeded in completely ensnaring the man's legs.

As he went down, he collapsed into the woman's, tripping her as well.

Of the two of them, the woman went down harder. She impacted so heavily Fin would be surprised if she hadn't fractured her jaw. Blood spurted from her mouth. The other man fell hard as well but managed to twist and land on his side.

Before he even hit the ground and Fin was on him.

As soon as he'd thrust the pole out, Fin had braced his leg against the wall. Like a loaded spring, he propelled himself toward the man that had been chasing him. With his hand in knife blade position, he jabbed his fingers into the man's pale throat. Unlike the woman, the man had time to see him coming, but it didn't matter.

Fin used his increased *Reaction* intentionally. To anyone looking, it looked like his whole body blurred. Before his target could even raise his arms in defense, Fin was on him.

The darker man's fingers hit his target's adam's apple. There was a moment of resistance, then his knife hand depressed the cartilage until there was a small *crunch*. It wasn't enough to completely block the windpipe, but the man was left gasping and flailing on the ground.

Like most fights, it ended in seconds.

A patient screamed from inside their room. Someone else yelled, "Security! Security! Someone get help!"

No one actually rushed to get involved themselves.

Who would?

Right after incapacitating his first target, Fin twisted his body. At the same time, he reached for the metal bedpan he'd set aside while preparing his ambush.

~REWARD~

Damn I wish I'd kept that hammer.

A bedpan was a crappy weapon, but it was hard and metal, and when your options came from a hospital cart, you did the best you could. What was important was that his ambush had worked. Once he bashed this bitch's face in, he'd-

"Oh shit!"

As Fin turned his head, he was shocked by what he saw.

Not the anticipated sight of a woman moaning and partially concussed on the ground, but instead a foot of gunmetal grey blade slicing through the air.

It was coming fast enough that he had no chance to dodge.

At least, that would have been the case a week ago.

Today, for the iota of time that time seemed slowed, he was able to watch the shining length of steel flow towards his neck with what seemed to be glacial inevitability.

The woman grinned fiercely knowing Fin would be too slow to react.

Except that he wasn't!

With a smile forming on his own face, Fin's body moved faster than he could even think.

Once again, his arm blurred slightly.

He'd thought he'd understood what his new *Reaction* threshold could do. It made him accelerate faster, right? That was only part of it.

Fin's hand started moving faster than should have been possible. Everyone knew their own body well, but anyone that had been combat trained knew their body intimately.

Most normal people could be surprised by sudden bouts of strength or speed in times of stress. They thought they were exceeding their limits, when really, they were just tapping into their true potential for the first time.

Fin wasn't like most people. The training he'd undergone during the War had unlocked his potential years before. His superiors and instructors had then pushed him to his limits more times than he could count. It was only through countless hours of sweat and pain that he'd truly surpassed his previous boundaries.

Every inch he'd progressed was earned through sweat and blood.

Every inch he moved forward was twice as difficult as the one before.

He wasn't an Olympian, but compared to a normal person, he was exceptional.

It all meant he had much better control over his body than the average Joe. He could move faster and more surely than most. His control let him do things that others would be astounded by. It also meant that he wouldn't have sudden surprising bursts of strength that exceeded his expectations. He knew exactly what his limits were.

Except, in this moment, his body was proving that he knew exactly dick.

As the dagger edge loomed larger in his sight, his body reacted faster than he'd ever moved before, even during the last fight against the Charlamagnes. Until now, his unconscious mind had still rebelled at this new reality he found himself in, limiting his performance.

In this current moment of life and death, the Element infusing his body combined with a lifetime of muscle memory, and for the first time fully accessed his capabilities. Each muscle in his body worked in conjunction to increase his speed.

If in the past it had taken months of work to expand his potential by an inch, in that split second, he moved a foot. His body jerked back and his head up. The woman's dagger passed under his chin, nearly close enough to shave.

Time sped back up.

Fin fell back across the body of the choking man, off balance, but still alive. The woman stared at him incredulously, not sure what had just happened. She was sure she was about to get a kill. She didn't care about her orders.

Nobody hurt Hans!

But then her target's body had blurred for just a split second, and somehow, he'd avoided her attack. That moment of shock cost her.

She wasn't able to dodge when Fin heel kicked her squarely in the mouth. Blood flew, and her front teeth, already loosened by her fall, shot back into her mouth, leaving a gaping, bloody hole.

She fell back with an angered cry.

Her partially fractured jaw well and truly cracked with a *click* that filled her head with battery acid.

Even in her pain, she remained a true warrior and swung her dagger at him again. She was not a machine, however. This attack was just a swipe of an injured animal, not the strike of a trained killer. Fin easily pulled his leg out of the way and rolled back.

The blond woman braced against one wall of the hallway, struggling to stand as quickly as possible. The stabbing pain in her head was making the edges of her vision blur. Fin elbowed the gasping man in the sternum making sure he stayed down a bit longer. The pained choking grew even more strained, and the man writhed on the ground, clutching at his throat. Fin's hand brushed something hard, and his eyes darted to the man's waist.

Who the hell with walked around in a bespoke suit with a dagger at their waist?

Who the *fuck* were these people?

Fin grabbed it from the man's belt sheath as he scrambled to his feet. The blade was identical to the one the woman was holding, a foot of double-edged steel with a simple bar crossguard.

In a second, he assessed it. This was an actual weapon, not a tool. Its purpose was to take human life. You wouldn't find it on a soldier, only a killer.

He stopped himself from mentally asking once more who was hunting him.

Fin and the blond woman got to their feet at nearly the same time. She stood on the other side of the hallway. It had been less than a minute since they'd met, but they'd already nourished a lifetime of hatred.

They locked eyes, his own bright and cold in his dark face, stars in the night. She stared back with fury, lip torn and mouth bloody, a large bruise forming on the anemic skin of her cheek. The left side of her mouth was slightly open, forced that way by her broken jaw. Her confederate continued to choke at their feet, too preoccupied with trying to breathe to do anything else.

With Fin's own gaze reflected in her eyes, murder dwelt there twice.

Fin knew he didn't have much time before the rest of the Icelandic soccer team got there. As it was, he was lucky he'd only come across two of them. If there had been a third, his little ambush would never have worked, and this would already be over. Killing these two hadn't been the original plan, but now that blades were out, he wasn't going to hold back.

Fin didn't know what her orders had been before they tussled, but there was no mistaking the look she was giving him now.

Only one of them was going to survive this.

~*DANGER*~

It was also clear now how powerful his improved *Reaction* could be.

He could use that to end her.

The only problem was he now knew something was keeping him from really using his new power when he went on the offensive. The best-case scenario would be for her to attack. Then, he could use his improved reflexes to catch her off guard. The problem was, time was on her side.

How could he get here to attack him?

Fin's face shifted, no longer cold.

The woman blinked. Was that excitement in his eyes?

It was.

Fin used *Violent Delights* for the first time.

Time froze.

He could not move, but he was able to see his Mark manifest on his forearm.

The bronze tattoo came into existence, jagged metal crowned with three drops of dark red blood.

One of those drops left his arm and splashed onto the forehead of the woman he was facing. Her eyes turned a monochromatic red, the pupil and irises replaced by a solid orb of crimson.

The effect faded away, leaving her outwardly unchanged.

The prompt Fin received proved that was not the case.

*You have made a **Hated Enemy**! **+20%** damage. You are now **Hated**!*

*Warning! A **Hated Enemy** will grow stronger through their enmity. **+10%** damage against you per day.*

Fin would have blinked if he could. He didn't know about that second part.

Time resumed.

From the woman's perspective, nothing had happened.

~REWARD~

She was just flooded with an intense hate for the man in front of her. The feeling dwarfed the murderous anger she'd felt before. Never, in her entire life, had she hated someone like she hated this mongrel!

A feeling of loathing thick enough to choke her overtook the woman. The sudden onrush of emotion, mixed with the despair she was already experiencing, short circuited her mind. A Pseudo-Mortal simply wasn't equipped to immediately process a magical alteration of their emotions. Fin didn't know it, but against most on Earth, the hatred inspired by *Violent Delights* was effectively an attack against the soul itself.

All Fin knew was that he'd never seen someone so easy to read.

The internal dissonance and quasi-stun debuff the woman suffered hadn't been Fin's intention, and he didn't even notice. Instead, he deliberately stared at her ruined mouth with a cocky grin, "Look, just because a menstruating hippo sat on your face, doesn't mean-"

Sadly, the world would never know how that zinger ended because she lunged at him with a mad scream. With her mouth all the way open, it became obvious why she sounded so crazy.

Half of her tongue had been bitten off.

The grin stayed on Fin's face, but his eyes remained deadly serious.

When most people said they didn't see a person's sex or race, they were usually full of shit.

He was an exception. He truly didn't see her as a woman.

All he saw was an asshole he was about to kill.

Fin swung his own blade to match her attack.

The weapons met, and he was surprised to find that her strength was the same as his, if not even a bit stronger. He had to outweigh her by a good thirty to forty pounds, and had three inches on her, but it was all he could do to hold her back when they locked blades.

She screamed at him over their braced daggers, blood spraying on his face, before she pulled back and swiped at him again. The two traded blows, the daggers making a steady staccato of *ting ting ting.* As they continued to battle, Fin's smile began to slip.

He was no stranger to knife fighting.

He'd hoped for a quick stab to incapacitate the woman, but he quickly found that not only was she was as strong as him, she was also more skilled with the blade and possibly a bit faster.

It was true that Fin wasn't at his peak.

His newly healed body had increased his physical capabilities, and his *Reaction* was incredible, but it was like getting into a sportscar for the first time.

He wasn't used to the power at his disposal.

When fighting the Charlamagnes, this hadn't been a problem. Not only was his body literally superior, but he was a better fighter than any of them. They may have served during the War, most did, but few had gotten the training that Fin had received.

At the end of the day, they were thugs.

This woman was different.

She was like him.

She was a killer.

That was why the disconnect between his mind and body was getting in the way this time.

The disjunction was small, but in a high intensity fight like this, even a 1% reduction in prowess could be deadly. As it was, the disruption between his new body and ingrained fighting instincts allowed his opponent to force a perilous stalemate as they traded blows.

To his surprise, what he was hoping would be a quick takedown was turning into a drawn out battle.

Fin wasn't the only one taken aback. Even in her maddened and pain addled state, his opponent couldn't help but be shocked.

How is he doing this?

Even when she increased the tempo of her attacks, he was able to keep up with her. Who was he?

In the House of the Ghost Lotus, she ranked 35th out of hundreds in short blade fighting, but this injured man, who was supposed to be a nobody with no backing, was blocking her every attempt to claim his life. The shame of it nearly drove her mad and brought even more fury to her blows.

Despite her increased ferocity, no matter how quickly she attacked Fin, for a split second, it felt like time stood still. In that fraction of a moment, he was able to decide on the right response. It wasn't that he was moving quicker the whole time, but it felt like his body was reacting as soon as he thought about something.

Reacting faster let him accelerate a bare centimeter before she did. In this fight where their blades were clashing at least once a second, his faster reaction time made all the difference.

It didn't make him a god, though.

After only a minute, he was already bleeding from a few small cuts that he'd just barely been able to deflect.

The sight of blood drove her even harder.

Fin met her bloodlust with his own, but was not at all happy about the messages he was getting.

*You have suffered a **miniscule** laceration. -0 HP*

*You have suffered a **minuscule** laceration. -0 HP*

Damage has accumulated! -1 HP

*You have suffered a **minor** laceration. -1 HP*

His improved body and unlocked Health were helping him, but unlocked HP didn't make him a god. The cuts he was suffering would chisel down his health if this continued on and he was already below 50%.

Even worse, he discovered something about her.

Fin had landed a few small cuts himself as they fought. That was to be expected. The first rule of a knife fight was that everyone in the fight got cut.

It turned out though, that she was cheating!

With no small amount of irritation, Fin discovered her shirt and suit weren't just tailored to look good.

They were made out of nanovar.

Another invention that came out of the Third War.

It was an extremely light weight synthetic material comprised of tightly interlocking nanotubules. Nanovar had high resistance to puncturing, pressure, heat and was poorly conductive, so it even provided some protection from shocks.

It was some of the best body armor available. A shirt woven from nanovar could stop a bullet just as well as 3rd-gen Kevlar but was as light as cotton.

Despite all of that, it was rarely seen. That was because the expenditure to make nanovar armor was insane. The suit the woman was wearing probably cost over 100,000 credits. You could buy a small house for what she was wearing.

Almost no one had the resources to go around Wick'd.

Who *were* these people?

No matter what the background of these blond bastards, Fin had bigger problems. This woman was better than him in a knife fight. She was also wearing body armor that he'd only be able to pierce with a full strength thrust at exactly the right angle. Even then, he might not penetrate too deeply.

This was all a good recipe for a shit sundae, and they both knew it. As they continued to trade blows, the ruined gash of her mouth opened in a bloody leer. She had reinforcements coming, and she knew she just needed to keep him occupied until they arrived. With the advantages she had, this battle was a foregone conclusion.

Even the man wheezing on the ground looked to be recovering over the past few seconds.

Fin knew he had to finish this fast, but he'd run out of moves!

In that moment it occurred to him. Why not flip the board?

Which was why Fin did something that you-just-didn't-do. He swung his free hand at her blade.

The look on her face showed a malevolent anticipation and she eagerly accelerated her weapon.

Unlike in the movies, you couldn't just grab a knife with your free hand. Even a basic kitchen knife could cut through flesh if it was moving fast enough. The daggers they were fighting with were anything but basic, and the edges of the foot long blades were probably sharp enough to slice falling silk.

Trying to grab someone else's dagger was almost always a deadly mistake. It would savage the muscles, slice through tendons and leave your hand a mangled mess faster than you could immobilize the moving blade. The resultant blood loss would make the end of the fight a forgone conclusion.

That is, unless you could match the angle of your hand perfectly to the angle of the attacking blade. Then you could knock your enemy's weapon to the side and create a small opening to counterattack.

Even a few degrees off and you'd be maimed.

With such a small degree of success, only an idiot would risk this.

Or a courageous man with a heightened reaction time…

Or an idiot with heighted reaction time.

The woman's dagger flew at Fin. With only a fraction of a second to respond, his wrist twisted to the precise degree required for his knife hand to parallel her blade. His hand blurred. To her shock and his elation, her weapon was batted away.

You have suffered a **small** laceration. -1 HP

It had cut a two-inch slice of skin free from the back of his hand. Her weapon continued past his wrist, cutting a bit deeper into the back of his forearm. The wound bled badly, but in the meantime, her dagger was knocked out of line. Battle joy filling him, his own blade flew forward.

This was it.

Fin's heart thudded, anticipating the feeling of his weapon sinking into her body. His dagger plunged directly at her heart. Even if her nanovar armor kept his strike from penetrating too deep, the heart was only a half inch beneath the skin. Well armored or not, it wouldn't save her.

Just before he claimed victory, something unexpected happened.

An inch from her chest, his dagger was stopped dead by a saucer sized circle of white energy that suddenly manifested into existence. His eyes widened in shock. She grinned at him in triumph, her ruined mouth bloody and misshapen. Not even the large gap of her missing front teeth could rob her joy.

She was invincible with her new power!

When the Wave had hit, she'd been Enabled along with almost every member of the Familia. Unlike many of them, she'd gained an ability.

She was Powered!

Ottoro's Luminous Shield *– Summon up to a +**10** shield of Light mana*

The ability was fueled by her mana, taking MP every second it was active. Experimentation had shown her she could make the shield larger or smaller at an additional mana cost. Blocking Fin's attack had cost her less than a tenth of her mana pool. She could block ten to fifteen more attacks before she ran dry. She still didn't know how he was moving so fast, but her shield appeared at the speed of thought.

She was a better fighter. With her shield protecting her, she could move even faster, forgoing defense for offense. She was better equipped, and she had reinforcements on the way.

The advantage was hers.

That meant he was hers.

Her eyes narrowed with deadly intent. She glared into Fin's eyes as her arm tensed, ready to finally plunge her blade into his chest!

Chapter 52: Cold Blood

F in had been shocked to see the shield appear.

Too bad for her, he was no stranger to life and death battles.

The unexpected was to be expected.

Maybe if he hadn't just spent the night working his own magic, he'd have been thrown off by seeing a magical shield pop into existence, but Fin was already mentally adjusting to this new reality.

Without wasting a moment, he pulled his dagger back. In the same motion, he threw it hard… directly behind him and into the neck of her companion.

The man had been starting to stand up, his breath still wheezing, but able to control his air again. All that stopped when a hilt sprouted from his throat.

The woman lost any semblance of composure. Her attack faltered as she involuntarily moved in a vain attempt to protect her friend. Fin had heard the two bantering, and it was clear they were close comrades, maybe more.

From her garbled scream of despair, Fin was guessing more.

The attack on the man hadn't truly been Fin switching targets, it had been a set up to his true attack. He had failed to match the woman physically, so he had to beat her mentally.

With no delay, the hand that had thrown the dagger lashed back at the woman in a blur. Fin didn't understand the rules of her shield, but he was hoping that it needed her to focus to bring it up. They'd been fighting for nearly

~DANGER~

a minute after all, and she hadn't summoned it before. There had to be a limit to it.

If it did appear, hopefully the damage buff would let him overcome it.

He needn't have worried.

With her mind being temporarily short circuited, coupled with his improved reaction time and her distraction, his fist connected with her ruined jaw.

With *Violent Delights'* 20% damage boost added in, her fate was sealed.

His arm blurred for a split second, as he threw everything he had into a hard jab to her fractured jaw. The blow connected this time with no shield stopping him. Either there was a delay in her using her power, or she'd been too distracted.

Fin didn't care.

He only cared that the pain he'd just caused her must have stunned her mind because she dropped like the sack of shit she was.

The fight had lasted for barely a minute, but Fin was panting and bleeding from several spots. His lacerated arm was letting blood flow freely onto the hallway floor.

Fin only allowed himself a single deep breath. She'd collapsed onto her face and wasn't moving. If her jaw wasn't completely broken before, it probably was now. Of course, that wasn't really a problem she'd need to worry about anymore.

With no regret, he grabbed the woman's dropped dagger.

Horrified faces were staring out from the various patients' rooms around him. The shrieks started back up a second later.

Leaning over her unconscious body, he grabbed a fistful of hair. He lifted her head unceremoniously and he plunged her own blade into her neck. The extra damage from her *Hated Enemy* status made the finally honed blade slide into her smooth as silk.

It felt more like cutting through tenderized meat rather than living flesh. The weapon grazed her esophagus as it sliced through her carotid artery and jugular.

Before pulling the sharp metal out, he pulled her hair again, twisting her neck slightly. The expected jet of bright red blood painted the white floor crimson. Several more spurts followed the first, each weaker than the last.

Fin didn't pause to watch.

In his experience, after the first two strong pumps, the risk of blood spatter dropped precipitously. He impassively dropped her head to impact the floor a final time with a faint *thud.*

In that moment, he didn't feel regret. He'd already killed the choking man with plenty of witnesses around. Whether it was the authorities or these pale bastards that came after him next, there was no going back.

It only made sense to put such a dangerous enemy down for good.

Neither did he celebrate her death.

The joy he gained from battle was never about the kill. It was the challenge. For some reason, after taking a life, he rarely felt anything but cold detachment. There simply wasn't room for anything in his heart and head except cold, clinical rationality.

While her heart pumped futilely to counteract her blood loss, he did a quick frisk. Her left pant pocket revealed a wallet. It was heavier than he was expecting, but only just. Fin threw it into his pillowcase. He'd need info on these bastards later.

Fin turned to the first man he'd killed.

The blonde's eyes stared sightlessly at the ceiling. Blood was already drying on his neck.

After a quick frisk, Fin grabbed the man's wallet as well. Then he retrieved the dagger from his victim's throat. Fin was surprised by how easily it slid out. It must have been sharper than he'd thought.

He grabbed the pillowcase with his belongings and almost started running again before pausing for a half moment in indecision.

Cursing himself for a greedy fool, he turned back and stripped the dead man of his suit coat. It was a risk, but if he had to fight again to get out of this hospital turned death trap, a good coat of nanovar armor could save his life. It took ten long seconds to strip the man and put the jacket on, but his gamble paid off.

Thankfully the Viking SOB had about the same build that he did, if a bit smaller.

Robbing the man had another unexpected benefit.

At the small of the corpse's back, Fin found a small brace of throwing knives. They were simple, steel lengths of metal without hilt or adornment. The end of each tapered to a sharp, triangular point.

They looked about the standard nine inches and change long, overall, no different from the type used by Confederation soldiers during the War. Most soldiers didn't bother training with throwing knives beyond the minimal requirements of basic training.

Fin's own training had been a bit more… extensive.

He wouldn't win any competitions, but he knew how to use them.

Fin was moving again before any more enemies appeared.

As he ran down the hall, the cuts on his hand and arms stung like hornets. The hallway was empty, but patients and hospital staff stared at him from patient rooms on both sides. Some stared in fear, but many were talking excitedly, their Links recording everything that happened.

Considering that he was rocking the latest in Versace nanovar over an open backed hospital gown, his black ass clapping in the wind, he probably looked quite dashing.

Yup. I'm definitely going viral.

Fuck.

A line of red droplets trailed behind him.

His goal was another stairwell at the end of the hall. He had to get out of this hospital, now!

Those bastards were definitely converging on him.

He wasn't really worried about hospital security, assuming they'd be as understaffed and apathetic as the guards in every hospital he'd ever been in.

Handling tweakers or the occasional schizophrenic was well within a security guard's wheelhouse, but dagger fights and magical powers was probably asking a bit much of them.

Which raised the question of just what that glowing shield had been all about. If he hadn't spent the previous night magically eating cancer, it would definitely have shocked the hell out of him.

He'd been dealing with his own brand of weird for the past few days though, so seeing a glowing disc pop into existence hadn't been enough to throw him off his game. That didn't mean it still hadn't been crazy to see a physical manifestation of magic up close and personal like that.

Did all of these Q-Tip looking freaks have powers?

Listening to the news and the nurses, he knew most people didn't have access to the interface. Social media was full of people debating if the Wave had even happened, so there was definitely no consensus on what had caused it. Scanning the Great Link for news had also been an exercise in futility.

You'd think that the sum total of the world's knowledge would be the place to go for information, but reality was sadly different. There were plenty of people talking about the Wave, but they all proclaimed their own theory was the only "true" one and that everyone else's was crap.

Scanning the Great Link had unearthed a full sack of nutjobs talking about every explanation imaginable. From alien invasions to mind control drugs in the water to mass hallucinations caused by the latest Link upgrade. One group was even talking about 5G, which apparently had something to do with old cellular telephone technology.

Surprisingly, he'd found almost no mention of the interface. That was how he knew that whatever had happened to him, hadn't happened to many. For a while, he'd even doubted his earlier assumption that he wasn't the only one the Wave had changed.

As of now, that question had been answered pretty definitively.

Other people had Abilities and, if that woman was any indication, theirs were more powerful than his. Or at least were more directly applicable to combat. Her shield had been impressive. His dagger hadn't just slowed down, it had stopped like he'd tried to stab a mountain.

That was better defense than body armor.

Without his improved *Reaction* Attribute, that fight with the woman could have easily gone the other way.

If all of these suit wearing albinos had powers as well… there was no way he was going to be able to take them all out in a fight.

Even if they didn't, if they were all wearing nanovar, he was screwed.

That was why as soon as he saw four coming around a corner, he didn't hesitate. He unsheathed one of the three throwing daggers he'd stolen and threw it in a smooth motion.

Many people thought you needed to throw a dagger as hard as you could. Point in fact, it took almost no pressure at all to pierce flesh. Merely brushing against a scalpel would part skin. A sharp dagger moving at speed through the air could bury itself up to the hilt if the angle was right.

With Fin's increased reaction time, his blade was flying before his target even registered his presence. By the time the man saw his arm move, the steel had already crossed half the distance. As Fin had been trained, he'd launched the dagger in a simple half turn throw.

In another situation, he'd have aimed mid chest. Knowing they were armored; his dagger was unerringly flying right into his target's eye.

His quarry was the budget superman who'd shattered the ice.

It wasn't an easy throw to make, but Fin knew it was perfect the moment it left his fingers. What he didn't know was that his stance, muscle contraction, even the humidity of the air, were all altered in minute ways to ever so slightly improve this ranged attack, courtesy of Fin's unlocked Dexterity.

Tattoos and piercings festooned his target's face.

His victim's eyes widened as he registered the attack, but with only Strength unlocked on his status page, there was no way he could move fast enough to dodge, especially not with his overly large frame.

Fin began to smile in that frozen moment.

He didn't know about any of the myriad metalaws affecting his action, but he did recognize the unique resonance of a perfect moment.

He couldn't miss!

Sadly, a moment later, Fin realized that, once again, he'd made an ass out "u" and "mption."

Before the dagger struck, one of the other men used a power. Right before Fin's throw landed, the guy blurred. Fin didn't even really understand what he had just seen. One moment, the guy had been standing several feet behind his muscle-bound target, and the next, he was in front of the terminator reject.

It wasn't just a split second of acceleration like his Reaction allowed him to do. This guy had moved more than two meters in an instant. It was like he was a speedster from a comic book.

White walker flash plucked the dagger out of the air when it was a bare inch from sinking into the eye of Fin's target.

  ~REWARD~

The muscle-bound man gulped audibly.

Everyone stopped, somewhat shocked by what had just happened. Even the guy who caught the blade just looked at it for a moment, as if he was just as surprised over his last second catch as everyone else. Then looked at Fin, and a sadistic smile grew on his face. He gestured with the dagger. The "come and get it," message was clear.

"Nope," Fin soundly declared.

That guy had moved more than five feet in a second! His improved *Reaction* speed was nothing compared to that. Fin's throw had been spot on and the blade had only needed a fraction of a second longer to land.

Put another way, the guy that had caught it had moved faster than a thrown dagger! Fin wasn't interested in round two with someone like that.

He turned around to run in the other direction. As soon as he did though, his heart dropped. Five more suited blondes were coming from the other end of the hallway.

He was trapped!

Chapter 53: Lightbulbs

S ola realized she was already on thin ice by secretly opposing the wergild. The Shadow had no love for the Lotus, not since the second war, but she was already in trouble with her Familia.

It would take only the work of a moment for her elders to review the command logs of the hospital and uncover that she had been slowing Jürgen's people down.

If one of the elders that still looked favorably upon her did the investigation, she'd get away with a chuckle and a slap on the wrist. If one of the elders gunning for her decided to investigate, then her actions were all the proof they'd need to throw her to the wolves. She might even be handed over to the Lotus.

Still, Jürgen had really pissed her off, which is why her fingers tapped on her link in a particular pattern, triggering a simple command.

After all, trouble might come to her any day, but she could shit on Jürgen's sundae right now.

***

Just as Fin was thinking it was time for a heroic last stand, and it would have been heroic, a metal door to his right cracked open with the sound of a releasing lock.

With no other option, he didn't question it. He just kicked it open and dove inside.

That quick action saved his freedom, and likely his life.

~DANGER~

As he entered the room, a *whirring* sound passed right over his head. It was the dagger he'd thrown coming back to him. It sailed just over his head, missing him by centimeters. The blade cut through the air fast enough to make a faint whistle. It had definitely come back at him faster than he'd thrown it.

As he slammed the door behind him, he heard a curse in German that Geneva translated.

"I said take him alive, you fools!"

Yup, Fin thought definitively, no shame in a strategic retreat.

Once he was inside the room, he saw that he'd finally had a bit of luck.

It was a pharm supply closet.

Simple medical supplies sat on the shelves that lined either wall. The back of the closet looked a bit like a series of metal panels with a built-in electric interface. He knew those panels could dispense any type of medicine patients would need. That included narcotics and other expensive meds, which was why hospitals typically protected these rooms with heavy doors…

He spun around looking at the door before thinking, "Yes!"

When Fin had slammed the door shut, he'd thought it had taken a bit of extra effort.

Now that he was doing his best to remember, he realized it had even made a faint *thunk* when it closed.

Most pharm closets were protected by a reinforced door, yet another legacy of the War.

Just like War Protocol, buildings were mandated to have reinforced rooms now in case of emergency. In hospitals, it just made sense to secure the highest value items that could easily be stolen.

Fin wasted no time, flipping up a plastic cover and slamming his hand against the large red button underneath. A series of faint *clicks* sounded along with an almost imperceptible electric hum showing the EM locks around the door had engaged.

Outside the door, he heard shouting and then a faint thud, almost definitely someone slamming their shoulder against the door, then muted cursing.

Fin grinned. He'd done it!

He'd kept those blond fuckers from getting him. Now all he had to do was wait until the authorities came to investigate why a War Protocol had been triggered.

Turning around, his eyes scanned the walls of his small safe haven.

His small, now exit-less, room with blood thirsty nazi-yakuza on the other side of the door.

"Well," he admitted, looking around like a trapped stallion, "this is less than ideal."

With no better options, he braced his back against the door and waited to see how this would all play out.

Heavy footsteps sounded outside of door, followed quickly by a thud that felt like a battering ram had hit it from the outside.

Fin was pretty sure the target of his dagger throw, the big guy that had shattered the ice on the floor before, was making his displeasure known. Even through the reinforced door, the force of that hit shot reverberations through the door, making his lacerated arm throb.

You have suffered 0 damage.*

Fin looked at the door in disbelief.

He was really getting tired of thinking this, but that shouldn't be possible.

Pharm closet doors weren't exactly bank vaults, but they were still three inches of solid steel sealed with no less than five electromagnetic locks. Someone slamming into one shouldn't do anything else except give that idiot a sore shoulder.

They shouldn't be able to rattle the door, let alone hit it hard enough that the transmitted force could hurt him.

Then again, the word "possible" was getting a major overhaul these days.

"Hey biggun," he yelled. "No hard feelings about the whole knife to the face thing. I mean, you're not going to hold a grudge, right?"

The response an even stronger slam against the door, and something Fin couldn't quite make out.

It sounded like "I am Klaus," but that made no sense, so he assumed the guy was speaking Finnish or something.

"Yeah, he's definitely holding a grudge," Fin muttered. He decided not to rebrace against the door.

Even though that freak was bashing the metal harder than a human should be able to, he shouldn't be able to get through the barrier anytime soon.

Besides, that last hit had kinda hurt.

On the other side of the door, a female spoke loud enough for him to hear her sadistic Alemannic tone, "Our patriarch is going to skin you alive you know. He said I can use what he takes off to make some boots. I have some jeans and a white top that would go great with that brown color." An unhinged laugh followed her taunt.

"You need therapy lady," Fin shouted back. Under his breath he muttered, "God damn, that's fucked up."

Feminine laughter came through the door right before another slam hit it. This time, the door creaked and *definitely* rattled before the locks reengaged.

Unfortunately, Fin had even more urgent problems to deal with.

You are bleeding. **-1 HP**

HP remaining: **23/58**

Crap.

Fin started to curse seeing his health was well under half now, then he remembered that was only because his Constitution was Threshold two. In his old body, the one he'd rocked for most of his life, he'd only be down by about 25%.

Fin grinned to himself. Amazing how easily you could get used to this superhero stuff.

He grabbed some gauze and tape from a shelf.

As he dressed his arm, Fin cast his gaze all around the room.

"What else can I do? What else can I do?"

He still felt relatively safe in the pharm closet, but wasn't quite as sure he could just hide in here until the calvary came.

One, evil Thumbelina Thor out there might just be able to beat down the door given enough time. The guy clearly had some sort of strength power, and who knew what the limit was.

And two, for all he knew, these suited bastards had some cops on the payroll. It would certainly explain why they were so brazen as to come after him like this in broad daylight.

There was at least one bit of good news.

You have stopped bleeding.

It looked like with the large wound taken care of, he wasn't actively losing HP anymore. He had plenty of smaller cuts, but those were just oozing blood.

That done, he turned his attention back to the larger issue.

"I'm stuck in a supply closet. And I need something to fight magic freaks. What do I do?" Saying it out loud made it seem obvious.

"I need to MacGyver it."

Looking around, unfortunately, there was no duct tape.

"Okay, plan B. I'll use magic."

Fin turned on his *Mana Sight*. Nothing in the room registered, only showing the same horrid emptiness he saw in other inanimate objects. Another thud against the door made him look over his shoulder.

And that's when he really started to curse.

His *Mana Sight* hadn't shown him anything in the room, but it was able to see through physical objects to a certain extent. The resolution dropped sharply, and he'd never have managed it before it was energized, but it extended just far enough now to give him a view of the hallway.

When he looked at the door, he just able to make out more than a dozen figures outside in the hall.

As he watched, he saw even more enter his visual range.

"Just keeps getting better and better," he spat.

While the number of enemies wasn't great, it was what he saw inside of them that was the real problem.

During the night, he'd scanned more than a dozen people with *Mana Sight.* He was able to examine the comatose patients in detail for hours. He'd found there was some variation in brightness of the mana pathways, how quickly the pulses of the light moved and how thick the lines were.

What he'd learned was that there was a clear difference between the mana lines in a sick person compared to his own pathways.

His were generally more vibrant and active than those of the patients in the ICU. The sickest patients' pathways looked like glow sticks that had been left on for hours and were about to fade completely. In contrast, Fin's mana skeleton looked freshly cracked neon blue.

Every time he'd drained a cancer of Life Element, the pathways of the person would get stronger. It even felt like the line of light stabilized, though he wasn't exactly sure exactly why he felt that way.

None of the patient's pathways, or his own, had ever approached the luminous brilliance of the cancers themselves, however. Those burned like the sun.

Which was what made Fin curse.

Now that he was able to really look, it was obvious.

Every single one of the blue stick figures on the other side of the door was shining like a lightbulb.

Chapter 54: Local News

DARK

*M*ana Sight was starting to feel like the local news. It wasn't doing anything but depressing him, so he turned it off. Fin hadn't given up on the idea that his new magical powers could help him though.

He turned to his other skill, *Mana Threads*.

Maybe I'm not using it to its full ability, he thought. Maybe *Mana Threads* lets me control anything with mana. Maybe, he thought with vigor, it will let me control them!

Throwing up an arm, palm out and fingers splayed, he accessed his skill. For good measure, he shouted, "*Mana Threads!*"

An invisible tendril shot from his hand. After increasing the skill level to four, his range had increased to a few feet, more than enough to reach through the door and touch an enemy on the other side.

The thuds against the door stopped. A disbelieving smile cracked over Fin's face. "I can't believe that wor-"

"What did he say?" came from the other side of the door.

"Who cares? Just keeping knocking the door down."

"I am Klaus."

Another thud rattled the door.

Dropping his arm, Fin was full of both regret and thanks.

He really wished that had worked.

On the other hand, no one saw him in that Sailor Moon pose, which could only be a win.

What had he even been thinking?

His *Mana Thread* had indeed reached the guy on the other side, but it had bounced off his target's skin immediately.

He might has well have thrown wet spaghetti at a peach.

Pushing inane thoughts out of his head, his mind raced to come up with something else to try. A light blinked in the corner of his vision. There were prompts waiting to be read. He brought them up, hoping for a way out of his situation.

*You have killed a **Level 0 Enabled** Human. XP blocked. 0 awarded.*

*You have killed a **Level 0 Powered** Human. XP blocked. 0 awarded.*

Well, on the bright side, it looked like killing other people wasn't a path to power. There were no shortage of psychos and ex-girlfriends who would happily go on a killing spree.

It still didn't help his situation unfortunately.

The only bright spot was it appeared his medical skills had come through.

You are no longer bleeding.

The gauze had stopped his health from falling any further. Which was definitely good news because he was down a major chunk after the fights.

Sadly, there were no more helpful prompts waiting to be read.

The thuds against the door continued. Worse, on the seventh, something changed.

This time, the door dented inward at one spot.

Fin stared at the curve that hadn't been there a second ago.

A curve in three inches of steel caused by a human body hitting it from the other side.

He just didn't have it in him to think 'that's not possible' again so he went with another classic trinity.

"What the fuck."

The thuds continued, and now every third hit created a new dent or worsened an old one.

Fin stared at the EM locks.

They were currently holding, but they rattled harder every time.

It was obvious the door wouldn't last forever.

As the minutes had passed, Fin had lost all hope on the police saving the day. If these people were able to do all of this and block his access to the Great Link, they were clearly heavily connected.

The fact that their mana pathways glowed that brightly made it even worse. It was clear now that he wasn't only being targeted by a powerful organization. These blond pricks were connected to the mana. All he could come up with was that he'd stumbled onto a secret organization that was somehow connected to the Wave, or at least had a better understanding of it than he had.

Still, Fin didn't give into despair.

He just needed to flip the board again.

But how?

Going back through everything he'd learned since the Wave, he recalled his quest rewards.

The first thing he came to was his healing herb.

As tempting as it was, his experience with absorbing magical items hadn't been great. He couldn't afford for the herb to put him into a medical coma while it healed him. He left that one unclaimed.

Thankfully, that wasn't his only reward.

He'd also learned a Technique.

Fin didn't know the significance of Technique needing a capital "T," but the prompt had hinted that using it to make an Elemental Splinter, whatever that was, could lead to greater power.

With no other options, it was that or nothing.

Fin decided to sit back down and put his back against the door. The thuds hurt, but it would at least give him some idea of what was happening as he shifted his consciousness over to the Cave of Whispers.

     ~REWARD~

No sooner had he entered the cavern than the steel door began to glow red.

***

On the other side of the door, Jürgen watched Klaus slamming his large body against the door. In another situation, he might have sat back and just watched his family member work. Klaus was one of the family's new Powered.

The man had had gained a transformation ability that increased his strength. Apparently it also turned him into an even bigger idiot. All he'd said since transforming was "I am Klaus!"

No matter what you asked him, the answer was, "I am Klaus!"

It was more than a little annoying.

"Annoyance" wasn't what Jürgen was experiencing now, however.

Point in fact, Jürgen was furious.

First dealing with that bitch of a shade, then having to undergo the embarrassment of having to call his superiors during a simple retrieval mission.

Not only that, but two of his subordinates had been killed. Deaths during missions were not inherently a bad thing. Culling weakness was a primary tenet of his Familia after all. The fact that one of them was Powered though would definitely impact his mission completion grade as a team leader.

While a main branch member might be chastised if they failed, his punishment would be far more severe.

It was only because of his third rank, *limited* Ability, *Scintillating Sight*, that a side branch family member like himself had been given command over main branch members in the first place.

The Familias were powerful, and widely feared. Even nations treated them with respect. That was because opposing them was, historically, a deadly mistake.

Unfortunately for Jürgen, that viciousness was also applied internally.

Each Familia divided the world into several Houses, and each House controlled a given geographic area. Familias fought other Familias whenever they could get away with it, and internal politics made violence within Familias a common occurrence as well. Houses would betray one another if there was enough benefit.

The competition within a House was no less fierce, and could, quite literally, turn deadly.

When he'd been given this task, Jürgen had rejoiced. Completing a mission that was personal to the patriarch was his ticket to a rapid rise in the family ranks. Conversely, if he failed…

Jürgen shivered. He didn't even want to think about that, and he definitely didn't want to think about the mistress's Red Room.

All this bastard had to do was surrender, so they could torture him to death, and he was not being compliant!

Jürgen had had enough!

"Get out of the way. It's time to finish this," he ordered in clipped German tones.

Light bloomed in his eyes right before twin, incandescent beams shot from them like lasers. As the energy blast started cutting through the door, Jürgen smiled victoriously.

Chapter 55: Hate

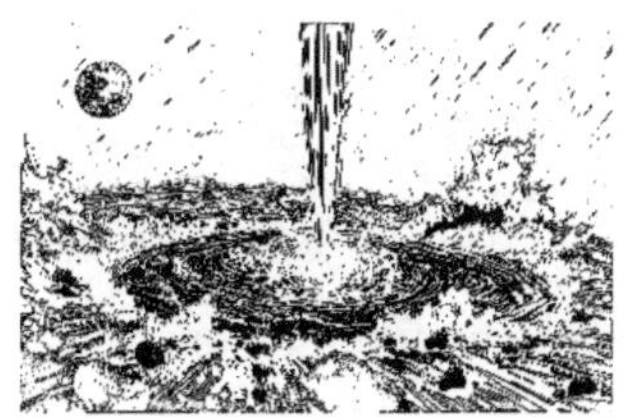

Feeling the fierce heat on his back, Fin popped out of his Cave of Whispers almost immediately. In alarm, he shifted to the side. To his intense surprise, he saw that the steel right behind where he'd just been sitting was glowing.

At first, all he could see was a baseball sized red spot.

In a single second it grew brighter and then a small orange dimple appeared in the middle. Scant seconds later, the metal on that spot began to bubble. Then the center of the bright spot began to run down the steel slab like heated slag. Right after that, two beams of red light shot through the door and cut into the pill dispenser at the back of the room!

The smell of burning hair filled the room.

"Shit. Shit!" Fin gasped, patting the side of his head, hard and fast. A piece of melted metal had splattered onto his head, setting some of his black curls on fire. Fin pulled out a clump of his own hair. The strands, along with a tiny piece of metal fell free, hitting the floor with a tiny *hiss*.

A few embers burned like hell on his scalp, but he'd avoid a direct hit from the lasers. Something he was supremely happy about as he saw the beams cut through the metal.

You have suffered a minor burn. **-1 HP**

"Really!" Fin shouted, jumping up to get as far from the deadly rays as the cramped confines of the storage closet allowed. "Laser beams! Who the hell brings laser beams into a hospital!"

~REWARD~

Who, the holy hell, were these guys?!?

"We're going to kill you!" came a shout from outside the room.

"Really Captain Obvious? What else do you want to tell me? That you've never satisfied a woman? We know!"

"You killed my sister," came another man's enraged scream.

"You'll find another date," Fin shouted back.

More furious yells came from the other side of door.

Jürgen continued his onslaught as his subordinates railed at the target.

The lasers cut through the door slowly, but surely. He'd created a two inch hole in the metal door when a headache hit him. He was able to ignore it at first, but he noticed that his mana pool started draining right after. It only took a few seconds for the blue bar to almost empty.

At that point, the pain ratcheted upwards dramatically.

With a grunt, he shut his eyes and turned his head away. The beams cut off abruptly.

Jürgen grasped his head with both hands, barely containing a groan of pain.

The other members of the Lotus Familia and Sola stared at him in surprise and astonishment.

Jürgen wasn't the only Powered there.

Sola, and three other Lotus on the capture squad, had been granted their own Abilities by the Wave, but none of them were able to summon the pure destruction they'd just witnessed Jürgen unleash.

The lasers disappearing also prompted Fin to look through the new hole in the door. He didn't get too close thanks to the edges still glowing hot.

Seeing everyone staring at one man in shock, while that same man held his head in pain, brought a horrible conclusion to Fin's mind.

They didn't have a laser weapon.

That guy *was* the laser weapon.

That's what he was facing.

The insanity and enormity of how monumentally fucked he was hit all at once.

He also took notice that there were more than twenty people out there along with his doctor. She didn't seem to be allied with them, standing to the side with an unhappy look on her face, but neither was she stopping them.

None of that was what really grabbed his attention though.

It was that everyone else was uniformly pale skinned, flaxen haired, beautiful, and wearing suits.

Seriously?

He wouldn't be surprised if these guys even shit blond.

A strange détente formed while the blond holding his head called out to one of his team members. The man walked up, placing a hand on who Fin assumed was the leader. Closing his eyes, a white light appeared on the man's hand. A few seconds later, the light winked out, leaving the subordinate looking drained.

In contrast, the leader straightened, all discomfort gone from his face. Opening his eyes, he looked at the door, and saw Fin peering out through the hole he'd cut.

Smirking, red lights kindled in Jürgen's eyes.

"Crap," Fin grumbled as he ducked back out of sight.

Two brilliant beams of fire shot through the hole again.

On the one hand, it was good to know that these guys weren't so well connected that they could pull out forbidden weaponry just to hunt lil' ol' him.

On the other hand, that guy could shoot frickin' laser beams out of his eyes! The fact that a single person had that kind of power was worse in its own way.

He'd already come across the woman with the energy shield, the muscle bound bastard, who he now thought actually *was* named Klaus, and the speedster. What other kind of powers did these bastards have?

From what he'd seen on the Great Link, very few people even had access to the information boxes, and yet a bunch of these inbred bastards had superpowers?

Did their powers all come from the Wave, or had these people always had these kind of abilities?

Whatever the case, he was still stuck in a small room with an albino superman cutting through the door. If the guy continued at the same rate, he'd cut a big enough hole to reach through and push unlock button in a few minutes.

Maybe, just maybe, that would give Fin enough time to go back into his Cave of Whispers and figure something out.

Thank god these guys weren't smart enough to just target the EM locks in the door frame. There were only five of them and it would let them in the room much faster than burning a hand sized hole through several inches of steel.

The lasers cut off for a moment, and Fin heard someone murmuring in the hallway.

Right after, the door started glowing orange again, centered on one of the locks.

"Well! Ain't you fuckers precious!" Fin spat.

The beams made short work of one of the locks and then moved onto the second.

Thinking quickly, Fin grabbed a saline bottle from the shelf, hoping that throwing the water on the hot metal would make the slag fuse in the door jam. Sadly, while the water *hissed* on contact with the metal, it didn't make a new lock that would keep out four hundred pound magical German.

"Yeah, that was dumb," Fin admitted looking at the empty bottle.

About five seconds later, the second lock began to bubble. It had just started to slag when the beams cut off again. Unfortunately, that had still been long enough to destroy the lock, just leaving three on the vertical part of the doorframe.

Still, Fin sighed in relief. The guy had run out of juice again. Not able to resist, he shouted out, "Can't keep it up, huh? That's embarrassing!"

Hearing his prey's mockery, words that cut a little too close to home though Jürgen would never admit it aloud, drove him nearly mad with rage. That didn't mean the target was wrong. The longer he used his *Scintillating Sight*, the faster his MP drained and the greater the pain he felt.

The mana infusion from his subordinate had helped, but Jürgen just didn't have enough control over his new ability. It felt like he was using an already overtaxed muscle.

He tried to summon fire with his eyes again, but the spike of pain shooting through his skull stopped that attempt in its tracks.

     ~REWARD~

Jürgen screeched in agony and gave a command.

"Knock the door down," he spat. "Get his ass out here!"

"I am Klaus!"

Jürgen opened his eyes, pain radiating through his head. His vision was narrowed, the overuse of his ability literally decreasing his vision. A thrill of panic shot through Jürgen's heart that the impediment might be permanent, but he shut that from his mind. Failure could hold consequences far more dire than losing half his sight.

The mistress might pluck the very eyes from his skull.

A thud echoed down the hallway and the door rattled far more than it had before. At least his previous efforts had not been in vain.

Destroying two of the locks had made Klaus's efforts more effective.

That barely made Jürgen feel any better, but there was nothing he could do.

Even if he could force maybe another couple seconds out of his ability and destroy the third lock, there was no way he'd be able to cut through the fourth. The first time his mana had bottomed out had made his head throb.

This current headache had almost knocked him out.

They also didn't have any other mana transfer glyphs.

They'd been lucky to requisition one at all.

As frustrating as it was, Jürgen knew he'd just have to let Klaus do his thing.

Jürgen forced himself to breathe.

With two locks destroyed, the door shouldn't hold up for long.

As thuds and "Klaus's" echoed around him, Jürgen's mind cleared a bit.

It was only at that moment, when he realized he was angrier than he should be right now.

True, he had reason to hate his target, even more than just hating those with inferior blood. This Fin Evers had killed two of his Familia, and worse, had the audacity to mock him.

There was also the fact that he was having to deal with this annoying shade bitch.

Still, this was just another mission.

Yet, it didn't feel that way. It felt personal.

He-

He *hated* the man on the other side of the door. For someone reason, more than was reasonable, Jürgen wanted to kill the target with his own hands. Almost more than he'd ever wanted to hurt anyone, he wanted to hurt Fin Evers.

Looking around, seeing the anger in the eyes of his family members, he realized he was not alone in that feeling. In fact, the only person in the hallway that didn't look ready for murder was the shade doctor.

What he didn't understand was that the Labyrinth itself was affecting the minds and emotions of his entire team. None of them could wait to slay an enemy they literally could not coexist with.

Even if he had understood, Jürgen knew that giving in to those feelings could not be allowed. Only the Red Room awaited him if anyone robbed the matriarch of her vengeance.

"Remember!" Jürgen commanded sharply. "The target is to be taken alive or risk our Lady's displeasure!"

When he'd started talking, some of the team had looked at him in anger, but the threat at the end had cowed them.

Seeing that, Jürgen centered his attention on his breathing. The man would be theirs soon enough. He'd turn him over to the patriarch, and then ask to watch as the mistress used her toys. That thought brought a smile to his face, one that couldn't be banished even by the latest, "I am Klaus."

Chapter 56: Inappropriate

Inside the room, Fin remained ducked down and braced against the door.

"Fuck, fuck, fuck," he muttered before bringing up his Cave of Whispers again.

He wasted no time summoning up his new technique.

In the darkness, four candle flames floated in the darkness. An additional six golden balls hovered off to the side along with a partially filled golden mote.

For the first time, Fin attempted to make an Elemental Splinter.

Following instructions that had been implanted within his mind only recently, but that he knew intimately, he exerted his will in a very specific manner. In response to his whim, a structure that looked like it was made out of glass manifested in front of him.

It was a clear rod with intricate tubules tracing through it like veins. Eight indentations were evenly spaced along its length. When he'd learned the Technique, some of the knowledge he'd gained let him know that each spot was made to hold an Elemental mote.

Sadly, he didn't know exactly what happened after that.

Looking into the darkness around him, he realized he now had a decision to make. Did he make an Elemental Splinter comprised of Fire or Life?

Happily, that decision took almost no time at all. He *needed* to fuck some people up, so, "From what I've tasted of desire, I hold with those who favor fire."

He'd just have to hope that the five motes of Fire he had left would be enough.

It turned out that visualizing the empty glyph was the easy part.

Moving the first mote of Fire Element into one of the eight slots on the glyph was a good deal harder.

When he'd cultivated Elemental motes with his Whisper ability, each round of cultivation had been harder than the one before. It was like he was trying to squeeze something into a vessel that was already full.

Wrangling the first mote of Fire Element to the glyph was far harder than the first round of Life cultivation, but fell short of the difficulty of breaking through a tertiary attribute Threshold. If he had to guess, it felt like the fifth or sixth round of cultivation.

That was because instead of moving the essence of the Element in a long tether, he was forced to move the Elemental mote en masse.

The entire flicking mote of Fire moved out of the darkness at once, fighting his will the entire way.

Thankfully, his Skill came to the rescue once more.

After it had moved a certain distance, he was able to wrap his mana thread around the mote like a lasso. After that, moving the candle flame was easy.

Thankfully his *Mana Threads* skill was now level four, so he was able to manipulate the mote out of the darkness faster, shortening the amount of time his mind was under strain.

Between his experience over the last day in the Cave of Whisper and *Mana Threads* leveling up, the increased resistance was still within his capabilities.

Fin concentrated and moved the first mote of Fire Element into the specified spot on the glyph. Once there, it felt like he had to mentally strain to push the mote through an invisible membrane. Focusing he both pushed with his mind and pulled with his mana threads. With a sensation of release, the membrane was pierced, and the flickering flame locked into place, turning into a round jewel of the same color.

Success!

He started moving the second mote of Fire Element. Sadly, and predictably, the difficulty increased notably.

If the first felt like sixth round before crossing the Threshold, this felt more like the fourth.

~REWARD~

It was within his capabilities despite the extra strain. In just another second it would be in the right spo-

A heavy thud against the door rocked his body out of place and completely made him lose his concentration. He even fell out of his Cave of Whispers.

Looking up, his stomach dropped. The top left side of the door, including one of the ruined EM locks, had ripped free from the wall.

All that held the door in place was three vertical EM locks and the bottom two hinges.

Fin was forced to make a split-second decision that he really, really didn't like.

The concentration needed to use the Elemental Splinter Technique was within his capabilities, but not if his body was being jostled by 'I am Klaus' slamming his big, dumb body against the door.

Which meant, Fin needed to sit away from the door if he had any hope of making this thing.

Which meant he'd have no idea what was happening while his consciousness was in the Cave of Whispers.

He'd already discovered that his sense of touch remained in contact with the real world, but all of his other senses could only experience what was happening in the darkness of the cavern.

There would be no way to know if they busted in or even if they were standing right over him.

Fin smiled.

I'm screwed either way.

Let's go for broke.

He had no idea what an Elemental Splinter would do, but it was all he had to work with in these last minutes of freedom.

Fin scooted back from the door.

Closing his eyes, he reentered the cavern.

Looking up, he breathed out in relief. It looked like the disruption hadn't wasted any of his Elemental motes. Four candle flames and six golden balls floated around him. Both the Fire mote he'd been working on, and the one he'd already put in place, had snapped back into the dark of the cave.

Focusing, he quickly grabbed a Fire Element. Not allowing even an iota of distraction, he pushed it into place. The second followed after, and the third was in place a few seconds later. When he attempted to grab the fourth, he was pushed almost to his limit.

It took just as much mental energy and concentration as he'd needed to do the last round of cultivation before crossing the second Threshold, if not more.

His mind strained, making it feel like he was splitting his focus. Fin may as well have been trying to multiply forty-three and seventeen while balancing on top of a large ball. A moment's distraction would make him lose his progression or fail completely.

With much effort, the fourth Fire mote snapped into place… and nothing happened.

"Dammit!" Fin cursed.

He'd known all along that the glyph had eight spots on it, but he was hoping the four motes of Fire Element would have done something.

Anything!

Anything that could help him get the hell out of here.

There wasn't another option now.

He'd need to add Life as well.

Fin reached out with both his mind and *Mana Threads* and pulled a glowing golden ball into the fifth position.

That had been the plan anyway.

The moment he tried to snap a golden sphere into the five spot, the entire crystal rod flashed ominously.

All Fin could do was blink before all four Fire motes and the Life ball he'd just manipulated shot back into the darkness. An echoing wave of force shot towards Fin and knocked him out of the circle of light.

The Cave of Whispers disappeared. Fin found himself back in the supply closet.

Then he vomited blood.

*You have suffered a backlash from inappropriate usage of **Life** and **Fire** Elements. -3 HP.*

*Remaining HP: **19/58***

"Gah!" Fin shouted, clawing the fingers of one hand into his chest.

Was he having a heart attack?

Another slam shook the door. Fin's eyes popped open just in time to see the corner with the detached hinge dip inward further.

A screw fell out of the middle hinge.

His protection wouldn't last much longer.

A second agonizing cough wracked Fin's body making him spit blood onto the floor yet again.

He heaved out a labored breath, feeling the pain in his chest.

"Yeah," he panted. "I think I broke something."

Another slam against the door was accompanied by another "I am Klaus" and the metal slab, his only shield against a painful death, bowed inward even more.

He didn't have time to feel pain.

Slamming a fist into the ground, Fin forced himself to settle his mind.

'Think!' he commanded himself.

Work the problem.

What just happened?

Closing his eyes, he reentered the cave.

He didn't immediately try to throw more Fire or Life Elements back into the glyph. Instead, he just made sure the orange flames and red balls were still waiting.

Seeing all ten were accounted for, he tried to remember what had happened.

Adding the Life Element had actually felt easier than adding fourth mote of Fire to the glyph. That had been until he'd snapped the golden ball in place.

Then "something" had happened.

Fin closed his eyes inside the cave, remove all possible stimuli so that he could focus on the memory.

He'd felt something strange for just a second before the glyph had flashed.

A vibration?

Yes, that was what it was.

Adding the Life Element had caused some sort of instability with the four motes of Fire Element he'd already added.

That is what had caused the glyph formation to fail.

Fin opened his eyes.

What had the prompt said?

An "inappropriate usage of Life and Fire Elements."

Didn't that mean there was an "appropriate" usage?

One interpretation of "inappropriate" could mean that Life and Fire weren't supposed to be combined into a single glyph, but Fin decided not to believe that.

Mostly because if he did ascribe to that belief, he'd be screwed.

Always best to choose an interpretation of reality that benefited you.

At least, that's what an ex had told him.

"Maybe it's about the order you add them," Fin murmured.

Wasting no more time, and trying not to think about Klaus knocking down the door in the real world, Fin summoned the clear rod of the glyph once more.

He snapped a Fire Element into place.

Next, he switched to Life.

With a smile on his face, he realized that adding the Life Element second took less focus than adding two Fires back to back. Instead of the difficulty increasing by two rounds of cultivation, it had instead increased by about one and change.

Fin smiled manically.

He was onto something.

Chapter 57: Cost of Power

Fin eagerly pulled a second Fire into slot three and then another Life into slot four.

There was no doubt about it now. Using two different Elements definitely decreased the mental focus needed.

Unfortunately, adding the fourth mote revealed another problem.

That vibration that had sundered the glyph all at once the first time was back.

Even though it had been harder to add four Fire Element in a row rather than two pairs of candlelight and gold, the glyph itself had felt completely solid after the four Fires were in place. The two pairs of Life and Fire felt like they were fighting against each other.

The first time, the vibration had been sudden and violent, enough to completely break his concentration and disrupt his technique. Thankfully, it looked like adding the Fire and Life Elements back to back didn't cause such a drastic reverberation. Instead, it was starting small and building with each added mote.

If adding four Fires had felt like drumming four different beats with both hands and feet, adding the two pairs was like drumming only two beats, but while hearing someone sing a different song completely offkey. And that tone deaf bastard was singing louder with each Element that snapped into place.

The discordant "song" wasn't just annoying. It reverberated through the technique, making Fin split his focus. After adding the second Life in the fourth position, it felt like the vibration in the glyph threatened to shake the motes free from their positions.

When Fin focused on them, they would settle back into place. If he didn't, it felt like they might fly back into the darkness.

Using only one Element took more intense focus to snap each into place, but once they were, they seemed pretty stable. It was difficult, but the challenge was only internal.

Using two Elements decreased the initial focus requirement, but added an external difficulty and a slight time aspect. The task got harder the longer he took to complete because the vibrations would continue to build.

Still, it wasn't anything Fin's trained mind couldn't handle.

Taking a deep breath, Fin reached out to the third mote of Fire.

He immediately felt the strain.

The mote floated out of the thickened darkness, but fought against his will the closer it got to the glyph. The strain was mental not physical, yet was just as real as if he was lifting weights. The closer it got to the glyph, the more difficult it became to split his focus on keeping the first four Elements in place and bringing the fifth one in.

The strain was now the same as if he'd placed four motes of the same Element in place.

Actually, it was even worse. Unlike when he'd only used Fire, he also had to contend with the dissonant reverberations of the motes he'd already placed in the glyph. The closer it got, the worse the discordance grew.

The mote continued to come closer at a sedate pace. Nothing he'd been able to figure out could make the motes travel from the darkness faster.

His *Mana Threads* Skill came to the rescue, pulling the mote the final distance.

With a last push of will, the red candlelight snapped into place on the glyph, filling the fifth position.

Thankfully, the discordance lessened somewhat once the mote was in place, but it was still worsening every second.

If he had been working this hard physically, sweat would have been pouring down his face in rivers.

Fin didn't dare risk a delay.

Not only hadn't he forgot that an idjit named Klaus was literally beating down the door to then beat him down afterwards, but the pain in his chest also hadn't disappeared after he suffered the last backlash.

That first failure had cost him three health points.

With the reverberations in the glyph already this bad, if he lost control, the resultant backlash might literally kill him.

Fin reached for the sixth mote.

He was shaking from the strain of focusing so hard.

Without the specialized training he'd received during the War, he doubted he would have made it even to this point.

On his first attempt at making the glyph, the mental difficulty of snapping the fifth mote into place had been like multiplying forty-one and twenty-eight while balancing on a ball. The mental strain wasn't as bad using two different Elements, but it wasn't far off.

The sixth mote was much worse.

The difficulty of maintaining his concentration felt like multiplying one hundred and thirteen by four hundred and sixty-one, but doing it aloud in a language you'd only started learning last week.

When you coupled that with also the needing to focus on keeping the earlier motes from vibrating out of place, Fin was stretched to his limit.

After hearing the sixth *snap* of the mote latching onto the clear rod, Fin didn't know how he'd do the fourth Fire Element, let alone the last mote to complete the glyph. Thankfully, his efforts to this point were rewarded.

*Congratulations! Your **Mana Threads** Skill can progress to level 5, but will require you to sacrifice **1 Power**. Do you wish to proceed?*

Fin didn't even have time to think about why this Skill level needed Power, while the others hadn't. He almost manically assented.

A sharp pain ripped through him, and he felt "less" in an indescribable way. It threatened to break his concentration, but out of pure spite, he persevered.

-1 Power

*Congratulations! **Mana Threads** has advanced to **Level 5**! Your ability to control and sense mana has increased.*

He'd been accumulating notifications while he worked, but had automatically minimized them, not being able to afford the distraction. It turns out that difficulty of making an Elemental Splinter had helped his Skill progress rapidly.

He'd just advanced two levels!

The pain passed quickly, and thankfully hadn't been without purpose. Knowledge flowed into Fin's mind, showing him he could stabilize his thread.

Just like with every other Skill level he'd reached, leveling up *Mana Threads* let him lengthen and strengthen a single thread.

Unlike before, he could now make a second one and combine them!

With a fierce and strained grin, he opened his left hand wide.

A thread that was nearly five feet long, double what he'd managed in the past, shot out from his palm. It was still short of where the Fire Element hung in the dark, but after mentally pulling on the flickering candle for a full minute, it reached his blue thread.

He eagerly began retracting his Skill, pulling the mote like a bucking fish on a hook. When it got to within a few feet, he opened both hands wide.

The existing blue lasso grew dimmer, and the Fire Element almost broke free. Before it could, a second thread shot out from Fin's right palm.

With a pair of threads encircling the mote, Fin's control grew more stable than ever before. The mote's struggles greatly decreased, and he pulled it the rest of the way to the glyph.

Fin heaved out a relieved breath.

Thanks to his leveled Skill, the difficulty was now less than it had been to manipulate the sixth mote. Not much less, and harder than manipulating the fifth, but definitely easier.

Staring, he pulled it closer until it reached the crystalline rod and snapped into place.

Fin mentally reached for the eighth and final mote.

It barely moved through the thick darkness.

He might as well have been pulling a tennis ball through mud.

Meanwhile, the vibrations were getting so bad that the glyph was blurring in front of him.

Fin remained undaunted.

His body in the cave, whether real or an avatar, started shaking uncontrollably from the strain, but Fin's eyes held only steel. The pain in his chest faded to the background. Worry about his enemies breaking down the door, his hope that this Elemental Splinter would somehow hold the key to his salvation, even the ache of losing Lauren, all fell away.

The only thing left was strength.

Inch by inch, Fin pulled the golden ball towards him from the depths of the cavern and towards the glyph. Just like every other time, the reverberations in the glyph worsened as the mote grew closer.

At five feet he lassoed it with his Skill and pulled with more than his will alone.

At two and half, he split his threads, wrestling the golden sphere even closer.

The vibrations had doubled in strength by the time the eighth was still two feet away. At a foot away, the reverberations were strong enough that Fin actually felt them in his teeth.

He didn't stop.

With a feeling of utter satisfaction, Fin pulled the last mote into the eighth position with a satisfaction that was palpable.

At long last, it was done!

Except that it wasn't.

As always, there was that final invisible barrier that needed to be overcome, the membrane that seemed to surround the glyph. As the vibrations had grown worse, it had become harder to overcome the membrane. The first seven times, his will had been enough to overcome the barrier.

The crucial difference here was that the vibrations worsened for two different reasons. One, the glyph shook harder with each node he successfully engaged and two, it got worse as time passed.

He'd taken too long to engage the eight mote.

The glyph was shaking almost twice as hard as it had been when he'd snapped the fourth Life sphere into place.

As he strained with all he had to cross the last inch of this marathon, the reverberations grew stronger, and then stronger still, until the entire glyph flashed ominously, just like it had before he'd suffered a backlash last time.

Fin struggled to stop the vibrations by a sheer force of will, but it barely quelled the instability. He even tried using a mana thread, wrapping around the rod like an octopus. The thread was severed almost immediately, shooting pain through his head.

It was all he could do to hold on to his consciousness.

The glyph shook so hard, that it became a blur in front of him, and it flashed again.

Flash.

Flash.

Flashflashflashflash.

Fin's eye's narrowed, not in fear, but in controlled anger.

"No."

Focusing on a particular spot beneath his throat, Fin accessed a power his conscious mind could not comprehend, but his essence knew intrinsically. A crystalline bell sounded.

Ting!

*Know this! You are **Forcing** an **Opportunity**. In accordance with your Actions and Essence, this Opportunity has been determined to be a lesser Heroic event. The cost for a **Forced Opportunity** will be 10x greater. Opportunities cannot be controlled. Do you wish to proceed?*

The prompt appeared and disappeared in less than a second. That was how long it took Fin to decide and almost unconsciously accept.

*The **Resonance** of your Cave of Whispers has increased by **37%** for the next **17** seconds.*

Vibrations flowed down both of his arms, through his hands, and towards the glyph hovering in front of him and beyond.

~DANGER~

They seemed to strike the walls of the cavern and then bounced back towards the glyph and the column of light.

As if with a mind of its own, his Cave of Whispers began to sing. It was the low hum of waves and the quite buzz of the swamp. It brought to mind the sharp crack of fracturing ice and the perfect stillness after death. His cavern provided a counterpoint to the destructive shaking of the glyph.

It was not enough to completely still the crystalline rod, but it was enough.

The flashing slowed.

Flashflashflashflash. Flashflash. Flash.

The vibrations continued to quell the reverberations until there was a final throb of light, but one completely different than the others. With a nearly audible *snap,* the membrane was overcome. The golden ball of Life Element turned into a golden jewel, finishing the crystalline lattice.

All eight gems on the glyph flashed together. Not with urgency this time, but in unity. Something inside him knew he'd succeeded.

The glyph began to change.

The end of the crystal rod bent upwards until they nearly formed a circle. Right before joining, the two poles bent outward again. Faint beams of light formed between the gems. Here a Fire joined to Fire. There a Life formed a connection with two other Life and a Fire. The beams seemed to pull on sections of the crystalline rod like tension wires, twisting it into a specific shape.

As it twisted, it shrank, by the initial size of several feet across to half that, then half again. The connections and twists of the rod happened faster than Fin could follow. In seconds, it had shrunk to the size of his pinky, then the size of his smallest nail.

Floating in the darkness, it shone brilliantly, rose gold luminance.

*You have lost **200** (20 + 10x penalty) magicka!*

Fin didn't care less about that cost because several more windows appeared.

~REWARD~

Congratulations! You have formed your first Elemental Splinter, unlocking a key to the greater powers of your Whisper ability!

*+**20** Magicka*

Assessing Elemental composition…

*This is a splinter of **Cleansing Fire***

Fin would have loved it if the description had stopped there.

Assessing Quality of Elemental Splinter…

Chapter 58: Fury

While Fin waited for his grade, hoping he'd passed, Jürgen stared at the other side of the door, his anger building every second.

There was only one thing standing between him and his prey.

A stupid fucking door.

A Light-damned slab of metal!

Staring at the dented gateway infuriated him.

If only his ability had lasted longer. If only he could make it stronger! He had already cut a foot through inches of solid steel. He was power personified!

And yet he was stopped by something as mundane as a door!

His anger continued to ratchet upward. He needed more power.

More!

A collection of horrible potential came together inside of Jürgen and birthed something new.

The taunting coming from his prey, the opposition from the Shadow, his fear of the consequences if he failed, and most of all, his Labyrinth fueled enmity, all combined to evoke something primal within him.

Ting!

~REWARD~

A prompt appeared accompanied by the sound of a crystal bell. He was so far gone into his rage that he agreed without even reading it.

Jürgen felt a strange vibration just beneath his throat. Not even recognizing what he was doing on a conscious level, the one hundred magicka he'd collected from a quest drained out of him to fuel a *Scarce Opportunity.*

A barrier broke inside of him, one that existed beyond the physical realm.

It was the last obstacle between him and his next step on the Path of Power. As it fell, he saw what was waiting on the other side. Like a smiling monster, Jürgen was filled with true fury for the first time in his life.

The feeling built until Jürgen could actually feel the heat inside his head.

*Congratulations! Your **Scarce Opportunity** has increased your hatred to true **Fury**!*

Fury has found synergy with your ability allowing you to cultivate it for the first time!

*You have unlocked your first Ability Aspect: **Furious Gaze**.*

*Furious Gaze – Use your soul energy to increase the strength of your **Scintillating Sight** ability. Using this Aspect will cause an increase in anger.*

*+**100** Magicka for cultivating an Ability for the first time.*

*Total Magicka: **100***

A wonderful vibration filled Jürgen's body as the magicka swept through it. The sensation was just as amazing as last time. The vibrations localized south of his throat, then half seemed to bleed out into the air.

As great as the magicka felt, Jürgen barely noticed either it or the prompt. The anger he'd originally possessed had been stoked into a rage.

The newly unlocked Aspect of his Ability compelled him to provide his fury a release. He stepped forward, pushing the other members of his family out of the way.

His eyes opened twice as wide as a human's should have been able to enlarge, and two points of light kindled in his pupils. With his emotion and magic fueling his new power, he managed a stronger attack than any he'd practiced at home!

Something snapped deep within him, and the reddish color in his eyes shifted to a bright pumpkin.

Beams of pure destruction kindled, while a withering bellow issued from his throat.

At that very moment, the magicka tithe that was the Earth's due was even now making its way to the nascent World Spirit, bringing the energy that had already been collected to a critical mass.

Little did Jürgen know, unlocking the first Aspect of his Ability, while bringing the power to complete his mission, would paradoxically lead to his defeat.

***

Meanwhile, inside the storage closet…

Fin was waiting with bated breath to see if his effort would really help him escape this death trap.

Assessing Quality of Elemental Splinter…

Quality is…

Trash!

Huh?

To Fin's surprise, he was immediately kicked out of his Cave of Whispers.

Looking down, he saw that he hadn't come back empty handed.

The Elemental Splinter was sitting in his palm.

The small crystal glowed softly in his hand. It was about an inch long, and tapered at both ends to a sharp point. It looked like two elongated triangular pyramids with their bases glued together.

One end was a shining gold while the other was a fiery orange-red.

He'd succeeded.

"Yes!" he shouted, pumping a fist in celebration. "Trash my ass!"

Now he just needed to figure out how to use this thing. Maybe he if he threw it through the door it'd explode like a grenade.

Yeah, that would be good right about now. He didn't think he'd been in the Cave of Whispers for more than a minute or so, but he still couldn't have much time before they broke down the door.

Speaking of which, Fin realized he'd been back in the real world for a couple seconds now and hadn't heard a thud. Not in his wildest dreams did he think they had just left. Rescue was not something he thought likely either.

It was theoretically possible for the police to have come, but a group that had the juice and balls to hunt him down a crowded hospital in broad daylight obviously wasn't afraid of the law. Even if a squad car had shown up, he didn't think the blondes would give him up. It would take a whole swat team to get him out of this.

Which raised the question, just what the hell were they do-

"What the fuck!" Fin shouted as two blazing orange beams of light cut through an EM lock.

The beams had drilled through the door almost as soon as he saw the metal glow.

The bastard on the other side of the door wasted no time, dragging his laser vision downward through the lock. The metal was cut at least three times as fast as before.

The beams burned so intensely they warped the air around them, like hot air in the desert.

Time was up!

He definitely didn't have time to figure out how to use the Element Splinter. The door would be open in less than ten seconds. Even if it could be used as a grenade, it was a tiny crystal. It didn't exactly have a pin he could pull.

A red-orange flash of light drew his gaze back to his hand. In the back of his head, he realized it wasn't the first pulse the crystal had emitted. It had flashed at almost the same time as the lasers cutting through the door.

He'd understandably been distracted.

But was the flash brighter this time?

Wait.

Why was his prompt notification flashing red too?

*You have created an **Elemental Splinter (trash)**. This cannot stay in your Cave of Whispers.*

*There is a **5%** chance of this Elemental Splinter exploding, releasing all the contained energy. This increases by **5%** every second.*

Oh shit! It *is* a grenade! How many seconds have passed?

Too many!

Crap!

Fin's arm flexed and threw it through the hole Jürgen had initially burned through the door.

His increased *Reaction* shot his hand forward in an instant and the crystal flew forward like a bullet. The unstable gem soared through the air, when suddenly, time froze.

Much like when the Wave washed over the Earth, he remained conscious, but the flow of the world ground to a halt.

~REWARD~

Chapter 59: Birth of a World

EARTH

In a womb of solid iron surrounded by molten metal, an innocent slumbered, waiting to be born.

Energy had slowly accumulated over the billions of years since its creation, but had never reached the level required for the child planet to awake.

This was the day that changed.

As consciousness bloomed, knowledge flowed from the Labyrinth into the waking World Spirit.

"Oh," it thought contentedly. "I'm a world."

In that moment, the Earth learned consciousness.

The iron sphere of the Earth's core turned crystalline in a single moment, the cocoon morphing into a chrysalis.

The World Spirit came to understand that its existence was not only confined to the iron orb. It was so much more.

Its awareness spread outward.

The spirit sighed happily upon coming into contact with the cozy molten iron flowing around it, offering both the security and comfort of a blanket.

"So warm and toasty," it thought merrily.

The World Spirit, innocent of all things, just glorified in its existence.

In that moment, the Earth learned Joy.

It dwelt in those warm and wonderful sensations until its consciousness expanded enough to ask questions. The first was, "Why do I know what 'warm'

~DANGER~

and 'toasty' mean?" Then it realized it did not matter how it knew, because to be warm and toasty was delightful.

Then it thought, "How do I know what 'delightful' means?"

Then it giggled, "I know what 'knowing' means!"

This continued on for a long while.

Such delight and wonder were completely normal for newly awakened worlds. When everything is new, everything is beautiful, and filled with delight.

This was why the Labyrinth always performed a limited cessation of Time when new World Spirits were birthed. The freeze lasted as long as it took a new world to full "stretch and wake up."

While many years would pass for the Earth itself, for its children, it would be like almost no time had passed at all.

Like all untainted, newly born creatures, it possessed only joy in its heart, and so all things were joyous.

Sadly, the purity of joy was too fragile to bear the weight of will.

The Earth's consciousness slowly expanded as its Energy drove it to leave its shell of the Earth's core, an instinct as ingrained as a chick leaving an egg.

The World Spirit explored through its various strata. It disturbed old creatures that had taken refuge within it while it was still only gaseous. The spirit tried to communicate, but the mighty denizens of the depths could not be pulled from their slumber.

After several centuries of trying, the curious spirit continued its search of its own body.

It came across old bones, forgotten cities and hidden rivers that had never known the touch of the sun. It was especially impressed with the last discovery, as the only liquid it had ever known before was the molten iron of its own nest.

The Earth had no idea that liquids came in different colors!

And that they could be… the spirit searched for the world until the Labyrinth supplied it, cold! It had no idea that "cold" was possible!

"Cold" was definitely not as cozy as "warm and toasty iron," but it was still happy that cold existed.

The world tuttled off, leaving the cold river behind, thinking, "I love that I can tuttle."

After long centuries, the Earth finally reached its surface. It took an understandably long time as the inside of the Earth, like the inside of us all, is fascinating and wondrous if given the proper time to explore.

When it did reach the surface however, the Earth was understandably shocked to learn that it was not alone. Other "me's" lived on top of it. After another century, it realized that the other "me's" did not think of themselves as part of it, they thought themselves as… apart… from… it.

That confusing paradox took several centuries to unravel, and the World Spirit was still not sure it had understood it when all was said and done.

What it did understand was that the number of "lives" that lived on her were so many that it could never fully count them. It also learned that the many white things just beneath its surface used to be other "me's" but they had… stopped… being.

It could not yet conceive of Death, as it had not yet truly experienced Time. It had come across me's that were sleeping, and it realized the bones were probably sleeping too. It knew that Time existed at this point and came to the conclusion that once it came back, sleeping me's would wake up. It resolved to check on the bones later, thinking they would be more interesting then.

The Earth swept its consciousness across its surface, finding so many interesting things everywhere she looked. It kept traveling upwards through the oceans until it felt a warm and cozy feeling again.

Looking "up," the Earth was particularly proud of itself for mastering that concept, it realized that there was light in that direction. It had found light in a few small places deep within itself, but nothing as brilliant as its warm and cozy iron core.

This light might be even brighter!

The Earth decided for the first time not to expand equally in every direction and instead send its consciousness directly upwards where it saw the light.

For the first time it saw the sun.

The Earth had never known awe before that moment. In that instant, it knew it was part of something greater than itself, and the knowledge brought it joy.

"I'm not alone. I'm not alone!" it shouted to itself in contentment and love.

~DANGER~

The other "me's" were nice to look at, but it could feel they were different from it. The sun though was a power and majesty like itself. The Earth wiggled and giggled, for the first time feeling warm and toasty both inside and out.

For decades it just lay under the frozen moment of Light shared by its sun, until it realized things could be even warmer and toastier.

There was a… it didn't know the word, and so Uncle Labby supplied it. There was a smudge keeping out the Light. For the first time, the World Spirit accessed its Energy reserves and willed the smudge away.

In that moment, all pollution in the atmosphere was removed. The Light was finally able to be seen without anything blocking it and the Earth delighted in its beauty.

At the same time, it suddenly felt weaker, and it did not like it.

The Earth cried out to Uncle Labby for help, and in that moment, as the Earth had made its Choice, as all new worlds inevitably did, it was provided with a helper.

"Who are you?" the Earth asked in a small voice.

The older World Spirit smiled kindly at the formless child. He was not without form. Instead, he looked like a very old man with shaggy white hair. It grew wildly all over his old face and when he spoke his voice sounded older still. Though his words carried the weight of ages, they were still strong as the strongest beast and as regal as the greatest king. Yet his tone was soft and filled with love which made the Earth feel warm and cozy again.

Sharing feelings of comfort, the old man said, "You can call me Arni, and I am very happy to meet you."

The Earth sighed contentedly and pressed its formless body against Arni. It felt warm and safe and was content.

For the next several years, Arni taught the Earth many things.

He educated it about Energy and why it felt so tired after it removed the pollution from its skies. The Earth learned it could do many things with its Energy because World Spirits were very special beings, but that if it used too much it might go to sleep again for a very long time.

The Earth promised it would try harder with the earnestness that only a child could convey.

That was the moment the Earth learned Caution and Fear.

The Earth began to spread its consciousness across the planet under Arni's watchful eye. It no longer called out to Uncle Labby. It did not need its uncle when Grandpa Arni was around. Sometimes it saw Grandpa Arni looking at it with an expression it did not understand. When it asked, Grandpa said his expression was called "sad."

When the Earth asked why Grandpa was sad, Arni just answered, "Nothing lasts forever, especially innocence."

The Earth did not understand that, but it didn't think it liked "sad," so it focused on being happy and learning more about the many "me's" all across its surface.

It explored all over, more carefully than before because it didn't want to fall asleep again. Not when there was so much, it searched for the word, beauty all around it. It never wanted to be without beauty again!

It marveled at the many "me's" it came across in all their shapes and colors.

Arni told it these were "lifeforms" and it learned they were different from "not lifeforms" because they glowed when it saw them. It liked the glows.

Arni also taught her the names of the many lifeforms. Trees and grass and worms and flies. And even tiny, tiny lifeforms called bacteria and, it searched for the word, viruses, even though Grandpa Arni said those were not real lifeforms unless they got enough Energy.

Confusion struck the Earth at that concept, something being real and not real. It didn't like that thought so it just pushed it aside. In that moment, the World Spirit learned Confusion and Irritation.

The Earth also came across some glows that had an extra spark just like it had. Their sparks weren't as bright as its and Arni's, but they were still nice and toasty!

There had been a few glows with sparks in its deeper levels, but on its surface there were…

It looked for the word…

Billions of bright sparks, dancing across its skin. They were beautiful!

Then it came to something that made it feel… wrong

The Earth had come upon the first Red Zone left by the Third War, an area made so toxic by the weapons used that human life could not exist there.

The World Spirit paused its exploration, spending more time in that area of its surface than it had ever spent on one place before. It knew its skin shouldn't look like this. Something had done this to it.

It also found what Grandpa Arni had taught her were called bones in that "wrong" place on her surface. It also knew now that the bones weren't sleeping. Grandpa Arni had gotten his "sad face" when he told it, but he never lied.

The Earth learned that the bones had once been lifeforms that had glowed. Maybe they had even sparked, but they never would again.

There were millions and millions of them in this one area.

The Earth knew that this area was wrong. This spot was ugly and bad! It didn't like it!

And in that moment, the Earth learned Judgement.

The World Spirit wanted to fix the bad area, like it had fixed the smudge that blocked the sun, but it didn't want to sleep again so it left it unchanged.

In that moment, the Earth learned Wisdom.

In that moment, the Earth learned Anger that something had hurt it.

As its consciousness continued to dwell over the red zone, it learned to hate whatever had hurt it.

In the next moment, it realized it wanted to hurt whatever had done this in return.

In that moment, the Earth learned Vengeance.

Through it all, Arni watched in sadness, at the paradise lost.

The Earth didn't like how it was feeling so it decided to move on.

Sadly, it came across more red zones. Its anger deepened, but then it arrived at a yellow zone. It could tell that its surface had been ugly before, but that now it was healing.

In that moment, the Earth learned Hope.

The Earth's consciousness continued to travel, exploring its highest heights and deepest depths. It traveled across its surface until the sunlight faded and was replaced by darkness.

　　　　　

The darkness did not scare it, most of its body was dark, but it did prefer cozy warmth. It considered staying in the light, but it wondered what was in the dark.

In that moment, the Earth learned Curiosity.

The Earth's mind and soul traveled across its body until it saw a new light, high above it. The light was different than the sun but was so beautiful still. Looking up, it saw the moon and cried out in delight.

Words came unbidden, "Little brother! Little brother!" the Earth cried out in delight.

It was so happy to see the moon, but the moon could not answer. If it would ever wake, that day was not today.

"Little brother, can you not see me?"

In that moment, the Earth learned Yearning.

In that moment, the Earth learned Disappointment.

The World Spirit moved on, searching itself and the space around it. For countless years, it was stuck in a moment of time with only itself, Grandpa Arni and the ever-watchful Labyrinth for company.

At times it laughed, though less as its consciousness grew. At times it cried. It expanded and contracted, growing and exploring. Until one day, it came to a realization. It liked being "more." It wanted to grow even further. It wanted to grow faster.

In that moment, the Earth learned Ambition.

In that moment, the Labyrinth knew it was ready and began to provide the Earth with prompts that would lead to its Ascendance, or its destruction.

Congratulations! You are now Aware!

Your Energy Density has reached Level 1.

You may now walk the Path of Power!

Due to your rapid speed of Advancement, there is a large Energy surplus from the Allotment provided to you as a new world.

Your share of this Allotment is 10%.

The Earth did not understand these concepts, but Grandpa Arni explained. A certain amount of Energy was given to worlds to nurture them to the next phase of their development. The Earth had done so well on its own though, that it didn't need all of the Energy. The Labyrinth was going to take most of it back, but would leave one out of every ten units as a reward.

The Earth finally understood. The Labyrinth was taking its Energy away!

In that moment, the Earth learned Greed.

It railed for several years at the injustice, and Grandpa Arni, like all wise grandfathers, just let the child wear itself out. Once the Earth was finally tuckered out, he sadly explained that reality was never fair, but must always be accepted.

Only through acceptance of what was could you change what is and perhaps, what would be.

Nearly a century passed as the Earth grappled with this harsh truth. In the end, it did come to accept that reality was bigger than itself… for now.

In that moment, the Earth's form grew much closer to completion.

In that moment, the Earth learned Guile.

More notifications came from the Labyrinth, asking what it would do with its surplus Energy.

At first, the Earth planned to bring all of the Energy to its core. If it did that, it would be "more," and that was always a good thing.

Grandpa Arni was thankfully there to provide counsel.

While the Earth thought 10% of its Allotment was a small amount, the truth was the Energy that entailed would destroy the young world's core in an instant if it was placed there all at once.

The Earth had already learned caution and so took its grandpa's words seriously.

Instead of trying to eat all the Energy, it followed his advice.

First, it spoke the words Grandpa Arni told it to say.

"Summon World Crown."

Just like that, a circle made of pure Probability appeared before it.

The Earth was immediately delighted because it didn't know it could do that.

Arni smiled benevolently, enjoying the delight over what he saw as a simple thing. A World Crown was merely the manifestation of a spirit's Blessings, yet to a cosmic child, it was like a coming of age gift.

*Would you like to **Energize** your **Blessings**?*

Without proper Energy, there is a high chance of your Blessings failing, fading or becoming subverted.

The Earth didn't like those last words and immediately agreed to put some of its extra Energy into its crown.

Arni continued to smile at it as a single white jewel appeared.

There was so much he didn't know about the little world, not even what its Blessing would be. The white jewel showed this child had been given a common Boon. It was not a great Blessing, but the Earth could still do wonderful things if given the right guidance. And the large amount of excess energy would maximize the Boon.

There were many mysteries he was eager to unravel regarding the Earth.

Why had a nascent World Spirit had been inducted to the Labyrinth?

And after being inducted as a null world, how had the Earth come so far so fast?

Perhaps most important, why could he detect a whiff of Chaos in her actions?

Whatever the answers to these questions, he felt a great connection to the emerging consciousness.

That in and of itself wasn't overly surprising.

He was an old spirit. One of the oldest, and he had walked many Paths.

Some of his strongest were the Paths of Inspiration and Might. He was so resonant in these Paths that he formed bonds with weaker World Spirits whose children would dream of him.

What was surprising was that he had answered when the Labyrinth had asked if any World Spirits would like to earn points fostering a new world.

While other worlds would scramble and scrap to reach the heights of this current Age, old monsters like himself had already won the Game of Ages more than once. They were typically content to let the younger generation learn folly on their own.

Arni still didn't know why he'd decided to take on this responsibility. He just knew it was something he had to do.

It had been a long time since he had last shepherded a new life, but he would give it his all.

Which was why as the white jewel shone brighter and brighter, he was already coming up with advice to help the Earth along. More Energy poured into the Blessing until it was maximized.

> The **Common** Blessing, **Instance Tokens**, has been Energized to… **Peak!**
> **150%** efficiency
> **+100%** chance to be maintained upon Ascension

Arni was just about to teach the Earth how to diffuse the excess Energy into outer space so that it could slowly consume it over the centuries to come, when, for the first time in Ages, he was surprised.

A second gem had started to form.

A double Blessing at birth?

Well, he thought with a smile, I guess this little world is special after all.

The Earth had no idea that having more than one Blessing was exceptional, or even what Blessings were, it just knew the jewels were beautiful. And it liked how they shined when it gave them Energy, so it kept doing so.

Under the gaze of the two World Spirits and the Labyrinth, the second blue gem began to shine. Soon, it blazed as bright as the white jewel, reaching the peak state as well.

> The **Limited** Blessing, **Lucid Abilities**, has been Energized to …**Peak!**
> **150%** efficiency

          ~REWARD~

> +100% chance to be maintained upon Ascention

Arni smiled like a proud papa. Two Blessings. Two!

And already maximized to Peak Energy before the Earth had even joined the Labyrinth. At first, he'd worried that the young spirit would be easy prey for predator worlds, but he wasn't concerned any longer.

In fact, with two-

The old World Spirit froze.

A third jewel was forming.

In its long history, it had seldom heard of a triple Blessing for a new world. The few times that had happened, great and terrible events had shaken the Labyrinth. The loss of life, not only of children, but of World Spirits themselves had been terrifying.

His own birth had been graced by three jewels.

Some of the Paths he had walked in his early days, then filled with Power and arrogance, still filled him with shame even now.

Arni intently watched the shape of the jewel form, and his stare grew even more intense as he saw its color.

Red.

It was a *rare* Blessing.

The gem glowed brighter until it too reached the peak. The lion's share of the Energy allotment was consumed to feed the gem, but with reserves still left, the Earth achieved its goal.

> The **Rare** Blessing, **Elemental Empowerment**, has been Energized to…
> **Peak**!
> **150%** efficiency
> **+100%** chance to be maintained upon Ascension

Pride had been replaced in Arni's heart.

Where once he felt joy, now he felt only wariness towards this young spirit who had reached heights during its birth what most worlds never achieved.

There was no doubt in Arni's mind.

He knew why he had been drawn to this child.

Something was wrong.

First it had been born early, and now it had a triple Blessing. And *somehow* the Earth had reached a milestone so early that it could energize all three to the peak?

This did not happen.

It should not happen.

A world like this could become worse than a predator. It could become a monster.

He had to do everything in his power to guide this child to Paths of peace. The devastation it and its children could unleash did not bear thinking about.

He opened his mouth to speak to it, but then froze.

Impossible.

A fourth jewel was forming, and it was the bright yellow of a *mythic*.

In his earlier days, Arni would have immediately slain any cosmic creature with this rich a heritage. Passing millennia had taught him wisdom, but he was still filled with apprehension.

Now, even if he had been moved to destroy this newly born calamity, as an Auriga, he could take no direct action against the Earth. The Labyrinth itself ensured that.

All he could do was watch, and whisper, as the Earth poured Energy into the yellow gem. With mixed feelings, he watched the jewel consume the rest of the Allotment, only reaching mid-grade.

The Mythic Blessing, Magicka, has been Energized to… Mid-grade
50% efficiency
25% chance to be maintained upon Ascension

The Earth was disappointed the last jewel wasn't as shiny as the first three, but it was still pretty. Following instinct, the young World Spirit merged with its crown, and the formless was given form.

Arni stared at the child in apprehension.

She stood before him in their collective world space, having chosen a body in line with the first humans that had evolved upon her. Her skin was the color of cocoa, and her hair was black as night. Full lips sat in a child's face, a promise of beauty that would one day be realized. Her eyes were luminous jewels, one made of a bottomless onyx and the other shining a brilliant gold.

Draped down her featureless body was a dress woven entirely of tiny leaves, each plucked from a different tree.

As he watched, she took her first steps, twirling and laughing in delight.

After a moment, she looked at her grandfather's old, wrinkled face, and thought he looked sad. Wanting to make him feel better, she smiled.

The sharp teeth she revealed did not bring the old World Spirit any peace.

"Grandpa Arni, I have a body!" she announced delightedly. Her words seemed to shake reality itself, Energy and promised Power held within them, far more than should ever be trusted in the hands of a child.

"Yes, you do," he replied with caution. Delicately, so as not to startle her, he said, "There are many things we must discuss, child."

"And there are so many things I want to know," she responded with hunger in her voice. Questions were flooding her, each tied to a desire. One curiosity felt more important than all the others somehow, so she asked about it first.

"Grandpa Arni, what's a Primordial of War?"

For the first time in eons, the elder World Spirit felt fear.

Chapter 60: Taxes

AIR

Though centuries had been lived by the world spirit, only seconds had passed for the denizens of Earth.

When time had first frozen, Fin had silently cursed, thinking one of his opponents had a time stop ability. They'd somehow figured out that his Elemental Splinter was going to explode, and they'd kept it in the room with him, so he'd blow up instead!

After seconds passed however, he noticed that while the golden flame colored crystal still glowed, the flashing had thankfully stopped.

After seven seconds, a series of glowing windows appeared in the vision of every single person around the world who was connected to the Labyrinth. Across the planet, new Enabled and Powered were created as well, though far less of the latter were made during this second awakening.

The windows were accompanied by the sensation of heavy vibration. What would shock people in the days to come was that everyone, Labyrinth connected or not, was able to feel the reverberation.

VRROOMMMM!

Global Announcement! Global Announcement! Global Announcement!

LET IT BE KNOWN!

Your Energy null world has corrected its deficiency, leading to an Energy surplus for the first time in its history!

World Energy Density: **Level 1**

414

*The increase of Energy in your world will have many consequences. One such effect is the emergence of short-lived gateways called **Instances** which will now appear in your world.*

*Find and conquer these **Instances** to increase your Power.*

*Ignore this **Opportunity** at your peril!*

*Know This! The emergence of Instances has unlocked a **Blessing** of your world: **Instance Tokens**!*

***Instance Tokens**: Many are the worlds and realities housed in Instances. Yet Instances can be hidden in the highest mountain bluff or the deepest ocean valley.*

Use these Tokens to find Instances.

Danger and Reward are close bedfellows!

Know This! Progressing the spread of Energy in your world shall be rewarded!

Those who ignore the needs of your world shall be punished!

This series of prompts flowed past his vision and into his mind despite the world remaining frozen.

In addition to the windows he was reading, an additional bit of knowledge was downloaded into Fin's mind.

The initial messages had been seen by everyone in the world connected to the Labyrinth. He had no idea how many people that meant, but he did know that those without an interface, who hadn't been Enabled, weren't told anything.

He also knew that the next prompts were customized for each person that was connected to the Labyrinth.

Congratulations! You have completed a Secret Quest of the World Ascencion Quest chain: **Cradle of Chaos**

Quest Grade: *Radiant Gold (A)*
Quest Rank: *Common*
Quest Type: *World Ascension*

The world you inhabit must thrive or be consumed like all beings of the Labyrinth. By your actions, you have helped to increase your world's Energy to Level 1.

Increasing the Energy of your world can greatly increase your chances of survival in the Labyrinth.

Energy is the foundation of Power. Power is to be praised!

Individual rewards will now be distributed to the denizens of your world based on their Energy contribution…

Of all the beings of your world, you have contributed the greatest amount of Energy via your magicka tithe!

Your Contribution is rated… **SSS**!

The Labyrinth has awarded you the highest rewards allowed for your Power Level of 0!

Do you wish to collect your Rewards?

Fin quickly thought "Yes," and a brightly glowing window took over his vision.

YOU HAVE EARNED

C-Grade Reward
- 150 Experience Points
- 100 Magicka

B-Grade Reward
- 188 Experience Points
- 200 Magicka
- 2 Silver Ducats

A-Grade Reward
- 225 Experience Points
- 300 Magicka
- 3 Silver Ducats

- 1 *Uncommon,* 2nd rank, Free Attribute Orb
-

S- Grade Reward
- All lower Grade Rewards Doubled!
- +100 Nobility Points! (150/100 to Noble Title)

SS-Grade Reward
- 1 time access to an Instance Labyrinth Shop

SSS-Grade Reward
- Skill Blessing

Special Reward for Quest Type: Secret World Ascension
- +100 World Favor Points

The torrent of information was almost overwhelming.

Still, none of it seemed nearly as interesting as his Elemental Splinter.

Correction, his *unstable trash* Elemental splinter.

It hung in the midair, not two feet away from him.

Thankfully, though he couldn't move, the magical grenade he'd just created also seemed stuck in time.

It also appeared that he was connected to it somehow. At least enough to know its worsening status.

20% chance to explode.

If you've never been told that a grenade only a couple feet from your face has a one in five chance of blowing up, you wouldn't quite get how stressful it can be.

Fin checked several times over the next few seconds, but thankfully the number remained at twenty-percent. After a half minute, he felt confident the number didn't mean a 20% chance to explode even though time was frozen.

He literally knew he wasn't lucky enough to avoid a one in five chance thirty times in a row.

With that worry paused for now, he forced himself to read the prompts again, hoping something, anything, in there would help him get out of this situation.

The first thing that struck him was how he'd been part of a yet another "secret" quest. Those things were popping up like mushrooms after a storm.

What this one had in common with the quest regarding his Life cultivation, seemed to be that pursuing power was rewarded. He thought back to one of the earliest notifications he'd received.

*Welcome to the **Age of Power***

There might be something to that.

What was the point to accumulating this Power, though? For that matter, what did it even mean that the world had leveled up? Was it a good or bad thing for humanity?

He was being pushed to gain more Power, but was he being encouraged to seize his destiny, or was he being fattened up for slaughter?

No matter what the world or the Labyrinth wanted, if it came for trouble one day, it would find him a hard nut to swallow!

Of course, before any of that, he had to get out of this damn storage closet!

Fin turned his attention to the rest of his rewards.

Experience points?

Leveling was still locked so that was no help.

Magicka?

The Opportunities that magicka created were amazing, but try as he might, Fin wasn't able to recreate whatever he'd done to make the Forced Opportunity, so it wouldn't help him right now.

Money?

Well, he was an American, so he'd always take more of that please, but not a help right now.

But what was this?

He'd gained enough points to be a noble?

Fin focused with hope in his soul!

Error! Nobility cannot be achieved by Pseudo-Mortals!

And once again, I've just got soap in my hole!

Not knowing how long he had until time resumed, he pushed down his irritation and went to the double-S reward, "Instance Labyrinth Shop."

Predictably, he received another red screen of death.

Error! This cannot be accessed outside of an Instance.

Of course not!

The last two rewards, the SSS and the Type-reward, were no joy either. Whatever a "Skill Blessing" was he didn't know how to access it, and 'World Favorability' was equally unhelpful.

So, Fin was stuck there frozen in time, his gaze occupied with a magical grenade that could go off at any second, a beam of orange death and destruction and his own, even more destructive, inner thoughts.

"What the fuck is the world even going to do with a level up?"

***

Fin didn't know how long he'd been stuck in time at this point. There was no real way to measure it, but it felt like hours.

While he'd been frozen, his active mind had been going nonstop. One concept his brain kept circling back to was the part of the world's level up message that had talked about donating a "magicka tithe."

Basically, every time he'd earned magicka, half had gone to the Earth.

That confirmed a suspicion he'd had for a while. Every time he'd gained magicka, he'd been filled euphoria while the vibrations spread through his body. After they concentrated beneath his throat though, it had always felt like half of the vibrations drained away.

It turned out he was right about that.

The magicka hadn't just disappeared. It had gone into the world itself. The Earth itself had taxed him each time. And it looked like those taxes had been used by the Earth to level up somehow.

That meant nearly every action he'd taken to strengthen himself, to grow his new powers, had increased the amount of Energy in the entire world. And not just him.

Everyone that had been given an Interface by the Wave had probably been increasing the world's energy accumulation as well.

What did that mean about his, and everyone on Earth's, relationship with the world? The prompt had called humans the Earth's "children." Based on how humanity had treated the planet, Fin wouldn't be surprised if 'mom' was tired of her kids trashing the house.

Historically that meant getting an all-expense paid ride to the army recruitment office, not that an orphan like him would know how moms really acted.

Jokes aside, Fin had come to a grim realization.

That even in a damn video game fantasy world you couldn't escape taxes.

Almost mockingly, right after that thought, his frozen purgatory was broken by a new series of prompts that proved, in Fin's humble opinion, that the Earth was a greedy lil' bugger.

Know This! Your world has also decided to offer its children the chance to purchase rewards using magicka as currency.

How goddamn altruistic, Fin thought. You just can't make this shit up.

We're not being kicked out of the house, but we are being given the 'opportunity' to start paying rent.

~REWARD~

Due to your SSS grade in the Secret Quest, Cradle of Chaos, you are allowed to purchase rewards up to the maximum rank, Limited, allowed by the Labyrinth for your State of Being.

Only 1 purchase can be made from each rank.

RANK	REWARD	MAGIKCA COST
Common	Attribute Orb (Common)	100
	Attribute Orb (Uncommon)	275
Uncommon	Instance Portal Token	200
	Personalized Instance Portal Token	550
Limited	Pouch of Holding (10 slots)	500
	Dimensional Ring (10 cubic yards)	1,100

Time will resume in 1 minute. You have that long to make your Choice or these rewards will be lost.

A counter ticking down in the corner of his vision.

'After all that time frozen, now I only get a minute to make my choice,' Fin thought in irritation.

Whatever, maybe I'll finally get something I can use against these sandy headed bastards.

Fin started reading the various options for about two seconds before going full 'Merica.

I'll just take it all.

Thinking that, he purchased the most expensive reward from each rank.

If not for his Primordial Quest chain and *Radiant Gold* grade in the Secret Quest, he wouldn't have had nearly enough magicka, but thankfully he had money to burn.

And in any case, Fin would have been happy if he'd just had enough magicka to buy one reward.

The portal token.

He didn't know where it would lead and didn't know why a "personalized" one would be better than the base model, but both options had the word "portal" in them.

Fin had read enough LitRPG books to know that he'd just been given a way out of here. Even if "Instances" sounded dodgy as all get out, it was better than here.

The twin beams of orange destruction that were frozen only a foot to the left argued that point better than anything. Nothing like staring at something that could slice you in half for hours on end to put a situation into perspective.

It was time to go.

Fin made his choice.

1,875 Magicka deducted

*You have acquired: **Attribute Orb** (Uncommon)*

*You have acquired: **Personalized Instance Portal Token***

*You have acquired: **Dimensional Ring** (10 cubic yards)*

Material Rewards will be available for the next 7 days

Total Magicka: 384

As soon as he'd purchased the rewards, the reverberations below his throat woke all at once. The vibrations felt so strong that it seemed like they should cause pain, but they didn't. Instead, the magicka effortlessly poured out of him like he'd opened a faucet.

To his surprise, once he'd made his choice, time resumed.

Not exactly a full minute, Fin thought in irritation. That feeling quickly fled however, as he noticed a difference in the air. It was like his skin had been

~REWARD~

parched and a wet breeze had blown in. His thinking was clearer than after pounding a triple espresso and he felt pure energy pouring into his body.

It was intoxication without inebriation.

It was rubbing aloe on a burn or loosening your belt after a big meal.

A faint sense of discomfort that he didn't even know he'd been ignoring his entire life was soothed to the barest extent, and that small succor was the greatest of all gifts.

He'd never known he could feel this way.

He'd never known.

Time seemed to slow once more, but this time it was not due to temporal energy or an action of the Labyrinth.

This was a sigh of the heart.

Fin, along with every being on Earth experienced a rebirth.

Truth echoed in his soul, and yet, there were no words.

There were no words.

No. Words.

Poetry.

His spirit wept in completion and joy.

They should have sent a poet.

So beautiful.

I had no idea.

A red flash drew his eye and broke the spell.

His heart finished exhaling beauty, and the ugliness of his chosen reality crashed back down around him.

Time resumed.

What he had experienced had changed him forever, but emotions of such purity were not meant for such an imperfect vessel. The amazing sense of universal connection disappeared, banished by the flashing of the crystal of Life and Fire flying towards the door.

Fin's mind hardened as he focused back on the here and now. The crystal sailed through the hole in the door. At the same moment, the twin beams of orange light winked out.

He was happy to see them go, but never did he think it was because his pursuers had chosen to show mercy.

'I'm just not the only one who was affected by the world's leveling.'

Fin shook his head. He didn't have time to worry about it. There was no doubt that the crystal's inner light had flashed brighter than it had before.

It was going to blow, and it'd be best if he wasn't here when it did. Accessing his interface, he fervently scanned for something he prayed was there.

Yes!

He accessed a new icon on his interface. As he did, a light blue sphere popped into existence, like a planet of latex paint.

You have found: Reliquary

Fin tapped it and a circular silver disc dropped into his hand. It had a white crystal in the middle. A script he couldn't read was embossed on both sides.

*You have found: **Personalized Instance Portal Token**. Do you wish to use it now?*

Yes, Fin thought furiously.

Nothing happened except a series of new prompts tried to pop up that he minimized to look at later.

He had to get out of here!

Unfortunately, the token didn't want to cooperate.

As one long second passed after another, absolutely nothing happened.

That wasn't exactly true.

A certain number went up.

40% chance to explode!

After the third second, a new sensation filled him.

Distinct from his intellectual caution regarding the Elemental crystal that now had a 45% chance to explode, but who was counting, there was an instinctual and ominous feeling coming from the other side of the door now.

He *had* to get out of here!

"Start! Begin! Take me! Fucking Ready Player One!" Fin shouted out in quick succession, not sure if there was some magic phrase was required to enter the Instance.

As the more seconds passed, the ominous vibe coming from the other side of the door grew to full blown dread.

65% chance to explode!

The Fire Element that made up the splinter had come from absorbing the explosion of a fuel cell. Fuel cell explosions had been known to destroy entire houses.

The Life Element was from cancer!

There was no way being near that thing when it blew was going to be healthy!

In panic, he focused back on the prompts waiting for him, hoping they had a way to activate the token. Indeed, there was something else he needed to decide before the token would trigger.

*As this is a **Personalized Instance Token**, you may choose one of three options to activate it.*

   1) H-

"Option one! Option one!" Fin spat. He could *feel* the energy in the splinter, even on the other side of the door, though he had no idea how.

It was felt… unstable.

Are you sure you wish to choos-

"Yes, gawdammit!"

75% chance to explode!

Good Luck!

Fin exhaled in relief.

Welcome to Hell

Wait, what?

***

That same moment, the people on either side of the nearly ruined storage room door were also being exposed to massive sources of energy, with widely divergent results.

On one side, the instance token changed appearance as soon as Fin read the last prompt. What had been a silver token with a white gem, morphed into a bronze token with a green gem. The script on the metal surrounding the jewel seemed to become more intricate as well.

Before Fin could register what the changes might mean, it shot out from his hand, like a lodestone to a magnet.

The instance token stopped moving as suddenly as it began. It slapped into empty air as if it was embedded in invisible clay.

It didn't just stop, though.

It impacted.

Striking something Fin couldn't see, the token slammed into reality itself, spreading cracks through the air. From his vantage point, it looked like his view of the storage closet wasn't actually three dimensional, but was instead a 2D picture of a storage closet.

The green jewel in the center of the token shot forward, leaving the bronze ring behind.

The gem shattered the picture of what Fin thought was the world.

Shards of what he had always called reality collapsed into the passage that would take him to a greater future.

He'd seen something like this once before.

The Wave had broken the entire sky, shards of blue flying upward like a shattered mirror.

The instance token was doing the same thing, but on a much smaller scale.

It was a repeat of an event that had occurred only days ago, but also a lifetime past.

This time, there were not entire universes behind the broken painting of the world. Instead, there was a green void with concentric and alternating rings of bronze and red leading into infinity. Each ring was both smooth, and yet also filled with innumerable scripts somehow. Fin could not read the language, but it irritated his mind with truths he was not yet ready to learn.

85% chance to explode!

The red of the rings conveyed an intangible menace, but Fin just bared his teeth in response to the silent threat.

Grabbing the pillowcases with his belongings, he dove into a brighter and more dangerous tomorrow.

***

On the other side of the door, most of his pursuers were still basking in the sublime feeling of the world's increased Energy concentration. It flooded their cells and the space between their molecules. At Energy level one, most denizens of the Labyrinth would still consider the Earth to be the harshest of deserts, a place that could literally not support most forms of "evolved" life.

To the men and women of Earth however, who had spent every moment of their lives on a null world, it was like divinity itself was being breathed into them.

Those who had lived on the moon would find the Sahara a true paradise.

That was why when a red and gold jewel flew through a certain door, it landed in the hallway without anyone noticing.

Even as it flashed brighter, the distracted scions of the Lotus and Shadow failed to understand their mortal peril.

In fact, only two of the people in the hallway had enough Power to finally detect the dangerous emanations coming from the crystal before it was too late.

Neither Sola nor Jürgen knew exactly what caught their attention.

After all, the gem's flashes were not very eye catching in the bright light of the hall. Whatever had drawn their gaze, once they saw the crystal, they knew on an instinctual level that they were looking at something both powerful and dangerous.

Summoning her Ability, Sola ducked around the corner of the hall. For good measure, she knelt down and created an ice wall with her ability. It was barely two feet high and no more than a few millimeters thick, but she poured everything she had into it.

Pain shot through her body as she overtaxed her reserves.

She paid it no heed.

As the wall thickened, the tips of her fingers turned black, unable to tolerate the ice energy she was channeling.

Jürgen, being directly in front of the now savaged door did not have that option. Instead, he grabbed Klaus. Placing the meat wall between him and the flashing jewel, the team leader snarled.

He didn't know why he should be so afraid of a tiny gem, but he had learned to trust his instincts. The muscular man barely had time to look back in irritation before the Elemental Splinter exploded.

Raw Fire and Life Element expanded violently in an explosion of golden flame. The floor beneath the gem melted immediately.

Radiating out from the ignition point, a conflagration was birthed.

Red flames with golden tips shot down the hallway in both directions. The heat made everyone inhale in pain, providing a wonderfully convenient passageway for the flames to follow. Incandescent Element coursed down the throats of several members of the Lotus Familia, first searing, then melting their lungs.

Flesh cooked and hair caught on fire. Klaus was lifted off his feet and slammed backwards, the front of his body a charred mess. Jürgen's own body was sandwiched between his meat shield and the wall.

Sola's own meager defense was shattered in an instant. Her summoned ice did serve to slightly weaken the blast, however, the Water Element of her ability cancelling out some of the destructive power of the blast.

Ultimately, she only suffered mild bruises and surface burns, despite blacking out for a moment.

In the aftermath, the Japanese woman clambered back onto her feet, barely wincing at the pain. Her perfect hair was completely askew, but she couldn't find a fuck to give.

She'd also suffered injuries from both the explosion and her unrestrained use of power, but it was nothing compared to the pain she'd endured in the past.

In line with her training, she did a quick self-evaluation.

Both arms were red and dusky from her elbows to her proximal interphalangeal joints. The front of both forearms were blistered from the heat. Distal to her PIPs, heat damage gave way to cold trauma. The very tips of her fingers were the black of dead flesh.

Pain washed through her in waves, but her honed mind would not be undone.

Especially since every breath was bringing more Energy, mana and vitality into her body. To most people on Earth, they would just feel better and have no idea why. To a member of a Familia, the increase in the Earth's Energy level meant so much more.

Her body had been altered by rituals similar to those that the Lotus Familia baptized their members with. Those rituals were costly, but they turned the Familias into something more than human. They brought health, beauty and potential. They also turned each family member into slaves, addicts that needed specialized food and support to fully function.

It was a need that had never fully been filled.

Until now.

Sola was a fallow field and at long last, the rain had come.

Every cell in her body eagerly drank.

The pain she was experiencing would make normal men and women double over in agony, but she was filled with wonder.

Besides, while it would cost her almost all of the coins she'd accumulated, her reserves would be enough to buy a healing glyph.

In a day or so, her injuries would all be gone.

As long as her family didn't kill her for what had happened here.

To that point, she walked around the corner to see just what had happened.

Looking down the corridor, Sola saw a sight that belonged in a war zone, not a hospital.

The area directly in front of the storage room looked like a bomb had gone off.

What wasn't cracked and dented was melted. The surrounding floor, walls and ceiling were all scored with scorch marks and soot.

Cracks spread out from the area, large enough that Sola was not sure this part of the hospital even remained structurally sound.

All of that only addressed the damage to the building.

The human cost was much higher.

Bodies lay in pieces.

They were crisped, scorched, cooked or all three.

One dismembered arm was still burning rosily, filling the hallway with the scent of barbeque pork.

~REWARD~

The few living members of the Lotus Familia mewled on the ground, some severely injured and others a bit less so, but only one man was still in combat shape.

Jürgen pushed his heavily muscled, and well-roasted, comrade off of him like so much trash. When he stood, his face was a mask of seething anger. Gone was the immaculate image of a man in control with a bespoke suit and well quaffed hair.

What was left, was a being of pure hate.

He spared not a glance at his fallen comrades, not even the one that had just saved his life, but instead glared at a blackened doorway.

The storage room he'd been trying to get into now lay bare, the door hanging onto the frame by the bottom hinge alone. Since chasing his prey into the closet, only minutes had passed, but it felt like hours.

Jürgen checked the room, expecting to find Fin either dead or unconscious.

Instead, what he saw made him feel like he aged years in a single second.

Hate tattooed itself in his heart and a seed of madness was planted in his mind.

Sola stepped over the dead and wounded with calculated dispassion. When she looked inside the room however, there was nothing detached about the joy that bloomed on her face.

It was empty.

Fin was not in the room, which meant she'd been right.

He *was* special!

Hanging in midair was a bronze circle with a gem in the middle. The gem was a rich green. A faint red haze surrounded the object.

For some reason that rouge color appeared sinister.

While Jürgen and Sola watched, brilliant flames consumed the disc, whatever it was. The fire flashed brightly before both it, and the item, vanished without a trace.

The two Powered, members of different Familias, merely stood there for long seconds, hearing the moans of the injured, both bloody but unbowed.

After a moment, Sola sniffed, before delicately and innocently asking, "He got away?"

Jürgen's fists squeezed so tight that blood bloomed in his palms.

Silence reigned until a tragic voice answered, "I… am… Klaus."

Chapter 61: We're "fine"

"*This is Reagan Watts, with World Confederation News. A bizarre phenomenon literally rocked the world yesterday. What has repeatedly been described as a "vibration" was felt at all points about the globe.*

This phenomenon, following on the heels of the questionable "Wave" event, which was reported days before, has worsened rumors of all kinds. There are also increased reports of chatter on the Great Link regarding people seeing holographic boxes appearing in their vision.

Some say this is proof that our reality is only a virtual simulation.

We reached out to former President Reeves who declined to comment.

From the office of the current President however, we have a very special guest, Dr Henry Wu, the Scientist General of the Western Confederation. Welcome Dr Wu."

The camera panned to a smooth faced Asian man with a soft voice and practiced smile, "It's always great to be here with you Rebecca. I'm so happy that I can share some good news with the people of the Western Confederation and the world. While there have been all sorts of conspiracy theories on the Great Link, actual scientists have made a pivotal discovery.

Dr Wu effortlessly changed the direction he was looking in response to a light coming on camera two, "Before anything else, let me just say, we are fine."

His smile radiated calm and safety, "I am happy to report that there is no cause for concern. We have determined that both the Wave, and the vibration felt yesterday, are all part of the same benign event.

The Wave has been determined to be the result of a series of extremely active solar flares that were clustered on a region of the sun that was facing the Earth. These flares released an amount of solar radiation that is on the far end

~DANGER~

of normal. While the amount is within the safety margin in regards to long term effects, in the short term there were some startling, but still benign, results."

"What caused this cluster of solar flares, Dr Wu?" Rebecca's voice held just the right tone. It blended concern over what she was hearing with relief that she was about to find out there was nothing to worry about. In the news business, she was setting her guest up for what was called, 'The Prestige.'

"While I can understand that the viewers might be concerned about the sun behaving abnormally, it is pretty big after all," Dr Wu chuckled benevolently, "the number of flares is actually no more out of the norm than seeing a hummingbird. Hummingbirds are all around us, but we just don't see them all the time. If you'd looked at the sun at the right moment, it would have just seemed a little brighter, though I wouldn't recommend doing that, of course," he chuckled again.

"Wise words," Rebecca chuckled back.

"The reason the solar flares triggered the Wave is a combination of three factors. The flares just happened to cluster in the right spot on the Sun, at the right time, and," he sighed dramatically.

"Go on doctor," Rebecca encouraged, her voice dripping with compassion.

"The third factor being our own negligence of this wonderful planet. The thinning of the ozone due to pollution and the harmful weapons used by the Eastern Bloc during the Third War left us vulnerable to the solar radiation the flares shot out into space."

"Even now we are paying the price for the atrocities committed by the Bloc," Rebecca cosigned with just the barest hint of cute anger.

"Yes," Henry nodded, "and yet, we must look towards the future and reconciliation. We are all, after all, united as children of this wonderful planet Earth."

Rebecca smiled warmly after her guest, just oh so inspired by his magnanimous approach to life.

"The important thing to remember," Dr Wu continued, "is that there is no danger. Now let me tell you what happened. The solar radiation swept over the planet and was a bit overwhelming for the senses. Anyone that has turned on a TV in the middle of the night knows how bright the screen can be. That's basically what happened.

With the thinning of the ozone layer, the specific amount and type of radiation released by the sun was able to 'stun' how our brain interpreted data for just a few seconds. The initial presentation of this disturbance was focused on the optic nerve and presented with an overload of information that the human mind perceived as a grey wave.

The residual boxes of light that some are reporting on the Great Link are the same thing. It's just that some people are more susceptible, just like how some people can't stand bright lights."

"That's me after a few apple-tinis," Rebecca added with a wink.

"Well, that's something completely different, though having tasted your apples before, I don't blame you," Dr Wu winked back.

A couple seconds of dead air passed as the two looked at each other before Henry coughed and kept explaining. "As I said, the Wave and the vibration were part of the same phenomenon. While the solar radiation acted on the perceptions of humans, it also had a small impact on the Earth itself. We are calling it an orbital wobble, and it was basically the Earth resetting its calibration after the wave of solar radiation passed.

This kind of thing may have happened millions of times throughout the history of the Earth. We were just lucky enough to enjoy the ride this time," Dr Wu rejoined, showing his pearly whites.

"Well, that is a massive relief," Rebecca exhaled happily.

"Even better, the orbital wobble seems to be part of the Earth's natural cycle. The solar radiation has actually cleared up the majority of pollution in the Earth's atmosphere, and, while I might get in trouble for ruining the surprise, even some Red Zones are showing signs of healing."

"Wait! The radiation was healing?"

"Yes Rebecca! And it might not be limited to healing the world. In Atlanta, GA, there are reports of an entire ward of cancer patients who went into remission overnight. The Wave might have been the best thing that ever happened to us."

"This is unprecedented," she smiled through ruby lips.

"Well," Henry replied with a smirk, "there is some *precedent. As you know, I'm a bit of nerd."*

Rebecca arched one eyebrow.

"There is a fantastic movie where Godzilla travels around spreading radiation and healing the planet with it."

"Are you telling me the Wave was like Godzilla, Henry?" Rebecca asked with a laugh.

"Well, not exactly," he admitted with a bashful chuckle. *"There aren't any giant lizards that eat people, but the beneficial effect is the same. And either way, it was just a great movie,"* he winked.

"Dr Wu, you are a treasure," she laughed gleefully, *"Thank you for sharing such amazing news."*

"I'm just happy to be here. To all the people of the Western Confederation and the world, we live in safe and amazing times that are only getting better!"

His smile blazed brighter than the Wave.

"Now Dr Wu, as I have you here, I would also love to get your opinion on..."

The rest of the show was filled with the inane banter that people had been trained to need and love. Before the end of the hour, "OrbitalWobble" was the number five hashtag on the Great Link.

Hundreds of other news shows and podcasts were filled with people agreeing, disagreeing, shouting and praying.

"Orbital wobble? Seriously? They're just making words up now."

"All words are made up!"

"That's not what I meant, you ignorant pleb! They're shitting on us and calling it chocolate sprinkles!"

"That's just gross."

"What's gross is that they think people are dumb enough to believe…"

Variations of that conversation played out for the next several days on the Great Link, triggering another wave of misinformation and argument, once again keeping the people under control. A flood of information had always proved more effective in hiding the truth than attempting to bury it in denial.

***

After the show, Rebecca and Henry shared a drink on his balcony. The two on again off again lovers had gotten to know each other well over the years.

Watching him take a long pull from the glass of single malt in his hand, Rebecca finally asked the question.

"Heny, off the record. What's the real deal?"

He stared at her hollowly before taking another long pull from his drink.

"Before anything else, let me just say, most people are fucked."

Rebecca blinked, "What?" She didn't know what she'd expected, but it hadn't been that.

"Remember when I said there aren't giant lizards that eat people?" he asked.

"Yeah?"

He just looked at her and polished off the rest of his drink.

Chapter 62: The One

LIfe

Awell-lit room sprung into existence, devoid of life or movement. It had not existed for more than ten seconds before the stillness was shattered.

A bronze object snapped into existence, starting the clock on the room's destruction.

Growing from a pinpoint to the size of a man's hand in an instant, it slammed into the air, fracturing reality.

To anyone observing, it would look like the token had flashed into existence and then smashed into midair. On impact, the world that had always seemed three dimensional was instead shown to be only a cleverly drawn painting. A facsimile that was now shown to be a lie as shards of reality fell in on itself.

On the other side was a field of hellish red energy framing a series of bronze rings.

A strange noise echoed in the room, the annoyed bellow of a planet sized baby with a full diaper. The sound grew louder and deeper like a reverse doppler effect.

In seconds, the message from another world could be clearly heard.

"Gaaaaaaaah!

A very small Fin shot out from the bronze and red rings, passed through the hole in the center of the bronze token, and collapsed unceremoniously onto the floor of the room.

With a sore back, he looked up and saw the floating portal token.

438

He realized that thinking was a bit difficult.

Honestly, he felt kind of drunk.

A green gem emerged from the bronze and red rings, flying at what looked like high speed. Despite its fast movement, it docked perfectly into the empty hole in the token, then the whole thing winked out of existence.

Random thoughts skittered across his addled mind, until it sunk in just where he was.

"Oh, I'm still in the supply closet."

Wait!

I'm still in the supply closet!

He hadn't gone anywhere!

The portal hadn't actually worked.

Which meant the Elemental Splinter was about to go off, and-

Those fuckers were still behind him!

Fin shot up from the ground, spinning with his dagger in his hand, "Come at me you piggly sons of bitc-"

The words died on his lips.

The door was completely whole.

Fin looked around confused.

He was definitely in the supply closet, but with his mind clearing, he realized he couldn't be in the *same* supply closet.

Now that he was paying attention, the differences became obvious. There were no scorch marks from the lasers. There was no blood on the floor and the scent of burning metal was gone from the air.

This wasn't the hospital storage room.

It just looked like it was. Flicking a blue plastic tub, Fin whistled in appreciation and amazement.

Except for the lack of damage, the closet had been replicated down to the last detail.

"What's happening?"

Then it hit him.

"Is this the Instance?"

Try as he might, Fin couldn't remember anything distinct after he'd entered the portal. He had a vague impression of movement, but no actual memories of the transportation. Soon, even that recollection faded.

All he could remember was jumping in, and then falling out.

He was pretty sure there hadn't been any actual pain from using the token until he'd hit the floor anyway, but arriving had been an extremely unsettling experience.

It had felt like…

Well, it had felt *exactly* like what he'd imagine being stretched, strained and compressed until you were shot out of a small hole would feel like if you turned off someone's pain receptors.

Was that how portals worked?

If so, then that was unacceptable.

Being squeezed through a hole the size of an acorn was something every man should only have to experience once.

Well… once with your *whole* body, his addled mind corrected.

Fin still felt a little drunk, but that slowly faded, and his ability to think clearly returned.

With clarity came a renewed sense of urgency.

Adrenalin shot through him again.

Had that prompt said, "Welcome to Hell?"

As in, "Hell" hell?

He pulled the window back up.

Good Luck!

*Welcome to **Hell Mode** of your **Uncommon** ranked Personalized Instance: **The Tunnels of Ritobah***

Fin wanted to strangle someone.

~*REWARD*~

While he was very happy not to be roasting in a fiery abyss, was there *really* no other way the prompt could have said that?

Maybe, "Welcome to your selected Mode, which please remember is called hell, which should not be confused an actual hellscape filled with demons."

Didn't seem too much to ask.

Either way, this was a load off.

Not that he'd been overly worried.

He wasn't a punk after all.

He was man… with what he'd been told were truly immaculate balls.

Fin marinated in that pillar of personality for a bit, then went back to his prompts.

The moment he started reading, he started swearing.

"WTF! I mean what, the actual, fuck!"

"What kind of a sick bastard puts the hardest option first!"

As this is a Personalized Instance Token, you may choose one of three options.

1) **Hell Mode (Tunnels of Ritobah)** *– Dangers are greatly strengthened. Almost none escape Hell.*
   a. **Minimum Success Condition**: *30 Zones*
   b. **Fail Penalty:** *Death*
   c. **Difficulty:** *Bronze Uncommon*
   d. **Reward:** *+100% Loot Quality and Quantity; Uncommon Treasure Chest (Quality: Unknown)*
   e. **Average World Energy:** *Peak Level 1*
2) **Advanced Mode (Waters of Ankarah)** *– Offers a greater challenge and higher rewards than Normal mode.*
   a. **Minimum Success Condition:** *20 Zones*
   b. **Fail Penalty:** *Loss of 1 Threshold from a randomly selected Primary Attribute*
   c. **Difficulty:** *Gold Common*
   d. **Reward:** *+30% Loot Quality and Quantity; Common Treasure Chest (Quality: Unknown)*
   e. **Average World Energy:** *Mid-Level 1*
3) **Normal Mode (Plains of Creedence)** *– This option is most in keeping with your current Power.*

> a. ***Minimum Success Condition:*** *10 Zones*
> b. ***Fail Penalty:*** *1 month Debuff: Weakness*
> c. ***Difficulty:*** *Silver Common*
> d. ***Reward:*** *No special conditions*
> e. ***Average World Energy:*** *Low Level 1*

While he'd read, Fin had been blinking fast enough for a morse code rap battle. What came next made his face freeze.

*Know This! As this is your first **Instance**, you are entitled to extra information.*

The likelihood of survival decreases sharply as the difficulty increases.

*At your current **Power Level** and **State of Being**, the survival chances of Instances are as follows:*

*Bronze Common < **50%***

*Silver Common < **20%***

*Gold Common < **5%***

*Bronze Uncommon > **0%***

Danger and Reward are close bedfellows. Choose wisely.

Fin looked at the earlier prompt, confirming that choosing Hell mode had upped the Instance's difficulty to *Bronze Uncommon*.

Slow nodding replaced fast blinking.

Cold anger replaced hot irritation.

"Can't even give a guy a decimal number for survival, huh? Just greater than zero?" Fin's nodding grew even slower and angrier, "Okay. Okay. That's fine."

He was going to shit in someone's cereal after all this was done. Until then, Fin resolved to learn everything he could. Moving too fast was how he'd ended up in "hell."

~*REWARD*~

Admittedly, when it had been a race between that dbag's laser vision and his own unstable magic grenade to see which would get to fricassee his juevos first, rushing through the portal token prompts had seemed like the right choice.

That didn't change the fact that he was currently outside of his depth, bleeding and in, what the prompts said, was basically a death trap.

It was time to slow things way down and be deliberate.

Fin's eyes hardened.

It didn't matter how low the life expectancy was for this place, or how many people it would normally kill.

If this place could slaughter nine hundred and ninety-nine thousand and nine hundred and ninety-nine people, it would find out he was that one-muthafucka-in-a-million.

Chapter 63: After Darkness

Fin took a more critical look at his surroundings.

Truth be told, he was a bit underwhelmed.

Even though this was his first Instance, the prompts had made it pretty clear that Instance Tokens were supposed to take him to another dimension or world or something.

Fin had expected to be in a meadow studded with wildflowers with a small demon talking to him. Or maybe in a forest being pursued by some type of mutated bear creature.

What he hadn't expected was to be taken back to the same damned supply room!

Fin forced himself to process what he knew.

Just as that laser beamed prick was going to cut his way into the storage closet, the Energy of the Earth had increased to a crucial level.

That had let the planet level up.

And, oh yeah, planets leveled up.

That was a thing now.

Not wasting time on the endless implications of that, Fin focused on what it meant for him personally.

Right before time had unfrozen, he'd experienced an amazing sensation, like every inch of his body had been soothed at once.

That had to be because of the world's leveling.

His body had craved the extra Energy on a fundamental level.

That made Fin realize something else.

That soothing feeling had grown even stronger after he'd jumped through the portal. He hadn't noticed at first, but, he took a deep breath, this felt amazing!

He intentionally took a deeper breath, and something primal within him shifted.

Without realizing it, his body began intentionally pulling more Energy from the environment into itself.

A dam was about to break.

He took another deep breath and let all other thoughts flee his mind.

"Oh my god," he exhaled slowly.

He started taking deep breaths as quickly as he could. Every time he did, he could feel "it."

Was this what it felt like to have more Energy?

Whatever it was he was sucking down, it permeated the air itself, and he wanted it all.

Without him realizing it, a new glyph was starting to form in his mind's eye.

Every breath brought more of it into his body.

He'd thought that things had felt great right after the Earth's Energy had increased, but this was even better!

Now that he was doing these breathing exercises, there was no doubt.

The Energy here was higher.

For long minutes, Fin just kept taking deep breaths, marveling at the sensation of his body waking up to its potential.

It was only after several minutes that he felt "full" for lack of a better word.

The moment that happened, he received a surprising prompt.

Hidden Debuff Removed: ***Energy Deficit***

Your entire existence has been lived in a state of bare subsistence. All beings have some Power, but your world suffered from a lack of Energy, constantly placing you in a cycle of loss and gain, For the first time, you have been given what your State of Being truly requires.

Free Energy can now be accumulated and converted into Power.

Fin blinked.

He'd lived in a deficit his entire life?

Based on how he was feeling, the amazing completeness that was washing through him, he couldn't muster an argument.

Everyone he'd ever met had been in a search for meaning. Some did it with religion, others with sex, love, drugs or money. Some found it in bloodshed and war, others in nurturing their children.

He himself had walked many paths. Orphan, soldier, killer, healer and lover, were only a few of them. In that moment, he realized while his experiences and emotions were real, he'd been driven onto each path by an intense yearning to be complete.

To achieve the very feeling currently coursing through him for the first time.

He'd been trying to hear the song of his heart his entire life.

It wasn't that he'd lacked what it took to be complete.

It was the Earth itself that hadn't given him what he needed.

He'd been searching for a key.

Until now, he'd been searching in the dark.

Maybe things would be different when he got back. Maybe everyone, the world round, would experience the revelation of completion and it would usher in a new golden age of peace and understanding.

Fin doubted it somehow, in fact, he was pretty sure things were going to go the other way.

That was a problem for tomorrow.

For now, he just enjoyed the feeling of his body being satiated for the first time in his life.

For the first time, he had what he needed.

And then he received too much.

Warning! *You have entered an environment with an Energy density much higher than your own!*

*Imbalance is **Severe.***

More Energy began to flood his cells, then the space between them, then his cells began to burst.

Energy +1

Energy +1

Energy +1

Energy +1

Energy +1

The sense of completeness was destroyed.

It was replaced by sharp, eviscerating lances of pain.

Warning! Your Free Energy has increased beyond what your State of Being can tolerate. You will experience discomfort until this Energy surplus is managed.

*Warning! You now have a **Minimal** Energy surplus*

Discomfort? Discomfort! This wasn't discomfort!

Energy continued to enter him. The prompts came about one a minute, every cheerful green line of text resigning him to sixty seconds of worsening agony.

Energy +1

Energy +1

Energy +1

Fin hunched over on the floor of the room, panting heavily.

And then it got worse.

Warning! Your Energy has increased beyond what your State of Being can endure.

You will start to accumulate damage!

*Warning! Your Energy Surplus has worsened to **Minor!***

Energy +1

Energy +1

Energy +1

Health -3

On the third cycle of Energy after the last prompt, blood gushed out of Fin's mouth. He lay prone on the ground, his feet spasming.

In this time of tragedy, Fin learned a danger of the Labyrinth.

The Energy of the world he'd fallen into was technically at the same level that Earth had just reached, but this world was at the cusp of reaching level two. As such, its Energy density had reached *peak* concentrations, while the Earth's was the lowest of the *low*.

Fin was experiencing an Energy density far greater than he had ever been exposed to before.

While the Laws of the Labyrinth could supersede many laws of the physical realm, they rarely completely replaced them.

~REWARD~

One natural law that was almost universally preserved was the concept of a gradient.

Therein lay the danger.

The high Energy world he'd portaled into had indeed saturated his cells, but Fin's Energy starved body was so barren compared to his new environment, that the flow did not stop. He had made the mistake of actively drawing it into him, and like a mosquito that couldn't detach, it was now going to make him burst.

All travelers of the Labyrinth learned a lesson that he was being taught now, Energy could lead to Power, but it nearly always led to pain.

Energy continued to pour into him, worsening his surplus.

Energy +1… +1… +1…

While he was initially losing health every three or four Energy, the damage frequency soon worsened every two or three.

*Warning! Your Energy Surplus has worsened to **Moderate***

Then every one.

*Warning! Your Energy Surplus has worsened to **Severe***

All beings that traversed the worlds of Labyrinth were exposed to this energy gradient, but rarely to this degree.

Almost no null worlds were inducted, and the few times that they were, the new Labyrinth worlds would gradually accumulate Energy over long years. This slow build let their children increase their Energy as well.

Magicka had changed that, allowing the Earth to reach Power Level 1 in days rather than decades.

This had brought the advent of Instances before its children were acclimated to their new, wider reality.

~DANGER~

All of that was beyond Fin's control, but the final cause of his agony was his fault alone.

Choosing Hell mode had taken him into the only *uncommon* Instance on Earth, and connected him to a world on the cusp of leveling.

Which all translated into Fin's body being torn apart by forces it was not prepared to receive.

Basically, it was first night in prison, but without the romance.

Energy continued to traverse his soul which lacked the tempering to channel such cosmic authority. The Energy continued to fill his body which was inadequate to house such majesty.

His mind was attacked as well, but here, Fin was not so easily overwhelmed. Just barely, his mind which had been tempered, trained and tortured for long years, snarled back at the river of Energy that threatened to carry him to oblivion.

It rejected the assumption that he was too weak to determine his own fate, and at the most crucial time, when others would have bowed in defeat, Fin did what all great men of history had done.

Anything and everything he could.

What he'd discovered, moment by agonizing moment, was that it took about a minute to absorb enough Energy for the prompt to say it had increased by one.

Once that green notification appeared, his body almost immediately began absorbing the next unit. If there was a way to stop the process once it began, Fin did not know how.

The key to that realization was the word "almost."

If he could head off the next influx of Energy before it began to fill him though, he just might survive.

When the next green prompt came, he made his move.

Energy +1

Fin chose not to just let it wash through him, but instead bend it to his will.

~*REWARD*~

Focusing on *Mana Threads*, he willed the Energy that had just started to enter his body to divert into his Skill instead of his own overflowing internal reservoir. The magical force resisted at first, almost like it wanted to follow its fellows and burst Fin from the inside, but his tenacious mind clamped down onto the Energy like a bulldog.

With all of his will, Fin forced the Energy into his Skill's *uncommon* Perk. The Energy slotted in, but nothing happened. Nearly frantic, Fin forced the next unit in as well, and was finally rewarded with a prompt!

Mana Efficiency Perk (Uncommon) improved!

*+1/10: All mana spent on **Mana Sense Skill** Tree 10% more effective*

*20 Magicka for improving an **Uncommon** Perk for the first time!*

While it was normally great getting the extra bonus of magicka for achieving something, the pleasing sensation of the vibrations were almost Fin's undoing. Between that, and the relief from having even a temporary break from influx of Energy, Fin lost his concentration.

He plunged back into the torrent of pain.

Energy +1

Health -1

Energy +1

Health -2

Baring his teeth like an animal, Fin struggled to hijack the process again.

What he'd done before by channeling the Energy into his Skill was to find just the right instant to divert the flow. If he succeeded, rather than glut him further, the Energy could be fed to his Skill, and he'd buy himself a minute where his pain just tortured him rather than got worse.

Unfortunately, his window of opportunity was measured in split seconds.

He failed, again and again and again.

Each failure was a lost point of health. Each failure saw him cough up blood, bleed from his eyes, ears, nose and anus. Anyone staring at Fin would feel pity for such a wretched soul, unless they looked in his eyes.

Then, they would feel fear.

After each failure, he endured a minute of torture, waiting for his next opportunity. At long last, he succeeded, and channeled more Energy into his Perk.

Mana Efficiency Perk (Uncommon) improved!

+2/10: All mana spent on Mana Sense Skill Tree 20% more effective

+3/10...

+4/10...

Every bit of Energy he was able to push into the skill, he improved the Perk and, apparently, the efficiency of *Mana Threads*. Small bits of knowledge entered his head with each success, changing his understanding of his Skill.

In the future, he knew it would cost him less mana to make threads.

As long as he had a future.

The Energy influx did not always obey his will, and he periodically lost control.

After each failure, he could only resign himself to a long minute of agony. His blood vessels burst, his muscles tore, and his synapses misfired. Almost anyone would have succumbed. That was not something Fin could live with. It wasn't something he could allow. Not after everything he had endured.

Not after everything he had done.

+5/10...

+6/10...

          ~REWARD~

It was working! Every addition to his Perk meant two Energy invest and two minutes of blissful relief from his pain worsening.

He was still glutted with Energy, but he'd stemmed the flow and was making headway.

Just as important, he was giving his agonized body time to acclimate to the increased Energy inside of him.

This marginally decreased his suffering. He latched onto that inch of progress, snarling into the void that it now belonged to him, and he would die before giving it up.

Time passed and Fin began to feel that the pressure of Energy from the environment had eased slightly, like a diver acclimating to the depths.

His body remained locked in pain and contraction, but his mind hardened even further. Fin poured more Energy into his Skill.

+7/10...

+8/10...

Energy +1

Health -1

+9/10...

He'd lost concentration once, and it had cost him another point of health, a resource that was far too close to being gone, but by the strength of his iron will, he maximized his Perk!

+10/10: All mana spent on Mana Sense Skill Tree is now 100% more effective.

Congratulations! You have maximized your first Perk!

No more Energy can be included in this Perk.

Maximizing the Perk had also gained him an Achievement.

You have gained an Achievement: **Perky!**

Fin minimized that immediately. He'd read it when it didn't feel like an alien was going to burst out of his chest.

His efforts had also earned him more magicka.

+20 Magicka for maximizing an Uncommon Perk for the first time!

Unlike last time, Fin had suspected the vibrations might come when he maxed out. Even though they were stronger, he wasn't thrown off his game. He'd mentally prepared for the extra stimulation.

Also, after the minutes of respite from his Energy increasing, the pain he was enduring improved just enough for him to unclench his jaw and take rough, agonal breaths.

Fin was able to maintain focus and keep the cycle of Power from beginning again.

He was also sure now that the flow of Energy into his body had slowed. It hadn't stopped, but it gave him hope that whatever was happening to him would end if he could only endure.

As soon as the first Perk maximized, Fin mentally forced the next bit of Energy into the *limited* one.

He immediately noticed a difference in what this higher ranked Perk demanded of him.

If adding Energy to the *Mana Efficiency* Perk had felt like pulling a dull knife through cold butter, improving his *Mana Stability* Perk felt like he was carving soap.

He would have to fight to get the Energy into it.

Fin's face broke into a manic grin.

As long as there was a fight, that's all he needed.

~REWARD~

Fin's mind was able to force the Energy inside, but the mental strain increased. Between that and the pain he was enduring, he had almost nothing left.

A race began, between will and his mind's ability to endure.

Mana Stability Perk (Limited) improved!

+1/15: All manifestations of the Mana Sense Skill Tree are 10% more resistant to outside influence.

+50 Magicka for improving a Limited Perk for the first time!

The *limited* Perk needed three Energy for every advancement. For most other denizens of the Labyrinth, this extra expense was a headache. For him, it was salvation.

Fin kept pouring his Energy into the Perk, hoping the Energy imbalance would subside.

+2/15...

+3/15...

+4/15...

A wave of exhaustion hit him.

Energy +1

Health -1

No!

+5/15...

His rallied focus faltered. It felt like he'd been up for two days!

Energy +1

Health -1

I will not allow this!

I will survive!

I will overcome!

+6/15...

Another prompt came, and the victory almost defeated him.

*Know This! The **Energy** imbalance between your **State of Being** and current environment has improved to **Moderate**.*

He'd been starting to hate the color green. Now he wished it was an M&M because he'd like to do dirty, dirty things to it!

With a nearly insane grin, he found his fighting spirit renewed.

One in a million!

Mana Stability Perk (Limited) improved!

+7/15: All manifestations of the Mana Sense Skill Tree are 90% more resistant to outside influence.

+8/15...

After earning the eighth point, Fin lost concentration again, or maybe he lost consciousness for a second. He couldn't really tell. He braced for

~REWARD~

another lance of pain to tear through him, but after a few seconds, he realized, it hadn't.

The prompt hadn't lied. The flow of Energy had really slowed.

He had a chance!

Fin dove back into improving his Perk, and, for the first time, chipped away at the Energy threatening to burst him like a balloon.

Energy -3

+9/15...

Energy -3

+10/15...

Energy -3

+11/15...

*Congratulations! Your Energy Surplus has improved to **Moderate***

Yes!

Fin didn't let up.

Energy -3

+12/15...

Energy -3

+13/15...

Energy -3

+14/15...

*Congratulations! Your Energy Surplus has improved to **Minor***

Mana Stability Perk (Limited) maximized!

~DANGER~

+15/15: All manifestations of the Mana Sense Skill Tree are 150% more resistant to outside influence.

Congratulations! You have maximized your Perk!

No more Energy can be included in this Perk.

+50 Magicka for maximizing a Limited Perk for the first time!

Vibrations filled him, but he barely noticed. He'd moved beyond exhaustion into instinct. He couldn't stop. He wouldn't.

Fin reached deep within himself and siphoned off his Energy.

The difficulty of investing into a *scarce* Perk shot up exponentially. Fin could hardly function, but he dug deep within and mustered the strength.

Energy -1

Energy -1

Energy -1

Energy -1

Energy -1

Mana Invasion Perk (Scarce) improved!

+1/25: All manifestations of the Mana Sense Skill Tree are 10% more likely to penetrate foreign mana and 10% harder to remove by foreign sources.

+100 Magicka for improving a Scarce Perk for the first time!

Vibrations spread through him as Fin gasped like a fish. He bit his lip hard enough to pour fresh blood into his mouth.

To his surprise, a new window appeared.

~REWARD~

Perky Achievement triggered. Would you like to spend 5 Energy to automatically gain an additional Progression Point in your Mana Invasion Perk?

"Oh god yes," Fin exhaled. A large glut of Energy left his body without needing any coaxing from him at all.

Energy -5

+2/25: All manifestations of the Mana Sense Skill Tree are 20% more likely to penetrate foreign mana and 20% harder to remove by foreign sources.

He cared not at all about advancing his Perk again, not when a beautiful green window was waiting right after.

*Congratulations! Your Energy Surplus has improved to **Minimal.** It is recommended to resolve this, as long term a Surplus may have detrimental effects.*

At long last, the Free Energy inside of Fin was reduced to a level that it wasn't actively threatening his life. He felt hollowed out and bloated all at once.

Eyes blood shot and soul weary, he lay on the ground, his vision dimming at the edges.

Fin slammed the back of his head against the floor, summoning pain again to banish weakness.

He couldn't lose consciousness. Not yet.

If he did, and his Energy surplus ratcheted back into dangerous levels…

That moment of distraction cost him.

Energy +1

No! This wasn't how he was going to go out!

For once, the Labyrinth agreed with him.

*Know This! The **Energy** imbalance between your **State of Being** and current environment has improved to **Minimal**.*

Spontaneous Energy consumption is now unlikely.

He'd done it.

He'd survived.

Fin lay there, at the entrance to a new world, covered in sweat and blood. Notifications blinked unread in the corner of his vision, and in the upper right of his interface, his health bar strobed red.

<u>3</u>/58 HP remaining

Despite all of that, as the darkness closed in on his vision once more, he summoned the last of his strength and spoke to whatever god or demon might be listening.

To whoever, or whatever, was responsible for bringing that grey beam to Earth, for triggering the death of his love, for pitting him against those blond sons of bitches, and finally, for making him suffer as soon as he took his first steps into the Labyrinth, he made a vow, a threat, and a promise all in one.

Each word was softer than the last as he lost his grip on the light.

"I'm not locked in here with you. You're locked in here with me."

Darkness fell.

Fin remained.

~ So ends Book 1 of Alpha ~

The Story Continues…

~REWARD~

<u>Thank you all for reading!</u>

Thank you for sharing your precious time perusing the insanity of my mind. I hope my words and worlds bring chuckles to your heart, peace to your soul and hope to your life.

Book 2 of Alpha will be coming early 2025.

And if you don't want to wait, there are nine other books you can enjoy immediately.

My first series, The Land, was voted one of the *Top 100 Series of All Time* in all genres by Audible.com

With over 200,000 5-star reviews it can't be all bad lol.

Please check out The Land, by Aleron Kong and God's Eye.

If you'd like updates, you can follow me on social media. My website is LitRPG.com

In either case, thank you again.

The Story Never Ends,

Aleron

You can make a massive difference!

As an indie author I don't have a publishing company behind me.

I have you!

As far as I'm concerned, that's more than enough.

Nothing helps as much as leaving a Review.

60 seconds of your time would help me for a **FOREVER**!

Even leaving some stars or just clicking "LIKE" on votes you agree with helps so much.

Thank you again!

I am honored to share my world with you.

~REWARD~

<u>How to Contact Aleron and check out additional books</u>

~DANGER~

I **LOVE** hearing from my readers so please reach out! I'm all OVER the net lol!

If you're looking for your next read, please try *The Land!*

The Land: Founding

The Land: Forging

The Land: Alliances

The Land: Catacombs

The Land: Swarm

The Land: Raiders

The Land: Predators

The Land: Monsters

Wall Street Journal Best Selling Series

Chosen *Top 100 Series of All Time* by Audible.com!

Chosen *Customer Favorite of the Year* by Audible.com!

Over 2,000,000 copies sold!

8 books and counting

⭐⭐⭐⭐⭐ AMAZING SERIES, AMAZING AUTHOR!

⭐⭐⭐⭐⭐ Pure Fantasy Gold!

⭐⭐⭐⭐⭐ Instant Classic and Still Going!

<u>Click HERE for a SNEAK PEAK</u>

And don't forget there is another book series waiting when you're done with
The Land!

God's Eye

<u>God's Eye: Awakening</u>

Top 5 of ALL books on Audible!

Top 5 of ALL books on Amazon!

<u>God's Eye - Awakening!</u>

<u>Click HERE for a SNEAK PEEK</u>

www.ingramcontent.com/pod-product-compliance
Lightning Source LLC
Chambersburg PA
CBHW060857140726
47996CB00001B/15